Bitter Sweet

A Novel by
Fhionna Mac

Moons Grove Press
British Columbia, Canada

Bitter Sweet

Copyright ©2019 by Fhionna Mac
ISBN-13 978-1-77143-389-1
First Edition

Library and Archives Canada Cataloguing in Publication
Title: Bitter sweet / a novel by Fhionna Mac.
Names: Mac, Fhionna, 1968- author.
Identifiers: Canadiana (print) 2019011861X | Canadiana (ebook) 20190118652 |
ISBN 9781771433891 (softcover) | ISBN 9781771433907 (PDF)
Classification: LCC PR6113.A2 B58 2019 | DDC 823/.92—dc23

Artwork credit: Front cover artwork © Fhionna Mac

Moons Grove Press is an imprint
of CCB Publishing: www.ccbpublishing.com

Moons Grove Press
British Columbia, Canada
www.moonsgrovepress.com

To my darling rabbit and my wonderful friends.
It's taken a while but I've finally finished.

Thank you to Paul and to Gloria for all your invaluable help.
I've learned so much.

PROLOGUE

He looked up at her and for the first time, possibly ever, couldn't fathom her feelings. Usually she had such an expressive face, especially her high arching eyebrow, but at that moment she seemed far away. He was always firmly in the present in her company, ready and waiting for the slightest hint of any need he could fulfil for her. He stared, even though he knew he shouldn't, but he couldn't draw his eyes away. At last, the smile he knew so well returned and he felt able to relax a little. His happiness was so dependent, no, wrapped up in hers that at times he felt it was all he could do to keep breathing.

* * *

Fhionna was in another time as she looked out of the heavily-leaded window, across the crisp lawn, to the rusty summer house with its glass panes cracked from the years of cold winters and the once sleek, white paint hanging from its beams like the flakes of snow that now covered the whole garden. How she'd loved it there, cherished her youth, playing in the summer house with the girl next door. She remembered Katie fondly, the way she bound her wrists with her mother's silk scarves. They were delicate and yet yielded such strength and power in their use as restraints. Fhionna, herself, had been described as such over the years. Strong and powerful yet graceful and gentle. Tender but with such a passion to dominate. Fond memories.

With a contented sigh she brought her mind back to the beautiful male that knelt on the rug a few feet away from where she stood. She glanced in his direction. His body really was magnificent. A strong body, with powerful legs and shoulders, and the tan of his skin contrasted against the pale coloured sheepskin. His face gave away his concern for her absence but as she smiled down on him his shoulders visibly reposed. She knew he wasn't scared of her, that he trusted her, but the slight tension in his muscles and the frown line on his brow told her he was worried he'd offended her in some way. The worst punishment she could ever bestow upon him would be her silence. Fhionna was well aware of this fact and, indeed, had trained him to respond in this way. This thought excited her greatly and she felt her face flush with passion towards him.

"Head bowed," she said, and he obeyed.

❧ Chapter 1 ☙

January 2012, Glasgow

Fhionna

I

Fhionna's fingers were stained and messy from the ink as she tried to fiddle with the printer paper that had somehow managed to get itself jammed, just when she was in a rush to get her instructions written out and sealed in an envelope. She smiled to herself as she thought about her secretary doing this job for her. This wasn't possible, of course. What would Jane have thought had she been asked to type out the instructions to:

Write a paragraph about why you want to serve me. Think about it very carefully because your answer will shape what happens to you. Once you have completed this task, strip and leave your clothes neatly folded in the corner of the room. Kneel by the door on all fours, without obstructing my entry.

As she struggled to get the page loose, she started to laugh, the corners of her eyes creasing along their already existent lines as her lips parted into what could almost be called a grin. Picturing dear Jane's face, shock and horror written all over it, made her worse. Tears were streaming down Fhionna's face and she couldn't see a damn thing. Somehow she managed to free it with one last tug and almost launched herself into the nearest chair. She was laughing so hard she thought she would explode. Her face hurt and it seemed quite impossible to stop, but stop she must. Thank goodness there was no one else around that day.

Trying desperately to compose herself, she got up from the chair and was relieved to see the instruction letter in her hand was still intact but unfortunately her stockings were not.

"Drat it," she mumbled, "I've got to be out of here in ten minutes."

Moving across to the old oak chest in the corner of the room, she slid a small brass key into the lock and opened the lid. Thankfully she'd remembered to buy a spare set of stockings because most of the time her memory wasn't that efficient and she forgot the simplest of things. Looking down at the delicate packet in her hands, she realised her fingers were still a complete mess. She crossed the room to the cloakroom and wiggled her fingers as she turned on the hot tap. Water gushed out and she did the best job she could, mildly scrubbing at the ink, trying not to make her long slim hands too red and blotchy, but deciding she would wear gloves anyway.

Fhionna returned to her office and sat gingerly on the edge of the chair that had saved her earlier. She removed the offending laddered nylons and slipped on the fresh pair, carefully smoothing them up her long, slim, legs, enjoying the feeling of the soft silk against her skin. They were an expensive pair, sent over from Paris, and she treasured little moments like these. They were so precious. She loved her life and she felt like the luckiest woman in the world.

* * *

Downstairs, she slipped out the front door and into the back seat of her fiery-red car.

"Home please, Tim."

"Yes, Ma'am."

They set off through the busy Glasgow streets and out into the beginnings of the countryside. The lights that had just buzzed into life were now being left behind. Pulling her thick velvet coat around her, Fhionna relaxed into the journey, enjoying the silhouettes of the trees that formed eerie and unusual shapes against the darkening sky. At times she would glance at Tim, the shape of his shoulders, the neatly cut hair appearing at the nape of his neck from underneath his cap, and she smiled as she realised how much he must be enjoying himself. He lived to serve and his talents were vast but she'd found out, quite quickly, that his real need was to lead a simple life, as chauffeur, servant, butler, in fact anything he could do to just be around her, in her presence.

His main gift to her, however, was his ability to take the lash like no other she'd found in her lifestyle as a dominant woman. His ability to absorb each blow, whether it was to his back or his buttocks, was astounding and all just for her pleasure. Tim wasn't a masochist so claimed no gratification from the pain he endured apart from the enjoyment of his Master. It amazed her just how different people were, their motivations, their wants, and their desires. Some being simple to accomplish, simple for her to provide, and others being much more complicated and, sad to say, unachievable. Certainly by her, at least.

As she watched him in the mirror, she noted he had an unusual, but not unpleasant, face. He wore a slight frown as he concentrated on the slippery wet roads, making sure, more than anything else, that his passenger was safe. She loved to observe his actions and his mannerisms. It was part of how she dominated her slaves. She learned their characters and their body language, and added it to the way she uniquely directed each of them in turn. She'd realised, from a very early age, she could provide happiness to others by dominating them, leading a most gratifying life herself. It gave her life purpose, real meaning, that not many people were lucky enough to find. She was very sure of that.

* * *

The driveway was long and winding and the large sandstone building up ahead in the distance was her old family home, which she'd moved into the year before. She thought about how hard her parents had worked to buy it and keep all their children clothed, fed, and warm. They hadn't been a rich family by any stretch of the imagination. It crossed her mind, at that moment, she must set Tim his next task: chopping wood for the fire. There was a storage bunker outside, under the side window. There were some logs and kindling left over from last winter but they wouldn't last long. She must send him out soon but it was raining heavily and the dark, thunderous clouds were scudding across the sky as if eager to shed even more of their heavy burden. The forecast was for snow that night but it hadn't happened yet. She would let him do it tomorrow.

She watched as he ran across the gravel path to open the large wooden door of the house before returning to open the car door for his Owner. She smiled at him as he held out his hand to steady her as she emerged, being very careful not to snag her stockings again. He would know to settle her comfortably in the living room where she could look out across the garden that ran all the way down to the summerhouse. She could then watch him bring her latest subject in through the impressive hallway and down the stairs to what used to be her childhood playroom. It had been redecorated since then, of course, many times over, and now it was a beautiful and lovingly created space, full of wonderful toys to control a willing submissive instead. She always loved this part, the part where her willing victim waited to be brought in to meet her, quivering like an autumn leaf about to be brought down suddenly by a powerful gust of wind.

* * *

With these and other thoughts running around in her mind, Fhionna settled down by the window and began to think about the room downstairs in more detail. A metal suspension frame hung from the ceiling that was capable of hoisting a fairly large adult completely off the floor. This was powered by an electric winch system because she'd discovered, through time, a manual device was too much like hard work. She'd definitely enjoyed the sound of the chains, though, as they ran their way through the loops and pulleys as the cranks were turned by hand. She missed that part of it, at least. There were also various whipping benches in the room, as well as a metal cage that stood upright in one corner and another that lay on its side for sleeping in. There was a wooden St Andrew's cross attached to the back wall, and dotted around the room were iron rings that served as anchor points for ropes or chains or restraints made up of various materials. Her own favourites to use were the soft leather wrist cuffs, which smelled of fresh linseed oil and creaked under the pressure of being tightened. She'd spent many a happy hour, even whole afternoons, in that room, sharing her passion for bondage and creating works of art, with her whips, on the bodies of her submissive play partners.

Just then, she heard the front door being opened along with two pairs of shoes sounding out loud and clear as they crossed the highly polished floor of the hallway. Tim had collected her latest victim and was leading him down to the chamber where he would be given the envelope containing the instructions she'd given so much effort to that afternoon. There were no audible voices but she hadn't really expected there to be, even though she listened for them anyway. Most of the submissives she decided to play with were too much in awe of their situation, feeling nervous about what was going to happen to them, that they had no words to utter to Tim. He was used to this, thankfully, and didn't break the silence to interrupt their thoughts.

She hadn't played with this male before and she wondered how quickly he would learn her ways and how to please her. She didn't take kindly to those who tried to top from the bottom, tried to control the play by making sure their needs were met before hers, or even above and beyond hers, sometimes. During their fairly frequent correspondence, however, he'd passed all her little tests, all the questions she'd asked him were answered and all the tasks she'd sent him to complete he'd done without any visible hesitation. He seemed well-educated, eager to please, honest, reliable, and very polite, but still in need of initiation into proper submission.

Fhionna knew that not many of the people she played with were going to become lifelong friends or slaves, for that matter, and was quite comfortable with this fact. If she could meet just one person who fulfilled both those roles at the same time then life would prove to be very happy. As it was, she'd met more than one and she considered herself to be extremely lucky.

II

"When I hold out my hand to be kissed I expect you to do so."

So far she was not impressed. He was kneeling on the floor, naked, as directed by the letter, and she'd made sure she'd given him enough time to finish writing the paragraph he'd been asked to complete but now she found that only a few lines had been written and they were very weak, at best.

"I give you credit for trying to do the task and for following the rest of my instructions, but the quality of your writing does not meet the desired standard. You were asked to think very carefully about why you wanted to serve me, and if this is the outcome of your profound thoughts then I believe you are not as intelligent as I presumed you to be."

Fhionna was always ultra-polite when playing with someone for the first time but could also feel herself become a little sarcastic when she thought the play partner wasn't actually going to be much fun. She certainly wasn't proud of the trait but knew herself well and accepted her own flaws.

She watched as the male slowly shuffled forward on his knees to kiss her leather clad hand. He was quite attractive but she had a feeling she was going to be disappointed by this play session. It would depend how he responded to her, of course, if he managed to relax enough to listen properly and if he were at all capable of learning from her years of experience. She believed he was willing to learn, that he truly wanted to submit, had an actual need for it, but she just wasn't sure whether or not the reality of play would match up to the fantasy he had built up in his mind.

As she raised his face up towards hers, she could see a glint of stubbornness in his dark eyes, but she enjoyed it.

"What do you have to say for your lack of imagination?"

The male shifted slightly and pulled his head out of her hand, moving backwards, although still on his knees. She took this as a sign that he would be a challenge, someone to conquer, but he was willing to play. Why else would he still be on his knees, after all?

"Well?"

He was obviously thinking about how to reply without causing further disapproval and this made her smile. She was delighted with the fact he was now about to try to give her a pleasing answer, while at the same time trying to save face.

With this, he moved forward once more and kissed the very tips of her fingers, not holding them with his own but placing his hands behind his back as he made the gesture.

Fhionna was happy to see some respect in his actions but distanced herself from him a little and decided that he needed some behavioural guidelines before she made any choices about the more tangible aspects of their play.

"First of all we will establish some rules. When you address me you shall call me Sir, as I prefer this term to Mistress. Secondly, while you are here, you shall be called Thing. Do you understand these basic rules so far?"

She watched him frown slightly but, at the same time, say, "Yes, Sir."

Reaching forward, she took his nipples in between her fingers and pulled him up off his knees. The male started to rise to his feet, somewhat unsteadily, and reached out to place his hands on her arms, to steady himself.

"Do not touch until you are allowed."

Thing, now fully upright, corrected himself and placed his hands behind his back again, wincing at the pain.

"Good. Now we're going to play a game."

Continuing to pinch his nipples, she pulled him down, almost to floor level, before raising him to his full height on tip toe. She repeated this action three times, pulling him quickly down into a squat, holding him there and pulling him back up, watching as he fought to remain in position each time, the strain from the pressure etched on his face.

"Such an easy way to test your eagerness to please and you did quite well. Kneel down, as before."

She removed her fingers and enjoyed the slow whistle of air that escaped from between his pursed lips. She also noticed his excitement.

Fhionna knew from their correspondence that he would like to try heavy-bondage, which diminished his senses, leaving him with the feeling of loss of control, to be fully at her mercy. She also knew she would enjoy the aesthetics of his slim body in bondage, with a blindfold, a gag, and his wrists bound, so she decided that he would be tied and put into the upright cage.

Crossing the room to pick her toys, she selected a latex blindfold that was padded for comfort, which also kept any light at bay, and a gag that was soft and supple and would fill his mouth, rendering anything but mere grunts or moans out of the question. The straps of the gag harness would snake up and over his face, parting at each side of his nose, and run round the side of his head, over his cheeks, to finally buckle at the back. The fine rope she chose to bind his body was silky and soft to the touch but it was strong, as long as she used the right loops and knots, and she could feel her own arousal growing as she ran her hands along its length.

"Stand up and come to me."

She watched him rise up from the floor and walk slowly towards her. He stopped in front of her but stayed silent, looking straight into her eyes, as if willing her to 'do her best.' A dare was being issued from a confident man but one who had never, to her knowledge, been in a similar position before. He was certainly trying to test her but she also thought he was maybe trying to be braver than he felt.

Without being told, he held his wrists out in front of his body to be tied and she watched his face as she started to coil the rope around them. He was grinning at her and she felt her amusement turn to slight annoyance. She placed the soft rubber blindfold over his eyes, pushed the gag into his mouth and then fixed the straps of the harness over his head. She wanted to see what he was capable of achieving. Maybe he could be made to cry. She certainly hoped so. She enjoyed making ego-laden submissives a little tearful.

The sight of this attractive male unable to do anything but dribble and listen to her instructions and obey them made Fhionna shiver. How she lived for such moments of blissful torture, especially to those who were as seemingly provocative as this one. She enjoyed a display of ego for one reason and one reason only and that was to bring it down to size. Otherwise it had no place in her pleasure. She found that the head-strong could usually be tamed and she loved the dance of it, as long as the submissive was actually capable of learning. Otherwise all too quickly it became boring.

Taking his wrists in her hands, she led him to the cage. The steel bars would be cold against his skin and she was looking forward to their initial contact.

"Place your hands above your head and feel for the bars at the top of the cage."

Thing did as he was told and grabbed onto them, as if for dear life, and, for the first time, she could actually see he was nervous.

Collecting more rope, she started to bind his whole body to the bars, listening to his breath rasp through the gag as its rate increased. She loved the feeling of power she had over him and his full potential suddenly became quite clear.

Thing moaned softly as the ropes tightened on his body, first round his arms, then around his chest as it circled his pecks where his nipples were standing to attention, like a girl's would when they were cold.

She enjoyed the feeling of his body against hers as she reached in to wind the rope round his waist, moving quickly and expertly, dangling its length down to his ankles and binding them, one at a time, at each side. He was now spread-eagle, in an upright position, hands tied to the bars at the top and his chest and waist tied to the bars at the back.

Fhionna stepped back, looked at his helpless body, and decided that his erection, now standing to attention, also needed to be bound. She felt Thing jump as she gripped his member in her gloved hands and wound some rope round his shaft and then down around his balls. She then pulled on the rope and tied it securely to the cage door after she'd closed it. He was now shaking slightly and his breathing was highly audible. She loved the sound of his gasps from behind the gag and felt her own sex respond to the sight of him. She very much wanted to break this male, to make him cry, make him shudder from the release she would eventually grant him. She wanted to watch him crumble before her as tears slid down his cheeks, gasping for air, and begging for mercy. But not yet.

She watched as he struggled to move his body forward to try and release some of the pressure on his bound erection.

"That won't do you any good, and perhaps by the end of our time together today you will be able to write a heartfelt and meaningful response to the task you were given."

As he groaned and nodded his head in response, she knew, even at this early stage of his torture, that he would be more compliant in future and that he may even learn some humility, in time. But for now, she wanted to lay claim to another part of his body. She really liked his large protruding nipples and wanted to see how much pain he could endure there. He'd done well, earlier, and she'd build it up slowly, knowing that her fingernails could ravage such tender skin. She thought that if anything would make him cry that it would be the eventual pain as she pulled her metal nipple clamps from them one by one, or perhaps at the same time, depending on how much he had accomplished.

Fhionna let the rope round his shaft slacken a little and listened to him sigh as the pressure decreased. He was panting and trying to wrestle free from his bonds but nothing happened, of course. He was tightly trussed and gave up after a few minutes.

Aware of his flagging energy, she reached through the bars of the cage to lightly touch his nipples. She felt him flinch, slightly, but was happy to see him surrender to the butter-soft leather that glided over them as he tried to get closer to her. She listened to him moan and noticed saliva escape from the bottom of the gag and run down his chest as he parted his lips a little. He also moved his hands as if in an attempt to wipe it away.

Feeling more sympathetic, she decided to give him some encouragement. "You're doing well. I love your large nipples. It makes me think that you're used to having them handled."

She inspected him as he inclined his head to hear her better and her excitement grew as he responded. She removed her gloves and ran her long, slender, fingers over his skin.

He seemed pleased at the contact and groaned as she started to pinch his nipples gently. She smiled as she increased her pressure and watched him wriggle. It appeared as though she'd found his weakness, a passion for receiving nipple torture. A passion she shared, in giving.

After a while, he was writhing in ecstasy but she knew that he still had a lot to give so decided to free him from the cage but to keep his hands bound. Slowly, she released his nipples from between her nails and listened to his sighs as he clearly didn't want her to stop. She laughed as he thrust himself forward to gain her attention.

"Don't be greedy."

Fhionna watched him sink back against the bars and attempt to wipe the dribble from his chin onto his arms, but failing to do so. She thought he looked defeated, almost, but realised he was just being moody at not having his own way. He had stiffened his body and was standing facing directly ahead, not like waiting for something else to happen but as if issuing another challenge, his ego obviously restored and his groans of ecstasy and his pleading noises quickly forgotten. She untied him and let the ropes fall away.

"Lower your head as you step out."

Doing as instructed, Thing stretched as he left the confined space behind. He was tall and elegant. Proud even. He flexed his muscles and let his arms come to rest straight down in front of his body, the rope still in place round his wrists.

"Move forward and kneel on the floor."

He did so with no argument, almost as if he thought that his experience was over, as if he was disappointed she hadn't continued his torture but at the same time confident that he'd bested her. She watched as he lowered himself to the ground and wait with what she knew was the kind of patience that's used when one waits for a long day to finish or a tiresome task to be completed, but she gently started to run her fingers over his nipples once more. She was pleased by his response as he swayed back and forth and murmured something, maybe a thank you, but actually more likely to be a comment or the command of 'harder.' Fhionna let go instantly and heard him grunt.

"Do you want more?"

She watched him nod his head before picking up nipple clamps from the nearby table. She paused to marvel at their tiny teeth. So intricately made. They positively gleamed in the light cast from the wall sconces.

Walking back to where she'd left him kneeling on the floor, she quickly attached them. Thing yelped and tried to pull away but she held them in place and quickly tightened their grip. She studied him as she pulled on the short chain that joined both clamps together and watched as his hands rose to hold onto her arms.

"Don't touch."

She was delighted when he removed his hands and began to sink lower to the floor.

"Lift yourself up onto your knees properly."

She increased the pressure of the clamps and let the tiny metal teeth bite into his tender flesh as she looked at him, considering his forehead now rested on her wrists. She allowed the contact and raised one hand to stroke his hair. This was the gesture that allowed his tears to flow. She knew that it wasn't just the pain itself but the tender action of her touch that had allowed him to give in. He'd finally submitted. There was no ego, no struggling, just release.

Fhionna felt it only fair to warn him that the removal of the clamps would be more painful than when they were being attached. This was caused by the rush of blood to his nipples. As she spoke, she admired his bare torso, glistening with drool as it ran like a small river down towards his groin. He was snivelling now, rather than crying openly, but the tears still glowed in the light as it shone on his face. She decided to show some mercy and removed them swiftly, watching him fall to the floor, curling up as if to protect himself, raising his arms up to his chest trying to bring himself comfort.

"Kneel up and lower your arms."

As he did so, she briefly placed a comforting hand on his shoulder before she removed the gag. Next she removed the ropes from round his wrists and then finally the blindfold.

Thing moved his stiff jaw from side to side, squinting as he raised his hand to protect his eyes from the dim light. Finally able to focus, he fixed her with his gaze before shuffling towards her on his knees, as he had done at the beginning of their play, but this time asking for permission to kiss her feet.

"Thank you, Sir."

She smiled down at him and was struck by the change in his demeanour, after only a short time together. She was quite confident that they would see each other again.

III

Once the front door was closed, Tim brought his Owner a glass of sherry. He knew that she often needed a little energy boost after such play times. He knocked on the door of her favourite room and quietly entered to find her on the window seat, once more.

"Thank you. You always know what I need."

Tim waited for further instructions so she asked him to run her a bath before making a start on dinner. She was suddenly very hungry but she needed to get out of her long dress and stilettos and refresh herself. She loved the feeling of slipping into the leather shoes but removing them always caused her some discomfort. She smiled as she stretched her toes, thoroughly amused and happy at the results of her play today. She wasn't entirely sure that he would turn out to be real slave material, someone who would be devoted to her every need, as much as it was possible given the general management life needed, but she was confident that they would have fun together again and she felt she'd made a little difference to his life. He'd certainly had his eyes opened to new possibilities and yet she wasn't convinced that she would be the right Dom for him, long-term, but time would tell.

Fhionna relaxed and sipped her sherry and enjoyed the burning sensation as it trickled down the back of her throat. She thought about how she'd purposefully not used his real name, had insisted on calling him 'Thing' instead of Martin. Somehow it had seemed more appropriate, as if she was willing him to become an object just for her pleasure.

Her thoughts were broken by a knock at the door before Tim entered and asked if there was anything she needed him to do before he started his chores in the kitchen.

"Yes, you may remove my stockings and rub my feet for a little while, please."

Tim, at once, took each delicate foot in his hands, removed the silk and smoothed out the stress from their soles, working away in silence until his Owner spoke.

"You may kiss my toes."

Shifting his position slightly, not expecting his Owner to have to move to accommodate his attentions, he now lay flat on his back on the floor with his hands tucked under his buttocks so that his devotion with his tongue was the only thing she should have to focus on.

He'd realised early on in their relationship that she liked a slave to perform a task to the best of their ability and without extraneous distractions. He knew, at that moment, she would only want to feel his mouth and would consider the attention of his hands to be unnecessary.

"Thank you, Tim. You may go and see to the bath now."

"Yes, Sir."

He raised himself up off the floor and left the room while his Master slowly removed the rest of her clothes and slipped into the velvet robe that he'd left on the chair beside the fireplace.

Fhionna loved an open fire, the flames dancing and crackling, creating shadows on the walls. The room was warm and suffused with a golden glow. She decided, though, that she would tear herself away from the fireside and climb the stairs to the bathroom before Tim found it necessary to come down to fetch her.

* * *

She found him on his knees beside the tub waving the water around to let it cool. When he heard her enter he turned off the taps and stood to greet her with a smile.

"It's ready, Master."

"Thank you. You can stay and wash me."

"Thank you, Sir."

Tim started to remove his clothing. He'd been taught that if she was naked in his presence that he should not remain dressed. Silently taking the soap in his hands, he rubbed it between them to gain a lather. He then began to wash her long elegant body, gently caressing her feet, her ankles, her calves and then her thighs. He lingered for a moment unsure of whether she would require any intimate touch but saw her close her eyes and part her thighs, as a signal for him to continue, so he slowly caressed the soft skin between her legs and up and over her neatly shaved mound, briefly touching her full and pouting lips. He was blushing and was relieved that his Owner wasn't watching him. He continued to gently caress and cleanse her soft, supple, body, moving slowly on to her belly and snaking upwards to her delicate breasts. He worked slowly and rhythmically in time to her shallow breaths, until he reached her slender neck.

With her eyes still closed, Fhionna raised her head into a position that allowed her slave to wash her hair.

Tim filled the crystal jug, which was always beside the bath, and let the water flow slowly over her head, her neck and down her back. He tenderly massaged her scalp with the lavender lotion she loved so much, rinsing the suds away and replacing the jug on the floor.

"Thank you. Go and attend to dinner, please. Wear your apron and your collar and nothing else."

As she watched him go downstairs she thought about how the next day would be a busy one. It was the 2nd of January, a Monday, and she had business to attend to. She enjoyed her work and had built up her small business from scratch. 'Window and Interior Displays,' her own pride and joy, now had six full-time employees, one of whom was her wonderful secretary. The others were all display artists who travelled the length and breadth of the UK to complete some of the most dazzling window displays she had ever seen, especially over the Christmas period. She was also particularly proud of her own creation, in the centre of Glasgow, in the window of Frasers, with its tall glass Christmas tree that glinted in the lights of Buchanan Street, and the old electric train set she'd saved from home, with which her brothers had enjoyed chasing poor old Benji the dog when they were little. It had been lovingly restored, for the occasion, and brought back so many wonderful memories, but she felt the best part of the display had been the white pottery statue of the little boy and girl opening their presents, which she'd positioned underneath the tree. It was simple and elegant and she loved it.

Fhionna closed her eyes. Christmas had been wonderful, and very hectic, but she needed to plan her team's activities for at least the next 4 months. This would mean scheduling and implementing displays for up to thirty shops, through Valentine's Day and the onset of spring and Easter. She loved to be busy but, at that moment, she was content to lie sleepily aware of her fresh, clean skin and enjoy the cooking aromas that drifted up from the kitchen. She smiled as she thought that she would instruct Tim to eat his meal from a bowl on the floor at her feet, as she sometimes liked him to do.

❧ Chapter 2 ❧

January 2012, New York

Aeneas

I

Aeneas was very proud of his Scottish heritage, even though he'd been born in Manhattan. He was proud of his unusual name, given to him by his parents whose own parents were Scottish. He knew that the name had meaning there and he'd tried to live up to its standard. It meant '*outstanding*' and he felt he'd done it justice, up until now. He'd never met his grandparents but he knew there were lots of Scots and Irish that lived in New York. In fact, most of the NYPD was of Irish descent.

Why this thought crossed his mind as he entered his office, to the cheers and shouts of '*Happy New Year*,' he wasn't quite sure. He was running late, as usual, but despite that, he felt that this was going to be a good year for him. He was travelling to Scotland next month for a business meeting that his ever-faithful personal assistant had arranged for him. Greg was a great guy but he was overly enthusiastic when it came to his travel arrangements, wanting to be responsible for every minute detail, and sometimes it ticked him off.

"I've booked you the executive suite at the Hotel Du Vin, Sir, right off the main road that leads down into the West End of Glasgow. I'm assuming that's suitable, Sir?"

"Yes, Greg, that's fine. Thank you."

At that moment, he just wanted to relax, drink his Scotch, and forget the strong urge of wanting to retire. He'd been in the banking industry for almost thirty years and he needed a change. He was looking for something new in his life but wasn't exactly sure what he wanted. He just knew that it had to be more fun than this and had to be pretty damn permanent to make him happy again.

With a deep sigh he downed his drink and headed over to the window. The sky wasn't clear. It was a very dark shade of grey, rather than a star-filled black, due to all the snow that crouched low in the clouds like flakes of dandruff on the shoulders of a giant, waiting to be brushed off. It had a heavy aura. He loved his office because it was based in a tall building that looked out on to Central Park, from 54th Street. He liked it there because he could see the sky and miles of the landscape and it wasn't the building or the city itself that was getting him down. He guessed it was just the lifestyle, too many parties to host, too many meetings to chair and too many people to fire now that the main business had been bought over by a company in Japan. That was the world of finance for you though, fickle at heart, and he was cheesed off with it. He wanted the world to stop, to let him off, to jump to safety before it started revolving again with all the crazy little lives starting up as normal.

Certain parts of his favourite poem would often come to mind when he had thoughts about shutting down the life he lived now. Not in a depressing way but more like in a, 'my life is passing too fast,' kind of way. Aeneas remembered that T. S. Eliot expressed the feeling perfectly in *Burnt Norton.* He thought it was about contradictions and how they can be reconciled, perhaps. He just needed breathing space, to have time to become himself, who he really wanted to be, and someone not based on the past or the future in the life he had now but to find another completely different life; where he could just 'be.' He knew he would sound ridiculous to anyone who dared to listen to thoughts like these but there they were, slap bang in the middle of his brain, as 2012 began in earnest.

* * *

It was Sunday the 1st of January and Aeneas had plans to meet up with his best friend for lunch. Hank loved this little tapas place that served the main dishes to you right off the hot plate in the centre of the room. It was Aeneas' turn to buy because it was Hank's birthday. He was turning fifty-two and was in need of some fun, not that lunch would cut it. They'd been friends since junior high and he had a feeling they'd both end up calling it a day early on Monday morning, with hangovers from hell and more than a few girls' phone numbers in each of their wallets. But that was Hank for you.

Aeneas loved him dearly and often wondered what his old friend would make of this need to not be living the life he had anymore. He would probably think he was nuts and point out that he would go stir crazy without his career for longer than a year. But that was just it, he felt like he'd made his mark in the financial world and that it didn't need his input anymore, not in any significant way. He knew he could tell Hank just about anything, though, so he'd take the plunge sooner rather than later.

For now, he walked happily along a street that was home to more than a few bars and restaurants, with each place vying for customers. One was offering a special offer of buy one meal and get the other one free, while another pronounced it had the best home cooked British food you could find in New York City, probably because the owners came from Leeds or somewhere in the north of England, he assumed. He turned the corner and started to jog the last block that would take him to their meeting place. It was just starting to snow and he didn't want to get soaked to the skin.

Arriving just in time to see Hank take his seat he waved over to catch his eye to let him know he was going to the restroom. He saw Hank wave back and settle in to order some wine, no doubt. Aeneas used the facilities and washed his hands, examining his cropped hair in the mirror above the sink and thinking that he should have trimmed his beard even though it was, by anyone else's standards, already quite short. He thought he looked quite young for his age and wondered what the day had in store for him. He knew that Hank would be in top form as his birthday was always an event to remember, even if it did fall on a Sunday this time.

Hank got up from his seat as he saw Aeneas moving towards him through the tables and chairs nestled together in the small area around the bar and past the central hot plate, which never ceased to entertain him.

"Hi, how you doin', good to see you."

They gave each other a half hug as they slapped each other on the back.

"Glad you could make it. Have I got some plans made for us tonight!"

Aeneas smiled. It was just as he'd figured so he'd have to go with the flow. At least his boss was aware of Hank's ritual birthday chaos and wouldn't be too upset when he failed to show for the seven o'clock meeting someone had scheduled. He made a mental note to fire them, whoever it was.

* * *

After many rounds in one of the clubs that lined the streets of Manhattan, Aeneas found the courage to bring up the subject of his discontentment. The conversation had got pretty serious, even though they were both a bit smashed, and he wanted Hank to know what was going on in his life. He didn't like keeping secrets from him, even though there was certainly more to tell than thinking about quitting his career. One step at a time though.

"Well, it's like this, how long can I work in this industry without completely burning out? I just feel that there's more to life than answering to a boss and at the same time being responsible for hundreds of people, all with really high expectations of financial gain, when, to be honest, some of them just aren't going to cut it. It feels like I'm two people, one who's the man I want to be but who's struggling to surface, and the other is the man who everyone else expects me to be, this reliable person who you can always depend on. That's all good, of course, but I feel like I'm drowning sometimes."

Hank was listening but he'd already figured out this was coming. He knew his friend too well to have missed the signs that Aeneas wasn't exactly happy, in a more general sense as well as in his career. He considered what to say and decided to just bite the bullet.

"I know, buddy. I've known for some time. You've made a lot of money and left some really important legacies behind in the deals you've done. As well as that, you've made some pretty crucial decisions that have paid off for the companies you've worked with. But I get it. It's just time to move on."

Hank was slurring his words slightly but he made sense just the same. Aeneas smiled at his friend and swayed closer to envelope him in a bear hug.

"I knew you would understand. Sorry I haven't told you before now. I should've guessed that you'd figure it out, though."

Hank smiled and raised his hand to one of the waiters to bring more drink.

"Let's celebrate. To me, another year older and as handsome as ever, and to you who's about to make some pretty interesting and life-changing decisions this year."

Aeneas raised his half empty glass in the air and echoed, "To us," just as the waitress brought them a bottle of champagne.

The liquid sparkled as it sloshed into their glasses and Aeneas held it up to the light above his head and watched the bubbles pop and fizz.

"You know, Hank, I'm travelling to Scotland next month and it might just be my last business trip for this company. I'm planning on staying a while, maybe tour the country a little. I've been before but I love Scotland and it would be a real shame not to sample as much of their single malt as I can while I'm in town."

Aeneas smiled. He noticed that Hank seemed to be pondering this news and was taking some time to respond.

"Whatever you decide to do with your life is fine by me. I'll always stick by you, but I can't help but get the feeling that there's more to this, 'wanting to quit,' than you're telling me."

Aeneas put his glass down rather shakily on the table top and looked at his friend. He guessed it was now time to let him know about some of his plans, but he couldn't bring himself to tell him the whole story. He did wonder when he'd have another opportunity to lay it out fully on the line but he just couldn't do it at that precise moment.

"There is more to tell, in fact, but I'm not sure you'd like it, to be honest. I want to retire, maybe go back to school, or do some travelling. One thing's for sure, I'm tired of working my butt off full-time, in an unforgiving industry. It saps your soul eventually."

Hank nodded and downed his champagne, not giving it a chance to be fully appreciated.

"I can tell you need a change but just be careful and take the time to make the right choices, is all I'm saying."

Aeneas nodded.

"When have you ever known me to make hasty decisions?" He

grinned and added, "But I know there's something more for me to explore. I'm not sure I can fill you in just now, I'm too drunk for a start, but I promise I'll tell you sometime soon."

* * *

Over the next week, Aeneas and Hank saw a lot of each other, sharing a meal together or attending fundraising events for the various charities they were both involved in. Aeneas thought Hank was a little more subdued than normal, but he knew that he would never make the first move in asking what his secret was. He also knew he wouldn't be able to keep it from him for much longer.

One night, at dinner, the time had come. He was nervous in case his old friend thought he was completely bonkers, or worse, wouldn't talk to him ever again. He was pretty sure the latter wouldn't happen, but he couldn't help feeling a little vulnerable.

"I leave for Europe in two weeks-time. I'm starting in Dublin then heading to London to catch up with some friends, then I'm going north to Glasgow for a few days."

Hank smiled at his friend.

"That's great. Had any more thoughts about what you'll do when you get back?"

"Of course. I've thought about little else, actually."

Aeneas sighed as he prepared to tell his best friend about his adventures in New York and in other parts of the world. Adventures that had left him restless but also with a yearning he hadn't been able to put into words before. How would he even start to explain his feelings and his needs to Hank? It dawned on Aeneas that he really wanted his friend's support but, with or without it, he was going to try and find what he really wanted and that was to find someone to belong to, to submit to, on some kind of semi-permanent basis.

"It's like this. For the past few years I've been living a double life. It's nothing bad. Just that it's made me feel impatient for change and left me with a need to explore."

Aeneas looked down at his hands as he said it but decided he should look Hank straight in the eyes, to gauge his reaction. He saw that Hank was gazing at him quizzically. He didn't think he look worried, as such, but he did appear slightly strained.

"Go on. You've started now. How hard can it be?"

Aeneas took the plunge and continued.

"You know, only too well, the stress of this business? Well I've been compensating by going all out in my sex life. I've had the most amazing hook-ups and experiences."

Hank spluttered his Coke across the table and started laughing. He wiped his chin with his napkin before he started speaking.

"Is that all? I thought you were about tell me you'd murdered someone or you were dealing arms, for God's sake."

Hank smirked and made waving gestures with his sticky hands for Aeneas to continue with his story, making it clear that he really hadn't thought those things but that he was nonetheless relieved that it was all about sex and nothing more.

Aeneas was laughing now too. He had to admit that it made him feel so much better to know that what he was going to say next was way down on Hank's list of possible deviancy.

"Ok, here goes. I've been seeing professional Dominatrix every time I've been away on business."

Hank smiled and said that while he knew what that was he was going to need more detail, only to take it slowly and not overload him all in one go.

Aeneas smiled back and was happy that the conversation was going so well. The weight was being lifted from his shoulders and he would be eternally grateful for that.

"I discovered when I was quite young that I loved dominant females. I guess it was when my math teacher used the belt on me when I was being disruptive in class." Aeneas smiled to himself at this memory and then continued, "I loved the way she looked, with that really short haircut and those seamed-stockings she wore with the tight skirts. I felt I had to act up to get her attention. It was as if my life depended on it."

Now they were both laughing hard, eyes wet with tears.

"Wow! You sure do know how to tell a story." Hank wiped his face and grinned at his friend. "So, what then?"

Aeneas continued, "Well, it never left me. I still am attracted to dominant women with short hair but it's much more than that. My whole sexual being is dependent on it now. In fact, it's not just my sexuality. There's a need in my life that has grown so much that, at times, it overwhelms me completely."

Aeneas was wide-eyed as he became more animated about expressing this secret to his best friend.

"I can't allow it to take over completely, but I need someone in my life to sort me out!"

Now they were both laughing again.

After a while, Hank used another napkin to dab at his wet cheeks and they sat in silence for a moment before he said, "Well, if that's what you need, buddy, then that's what you need. I, myself, would tend to be more dominant but I can see why you would want to be submissive. It rather suits you."

Aeneas was amazed that Hank had even used the word submissive but there it was, the word that described his feelings and, hopefully, something positive in his soon to be, new, life. What could he possibly say now that would express how much he felt he owed his friend by just being allowed to express his feelings? It was incredible. He wasn't sure how he was going to make it happen yet but the fact that it was now out in the open was awesome.

Instead of speaking, he just smiled at Hank as they finished their meal together. Eventually they both joked about how long it had taken Aeneas to let the cat out of the bag. He'd only known him most of his life, after all.

II

He wasn't sure how the past week had actually unfolded. It seemed mostly a blur. He felt excited, nervous and confused, all at the same time. He didn't know how he was ever going to manage to feel normal again. It was like his skin was tingling, the hairs on his arms seemed permanently raised in anticipation of something. He knew this 'something' wouldn't come from Hank himself, but he couldn't quite shake the feeling that Hank might feature in his future happiness now that he'd let slip about his desires.

There was a lot to think about, certainly. He would have to tell his friend about some of the adventures he'd been on in the past. It would most likely have to be on another of his famous get-togethers, certainly over a few pints at least. He had more than a few tales to tell, that was for sure. Over the past seven years or so he'd travelled a lot and met and played with more than his fair share of Dominatrix, some of whom he'd enjoyed being with and others not so much. He'd found that, over the years of play scenes, very few had that real spark, an almost tangible aura of Dominance, one that needed no words to explain but just existed.

When it came down to it, it was all very well letting these thoughts run around his head, but how on earth would he put them into words if he got the chance to do so? He'd always got the impression that when he met such a person, a woman who would instinctively be able to see his submissive core without having to ask for petty details, that she would want him to serve her. That she would realise what a special gift his submission could be. But he guessed he was fooling himself. How could such a person exist, right? He was crazy to think there was a Dom out there that was a veritable mind reader. Aeneas laughed at himself. What an ego he had. Even if there was such a person, someone with enough experience, at least, to recognise a true need to submit, who was to say that she would want him? But he couldn't help it. There'd been so many times that he'd run the scene over in his mind, how she would look, how he would respond to her commands. But did the fantasy ever match the reality? He thought that it must, or what was the point of even trying to find someone to belong to in this way? Surely there must be a person out there in the big-wide-world whom he could serve, devote himself to, pamper and cherish, in his submission to them.

Aeneas was relieved at being able to spend the day at home because at the moment he wouldn't survive a full day in the office. Not without going completely crazy. He got up from the bed to stretch his legs and wandered over to the window. He saw that the garden was still covered in snow, and when he touched his fingers to the frosted glass the cold seemed to comfort him somehow. He needed a walk, even if he was to freeze to death. So, switching off his computer, he watched the screen blink its response and shut down before he ran downstairs two at a time, full of energy at the thought of crunching through the solid whiteness outside. He located his coat and hat on the end of the wooden banister and headed to the hall closet to find his gloves and scarf. After making sure he'd picked up his keys, he flung the door open like an excited child. Outside, he stood looking up at his home for a minute, realising what he'd accomplished by working so hard most of his life, and then turned and walked towards the forest, which started at the end of his long driveway.

As he walked down the hill, he realised Toby would be at the house soon and he'd forgotten to leave him a note to go shopping and to make sure he picked up his suits from the drycleaners but he didn't feel it necessary to go back. Good old Toby. He'd probably know what was required of him for the day. He'd probably checked the cupboards and the refrigerator, already, and noticed the stubs of the collection tickets lying on the hall table.

Jogging down the hill, he smiled to himself at how boy-like he felt. Sometimes he just loved to abandon being a responsible grownup, with all its complications, and do something simple like enjoy the freedom to roam the grounds of his home. This was what he wanted, what he craved. Simply to be allowed the space to be himself, which extended into serving someone. He wanted the freedom to feel owned and loved and cared for, by ultimately giving up his selfishness to fulfil the wishes of that person. To have that choice in the first place. As it was, he felt stuck, like in quicksand, sinking slowly into dark mush and unable to pull free. Free. The word really did seem to punctuate his every thought, and he felt a little like a broken record, but it was gnawing away at his insides.

Out of breath from all the running around, he sat down heavily on a large frosty tree stump. He was fit but not as young as he used to be, that was for sure. He looked out into the distance at the clear, pale sky and another section of the T. S. Eliot verse came to mind. Aeneas was certain he'd seen into the future and plucked feelings from his heart. His poem expressed how he felt at that moment, to be released from his overwhelming need, released from his own motivations and actions by serving another human being. Embracing the terror and the delight, and all that it may entail. He didn't know what it would involve but he did know he was ready for it to happen, whatever 'it' was. He didn't think he wanted his whole life to be taken over but to have that very special presence in his life would be awesome.

Because of his past dalliances with Dominatrix from all over America and Europe he knew enough about what it was he enjoyed, what his own preferences for play were. He'd always enjoyed severe nipple torture, for a start, but the point for him now was to change his life significantly by giving himself over for another's pleasure, rather than his own. He knew, also, that this person would need to care for him and not just be 'going through the motions' in some scene that had no meaning to either of them. There must be a mutual respect and trust or else how could it possibly work. She would need to be intelligent and attractive to him too.

Aeneas stopped himself in mid flow as he realised that what he was in the middle of creating was his very own little checklist, exactly what he didn't want to do. Exactly what he was trying to escape from in finding someone to offer himself to in real servitude. It was all too easy to lapse into the mind-set of what he knew was described as 'topping from the bottom' in fetish circles. He'd been guilty of it before but also realised that it was, essentially, through an ultimate lack of respect for the capabilities of the Dom he was playing with. A fault of his own, undoubtedly, to be very quick to judge and lack attention if he decided that the person he played with was not, at the very least, his equal. He reprimanded himself for being so self-absorbed. He knew it was a failing and one that he'd have to work on.

He decided it was time to head home as he realised that the sky was turning from pale blue to a shade of grey that resembled the smoke from a winter fire, set outdoors. He'd driven himself mad with jumbled thoughts that whirled around with no real place to rest. He felt as though he was possessed, to the point of no return. So, making the decision there and then that he'd initiate a search into the fetish scene in Europe before he travelled to Scotland, he ran back up the driveway leaving the trees to rustle their judgement in the background.

Aeneas reached his front door just as Toby was returning from the tasks he'd hoped he'd had the initiative to complete on his own.

"Ah, Toby, good man. I forgot to leave you a note."

"What would you do without me? Just as well it's not just you rattling around in this big old house of yours."

Aeneas smiled and clapped him on the back.

"You're right of course. If it was just me here then I'd have starved to death long ago and been reduced to a threadbare tracksuit into the bargain."

Reaching out, he helped take the shopping into the kitchen and set it down on the counter. Dear Toby, he was getting old. Aeneas realised he'd been his handyman and housekeeper for the past twenty years. Or maybe even more. He also knew his birthday was coming up in April and he wanted to get him something special. He'd mentioned to him on several occasions that he should have his own cottage built on the grounds of the house, somewhere he could call his own and perhaps be comfortable enough to retire there while still being close by. Perhaps this was something that he could look into and then present the plans to him nearer to the time.

"What would you like for supper?" Toby was asking now, breaking into Aeneas' thoughts. "I bought some of that pasta salad dish you like from the deli and there's a beautiful salmon here too."

"That sounds great. I'm just going upstairs to the office for a while, but I'll be back down in an hour or two."

As he said it, he turned away and bounded up the stairs like a leaping gazelle. Toby called out after him to ask if there was a specific time he wanted him to cook the fish because it would only take twenty minutes or so, but Aeneas hadn't heard him because he was already sitting at his computer screen and bringing up interesting websites about fetish clubs and events in Europe, and Scotland in particular.

As the screen filled with list upon list of fetish contacts, it became painfully obvious that there were very few party listings and just too many Dominatrix that were offering all the usual activities. One Dom's site actually showed her in pictures with her breasts out, flexing a riding crop in her hand, and beckoning with her finger to 'come play with Mistress Annabelle.' Aeneas laughed. He thought it looked like the posters you see for joining up: '*Your Country Needs You.*' He wondered how she could possibly take herself seriously as a Dom and have pictures of herself in such obvious and actually quite demeaning poses.

Moving the mouse, he clicked on a few more sites but was only disappointed. He thought there must be another way to meet genuine people, someone who he could make happy and, therefore, make himself happy too. Closing down the list of sites, he thought he'd better make his search more specific but didn't know what to type in. It wasn't as if he knew of any fetish clubs or events he could search for. He thought for a minute and then put fingers to keys and tapped out the phrase, 'fetish clubs in Glasgow.' That should do it. The Scots had to be into fetish too. Aeneas grinned as images of submissive men in kilts and Dominant women in tartan dresses filled his head. He watched, still smiling to himself, as a few websites of interest appeared on the screen. There was one in particular, however, that caught his eye. 'Violate.' It was a fetish club not too far from where he would be staying in the west end, so he clicked on the entry tab and went through all the usual consensual questions, like:

'Are you over 18? Some of the content of this site is sexually explicit; click agree to confirm your continued interest. You will be asked for some personal details and to create a password before being allowed entry to the personal listings or gallery area.'

Aeneas was impressed by the professionalism of the site and felt excited. He quickly filled in his details, submissive orientation, age and gender, created his password, and gained entry to the personal column. He felt nervous as he scanned the entries but was also hopeful.

Just as he was scrolling down the second page, he noticed a posting from a guy called Martin who appeared to be rambling on about serving this Dominant woman for the first time and how amazing she was. He clicked on it and read on about how he was brought to his knees, even though he had been cocky to start with and thought that he was in control. He also said that by the end of a few hours he was actually crying and kissing her feet and how amazing the feeling was, being overpowered in this way. He continued to greedily suck in all the details this guy had written and wondered how on earth he could meet this woman. Martin hadn't given a name, except his own, and there were no details suggesting that she was a professional Dom.

In a flash decision, he clicked on the posting and replied to the entry. He thought he'd say how much he'd enjoyed the post and enquire about attending the club. He didn't want to seem too pushy so he didn't mention anything about the woman. At the end of the day, he would have made contact with someone who was starting to live his dream, it seemed, and he was over the moon at maybe having found people to talk to about his own desires.

Aeneas tapped in the final sentence of the reply and pressed send. The computer made a little whooshing sound and it was gone. Just then, Toby called up to him from the bottom of the staircase to say that supper was ready. Aeneas smiled and closed the lid of the laptop to let the screen rest for now and got up from his chair to head down to join Toby at the dining table. He felt a little wound up at having to sit through the meal knowing that he'd made his first move towards experiencing something new. It was an incredible feeling to have found this group of people on the other side of the Atlantic, people who took themselves seriously and seemed to live a fetish lifestyle out in the open, and also to know that he would be travelling there so soon.

His stomach tightened at the thought as he greeted Toby in the kitchen and commented on how good the fish looked.

"Wow! That looks great, Toby, Thank you."

Aeneas sat down and picked up his knife and fork. Dinner really did look excellent but his mind was elsewhere. Toby was in for very little in the way of conversation tonight.

❧ Chapter 3 ❧

February 2012, Glasgow

A Special Event

I

Fhionna was excited because it was Saturday and another club night had rolled around but mainly because it was her birthday. She noticed that it was already getting dark outside and in the corner of the room the old cuckoo clock from the Black Forest was due to strike four. She loved the dear old thing. She'd picked it up on a trip there once and had made arrangements for it to be sent back to Scotland for her. There was no way she could have transported the thing herself. She looked at it and realized that the wood was faded and that it was more than a little bit worn around the edges, with the paintwork dim instead of vibrant and cheerful, as it once was. The little bird had broken years ago and she'd had it replaced with a crouching figure, draped in chains, with whip marks on his back. It had been made for her by her artist friend. She mainly did paintings of figures in some kind of bondage or of heads in masks or with their mouths gagged. This had been a challenge for her, as she wasn't a sculptor, but she'd wanted to do it and had produced a wonderful little miniature figure and Tim had managed to wire it into place. It had been a great day. They'd celebrated by drinking good wine and eating imported cheeses while waiting for the clock to strike. What bliss. So much fun.

She was waiting, with very little visible patience, for Tim to bring her the parcel he'd been sent to collect from the village post office. It was a new outfit for the club attendance that night and she was eager to make sure it fit. She wanted to look perfect because it was her birthday celebration and all her friends would be expecting her to be wearing something quite extravagant, as she always did on special occasions.

At last, she heard the car approaching. She heard Tim close the car boot and shuffle about with some obvious difficulty so she thought she'd do him a kindness and help him.

Tim blushed as the door of the house opened just as he was trying to fumble with the handle.

"Thank you, Master," he said, as he walked past her and into the living room.

Fhionna almost skipped into the room behind him. She absolutely adored shopping and the more luxurious the outfit or accessories, the better. This time, though, it was something very special. It had been sent up from London and was handmade to her exact measurements. She knew the leather would be soft and supple because she'd received other garments from this firm of tailors and she was always amazed at just how beautiful each creation really was when it arrived. Her friend often helped out by sending them sketches of long flowing dresses or listened to her ideas about an outfit, making drawings to match them, and the most wonderful clothes would grow from these nuggets of enthusiastic imagination.

Heading straight towards the largest of the boxes, she released the satin ribbon that held the lid in place. She noticed that Tim started to exit the room to give her some privacy but she instructed him to stay because she would need his help. Excitedly, she lifted the lid and carefully removed the tissue paper inside.

"Pull the dress out, please, while I undress."

"Yes, Master."

Slowly he lifted it from the box and held it up for his Owner to view. Fhionna clapped her hands together and grinned broadly.

"Oh, Tim, it's perfect! Undo the buttons down the back for me."

Tim did as instructed while she watched like a child on Christmas morning as her presents were passed to her from under the tree. He held the dress up for her to step into, then helped her slip her arms into the long sleeves before starting to refasten all the buttons down to the waistline. The buttons went to the floor but the lower half were just for effect, copying and elongating the ridges of her slender spine.

When he'd finished, he collected the long dressing mirror she liked kept in the corner of the room and placed it in front of his Master so she could see the full effect. He thought the colour suited her dark hair and her slightly tanned complexion. The deep red folds of leather hung elegantly from her slim waist and dropped to the floor. The bodice of the dress moulded itself to her slim curves, while the mandarin collar climbed her elegant neck, framing her jawline. There was a deep V-shape that extended from the collar to the top of her breasts and the long sleeves tapered to a narrow end on each wrist.

Fhionna stared at her reflection and was amazed at the transformation that had taken place, just by the dress alone. But there was still one box to open. The finishing touch to the outfit. The pièce de résistance.

"Bring me the other box, please."

"Yes, Sir."

Tim moved to get the smaller package. It was thin and long and at first he thought it might be gloves. He placed the box on a little table beside the mirror.

"Open it for me, then place the cape round my shoulders."

She caught his eye in the mirror and smiled as she acknowledged the change in title. He knew she loved to be called Sir and by doing so had made it obvious that he'd noticed her excitement. He was a truly attentive slave and she loved him for it.

As instructed, he lifted the item from the box and placed it round her shoulders. The dark red and copper feathers of the short cape draped beautifully around her neck and down the front at each side of the deep V. It also draped a short distance down her back but not so as to cover the delicate buttons.

"Magnificent, Sir."

She laughed. "I feel amazing. It's wonderful, isn't it?"

He smiled at her glowing reflection in the mirror. He enjoyed her happiness. Mostly she was very easy to please. There had been very few moments over the years when he'd felt her anger, but when he had it made him weep with sorrow to have let her down. But at that moment he was truly happy to be sharing her obvious joy.

* * *

Aeneas strolled through the park. He was really here. Glasgow was a great place and this part of the city was his absolute favourite. He loved the botanic gardens, specifically the orchid houses, with their warmth and the tall glass ceilings that gave perfect views of the sky above. He enjoyed the tiny flowers of the Dendrobium orchid, which looked like tiny spiders, and the Cymbidium, that were very large and showy, the perfect antithesis of the others. Perhaps his favourite, though, were the Masdevallia, which didn't really look like you'd expect orchids to look at all. He thought that they looked a little like kites in flight, the flesh of the flower stretched tightly over a dainty skeleton of tendrils. Such beauty, seemingly fragile but almost always stronger than they looked. Perhaps like a woman. He laughed at his comparison. Where had that come from? But he guessed that his thoughts were now straying to his upcoming visit to the fetish club that night. He was so nervous about it he'd forgotten to buy a gift for the club owner, a Dominant woman called Fhionna, whom he'd learned of through more communications with Martin. It seemed that this was the woman Martin had written about. Once he'd found this out, he'd searched for any other comments about her and had found a few but none from the woman herself. This just served to make her more interesting to him, of course. Mysterious and powerful, not needing to be seen as publically involved in her own club website but rather to watch from afar? The thought that he might actually meet her in person made him physically sweat.

As he looked at the flowers, he suddenly decided he'd go for a long run before showering and dressing to attend the club. He was in good shape but wanted to feel that he looked his best. First of all though, he had to get her a gift because when he'd logged on that morning Martin had sent him a message saying that it was her birthday and that more than 300 people would be in attendance. Aeneas guessed this was a lot for a small city like Glasgow, and Martin had hinted as much just by the way he expressed himself when he wrote about it. He could tell that he was excited too. He'd implied that most of the people in attendance that night would be there to see Fhionna, specifically, and that it might be difficult to meet her at all but that he shouldn't go empty handed, just in case. Aeneas wouldn't have dreamed of doing such a thing, anyway, but found himself inspired by the beauty around him at that moment. He decided that an orchid would be perfect but perhaps not the large showy variety.

Feeling that he was going to end up being late, he hurried out of the hothouse building, then the park itself, and onto Buyers Road. Surely he must find what he was looking for there? Walking quickly down the street he saw a cute little florist with exotic plants and flowers in the window and felt thankful for such a good omen. As he opened the door of the shop, a tiny bell jingled to signal his arrival. God how he loved Europeans and their quaint little ways. You just wouldn't find that in Manhattan. Some of the more 'secret' shops he'd visited had a type of customer-entry-system but these tended to be electronic devises with buttons that you had to press to signal that you wanted in. Inside there would usually be a camera so that the storekeeper could choose whether to let you in or not. He'd been to one just like it before he left New York, to pick up an outfit suitable for tonight's festivities.

Bringing his thoughts back to the task at hand, he gazed at the variety of blooms in different coloured vases and at the intricate, and sometimes suggestive, statues that adorned the walls. He instinctively liked this place.

Just as he was wondering what to choose, a fair-haired girl stepped out through a heavy curtain at the back of the shop.

"Hi, is there something special you're looking for?"

Aeneas turned towards her and took in her delicate features.

"Hi. Yeah sure. I'm looking for an orchid actually. Do you have any in stock?"

The girl smiled and led him to a corner near the curtain where a table full of orchids stood.

"As you can see, they're quite popular. I get the impression that people are inspired by the gardens at the top of the road." She smiled again before continuing, "Do you know about orchids or would you like my help?"

"Oh, you're help, please, but I'd like something delicate, with flowers that aren't too dramatic."

The girl picked up a beautiful gold pot that contained a striking white orchid, which had thousands of tiny flowers on individual stems.

"A Dendrobium, if I'm not mistaken."

"Yes. I'm impressed."

Aeneas thought that her choice was perfect and decided that he need look no further.

"A great choice, thank you. I'm hoping the lady I present it too will find it as beautiful as I do."

The girl said that she knew she would love it and wrapped it in a pale gold paper that matched the shade of the pot exactly, adding a white silk ribbon near the base. Aeneas thanked her and left feeling very pleased with himself. He dearly hoped that he'd get a chance to give Fhionna her gift himself. Martin had suggested he may be able to help out by introducing him to her but if it didn't happen then he'd be completely on his own.

* * *

It was getting quite late and she still had to bathe. Tim had treated her to dinner, seated at a lovely little table in her favourite restaurant in the nearby village. It had been her birthday present and she'd loved it. Now that they were home, she knew she still had things to do but she couldn't help but gaze out the window at the garden. It was lovingly bathed in bright starlight. She knew it was cold outside but the snow had melted. She loved the snow, though, as it gave her an excuse to wear her fur coat. It wasn't real fur, of course, as some cruelty was just uncalled for. She laughed at the irony of this thought. Here she was, one of the most sadistic women on the planet, she was quite sure, gaining pleasure from the pain of the men and women who presented themselves to her to be controlled and yet she could never hurt an animal. The human ability to reason and consent was, of course, the crux of the matter and the most important part of any interaction or relationship.

As a jumble of thoughts flowed through her head, she decided she must try and calm down. She felt a little overexcited. It was definitely time to relax in a nice hot bath and think about the fun she would have in a little while. It was always an adventure because you didn't know who you might meet and couldn't predict what would happen, even if the play area of the club was strictly controlled. Sometimes couples who came to the club together would leave separately or with someone else entirely. Sometimes someone would have the experience of their life, meet the perfect Dom or slave, and have a long-term contract forged; a bit like a marriage but with no legal binding element. Contracts like these often included the enactment of a ceremony and Fhionna loved it when she could facilitate. In fact, there was one due to take place in May. Sophia, her friend, a Dominant woman, was to collar her submissive, Spike, making him into her full-time slave. It was to be an event to remember.

She sighed a little at the thought of her two friends starting out on their new relationship together and secretly wished them the happiness they sought in each other. But now it was time she called for Tim and instructed him to run her bath. She wasn't quite in the mood to be bathed tonight but rather just to float in bubbles and let her imagination run along on its own.

* * *

As she sank into the deep water, she picked up the glass of wine that was there waiting for her. The blood red liquid matched her mood. She closed her eyes and images of past encounters flitted through her head like the pages of a book being turned. Her memory didn't usually present itself in this manner, normally images just drifted in and out, but tonight it felt like she could actually control their selection, like finding a favourite section of a story and reading it over and over again until an image was created that somehow matched the words exactly.

The image she chose was of Bunty. She smiled as she mentally ran her fingers over the curve of her hips, moving her hands up towards her smooth pert breasts, and eventually tangling her fingers in the thick golden hair that waved and curled, winding its way down over her pale white skin. She was a creature of real beauty and had a stubborn streak, which Fhionna found challenging, but she loved her. Completely.

Fhionna opened her eyes and sipped from the glass in her hand. Bunty would be there tonight, of course, even though she didn't like to attend many clubs these days. There was a time when she was the belle of the ball, and attracted everyone's attention, male and female, but now she craved purely private play time. It was much more intimate and intense. She'd experienced her passion and thirst for punishment many times, of course, and quite often Bunty deserved it. She loved how her partner became wanton with desire, thrusting her bottom out to be caned, her eyes narrowed as if shy or sly perhaps, touching her own nipples, tweaking them into life and groaning with pleasure because she wanted to create her own arousal but give herself over for control at the same time. She knew that play, for Bunty, was complicated. She knew she loved her Owner with all her heart. She was her universe, her lover, her Master, her best friend, and yet she was amazed that she still found it difficult to submit at times. But when she did submit, and they reached a mutual place of desire and need and thirst for satisfaction, it was truly magical. There was no other feeling like it on earth.

Grudgingly bringing her mind back to the present, she knew it was time to get ready for the party. Turning forty wasn't such a big deal. She had grown in self-awareness, was at a point in her life that she knew exactly who she was, what she wanted, and how to get it. She felt confident and probably at her most sexy. She laughed. Sexy at forty. It wasn't something she'd expected to feel and it was probably more to do with the fact that she gave off a radiance, of sorts. A kind of self-confidence that wasn't ego related. She didn't need others' opinions to make her feel whole as a person and she'd certainly never let anyone dictate what she could or couldn't do with her life. She felt that it was more like an awareness of the love she desired to share. There was no arrogance, only an understanding that because she knew herself so well she could help others find themselves in the same way. She wanted to help others believe in themselves, to love themselves, and therefore love others and be happy.

Fhionna rang a little bell and waited.

"Come and help me, please, Tim. I've been in the bath for far too long and now I'm sure I look like a wrinkled prune. Help me get dressed and then we must go. You should wear your leather kilt tonight and your dress-shirt with the onyx studs and cufflinks I gave you."

"Yes, Sir. I'll fetch them."

After helping his Master from the tub, Tim held up the fluffy rose-scented towel that she enjoyed and wrapped it around her with his eyes averted.

"You can be so shy sometimes. Thank you. Now you must get ready too, while I dry myself, then come to my bedroom to fasten all the buttons on my gown."

Tim did as he was told. He could tell she was happy and a little distracted. Usually his Owner would take a lingering pleasure in giving him instructions to dry her skin, apply lotion to her long, slender legs, and paint her toenails, sending him back and forth from her dressing table until she chose a suitable colour of varnish. Tonight, it seemed, she was independent but content to be so. Tim knew his next task would be to arrange for another driver to pick them up and take them to the club. He was being allowed some time off from his duties as chauffeur, even though he didn't really want or need any. To be of service was his whole existence but he was grateful that she was a thoughtful and, ultimately, kind person. He could never have devoted himself to someone who was heartless or unthinking, unaware or unconcerned about the consequences of their actions.

Tonight was a very special occasion and he may not see much of her at all. He was used to others seeking her attentions, though. Fhionna was quite unique in her approach to life. She always gave her time to those who wanted to ask her questions, or simply to chat to people who wanted her friendship, for whatever reason. This Violate would be no different, he suspected, but perhaps even busier because of her birthday, and he was aware that she may need some respite. He was proud to be the one she would call on, along with Bunty, if she needed to rest or be quiet for a while. It would be a late night and she would be tired by the end of it but her two devoted slaves would be there to look after her.

II

Violate started at eight o'clock and it was now nine. It usually ran on till two in the morning, or sometimes later, or involved a kind of unofficial after party event. Fhionna wasn't sure how late she would stay. It would depend on the people she talked to and met that night. Each time was very different, even after having run the event for fifteen years. It could still reveal surprises and she loved that about it. She was glad she didn't actually have to be involved in setting it up herself anymore. She had managers to do that for her which meant she could just enjoy the ambiance and arrive and leave when she wanted to, without having to worry about how the dungeon equipment was dismantled, how people would get home after the club, or worry about paying all the bar staff and bouncers. It was all done for her, these days, and then she was presented with the receipts and contact numbers of people her staff thought she might find interesting in some way. One benefit of having close friends and subs as her management team was that they knew her tastes very well, who she would find interesting enough to play with or people who had good business ideas who she felt she could help out or join forces with. Sometimes she made lifelong friendships from being introduced to people, rather than by bumping into them herself. Usually she was just so busy either chatting to her friends, or playing in the dungeon room, that she rarely had the time to mingle as much as she'd like to.

Fhionna sank back into the leather seat of Bunty's car as she let her mind wander. They were nearly there and she was very excited about the party.

"Are you ok, Master?"

"Yes, thank you, Tim. I'm enjoying the thought of meeting new people tonight and I feel fabulous in my new gown."

Tim smiled and continued to look out the window as they made their way through the wet streets of Glasgow. It wasn't often he was allowed to sit in the back with his Owner and so he enjoyed this rare occasion of being able to be beside her, rather than being in the driver's seat. Bunty had been happy to drive and Tim was pleased he'd asked her first, before just booking a taxi. She'd said she could only stay for an hour or two that night and offered to drive them both there and arrange for a taxi to take them back to Fhionna's house afterwards, as her treat. He knew Bunty had already had the most wonderful play with their Master, and given her a birthday present, so she wouldn't mind her slave's early departure.

As they pulled up outside the gates of the club, Fhionna watched Bunty wind down the window and press the button on the panel at the entrance to speak to one of the staff inside. She watched the gates slowly spread apart and enjoyed the short drive down the private lane but was absolutely thrilled when she saw that someone had arranged to have flaming torches lit outside the door. She grinned and said, "Wonderful," out loud, to no-one in particular.

Tim smiled too and was pleased that his efforts were appreciated. He'd managed to contact Louise to ask her if she thought it was possible and they'd met a few weeks ago to plan it all out. Louise was one of Fhionna's subs and managers of Violate and she would be happy that her Master was so delighted with the outcome. It did look fantastic. The flames were high and seemed to leap up the front of the building, staining the blackness of the night sky with streaks of gold and orange.

Bunty jumped out and opened the car door for her Master, just as Tim was opening his own. He came round to her side to help her arrange her outfit, smoothing down the soft leather folds of her dress and the feathers of the shoulder cape.

"Thank you both for all your help, now let's get inside."

Fhionna led the way up the stone steps and through the tall glass doors that had been etched with the symbol of the club. The emblem was made up of an 'O' shape that had grown a spikey tail and a pair of small pointed horns. It was very marketable too, as it turned out.

She smiled and glanced back at her loyal slaves, who followed on behind. They were grinning like Cheshire cats as they knew the entertainment they'd arranged would make her laugh and couldn't wait to see her face. She happened to be special in a lot of people's lives and they wanted to make it the best night ever.

* * *

Aeneas hoped that the outfit he'd chosen in New York was appropriate. He'd checked with Violate's website to see the dress code but felt it was much harder for a male than a female to choose something that helped him look submissive yet didn't stand out too much or make him look silly. He really didn't want to start out on the wrong foot. He hadn't found someone to issue him with an Ownership collar, yet, but he hoped, one day, to be able to wear something round his neck that a woman had chosen for him as a sign of their bond. Surely it wasn't too much to ask?

He smiled to himself as he did up his leather trousers and bent over to fasten his boots. The top he'd chosen was a leather chest harness. He thought he'd made the right choice but now he wasn't so sure. The harness was certainly in the spirit of the club and the trousers looked good but maybe he looked more like a gay, Dom, bear than a straight sub. Ah well, he'd chosen them now. He figured that he wouldn't be completely satisfied with anything that he'd chosen to buy anyway. He was way too nervous to think things through properly.

Gathering the things he needed from the dresser, the last thing he picked up was the orchid. He couldn't forget that! One final check and he was out the door and heading down to the lobby. He'd booked a taxi but didn't really know how long the journey would take. It had just turned ten o'clock and he was sure the party would be well underway by now.

It was raining slightly but he was glad it wasn't as heavy as before. The taxi driver had done his best not to look Aeneas up and down as he got into the back seat of the cab but in the end curiosity won him over.

"Off somewhere nice are we, Sir?"

Aeneas smiled at him and said that he was indeed and that he was hoping to have a very special night. As it turned out, the cabby, 'Fred,' knew about Violate as he often ferried people to and fro in various 'stages of undress,' as he put it. Aeneas laughed and said that he was looking forward to it even more now. They chatted a little about America and about Glasgow but Aeneas wasn't really in the mood for small talk.

When they arrived, he paid his fare and jumped out. He smiled and waved at the back of the cab as it drove away. Taking a deep breath, he went to pull on the handle of the huge glass door in front of him but instead the door was opened by a curvy woman with a big smile on her face.

"Hi. This your first time?" She was laughing at him but not in an un-kind way.

"It is, yes, but I'm glad to be here, even if I feel like I'm entering the lion's den."

He smiled back and couldn't help but laugh too.

"I'm Louise. Just hold on a minute and I'll call through for someone to come and collect you. Can't have our foreign visitor just being left to wander about on his own. I'd get into so much trouble."

Aeneas thanked her but she'd already picked up the walky-talky and was speaking into it, interrupting the crackling static.

"Tim will show you around. There's a cloakroom, a dance floor, the main bar and a quiet room upstairs that's reserved for chatting. The all-important dungeon room is downstairs. That's the room that gets the most attention but it doesn't start to fill up with players until after ten-thirty usually."

Aeneas was just about to comment that it was nearly that time now when he sensed someone hovering at his elbow.

"Hi. I'm Tim. Follow me. We can start upstairs at the cloakroom and you can leave your bag and coat. I see you're already dressed the part."

Aeneas smiled rather nervously, feeling butterflies in his stomach at the mention of his outfit. He thanked Louise for her help and followed Tim into the depths of the club, on through a long hallway and up a flight of stairs.

Tim smiled up at the large man. He was much taller than he was and he liked the look of him.

"Which part of the US are you from?"

Aeneas realized that he hadn't introduced himself.

"Hi, I'm Aeneas. I'm from Manhattan."

He thought it sounded a bit like he was joining in an AA meeting rather than a friendly hello, but he guessed Tim would know he was nervous.

"Good name. I was in Manhattan when I was in the merchant navy as a young man. Many years ago now but I'd love to go back there sometime. Can I take your things for you?"

Tim took his jacket and went to take his bag. Aeneas wasn't sure but he thought that Tim might be flirting with him a little.

"Oh sure, thank you. That would be great. I just have to get something out of it first. I have a gift for the owner of the club. I was told by one of Violate's members that it was her birthday. I'd love to be able to give her it myself, though. Do you think that might be possible?"

"Let me hold your bag while you get it out and then I'll see where she is and, if I can, I'll introduce you."

Aeneas was amazed at the offer. He hadn't expected it to be as simple as that.

"That's very kind of you. I've been talking to a guy online called Martin and he said he would try and introduce me but I'll accept your generous offer, if you don't mind."

"I don't mind at all. It's not as likely that Martin would be able to do that anyway." Tim chuckled and continued, "I know her extremely well, you see."

Aeneas felt a little out of his league and told Tim that he was so nervous about meeting Fhionna that any help he could get would make him truly grateful.

"It's ok, she won't bite. She's actually a really nice person. I think she will like the look of you too. If you hadn't been so tall and muscular I might have thought twice about making the offer but, as it is, I think you'll be right up her street."

Tim was grinning like a Cheshire cat as he clapped Aeneas on the back.

"Come on. Let's see if we can find her. I'm guessing she'll be in the dungeon room somewhere, as she almost lives in there, but I've got the night off to enjoy myself tonight so I've had a chance to watch some fun and chat to people. Usually I'm at her side all night, which is where I love to be, but it makes a change to be able to roam a little. I have a radio with me in case I'm needed, though."

Aeneas followed on behind as he was taken through to the main dungeon. He liked the way that the walls were painted black and noticed there were silver stars plastered all over the ceiling in the hallway, which shimmered and glistened. He also saw the discrete lighting embedded in the walls that threw a few beams upwards and made quite a dramatic effect.

Watching the stars twinkle, for a moment, before moving his eyes onto Tim, he tried not to lose him in the crowd that was forming. He figured he must be Fhionna's slave, maybe even just one of them, but definitely a person to get to know better if he was ever to be part of her inner circle.

"This is Fhionna's favourite room. Am I right in assuming you're submissive?"

"What gave it away?"

Tim said that it was the slightly startled look of fear on his face that was the real clue.

"Yeah sure. I guess that's a dead giveaway. You've seen that expression before, right?"

"Yes, many times. Here we go then. Are you ready?"

Aeneas said, "As I'll ever be," and followed Tim into the dungeon, clutching the orchid between his shaking hands.

Aeneas was amazed. "Wow. What an awesome room."

Tim smiled and started to explain some of the pieces of equipment that lined two of the walls and then the ones that stood freely in the centre of the room. He explained that all the equipment belonged to Fhionna and that it was stored at the club long-term. He also explained that she was well known in the fetish scene in Scotland and in parts of the north of England and in London too. He said that she'd been in the fetish scene for about twenty years, even though he'd only known her for about seventeen of them.

"Wow! Oops, there I go again."

Aeneas was shocked he'd known her so long.

Tim confirmed his earlier thought, that he was her slave, and that serving her was his life but that she also had a slave called Bunty, whom she'd know even longer and who was her partner.

"Fhionna married her in a ceremony here. They don't live together, though. She isn't keen for people outside the fetish scene to know that she's bisexual. I think the people she employs in her business wouldn't give a damn, personally, but she says it suits Bunty too, to remain discrete."

Aeneas got the impression that she was a complex person. Well, maybe not complicated but certainly led an interesting life. Maybe, just maybe, he could get to know her a little. Maybe spend some time with her while he was over here for the next few days.

At that moment in time, though, he felt like he was struggling to take it all in. He was about to ask Tim more about the play that took place in the dungeon room when he saw him stop and look over into the back corner of the room. Following his gaze, he realized that the figure he was watching must be Fhionna and he felt his body involuntarily stiffen. There she was, the woman whom it had become his priority to find. She was standing a few feet away and he couldn't quite believe he was about to meet her. He wondered if he was actually awake and resisted the temptation to pinch himself.

Tim looked up at Aeneas and could tell by his face he was scared but also in awe of it all, of being at Violate for the first time, in awe of being in amongst people who weren't afraid to show their real selves to each other, but most of all in awe of her as she laughed with her friends, obviously enjoying herself.

"You'll be fine. Just follow my lead."

But Aeneas wasn't so sure. How could he just walk over and join her group of intimate friends? He caught hold of Tim's arm before he could lead him across the floor.

"I'm not sure I can do this. I'm too nervous, I think."

Tim stopped and said, in a mock American accent, "Sure you can, buddy," before he laughed and returned to his normal, polite English accent.

"Don't worry. You're with me. She'll take notice of you, I promise."

"Well, that's kinda the problem. What if I'm not up to her standard? What if she says, 'Lovely to meet you,' but politely turns away? What if…"

"You're panicking. None of that will happen. I know her type and you're definitely it."

Aeneas let Tim take him by the hand and didn't flinch, as he thought he might have done. He let him keep hold of it as he led him across the dungeon floor, through the middle of the equipment, avoiding all the people gathered around the edges of the room behind the rope that indicated a boundary for viewing purposes. He wondered what on earth they must have thought at seeing a large man being dragged across the room but realized that not many people would probably have noticed. Even if they had, was it so unusual in a place like Violate?

Suddenly, Tim was pulling him down to his height and whispering in his ear that if Fhionna offered him her hand to shake that he should actually kiss it instead. He said she'd love that.

Aeneas nodded that he understood and let Tim lead him the rest of the way.

* * *

"Well," Fhionna was saying as they arrived in front of her, "that's a matter of taste!"

Tim stood silently, presumably not wanting to interrupt her conversation, but at the same time he was smiling at her and keeping hold of Aeneas' hand like he was the gift to be presented, rather than a man with a one in his hands.

Slowly, she realized that Tim was there, waiting for her attention, so smiled at her friends and said, "I think Tim needs me."

"This is Aeneas, all the way from Manhattan. I think you may like him, Sir."

She turned her full gaze upon Tim's companion and held out her hand to introduce herself.

"Hello, Aeneas, what a long way you've travelled. I'm Fhionna, pleased to meet you."

As instructed, Aeneas took her fingers in his hand and kissed their tips.

"I'm so pleased to be allowed into your company Ma'am," he said and released her fingers after what he thought was an appropriate amount of time. To be honest, he had no clue as to what was appropriate but he hoped he'd got it right.

"What lovely manners. I see Tim has taught you well already."

Fhionna flashed a smile in Tim's direction and watched him blush.

"What a beautiful orchid, Aeneas. I do hope it's for me."

She grinned as she saw him wince and hold out the plant that now seemed so out of place he felt he had to explain it.

"It is, Ma'am. I hope you like it. It seems such a small token on your birthday but I hope it brings you some pleasure. I found a great little shop in the west-end and felt inspired by the orchids in the hothouses of the Botanic Gardens."

Aeneas paused, aware that he was starting to babble.

"It's perfect. Thank you. I adore orchids. My favourite flower, in fact. I hope you enjoy your evening. Are you staying in Glasgow long?"

"Thank you, Ma'am. I'm staying for three days. I have business here but I also found Violate online. Martin was writing about his meeting with you and it made me want to fly over on the next flight. Sorry. I hope you don't mind me telling you that. I tend to talk too much when I'm nervous."

"Not at all. I'm flattered that you put so much effort into trying to make it happen. Perhaps we can have a chat in the quiet room upstairs. It's very noisy through here."

Aeneas said that he would be honoured.

Fhionna glanced at Tim and nodded so he knew that she was happy to be left alone with this new male companion.

"Would it be too much of an imposition for me to attach a lead to the ring on your chest harness and lead you away?"

Aeneas turned bright red and whispered, "No, Ma'am. Thank you, Ma'am."

Happy to see he was eager to please, she slowly removed a chain with a large ring at its end from the many that hung around Tim's waist, at the top of his kilt, waiting for just such an occasion. She attached it to the metal loop on Aeneas' chest harness, which hung between his nipples.

"Please place your hands behind your back and keep your head slightly lowered."

Aeneas was amazed and thrilled, all at the same time, and immediately did as he was told. She certainly knew what she wanted and didn't waste any time getting to the point.

Fhionna was excited to have such a handsome creature on the end of a chain as she led him, slowly, back through the dungeon, through the starry hallway, and up the stairs to a room that was quiet. She felt that this might be the start of something exciting and watched her friends smile and wink at her as she walked by them, grinning.

❧ Chapter 4 ❧

March 2012, Between Cities

Devotion

I

It felt like the past couple of weeks had been nothing but a whirlwind of emotions. Aeneas' mind was all over the place, not being able to concentrate on even the simplest of tasks at work for thinking about her. The evening at Violate the previous month had been wonderful. He'd chatted with Fhionna for nearly two hours, about both their lives and passions and what they hoped to accomplish in the future, before she'd eventually snaked her hands down to his nipples and gently played with them between her fingers. He remembered he'd been kneeling in front of her with his hands behind his back the whole time and that while his body was certainly stiff and sore, when he was finally allowed to stand, he was also in heaven at having found such a wonderful and naturally dominant woman he might be able to make happy, in some way.

Now, in his office, it felt like it had all been some kind of dream. But he knew it was real because he still had the marks and the healed over scabs on his nipples from where he'd been tortured by her long fingernails. Her words to him at the end of the night ran through his mind…

"I'll give you tasks to complete and you will prove your worthiness to serve me, if that's what you want?"

And they still sent an excited shiver down his spine.

Aeneas had thought long and hard about the first task she'd given him to complete: to find a poem, with which to honour her, or put pen to paper and write a verse himself. He'd tried to write one of his own but feared it wouldn't be good enough, that it may not do her graceful beauty justice or, indeed, denote the power she already had over him. He knew from the hours of chat at Violate that she was well-educated and had a love of poetry from the nineteenth century, so he set himself the extended task of finding an appropriate tribute from this time period. This would prove difficult, though, as he'd no idea where to start. He'd wondered if it would be cheating to seek Tim's advice but decided it wouldn't be totally honest to seek help with his first assignment so decided to visit the library that afternoon. It had also crossed his mind that Tim might actually tell Fhionna he'd written to him asking for advice. He couldn't imagine what the outcome of that would be but it wasn't a good idea to get it wrong, at this stage. Part of his submissive nature was to be the best slave he could possibly be and even now, at the start of something so new, he would rather die than disappoint her.

When three o'clock came, he told Greg he was going out.

"Where will I say you are, Sir? Should anyone ask."

Aeneas sighed. He knew he was just doing his job but it got on his nerves to have to answer questions about where he would be and what he was doing, all the time, when he just needed to be left alone for an hour or two.

"Just out and unreachable for a while."

Greg took the hint and assured his boss that he wouldn't be disturbed.

"Thank you. Oh, and make sure that my calendar has a trip to Glasgow booked in for next week please."

His assistant opened his mouth to ask for more detail but thought better of it as Aeneas shot him a glance that suggested he should think carefully before asking any further questions at that particular moment in time.

Aeneas grabbed his jacket from the back of his chair and walked towards the door, putting his arms into the sleeves as he did so.

"I'd like to stay at the same hotel, if possible, and the dates should be over the weekend. If I have to come back on the Monday then that's ok, as long as I have two whole days there."

Greg acknowledged his task and thought that the Glasgow business deal must be really important to be going back after just three weeks. The following weekend was the seventeenth of March, and so he supposed it was actually a full month. But still, it wasn't like his boss to devote time to something unless it was a worthwhile project. He was known for finding new deals and setting them up then letting them develop in someone else's hands, if they were capable.

Striding out the door, Aeneas thought that he would probably be bombarded with questions when he got back but his focus had to be elsewhere. He knew it would take him a while to find suitable poetry but he was determined not to fail. It felt that his whole future happiness now depended on this single task and he wasn't about to let anything interrupt him.

The poem he finally selected was by Charles Baudelaire. It seemed appropriate somehow, even though he had never in his life attempted to analyse poetry. He loved to write short stories in his spare time, but he didn't get to do much of that these days.

The verse had been written in French but the English translation was published beside it, which was just as well. It was the title of the collection of verses which caught his eye. *Fleur du Mal*; Flowers of Evil, and the single poem within it called, *To a Passerby*, was perfect. It described the male mania, the woman's hold over him, and the sexuality that was imagined as he described her:

'Graceful, noble, with a statue's form. And I drank, trembling as a madman thrills, from her eyes, ashen sky where brooded storm, that softness that fascinates, the pleasure that kills… I am suddenly reborn from your swift glance.'

It felt like it had been waiting there for years, just for him to find it. It described how he felt as her eyes bore into him when he was allowed to be close to her in that first and only meeting so far. The intellect in her grey eyes, the way her brow had risen as if in enquiry to a comment he had made that might not be appropriate. She had secured his devotion, even then.

* * *

Fhionna was delighted with how her birthday event turned out. Not only had there been an erotic floor show but fire eaters and jugglers had roamed through the club, showing off their talents. It had been an amazing evening. Tim and Bunty had joined forces to arrange all the entertainment and she would need to thank them properly, but, for now, she let her mind wander and decided to oil the leather equipment in the dungeon. Usually she asked one of her slaves to keep it clean and fresh but she just felt she wanted to be in that particular room because it brought her comfort somehow.

She thought how strange it was that a smell could conjure up a vivid image in her mind, much like a piece of music could. The strong smell of the leather, in particular, always managed to help her relax and remember a play scene she had enjoyed. She did love the raw animal magic of a muscled male, tethered and bound, maybe with a long bit-gag in his mouth, snorting through his nose like a wild animal as she teased, caressed and tortured him in some way. She found it very easy and enjoyable to lightly pinch or scratch the skin of a human stallion, pretending that he really was her pet, her beast, to train him to serve her. Often the thought of a handsome male squirming and pulling at his bonds to escape her needle-like fingernails was all it took to make her excited. She could feel the dampness between her thighs now, as she thought about it.

Shifting her weight, slightly, she picked up a cloth, added some linseed oil, and applied it to the beautiful saddle she'd bought from a stable in Texas. She always enjoyed watching a pattern emerge. She laughed to herself as she thought of Aeneas wearing it, being made to crawl around the dungeon floor with her on his back, a bit in his mouth and a butt-plug tail inserted so that he could swish it on demand.

The image of his tall athletic body popped into her head and she purred with excitement. He'd definitely been the best birthday present of the night, and she made a mental note to reward Tim for recognising his worth. She would let him choose between three things: to bathe her, to sleep at her feet overnight, or to appear at a fetish club together that wasn't her own. She wondered which one he would choose. Fhionna knew he loved to spend time with her alone, sharing a closeness that came from many years of servitude, but she also knew he loved to be shown off in a more public arena, his ability to take the lash rivalled by no other.

As she tidied up the last of the equipment and closed the door to the dungeon behind her, she had the sensation of feeling lost, a bit disconnected. She'd no idea what time it was but her tummy rumbled and told her that it was time to eat.

Walking back up the stairs, she thought she'd make some hot chocolate, a little treat that would settle her down for the night while she read her book, perhaps, or looked over the photos taken at Violate last month to see which ones she would pick for the website. She always felt it was important to have selected the images of her friends and people having fun, herself. Nothing distasteful but glimpses of a stiletto heel, a leather clad amazon figure, or the tails of a whip moving through the air before reaching their soft, fleshy target.

Reaching the kitchen, she glanced at the clock above the stove and was surprised to see that it was already ten o'clock. She had no idea it was that late. Fhionna took comfort from the little details of boiling the water in her rather ancient kettle which sat on top of the large range. She liked the squeaky clean surface of the china mug that Martin had bought her as a gift the second time he met her. She liked it, though she thought it was an unusual thing to give her. Usually submissives whom she chose to play with brought her things like stockings or boxes of chocolates, not very original but still enjoyable. The cup, however, was thoughtful. It was tall and elegant, pure white, with gold lettering that spelled out the word 'Mistress.' It was really a coffee cup, she thought, as it had a stem and a flat base, a bit like the glasses they used in stylish cafés in France or Italy.

When the whistle blew, she emptied a generous quantity of chocolate powder and sugar into the mug then lifted the kettle and watched as the water tumbled from its spout. She picked up a little silver spoon that sat on the counter and stirred the mixture, making sure it had melted together before adding just a drop of milk. Perfect.

Happy with her choice, she left the kitchen, switched off the light, and headed upstairs to her bedroom being careful not to spill any on the floorboards as she went. She smiled to herself as she thought that it didn't matter too much if she did spill some because Tim would clean it up for her in the morning. He would, no doubt, find it as soon as he came through the front door.

* * *

Aeneas was running late and he fumbled about in his bag to find his passport. He'd checked over the arrangements that Greg had made and was now patting himself down to make sure nothing important was being left behind. The poem he'd selected and copied out in the library the week before was safely tucked into his inner jacket pocket. He'd rather not start out by losing it or forgetting to bring it. Even though he had only been in Fhionna's presence for a few hours he knew, instinctively, he shouldn't disappoint her. She seemed to be a caring, gentle person but he got the impression that she could be sadistic, even if not entirely merciless, in administering her slave's punishments. He thought about her as he closed his bag and picked up his house keys from the coffee table. He thought about her high cheek bones, slim neck, and her elegant fingers that had pulled and pinched at his large nipples. He was excited about seeing her again.

It was going to be a long flight but he was feeling wide awake. He couldn't help it but knew he'd end up tired when he arrived in Glasgow in the early hours of the morning. He never got used to how he could start a journey one day and then, after only a few hours flight, could be in a totally different country and time zone, making it difficult to adjust to things like meal times and sleep patterns. He'd travelled extensively due to the nature of his business but he guessed it was only natural to feel a little mixed up and more than a little restless on a trip like this. He was prepared for these changes, as much as he could be, but the added adventure of meeting her again, after only a few weeks, was bound to take its toll on his sleep during the flight.

Tim was meeting him at the other end and he was also a little nervous at having to make conversation with him. Aeneas felt like he knew the man pretty well, already, and he definitely respected him for making him feel so welcome at the club, and for making sure he met Fhionna properly that night, so he wasn't sure why he was hesitant now. He thought it was probably because he was unsure of what lay ahead and Tim would know a lot more than he did.

* * *

The flight landed on time and Aeneas gathered his belongings together, checking the poem was still there, as a nervous kid might check he hadn't forgotten his Gameboy. Everything was present and correct so all he had to do now was leave the plane.

As he headed towards baggage collection he could see Tim waiting for him, checking his watch. It hadn't really crossed his mind he might be on a tight schedule but the thought excited Aeneas. It was arousing to think that Fhionna would expect to know where they both were and what they were doing. Perhaps the next few days were going to be full of instructions like these. Tim, of course, would be used to it but he wasn't. He was more used to giving out orders than following them and hoped he could live up to her expectations.

Cases in tow, he held out his hand and thanked Tim for picking him up.

"No problem at all. I'm under strict orders to make sure you're safe and comfortable." Tim smiled as he grasped Aeneas' hand and added, "Master made it clear I'm to keep an eye on you."

He laughed, as he knew his Owner was excited to have Aeneas back in the country to serve her. She'd made plans and wanted to make sure he was rested and up to the challenges ahead.

"I'm quite sure she has some events scheduled that will test your endurance so make sure you get some sleep and have some good food in your belly."

Aeneas smiled back, rather nervously.

"Can you help me do the right things and says the right words?"

Tim said he should just be himself, as honesty was always the best policy, and if Fhionna had something to say or felt he needed guidance or correction that she would undoubtedly let him know.

Aeneas wasn't sure if he was comforted by these words but he was here to serve and was determined to do his best to make her happy, whatever it entailed.

II

Fhionna stretched like a cat, lengthening her fingers like claws and arching her back up off the mattress. Another beautiful winter's day, and the sun was pouring in through her bedroom window, chasing away shadow creatures that lurked in the dark recesses. She loved the winter sun. There was something ethereal about it. It was a thin light, not full blown like the hot sun of summer but, rather, it shimmered and gently folded itself into the corners of the room.

Wrapping a silk robe round her naked form as she slipped from the bed, she thought about how Tim always left a clean one for her each day. She enjoyed the fresh scent of the fabric and the feeling as it made contact with her thighs as she walked towards the window. Her room was directly above the living room downstairs and so shared the same view out over the garden. There were other rooms she could have picked but the lawn at the front of the house had always been her favourite view.

Today she was meeting the American male for lunch. She hoped he would turn out to be worth all the effort she was prepared to make in training him to serve her. It was only ten o'clock so their meeting was a few hours away yet. She'd planned an ordinary get-together, perhaps just chatting in one of the local village pubs, but then she'd changed her mind and decided that she would test him straightaway. She knew he was here for a few days and she was going to use him as much as she could, without scaring him away. Hopefully.

Fhionna laughed as she thought about the adventures that lay ahead and today was only the beginning. Tim would collect her and then pick up Aeneas from his hotel and they would travel into Glasgow city centre to a little place she knew where they could chat openly about all things fetish. The place didn't have a name on the outside of the building, to be discrete, but word of mouth made it one of the most popular places in the city to take a slave to dine. It was owned by a couple, George and Wayne, who had been partners for many years and enjoyed each other in a Dom/sub relationship, but they also had an interest in promoting the lifestyle outside of their cosy twosome. The result of this was the bistro they ran together where Dominants and their slaves or human pets could be themselves, outside of their homes and their bedrooms. Fhionna considered herself extremely lucky, of course, that she had her own home with the dungeon she'd installed but it was good to be able to venture out into the city and be accepted by people with similar tastes, outside of Violate parties. It was wonderful to be able to be out in the daylight and be as kinky as you wanted to be, without disturbing the regular Glasgow inhabitants.

Tim arrived to find an excited Owner waiting for him in the living room. It had just gone noon and the little wooden slave was doing his best to keep time as he popped out from his place of eternal bondage.

"How did Aeneas react last night when you picked him up? Was he nervous?"

"Yes, Sir. It was all he could do to keep himself from visibly shaking. I believe he is extremely excited too, though, Sir."

Fhionna smiled at Tim as he told her how Aeneas had pleaded with him to keep him surefooted in his meeting with her and how he'd not slept a wink on the plane for worrying about making mistakes. It was all very amusing and she loved the fact that Tim was enjoying relating the tale to her so much.

"Let's not keep him terrified for much longer."

Opening the passenger door, Tim helped her into her seat, making sure her long coat didn't catch on the frame. He'd let this happen before and remembered the consequences all too well. He'd received a sound thrashing with the cane because the velvet had been almost beyond repair. Luckily he'd been able to fix the damage by sending it to the tailor his Master used for her club outfits, but his backside had taken more time to heal than it had taken to mend the coat.

"Your effort to take care of my coat, this time, is duly noted."

Tim blushed. "I'll never make that mistake again, not meaning to be cheeky, Sir."

"I'm sure your buttocks still remember the sting of the cane, don't they?"

"Yes, Sir, they do."

Tim smiled at her, with warmth, as she settled back into the leather interior, ready to begin another little adventure.

* * *

Aeneas lay on his back in the darkness, sensing that something huge was about to happen. He hung his head off the side of the bed, feeling the skin of his cheeks slide down towards the floor and the veins in his neck throb with the exertion of pumping blood in a strange direction. Today was the day he was to meet Fhionna for lunch. He was to be ready by one o'clock so he had plenty of time. Admittedly, he'd slept longer than planned but now he had to wake up and make sure he presented himself properly.

Pulling himself up off the mattress, he padded his way across the room to the bathroom. The large roll top bath looked very inviting but he didn't really have the time to spare to indulge in its luxury. So, deciding to jump into the shower instead, he ran the water till it grew hot and trimmed his beard to an appropriate tidy stubble before entering the frosted glass cubicle. He loved this hotel. It was old fashioned with its heavy damask curtains and four-poster beds. The service was always first class and he liked to indulge himself with the finer things in life.

Back in the bedroom, he noticed that the sun was shining and thought how appropriate it was. A lovely start to an exciting day. He looked at his watch and realized that Fhionna and Tim would be arriving soon so ran around the room trying to work out what to wear and piling what he discarded back into either his case or the wardrobe. He wanted to look his best for her and knew that the white linen shirt suited him so decided to wear it with his dark blue suit and his heavy navy overcoat for warmth against the cold, Scottish air.

Finally, he draped the pale grey cashmere scarf around his neck and bent down to tie the laces of his black Italian leather shoes. He felt sexy and handsome and hoped she would think the same. He was glad Tim was going to be there for lunch but also hoped he would have some time alone with her. He didn't actually know what was in store for him, though, so he decided he should just breathe deeply and try to relax rather than try to second guess his fate.

Just as Aeneas was taking his third deep breath, in through his nose and releasing it slowly out though his parted lips, as his yoga instructor had taught him to do, he heard a knock on his room door. He walked slowly towards it, trying to keep calm but failing miserably, and opened it to find Tim standing there.

"Are you ready? Sir is waiting in the car so I'd be quick if I were you."

"I guess I am but I feel like I've forgotten something. I've checked my pockets about a million times."

When they were outside, Tim opened the back passenger door and gestured for Aeneas to get in.

"Good morning, Ma'am. It's so good to see you again. I'm rather nervous so please forgive my trembling."

Fhionna smiled and held out her hand.

Aeneas leaned forward and kissed the tips of her slender fingers, as he'd done the month before.

"I hope you don't mind, but can I ask where we're going? It might help me calm down."

"Certainly, we're going to a private little place I know where the food is wonderful and the company of the people is even better."

As she didn't venture any further in way of a description, Aeneas stayed quiet.

Within minutes, Tim pulled the car to a standstill outside a tall building that looked really old to Aeneas. Manhattan had some old, beautiful buildings too but nothing quite like this.

He gazed out the window as Tim came round to his Owner's side of the car and opened the door. As he didn't come round to his side Aeneas quickly jumped out and burst into a little trot to keep up.

Fhionna looked back over her shoulder to make sure Aeneas got the message and smiled as she saw him trip over the pavement. "Don't fall, you'll dirty your good suit."

Tim smiled at him, said that he was in for a treat and he should try to do as he was told quickly and without argument, although he may wish he hadn't worn his best clothes.

Aeneas struggled to stay calm as he nodded his head and could only just whisper to Tim that he was scared.

"You'll be perfectly fine. Just do your best. That's what really matters to her. If in doubt then do what I do."

Aeneas nodded again, finding that words wouldn't form themselves in any sort of coherent sequence.

Tim laughed and, realizing that Fhionna was already out of sight, hurried in after her, taking Aeneas by the hand and pulling him forward.

* * *

The room was amazing. The walls were very high and were painted the colour of a blue summer sky, which was completely unexpected. The building, itself, wouldn't have looked out of place in an old black and white horror movie but this was its antithesis, with its white flowing curtains and the hand carved chairs and tables, obviously made from natural tree trunks, only lightly shaped, sanded and varnished so that they kept most of their original charm.

Aeneas felt himself being led towards a table by a window but on closer inspection realized it wasn't a window at all but a section of wall that was painted white behind the white drapes. The effect was quite clever and he wondered how on earth the owners had thought up the décor.

Fhionna smiled and handed her coat to the waitress who'd appeared at her side.

"Hello, Michelle. This is Aeneas, and Tim you already know. If you would be kind enough to hang our coats and bring two large dog bowls please. Thank you."

Aeneas blinked at Michelle then looked at Tim, who he noticed was grinning from ear to ear as he removed two leather dog collars from his coat pocket before handing it over.

Aeneas could feel Fhionna's eyes on him and went red.

"Yes, I did ask for dog bowls. Sit at my feet on the floor, beside Tim, please."

Totally in shock, Aeneas managed to sort of stumble to the floor beside the leg of the table and her stiletto. Tim positioned himself at the other side then lifted himself up slightly so his Owner could place the collar round his neck then sank back down. Aeneas watched him and when she turned to him he copied Tim's actions, still amazed at what was happening.

She smiled down at him and said he was doing very well. Her attention then moved to her handbag as she removed two long silver chains with clasps on each end. As before, Aeneas watched as Tim raised himself up off the floor slightly so she could attach one end of the chain to his collar and clip the other end through a discretely placed metal loop under the table top. It would seem that Tim was now secured in place and she expected him to be too.

"I don't suppose you've ever eaten your lunch from a bowl on the floor, have you, Aeneas?"

"No, Ma'am. I haven't."

"And how does it make you feel?"

Bowing his head, he managed to mumble that he felt totally humiliated.

She smiled down at him and lifted his chin with her fingers.

"That's not my intention. You're among friends and people who live and breathe this type of lifestyle so try and relax. As you can see, Tim has been here many times so if you're feeling unsure then watch what he does and copy him."

Aeneas managed to say, "Yes, Ma'am, thank you," before freeing himself from her grip.

Tim noticed he'd moved his head away before she'd released him properly and looked at her face to gauge her reaction. He watched her lower herself down to Aeneas' ear and speak quietly into it. He'd thought lunch in this particular place might be too much for Aeneas to handle, on his first outing, but he knew she'd wanted to test him to see whether he'd do as he was told or would rebel and leave. To his relief, and to her great pleasure, he seemed to be just about coping and didn't bolt for the door.

Fhionna stroked Aeneas' hair and was thrilled when he rested his head on her hand. A sign of real affection, which he must have dredged up from the depths of his submission, and felt excited at the sight of this male bending to her will, in such a way, on their first proper encounter.

Lifting his head from her hand she said they should order some food. She asked Aeneas if he had any allergies and when he said he didn't she smiled down at him and proceeded to choose for the three of them.

Michelle appeared at the table in perfect timing and took the order, not phased that Fhionna was the one ordering all the food.

"Will your pets be allowed cutlery today, Madame, and are they permitted water bowls?"

Fhionna smiled and handed her back the menu.

"They shall eat with their fingers and yes, they're allowed water bowls, thank you."

"Very good, Madame."

Aeneas actually felt near to tears. He was struggling to take it all in and was mortified at being treated like an animal. His face and neck burned with embarrassment but he was also determined not to fail. He would put up with it but wondered what could possibly happen in the next four days and if he would be able to cope.

III

Later that afternoon, back in his hotel room, after 3 hours of feeling utterly humiliated, Aeneas had another task to complete. It seemed that she wanted to know his thoughts about his training, while he was here, as she'd asked him to keep a journal every day. She'd said it could have as many or as few entries as he wanted to write as long as they were honest and heartfelt, relaying his emotions. She'd also said that she would not punish him for anything he wrote in it.

When he'd left the car, Tim had given him a notepad and a pen to complete the task and said he would collect him the next morning at eleven. Aeneas managed to thank Fhionna for her company and walked quickly to his room. He felt angry and frustrated and wasn't quite sure if he wanted to continue down this path. He threw the notepad onto the bed and undressed. He wanted, more than anything else, at that point, to enjoy the luxury of the roll top bath. He felt he'd earned it after the day he'd endured.

Just as he stripped to the waist and stretched his muscles out to relax them, there was a knock on the door. He wondered who on earth it could be. He didn't want to be disturbed and would make sure the person knew it before they left.

Striding across the room, he yanked the door open and barked 'yes' at the person on the other side. He nearly fainted when he realised it was Fhionna and, unsure what to do next, he took two steps back and apologised for his rudeness.

"Bend down and kiss my feet, Aeneas."

Aeneas looked at the woman who stood before him and saw that her eyebrow was arched high into her hairline as she observed him with interest. He faltered. He knew if he didn't do what she asked he'd definitely return home defeated. Fighting the urge to let his ego win, Aeneas slowly moved to the floor and kissed her feet.

"I apologise for my rudeness again, Ma'am. I had no idea it would be you at my door."

Fhionna smiled. "I hope you'll be more careful in future! You may get up."

Aeneas rose from the floor and managed a small smile. He was very tired, all of a sudden.

"Please come in."

As she entered the room and looked around, she removed her gloves and took her place on a sofa that occupied the space of a huge bay window.

"I wanted to let you know I'm very proud of you and that you handled this afternoon very well. I repeat that it wasn't done to humiliate you, but I was interested to see how you handled yourself." Fhionna patted the seat beside her. "Come sit beside me, Aeneas."

Aeneas moved towards her and found himself bending to sit on the floor. He didn't really know why, when she'd asked him to be beside her, but it seemed the right thing to do.

She held out her hand and Aeneas gently took hold of her fingers and kissed them. "I wanted to make sure you were alright as you seemed upset and to tell you we will have dungeon time together tomorrow. This may seem a lot to take in at the moment but I want to train you as my slave."

Aeneas couldn't quite believe his ears. Could this be happening after just one day? His head was spinning and he couldn't answer her.

"This is a big step, Aeneas. If, in the morning, you've decided you don't wish to carry on then let Tim know when he comes to collect you. If you do, however, I will expect to receive a significant journal entry and for you to be brought to my home for the rest of the day."

Aeneas nodded his understanding. "I will do as you ask and give my continued service to you a great deal of thought. I will write the journal either way and leave it for you to read, should I decide to stay or to go home, Ma'am."

Fhionna smiled a sad little smile as she wondered whether or not he'd stay and start training for the life she knew he wanted or retreat to a place where he felt safe.

Aeneas rose to his feet too and walked her to the door, taking the poem from the pocket of his jacket as he did so. "Thank you, Ma'am, for all your attention. I would like to say that I've enjoyed it all but it wouldn't be completely honest. I respect you and promise to think about nothing else but your offer. Here's the poem you requested. Good night, Ma'am."

"Thank you. Goodnight." Fhionna took it and walked towards the lift, wondering if she would see him again.

Aeneas crossed the room and sank down onto the bed. He had a lot to think about. This beautiful, dominant, intelligent woman was offering him what he'd always wanted and here he was doubting himself; doubting whether he could pursue the lifestyle properly. He knew himself well, though. He'd have to commit to her fully or else not at all and she'd expect the same. She was a woman who was used to her own way, but she seemed to care about him and this made all the difference. She wasn't just interested in using him up and spitting him out like so many dominant women he'd met over the years. She seemed genuinely concerned for his happiness as her slave. He knew she would push him to his limits, and beyond, but he felt she would look after him and cherish him while she did it. He also knew he'd be punished and have to receive pain but felt she would be fair in her judgements. Aeneas wondered how he could possibly devote his life to slavery but also wondered how he could reject this amazing opportunity.

* * *

"What do you think, Tim? Have I pushed him too far? He has the makings of a truly wonderful slave and I needed to test him. Sometimes when someone is so new to the reality of being a slave, though, it's hard to impart just how important this lifestyle is and there's no other way to do it but to make them feel that they'll either sink or swim straightaway."

Fhionna was rambling on but she wanted Tim's opinion. She knew he would always be honest with her, even while trying to be diplomatic. She also knew Tim hated it when she asked him such hard questions, but she'd always told him she would never punish him for having an opinion. Maybe he felt, one day, she might decide he'd crossed a line and change her mind but she was sure he felt she'd always respected him, and so a promise was a promise, even if she didn't always agree with what he said.

As these thoughts skipped through her brain, she saw Tim wince in the mirror as he helped her undress; the sound of water running into the tub in the background. She laughed. "I want to hear what you have to say about how I treated Aeneas today and if you think he'll stay."

Tim sighed, he couldn't help himself, and when he stood up to undo the last button at the back of her dress he caught her eye but quickly looked away again.

"You're going to say I was too hard on him, aren't you!"

"No, Master, well, maybe a little, Sir. I believe he's quite a powerful man in America and while he may have fantasised about a chance like this he may not be able to actually go through with it for real. I don't mean to criticise, I would never do that, and you have been training slaves for a long time, but I feel he may not quite be ready for life as a slave."

It was her turn to let out a little sigh and Tim tensed.

"I think you're right. I may have expected too much too soon. He said he'd write his journal no matter what his final decision was so at least that's something. It means he's a thinker and I like that. He's not afraid of his emotions and I like that too. I hope he has the courage to follow through but I suppose time will tell."

Fhionna wanted to continue their conversation but asked him to fetch the poem Aeneas had given her instead.

"I'm looking forward to seeing what he chose. He may even have attempted to take pen to paper himself."

Tim smiled and left it by the bath for his Owner to read before heading to the kitchen. If she wanted him she would ring.

* * *

The next morning, Tim turned up at Aeneas' hotel room as directed. He knew his Owner was excited and a little nervous, although she would never admit to this last feeling. He smiled to himself as he approached the door and imagined her in the living room at home, with the fire blazing in the hearth. He'd left her lying comfortably on her favourite sofa, with breakfast on a tray at her side and her computer on her lap, the screen's artificial glow outdone by the light of the flames from the fire. Now, as he approached to knock, he wondered if he would be handed the journal and nothing else, maybe even witness a packed case on the bed, or would Aeneas be ready and waiting to continue his training. Tim couldn't help but feel a little excited himself.

Straightening his tie, which he always did when he was slightly anxious, he rapped on the door. It seemed like such a long time before it opened but when it did Aeneas stood before him, smiling, with journal in hand and his coat on.

"Well I may be a complete fool," he said, "but what the hell. I have to do it!"

Tim laughed. "Congratulations. A very good decision, even though I'm pretty sure you don't know what you're letting yourself in for!"

"No, I don't, but I guess that's part of it, isn't it, giving yourself completely to someone else for control."

Tim took the bag from the other man's shoulder and said, "Let's go then. Sir will be thrilled."

* * *

Fhionna felt a little on edge but she occupied herself with sorting out the photos for the club website. She remembered that she was going to do this before but never got around to it. It seemed the perfect activity to distract her from thinking about whether or not Aeneas would become hers. She had to admit, she would be more than a little disappointed if he were to return home and all she had left was his writing and the verse to remind her of the mistake she'd made in pushing him too hard. She felt she sometimes got the balance wrong, misjudging the depths to which a submissive might descend in order to pursue the lifestyle they craved. This didn't happen often, thank goodness. She was usually a very good judge of character but maybe this was one of those rare occasions. It would be a real pity if such a handsome man escaped her loving control.

These thoughts ticked through her mind and when she looked at the clock it was already eleven. In about five minutes or so she would have her answer because Tim would be texting to let her know if Aeneas was with him or not. Trying to be patient, she slid the breakfast tray under the sofa with her foot and closed the lid on her laptop at the same time. She rose from the couch and nestled closer to the fire, watching the flames dance their way up the chimney, radiating heat that comforted and consoled.

Fhionna picked up her phone and, as she did, it vibrated in her hand. She gazed down at it and swiped her finger across the screen to unlock it, to read the text from Tim:

Dear Sir, I have the package. The journal is in my possession and so is its creator. May I be the first to congratulate you on your new conquest!

Absolutely delighted, she clapped her hands together with excitement. A surge of joy ran through her body, making her shiver. She would run upstairs and shower but first she must answer Tim's wonderful text:

Wonderful news. I am absolutely delighted. When you arrive, leave the journal in the living room before taking him down to the dungeon. Tell him to strip. You may ask him if he would like a cup of tea or a small whisky to calm his nerves. He may wander around the room so there's no need to instruct him to kneel and wait.

Pressing 'send' and throwing the phone down onto the sofa as she passed it, Fhionna almost ran from the room like an excited child. Upstairs she showered and chose her outfit, one that flowed down the full length of her body, the white silk almost virginal as it hung in delicate folds from her slim hips. The sleeves were long and edged with lace. The bodice was fitted and the neckline plunged down, over her breasts, to where an empire line would normally be. The gown was delicate but somehow exuded power when she wore it. She decided she would also remain barefoot and wondered if Aeneas would make a comment or be far too nervous to even notice.

* * *

Downstairs the door opened and Tim brought Aeneas into the house. He watched him as he silently looked around the great hall of Fhionna's home. Up until that point, Aeneas had talked his ear off and asked so many questions during the car ride that Tim, eventually, had to ask him to be quiet for a little while. He smiled at Aeneas when he said it, though, and Aeneas smiled back, apologising for being so excited and rambling on so much.

"Let me take your journal and leave it in the living room. I've been given instructions to follow so you should do as I ask, please."

"Yes, Tim. I won't let you down either."

"Good, because I might get punished and if I did I wouldn't want you to feel responsible. It's one thing to get punished for one's own errors but to be made to watch someone else suffer because of them is quite another matter."

* * *

Fhionna opened her bedroom door so she could listen to both her slaves talking quietly in the hall below. She couldn't really hear what they were saying but she knew Tim would be trying to advise Aeneas, giving him little hints on protocol. Once she'd heard them continue down to the dungeon room, she moved to the staircase, her bare feet making no sound as she descended. She was eager to read what he'd written because she was sure he'd be expressive.

As expected, the journal was on the hearth. She sat on the floor with her legs curled underneath her, picked up the notepad and turned to the first page. She was pleased to see she wouldn't be disappointed.

Dear Madame,

There are few words that could truly express my humiliation yesterday but I will try my best. I had never dreamed of being in such a position, being chained to a table, having to sit on the floor and eat like an animal. I found it very distressing mainly because it was so unexpected. I am a very determined person, however, and did not want to fail the test.

It is this fact, more than the physicality of the test itself, that I wish to write about. I thought about why this was the case, why did I want to succeed so much? I thought about the possibility that it may have been pure determination only, a stubbornness not to be broken, but this is not the case. I came to realize that it was, in fact, because I didn't want to let you down and this was a revelation.

While I have dreamed about service to someone like you, I have never experienced it in this way before. I have played with other dominant women and have served them, I hope, to acceptable levels, but this experience was totally new to me. I found myself actually wanting to succeed just for you, not to serve my own ego.

My submission has never been selfless in this way. Ever! The humiliation was very hard to bear, even though you promised this was not the aim of the experience. Perhaps it's because of this promise, or partly, at least, that I've come to realize that to be in your service is where I belong.

Making you happy, Ma'am, is more important to me than anything else, it would seem.

Fhionna read the words Aeneas had written once more before placing the notepad back onto the tiles where she'd found it. She sighed softly and marvelled at how he'd managed to express his feelings so eloquently. Not many of the men she'd met over the years possessed such skill and, more often than not, had run from their submissive selves. She was impressed by his words but now it was definitely time to play, to see what he could do to match them.

* * *

When she walked in, Aeneas was naked and kneeling on the floor but looking up at the pictures on the walls. She sometimes forgot they were there. Most of the scenes were of servitude of some kind and images of bodies in various degrees of bondage, which thrilled her. She'd taken the photos herself, during play, and each one brought with it a wonderful memory, even though she hadn't looked at them properly for quite some time. Some of the other photographs were of her, in full Dominant glory, and she followed his gaze to one that depicted her wearing her long, black, leather dress-coat with the white leather collar and cuffs, sitting on a rubber-draped chair and holding a long cane in her gloved hands. She knew she looked pretty severe and wondered what Aeneas was thinking as he stared at it.

Aeneas hadn't realised she was in the room and he jumped when he noticed she was watching him. "I'm sorry. I was miles away. I was thinking about the pain you could inflict with the cane you're holding."

Fhionna smiled. "Do you like the picture?"

He said that he loved it, but it made him feel both nervous and excited and probably more the former than the latter.

She laughed. "I love it too, although I look very serious. Perhaps a little smile would have been better?"

"Oh no, Ma'am. You look the perfect picture of Dominance as it is; the way your legs emerge elegantly from the soft folds of the leather dress, the gloves show off your slender fingers and hands beautifully, and your breasts are just visible in the deep V of the neckline."

Aeneas looked up at Fhionna and blushed as he realised what he'd said and hoped she wouldn't take offence at such intimate comments about her body. But she smiled down at him and thanked him for the lovely compliments.

Walking further into the room she noticed an empty whisky glass sitting on the floor in the corner, where his clothes lay neatly folded and out of the way of any equipment.

"I see you've enjoyed a wee nip of courage."

Fhionna laughed as Aeneas grinned up at her and said he'd enjoyed it and that it had definitely been needed.

"Well, now that you've been prepped, we shall begin. You will start by calling me Master or Sir. I will also, by the end of our play today, have chosen a new slave name for you. I will use a mixture of your real name and your slave name, as I feel is appropriate."

Aeneas bowed his head slightly and said, "Yes, Ma'am, er, Master. Sorry, Master."

Fhionna continued, "Place your hands behind your back at all times when in my company in the dungeon or the restaurant or the club. I will introduce you to my friends using your slave name."

She paused as she looked at him and was pleased to see he'd already placed his hands behind his back. He was going to be a quick learner. Sometimes, in past play times, she'd had to tell her submissive to do something more than once.

"You'll be allowed to tell me, at some point, how you've served others and what you found to be the most exciting aspects of play. Our short time at Violate suggests you love nipple torture, as much as I do, so you're lucky."

Aeneas asked for permission to speak, which Fhionna found adorable.

"Master, may I just say that I am yours to command and I will always do my best to please you, but I'm not perfect and may fail sometimes. Nipple torture is indeed my favourite type of pain and pleasure mix but please use me as you see fit."

"I certainly will but I appreciate your candour. Stand up and go over to the spanking bench."

Aeneas did as instructed, remembering to keep his hands where they were, and leaned over the red leather bench. It felt cold and he wasn't sure what to do next. It crossed his mind that she might find it difficult to do anything to him with his hands behind his back but he daren't move them either. It was as if she'd read his thoughts, though, because she told him to place his arms down the sides and fastened them there. Next, he felt her touch on his ankles as she strapped them into place. Then his knees and thighs were secured and, lastly, a large flat leather brace was fitted over his lower back. Aeneas felt it tighten. He knew instantly that this device would allow for very little movement and felt a slight panic rise in his throat.

Fhionna moved to his head and spoke to him. "I'm about to place a gag in your mouth. I like to hear a slave moan as I work my magic on his body. Some sensations will be pleasurable and some less so. I'll look after you, so try not to struggle, but I'll also be testing your boundaries and pain threshold." She smiled down at him and lifted his head with her hand, parting his lips with her fingers to open his mouth more fully.

Aeneas felt her push a phallic shaped gag between his lips and choked a little as it filled his mouth. He felt foolish as she strapped it in place behind his head and he started to dribble almost immediately.

"How beautiful you look. So shy and nervous."

Aeneas dipped his head as she spoke to him but she raised it again to make him look into her eyes.

"I'll begin with a light spanking, by hand, and work my way up through my various paddles and straps. You might be able to take the cane by the end of our play time today so try your best."

He nodded slowly and bowed his head again, feeling tears forming in the corners of his eyes. He didn't know why he was upset. Perhaps it was just so real, all of a sudden. Maybe he was overwhelmed by her caring concern for him to succeed and make her proud of him.

With his face flat against the bench, he could smell the wax and feel his own saliva dribbling onto his chin. Soon it would form a pool under his face and neck and would be uncomfortable to lie in. It seemed like he wasn't being given a blindfold and he didn't know if this made his predicament worse or not. He felt that being unable to see what she was about to do to him might be of benefit but also knowing what implement she had in her hand might cause him to panic.

Fhionna reached down and stroked his hair, lovingly. She wiped the drool from under his chin and the tears from his cheeks.

Aeneas knew this was a signal, she was ready to begin his torture. He nuzzled his head into her hand, briefly, to say thank you and then settled down, as much as he could, to receive what she wanted to give.

*   *   *

Aeneas' cheeks were red and fiery from the spanking but she'd warned him it was just a warm up. He knew this from previous experiences of being spanked and paddled but he'd never felt it so intensely before. It wasn't that she was stronger than anyone else he'd visited for a session but more the emotion involved. The need to do well was so overpowering that it made every touch feel electric; heightened in some way.

He felt her move to his head, once more, and bend to whisper in his ear that he was doing well. She moved away, presumably to fetch a paddle or belt of some kind but he didn't have the nerve to look and see what she'd picked up. He waited what seemed like an age and then felt pain radiate through his buttocks. A loud 'whack' filled the room as the implement was brought down onto his flesh. Aeneas jumped a little but there wasn't much room to manoeuvre. Quickly another blow landed. Aeneas groaned and made a growling noise as the second blow hit home. He wriggled his buttocks, trying to cool them before the next inevitable stroke.

"Squirm all you want but it won't do any good."

Aeneas growled a little. He wondered if he was completely mad to have placed himself in this position.

She laughed and said she had his new name, already. In that moment of growling he became her dog.

Aeneas found he could raise his head just enough to view her in the long mirror that stood in front of the bench. He tried to free his arms and legs but it was impossible. He felt humiliated at having such a stupid animal name given to him.

Fhionna patiently waited for him to stop. "That's enough, Dog. I understand you don't like your slave name but that's just too bad."

She noticed he'd turned his head away from her as a third stroke landed square on his pink buttocks, then a fourth, a fifth, and sixth until she stopped to look at his reflection. He didn't move and seemed not to care what was happening to him. She walked round to his head and stroked his hair but he didn't respond.

"Huffiness is unacceptable, so get yourself out of it right now."

He turned his head and looked at her sulkily.

She placed her hand on his cheek and he slowly, grudgingly rubbed it against her palm.

"That's better. I'm nowhere near finished yet." She walked back to the rack of whips, paddles and canes and picked up a long leather belt with a wooden handle. This was her particular favourite.

She was breathing heavily from the exertion of wielding the strap but also from desire. Dog had wriggled, wagged, squirmed and moaned his way through his test with the belt and she was excited. His buttocks were now a very dark red with more than a hint of purple forming at the inner crease of his cheeks. She was impressed. She didn't mind silent slaves but she always preferred some reaction. It was definitely more fun but also a good way to evaluate; allowing her to gauge how much they could take.

Not stopping to talk to Dog, she selected a large paddle that was made of rubber and had holes bored into its flat surface to let the air pass through. It would feel heavy on his buttocks, making a thudding sound as it landed, but it would also feel stingy in the aftermath of each stroke. Over the years she'd accumulated many toys, assessed many play sessions, and knew her equipment very well. It was important to know what marks they left behind on the skin and be able to appraise how they felt to the slave receiving them.

She raised her arm to administer the first blow to her new pet and watched him carefully as he tensed his buttocks and braced himself for what was to come.

"Breathe slowly and deeply and try to unclench your buttocks. It'll be easier to absorb the pain."

She brought the paddle down swiftly onto his buttocks and grinned as she heard him yelp through the soft gag.

"A few more strokes and then you can rest."

Five more were completed and by the end of them Aeneas was utterly exhausted.

She unfastened all the straps that held him captive and instructed him to kneel at her feet as she moved to the nearest seat. She watched as Aeneas got up and slowly crawled across the floor. He collapsed at her feet and held onto them as he sobbed.

"You did really well. Get some rest and write in your journal before we continue."

She left the room feeling like she was drifting on a cloud. She was really happy with his efforts, so far.

Reaching the door of the living room she pushed it open and walked across to the fireplace to retrieve Aeneas' journal. As she turned round to leave, Tim was standing in the doorway.

"Is everything ok, Master?"

He was aware he sounded a little anxious but he wasn't sure how she was feeling. He could normally tell by the way she moved and by the expression on her face, of course, but at the moment it was difficult to read.

"Come in. It's going well, thank you. I've just given Aeneas his new slave name. It's quite extraordinary really. It just came to me as we were playing. His new name is Dog."

Tim smiled. "What a great name. Can I do anything for you?"

Fhionna smiled, said that she didn't need anything, then left the living room and made her way back downstairs to the dungeon, where she found Aeneas in the same position as she'd left him.

"You may get up now. Kneel up."

Aeneas did as he was told and bowed his head, feeling embarrassed at the drool on his chin and chest, the carpet marks on his face, and his bruised buttocks on display.

"I'm going to leave your gag in place because I like it. I expect you to write a little about what has just happened and I'll come back in half an hour to continue your training."

She stroked his face gently and gave him the pad and a pen.

Aeneas took them but didn't fully raise his head to look at her as she left the room. He was already thinking about the words he'd use to try and explain how he felt.

* * *

Aeneas was shaking but he didn't feel cold. He guessed it was the adrenalin rushing through his body. He wished he could take the goddamn gag out but knew that he shouldn't. He felt he couldn't, not because he was scared of the consequences, of being found out, but because he would feel guilty at being dishonest. She'd said she wanted it to remain in place and to remove it would be against her wishes. He thought it was astonishing how much he wanted to please her, already.

Dear Sir,

At this moment in time, I want to take this gag out of my mouth but I won't because it's what you love. This is amazing to me. I kneel here after only an hour or so in your dungeon and already I have a new name and significant bruising on my backside.

The feeling of submitting to your whim is like nothing else I've ever felt before. It makes me feel free to be able to give myself to you but also scares the crap out of me too. Sorry for the language but I want to be completely honest. I'm sure that the beating I've had as my test so far is light compared to what you've inflicted before, with your other slaves, but I can assure you that I felt it.

I'll try to make you happy and hope this journal entry pleases you, Master.

Aeneas quickly read through what he'd written and then closed the pad. He'd no real sense of the time and guessed that she'd be back soon. Wiping his chin to make himself slightly more comfortable, he placed his hands on his buttocks to try to feel the marks that were there. He could feel raised flesh, slightly hard and hot on the surface, but there were no welts, of course. He'd never been caned but had watched online clips of it being done before, and hoped that he'd be spared that as part of his test today.

Aeneas re-opened his journal and continued to write quickly.

Sir,

I hope you don't mind but I touched my backside to try and feel the marks you left. I'm surprised to find that I want marks from you and I like the feeling of swollen skin. I'm also a little shy to say I would like more and maybe to feel your cane but I'm not sure I could manage it. I, of course, will do as you command. I make no request of you but only give you my thoughts in my journal.

Aeneas hoped this last piece of writing was acceptable but heard footsteps on the stairs before he could add anything else. He closed the pad and resumed a position he hoped would please her by bowing his head and placing his hands behind his back, after laying the journal in front of his knees.

The door opened and Tim entered, bringing a glass of water.

"Hi, Dog. I've brought you something to drink. Master thought you might be thirsty but wants you to replace your gag when you've had it."

Aeneas raised his head and blushed as he unfastened the strap at the back of his head.

"I am thirsty, thank you. You called me Dog! News travels fast around here."

Tim laughed. "Yes, it does! I was given a slave name years ago but I think she just likes the sound of my own name because she calls me Tim all the time. Like a posh butler, I suppose."

Aeneas smiled and asked what his slave name was.

"Ah, well, that would be telling but safe to say it's not as cute as the name Dog, even though it is an animal, of sorts. Consider yourself lucky in that respect."

Tim smiled, took the empty glass and said, "Keep up the good work," as he left the room.

Aeneas placed the gag back into his mouth, bowed his head, and waited for his new Master's return.

* * *

Fhionna wanted to look through his journal but decided it would be better to read the completed entries at the end of the day. She planned to let him write at various intervals, when she let him rest. She felt she would achieve a more complete picture of her new slave and how his mind worked by reading it all in one sitting.

She picked up the pad but instead of sitting to read it she moved it to one side, for later consumption. She lifted Dog's head so he could look at her and, without a word, moved her hands down over his head, his shoulders, and then his chest, and took his nipples in her hands. She loved the way he moaned when she touched them.

Letting them go after caressing them for a few seconds, she moved to the wall where ropes and chains hung, dangling in measured lengths. She returned with four lengths of rope and began to bind Aeneas' body where he knelt. First, she took his hands in hers and clasped them together before binding them tightly, making circles round his wrists and passing the rope between them. Next, she bound his ankles together in the same way then moved up and tied his thighs together. The last piece of rope was a little longer and she used this to bind his arms to his torso, circling his chest. She felt like she wanted to test his nipples properly. She'd enjoyed them at Violate and wanted to see how much he could endure.

There were two sets of clamps. One set was more vicious than the other, with metal teeth that dug into the flesh. The kinder clamps were long metal strips, like slender pincers, that were tipped in rubber and could be tightened by pushing a little metal loop up or down the shaft of each one. These clamps were also attached to a chain that connected them together. She knew they would cause very different kinds of pain but both would be intense, in their own way. She selected the more gentle pair and noticed Aeneas watching her intently. She would be kind and warm up his nipples by rolling them between her fingers then tweak them gently into life.

Dog moaned loudly, thrusting his bound body into her hands as much as he could. He always felt slutty when his nipples were the focus of a Dom's interest and now that he knew he was being trained by his new Owner, it seemed to heighten his arousal even more.

Fhionna laughed as his member bobbed up and down in front of him, yearning for attention. She enjoyed watching him as he looked at her with his eyes half closed, making low growling sounds through the gag that continued to fill his mouth. She smiled as his face flushed, feeling embarrassed probably at his predicament, but not being able to help himself move towards her hands, revelling in her pinching nails.

Suddenly she let them go and watched as he fell forward slightly. He'd been leaning against her hands and lost his balance as she moved.

"What a cute pet you are. I want to see how much pain your nipples can take."

Placing the clamps with the rubber tips onto his erect fleshy mounds, she put each metal strip into place at the top and bottom of each nipple and pushed the little silver circle slowly up towards his chest. Aeneas groaned loudly and tried to pull away, much to her pleasure.

"I wouldn't do that if I were you. It'll hurt more if they're pulled off by jerking your body backwards."

Aeneas took the hint and moved back towards his Master, wincing as she held the chain that ran between the clamps. Slowly, but deliberately, she placed just one finger inside the arc of the chain and ran it from one side to the other, pulling it out at the same time. She enjoyed his moans and whimpers as it slackened then tightened, and repeated the action.

"Is it sore, Dog?"

Aeneas could do nothing but nod his head a little in confirmation.

"That's good. You'll be trying the more severe clamps soon."

She looked at his face to gauge his fear. She was pleased to see his eyes widen and hear his breath quicken slightly. She thought she noticed a few tiny beads of sweat forming on his brow too.

"Brace yourself. I'm about to remove them."

With these words, Aeneas' torso stiffened as each nipple was released from the device. His howls filled the room as he lunged backwards when the first one came off, causing the second clamp to detach on its own. He shrieked again as the clamps fell off and he sank down onto the floor beside them.

"Kneel up. That last surge of pain was your own fault and you'll be punished for moving away."

Aeneas struggled onto his knees as the ropes dug into his flesh and prevented any easy movement. Once in position he managed to bow his head but he was sweating and his nipples were engorged with blood.

"You did well. I can tell you did your best so I'm not going to use the severe clamps just now."

She watched him nod and listened to him panting, trying to slow his breathing down.

"I'm going to give you your punishment now, to get it over with. Put your forehead on the floor."

Aeneas looked up at her and shook his head, growling loudly.

"Are you saying no to me, Dog?" Fhionna was slightly amused at this show of stubborn bravery but also wondered, briefly, if it was going to be too much for him to take. She felt she had no choice but to continue, now that she'd made the statement. She wouldn't allow him to think he could change her mind simply by growling at her.

"I must insist, now place your forehead on the ground." She watched him for a moment but he didn't meet her gaze.

Aeneas finally did as he was told and, with much difficulty, placed his forehead on the floor.

"Thank you. Now your buttocks are nice and high to receive the cane. You'll receive two strokes for pulling away from me and making your pain worse."

Fhionna walked quickly to retrieve a cane and brought it back to where her trainee slave knelt on the floor. He was obviously in some discomfort but he stayed in place, the ropes leaving red grooves on his body and his buttocks raised and exposed.

"Two strokes and then you can rest."

Quick as a flash, she raised her arm and brought the cane down onto his fleshy buttocks. Raising it above her head once more, she administered the second blow before he had time to move away.

She smiled as she watched him fall over onto his side and realised he was crying.

"You're a very emotional creature but I'll enjoy your tears."

Fhionna sat in front of him and smiled down on his broken body. After a while she bent to untie him and remove the gag from his mouth.

"Compose yourself and when you're ready write in your journal."

With these words she left the room, happy with the pain she'd caused him but also his earlier excitement at her touch.

* * *

It was some time before Aeneas was able to sit up. He was alone again but he couldn't bear to touch his chest. Instead he looked at his arms and legs and saw blue and purple stains under the skin's surface. "That hurt like a bitch." He started laughing even though he didn't know why. He laughed so hard that he wasn't surprised when Tim came into the room and asked if everything was alright.

"Yeah, I think so. I'm not sure to be honest. I'm still in one piece but I'm very sore and more than a little tired. I guess I'm just realising I belong to a sadist!"

Tim smiled and said that Fhionna's love of pain-giving made her a powerful force to be reckoned with and that being her slave wasn't always easy. He also said she was very loving too, though, and if he'd done well he would, eventually, be rewarded.

Aeneas guessed that his tests weren't over but he'd no idea what would happen next. He sincerely hoped it wouldn't be more pain but couldn't think what else they would be.

"Thanks for checking on me but I have to write in my journal again, and after seeing what Master is capable of I really don't want to piss her off by not having it done in time."

Tim left him to it and Aeneas picked up the pad and pen and tried to make himself comfortable on the floor, even though his backside hurt like hell and every move made him aware of his erect and tender nipples. He wondered what he could possibly write about this latest experience but thought that honesty was always the best policy.

Master,

Thank you for the water break. It was needed and you are very considerate. It was good to take the gag out of my mouth for a short time. I like the feeling of the gag but it does make me dribble a lot. You probably enjoy this, though, as it truly makes me your animal.

I must say that the nipple torture was divine when you had them between your fingers. You noticed how excited I got and made sure I was suitably embarrassed. The clamps were difficult but thank you for using the less severe device. Again, very considerate. My apologies for straining against them and I was a bit upset I got punishment for that, but I learned my lesson and won't do it again.

I realize you hadn't looked at my journal before issuing my punishment and so I'm sure you will laugh when you do read it. The cane was the last straw and it broke me. Yes, I am a very emotional person but maybe you will enjoy making me cry? I hope so as I believe it may happen quite often.

Tim came to check on me but maybe you sent him to see what all the fuss was about. I was laughing at my predicament and the reality of being a new slave. I have never been a proper slave before but I hope you are pleased with me, overall.

The cane will leave welts and this makes me happy. I feel that if I'm going to go through pain for you that I at least want marks at the end of it, as a badge of honor.

You are my new sadistic and beautiful Lord and I hope I can live up to your expectations of me.

Aeneas read through what he'd written, closed the pad, and placed it in front of him as before, kneeling back in position to wait for Fhionna's return. He heard the door to the dungeon open and thought it might be Tim again but it was his Master. As she came into the room he felt his breathing rate increase. This was probably going to be a regular occurrence so he might as well get used to it. She probably noticed it too, as she seemed to miss nothing. He felt sore and a little tired and longed for a chance to chat for a while but focused his attention on her beautiful bare feet as she spoke to him.

"We've been here for a few hours now and I'm hungry so we shall go and eat. I'm also aware you may be tired so a break will do you the world of good."

Aeneas smiled and bent his head to lay it on his Owner's feet as a thank you. She must have understood the gesture because she said he was welcome and to follow her upstairs. He was relieved and surprised he was going to be allowed to eat with her and not on his own, in the dungeon.

* * *

In the kitchen, Tim had been working hard to prepare a lovely meal. He'd spread the table with an intricate lace cloth and matching napkins. There were also silver candlesticks in the centre and a bowl of fresh flowers from the florist in the village. He knew that lilacs were among his Owner's favourites and filled a deep bowl with the purple blooms. He'd prepared a thick winter vegetable soup, to be followed by roast chicken and felt quite proud of his attention to detail. He knew his Owner would be thrilled. In some ways she was very easy to please but perhaps Dog wouldn't agree right now.

As he was making the gravy and boiling the kettle again in case she wanted tea, the door opened and Fhionna came in, closely followed by a crawling Dog on a lead.

"What a beautiful table you've created. You're spoiling me. Thank you. Such beautiful flowers. Let's light the candles since it's getting dark outside."

She walked to the table, pulling Aeneas behind her, and sat down as Tim lit the candles. She bent down to release Dog from his lead and Tim placed a bowl on the floor beside his Master's feet.

Aeneas thanked him and let out a little sigh as he realised he was still to be her animal.

Fhionna heard it and pulled him closer to her legs, so much so that he choked a little as she held him strongly in place by his neck.

"You are my pet-slave, Aeneas. Animals and new salves eat under the table, especially on their first day in service. Do you understand?"

Aeneas nodded and managed a feeble, "Yes, Master," before being released from her grip and allowed to sit back down on the floor properly.

"You may eat it with your hands and lap with your tongue, as you did in the restaurant."

Tim brought the soup to the table in a large silver terrine and ladled some into his Owner's white china bowl before adding some to his own and then, lastly, adding some to the dog bowl.

Tim winked at Dog and Dog managed a little smile in return.

"This is wonderful soup. Very tasty."

Fhionna laughed as Tim made some comment about 'being well trained.'

Aeneas had been ignored, so far, but soon felt his Master's hand reach down to stroke his hair. A simple, friendly gesture but also one that was full of Dominance and Ownership. It made him shiver slightly and he felt his member grow hard. He saw that Tim had noticed it but Fhionna hadn't, which he hoped would remain the case. He wondered if Tim would point it out but was somewhat relieved when he showed no interest in telling on him, so Aeneas fidgeted until his member was more hidden between his thighs and listened to her talk.

"What an exciting day it's been. Dog is doing well in his training. Come and sit down and enjoy your lunch."

Tim smiled and said, "Yes, Sir," because he knew she was doing this little play scene on purpose. It wasn't often he got to sit at the table with her so he just went with the flow and enjoyed the attention.

As she continued to chat, Aeneas tried his best to eat the soup by picking out the solid vegetables with his fingers. The liquid would prove more difficult, though, so he lifted the bowl to his face, tried to tip it forward to let the goo slide towards him, but missed aim completely and the contents emptied down his chest instead.

"What a silly animal you are! Fetch Dog a damp cloth, please."

Doing as instructed, Tim got up from the table, ran a dishcloth under the tap and handed it to Aeneas but he couldn't help but laugh. Fhionna laughed too and Aeneas was glad she didn't seem upset by his messiness.

"When you get home, buy a small hard-backed notepad. Once you have it, find a picture of a dog in a collar, print it out and stick it to the front of the book. You will also write 'punishment book' at the top on the inside cover. Is that clear?"

Aeneas said, "Yes, Master," and handed Tim the soggy cloth.

Tim was still laughing when he returned to the table. "Are you ready for the second course, Sir?"

Fhionna said that she was so he brought the chicken to the table and started to carve.

Aeneas sat with his thighs closed on the floor and paid silent attention to what was happening. He watched her as she waited for Tim to add some chicken and roast potatoes to her plate, before fetching the gravy boat. He then saw him bend down to add chicken to his bowl and smother it in thick brown paste. He was staring at the food when he registered his Master's voice giving him an instruction.

"This time, put your face in the bowl and eat it with your mouth only."

Aeneas whispered, "Yes, Sir," and put his face in the bowl. The gravy was hot and burnt his lips and nose but he persevered, making the most awful slurping noises imaginable.

"What a noise you're making!"

Aeneas put his face deeper into the bowl and growled a little bit under his breath. This was becoming common practice. He felt like he was being conditioned to respond by growling. He really did feel like an animal but thought that as long as he was 'her' animal he could cope. This sudden surge of attachment surprised him. He hadn't known her long and yet the thought was there: As long as he was her animal!

* * *

The meal had been fun. Fhionna had ignored Aeneas most of the time, addressing Tim instead. She knew he'd find it amusing, though, because he wasn't used to having her full attention like that. He would probably guess she was doing it on purpose but she knew he would do anything for her pleasure and would play along. And he did, marvellously.

After dinner, she decided to let Dog rest so she sent them both down to the dungeon room where she asked Tim to put steel manacles on Aeneas' ankles and run a length of chain from the restraints to the wall, passing through the bars of the cage he'd sleep in. Secured in this way, she knew he'd continue to feel like a dog but be able to rest and recuperate a little. She smiled to herself as she imagined him trying to sleep but thought he might be too wound up. She'd actually arranged a little gift for him and hoped it would help him to relax. In the meantime, she would retire to her room, have a shower, and plan some club night activities.

Tim reattached his fellow slave's lead and led him downstairs. Pushing open the dungeon door and letting Aeneas stand up, he said, "I think you did really well. I won't tell Master about your excitement at the table but it might cost you."

Tim laughed when he saw the surprised look on Aeneas' face.

"I'm only joking. I'm your friend and I hope you know that."

Aeneas said that he did.

"That's good because I feel like I can trust you completely. I think this is going to be important because our Owner likes to watch her male slaves play together, if you get my gist?"

Aeneas said he thought he understood but he'd never been with another man before.

"That won't matter, I'm afraid, but I thought I'd better prepare you for it as it might become an issue, especially if she's aware of how well we get on together. She allows me a lot of freedom to come check on you and instigates little moments for us to bond. I'm quite sure it's done with a purpose behind it, even though she is very caring too."

Aeneas was surprised by these words. "You really think so? Wow! I guess I hadn't figured that out. I'm not sure how I feel about that, but I guess I've got some time to think it through. I do like you a lot, Tim, but I hadn't imagined us being together in 'that' way. How would you feel about it?" He felt like he should ask the question but he already had a good idea what the answer would be.

"I would enjoy it because I like you and you are handsome and I want to make my Owner happy." Tim blushed. "Anyway, I've to set you up in your bed to get some rest."

With that, Tim led Aeneas across the room and then took some large manacles off the wall.

"Separate your legs for me, please."

Aeneas did as instructed and soon felt the cold metal close around his ankles, one by one. They felt heavy and uncomfortable and he wondered how on earth he would be able to rest with these cumbersome things on his body. But there was more to come, he discovered, as Tim then told him to enter the cage.

Aeneas crawled in and discovered a soft rubber mattress. He was quite sure it hadn't been there before and assumed Tim must have placed it there at some point but he wasn't sure when he would have had the chance.

These thoughts occupied his mind as he was padlocked in place and long chains were stretched out through the bars so that they would reach the wall. Tim clipped them into place, out of reach, and returned to lock the door. Aeneas smiled at him and couldn't help but make a comment.

"Master believes in keeping her slaves secure!"

Tim smiled back and said she enjoyed the sight of her male subjects in chains and may want to come down and watch him while he slept, if he could sleep.

Dog said he didn't know if he'd be able to sleep or not but a chance to rest was definitely needed and appreciated.

Tim was just closing the cage door when the dungeon door opened. Aeneas was still and silent as he watched it swing open but the other man just glanced over his shoulder then went back to what he was doing. It wasn't Master, as he'd expected, but Louise, mostly naked apart from a thin gold collar round her neck and matching ankle cuffs. He noticed they resembled the colour of her hair and thought she looked stunning.

Aeneas looked at Tim, wondering what was going on but he only smiled at him and said, "Enjoy," before leaving them to it.

Louise walked towards the cage and slid a bolt across on the side of it, which opened a panel. "Hello, Dog," she said, but she didn't allow him to respond before she had placed her lips on his thighs, kissing upwards from his knees to his groin and then onto his member.

Aeneas gasped. He didn't know what to do but his member did. Slowly he was brought to a full and enthusiastic erection by her soft lips and strong tongue as it flicked and licked its way up and down his shaft. Aeneas laid back as flat as he could, allowing this pretty woman to work her magic on him. He guessed that his new Master had sent her and Louise obviously seemed to be enjoying it.

It didn't take long for the surprise and shock of the situation to pass and Aeneas moaned loudly as she caressed and sucked him to completion. With a loud grunt he came, still feeling a little bewildered.

As she moved out of the cage and locked the door, Aeneas looked up at her, shivering slightly from the waves of his orgasm.

"This is going to sound lame but thank you."

Louise grinned and said it was her pleasure.

Dog couldn't help but ask if she'd enjoyed it because he hoped that she had.

"I liked you the first time I saw you at Violate and I'm afraid I developed a little bit of a crush on you." She blushed, but continued, "Master knew I liked you because Tim said that I had a 'glazed' look on my face when I met you. Tim knows me pretty well. He knows when I get that look on my face that I'm in lust. I guess she wanted me to have the opportunity to entertain you because she knew I would like to and I'm particularly skilled at it."

Louise laughed and shook out her hair so that it covered her face as she went pink.

Aeneas laughed too. "You're very good at it." He grinned at her. "I think our Owner wanted to make sure we are both happy in her service. I haven't met a woman like her before. She can be so sadistic but is just such a lovely person. I don't think many people exist like that in the world. Kind of a strange paradox, really. Very confusing, at times."

Louise parted her mane, slightly, and looked at Aeneas. "Yes, she's very unusual but her gentle side makes her even more powerful, I think."

Aeneas thought about this for a moment and said that she was right, it did.

* * *

Upstairs, Fhionna made some preliminary scribbles about possible club events for the next two months but was aware that Louise would have paid Dog a visit by now and smiled to herself. She loved to keep her pets happy. If they were happy then she got so much more out of them. They tried so much harder to please her, in return. She was aware Aeneas was going home the next day and she wanted to use him as much as possible while he was here. She would let him rest for the remainder of the afternoon but tonight would be a different matter. She hoped his orgasm might help him sleep because he would need the energy.

❧ Chapter 5 ❧

April 2012, Manhattan

A Realisation

I

Aeneas had left for the flight home early that morning and leaving his new Owner had been very difficult. After having just boarded the plane, he thought about how she'd used and abused him the previous night, even after his tests during the day. She'd shown him no mercy by torturing his nipples till they bled, using the severe clamps, whipping his back till it had blackened marks and purple bruising showing across his shoulder blades and, finally, had caned him, leaving six clean welts on his backside before making him take a hot shower while she watched him try to avoid contact with the water. She'd then locked him in his cage for the rest of the night. He was exhausted and his body ached all over. He knew this was a combination of the marks and welts on his skin, making it feel tight and sore, but also the confinement of the cage because he couldn't quite fit his tall body into it in a fully laid out position. He'd had to curl up, slightly, for most of the night but he guessed she would have known that.

Even after all this, he felt he didn't want to leave. He knew his body might not have coped with such an onslaught of torture for more than a day or two but he felt like he would miss it, also. He certainly had plenty of reminders but knew they would fade. He'd maybe have them for a week or two but after that he would have to rely on his memory. Master had, however, given him the task of writing another journal entry and he decided he would do it on the flight, while he felt able to. It was a long journey home and he wouldn't sleep much anyway.

Aeneas unfastened his seatbelt and stood up to retrieve his

backpack from the overhead locker. Sitting down again, he rummaged around in it till he found the pad and pen he'd been given, and started to write.

I'm not quite sure where to start, Master. My mind is ablaze with all that has happened to me in the short two days in Glasgow with you. I believe you haven't read my journal at all yet. I thought you might have done so while I slept in my cage last night but when I woke this morning, and was freed by Tim, I noticed it was still in the dungeon room where I'd left it.

Anyway, I now obey your wishes and write in my journal for the fourth time and will try to express myself as openly as possible. I will always be honest, as befits my personality, and also because I know you would expect it.

I sit here, on the flight home, and I can feel the marks on my shoulders as I move around. I have never experienced the lash or flogger before and it surprised me by the way it thudded and then stung.

The pain has decreased, somewhat, but the welts on my backside are still the most tender. I'm actually amazed that I didn't weep at your feet again last night, when our time together was over, but I guess I was just too tired.

The most important part, for me, is that I made you happy and I know I did by how you said goodbye this morning. I think what surprised me most about our parting was when you hugged me. I hadn't expected it and I'm sorry that I flinched. I saw you smile, though, so I guess you probably enjoyed that too. You are truly unique.

I don't have much to say about the tests you put me through as I don't want to just repeat in words what happened in action, even though this might indeed be impossible anyway. I just want to express how wonderful it was to be in your control and I will do my best to fulfill any tasks you see fit to give me while I am in my own country.

You said that you want me to write to you and send it by airmail because you would love to receive letters, and maybe even my journal entries, so I will do my best to write about my life in ways you would find interesting.

I think I've changed a lot in the past eight weeks, or so, and now that I've found you I can never let you go out of my life. Some practical changes will need to be made, in my work life, to make sure I can devote to your wishes properly, but I'll attend to them and let you know.

I owe you so much for being my rescuer.

Your devoted Dog.

Aeneas reread what he'd written and was satisfied it was honest and heartfelt. He was so tired that he felt he'd manage to sleep a little after all, so he closed the pad and shoved it back into the rucksack before placing it under the seat in front of him and pulling the lever to make his chair recline. Aeneas closed his eyes.

* * *

Back at home, Toby was there to greet him.

"A pleasant trip, Sir?"

Aeneas said it had been fantastic and saw Toby's eyebrow raise in surprise.

"Ah, I see, Sir," he smiled but said nothing more.

Reaching the car, he opened the door for his boss, closed it, put his bag in the boot, and positioned himself in the driving seat. He then adjusted the mirror slightly so he could see Aeneas' face more clearly.

"Beg your pardon for being so forward but what's the lady's name?"

Toby grinned at him in the mirror and Aeneas had to laugh.

"There's no fooling you, is there!"

He smiled and said he was glad that Aeneas looked so happy, even though a little tired.

Aeneas thought he didn't know the half of it but replied that he'd met someone online, her name was Fhionna and he'd gone to meet her, the only problem being that she lived in Scotland.

"Scotland, of all places. Could you not have found someone a bit nearer to home, Sir?"

Aeneas was used to Toby's straight talking ways and said it was better that she lived some distance away because it made it exciting to travel to see her and he wasn't sure he wanted to date another American woman anyway. Aeneas smiled to himself as he thought how much the words date or dating were completely inappropriate, under the circumstances. He was actually laughing as he pictured himself manacled and caged overnight, beaten and bruised, and wondered what Toby would think of such a 'date.'

The rest of the journey home was fairly quiet, each man deep in their own thoughts. Aeneas, turning over in his mind his new name, while God only knew what Toby thought about the news of a new 'girlfriend in Scotland.'

Back at the house, he opened the boot to get his bag while Toby unlocked the front door. He watched the other man as he fussed over making sure the lights were on and went upstairs, presumably to light the fire in his study. Even though the weather was a lot milder now, there was still a chill in the air.

It was still only ten o'clock in the morning, he realised. It sometimes felt like being in a time warp, travelling between countries with five hours difference between them. The fact that he had the rest of the day to himself made him feel excited somehow, as he could lounge about the house, look at the Violate website to see what was going on, and generally think about the last few days and what they meant. He was also dying to check out his butt and back marks in the long dressing mirror in his room. He would certainly let his new Master know that he was home safely and missing her already. He was sure she would like that.

With all these thoughts whirling about in his head, Aeneas followed Toby into the house and went straight up to his room. Toby asked him if he wanted anything from the kitchen and he said he would come down for some lunch in a few hours but he wasn't hungry at the moment. Toby nodded and left him to it, closing the door gently behind him as he went into the kitchen.

When Aeneas was alone in his room, he went into the bathroom to run the shower and began to disrobe, slowly and gingerly removing his shirt because of his aching shoulders. He thought about his Master's face smiling at him as he grimaced taking off his clothes and stepped into the cubicle. The water beat down on his skin and he almost howled from the contact. He would have to cancel his plans to meet Hank for a sauna and swim tomorrow, that was for sure. He'd forgotten about their plans together but it wasn't as if he could ask his Master to please not beat his back as he wanted to swim in public.

Aeneas smiled and washed himself, rather delicately, before he wrapped himself in his robe and settled down in front of his computer. The screen pinged into life as he turned it on and he logged into the personal section of the Violate website. He rubbed a towel over his short hair while he scanned the site for people he might know. The first person he noticed was Martin so he typed a polite hello message saying he would be back to Violate sometime soon, he hoped. He told him about some of the adventures he'd just experienced and how he was Fhionna's newest slave. He wondered if he should tell Martin, as it might make him jealous, but decided he would probably find out anyway and that it was better straight from the dog's mouth, as it were.

Once he'd sent the email to Martin he continued to scan the pages for anyone else familiar. It was nice to feel like he had a Scottish family, even if in very unconventional terms. He smiled as he thought about being owned by a Scottish Master. Somehow it just seemed appropriate.

Next he noticed an entry from Louise and it was addressed directly to him. Fhionna must have given her his details for the title of the message read, 'Dear Dog, hope you are safely home.' He laughed as he clicked to open the full message:

Dear Dog,

I've been given permission to make contact with you. I can't tell you how much I enjoyed being given orders to give you your little treat while you were here. It's always a delight for me too, to be allowed to bring a little pleasure to a handsome slave.

Now I'm blushing and I might get into trouble if Master reads this email. As you are her new property, I guess she'll be very careful about who she lets make contact. I think both Martin and Tim have permission but I can't think of anyone else that has.

This is a little warning, Dog, to be careful who you talk to on this site, or any other site, for that matter, as not all people are upfront in their intentions and some are blatantly on the lookout to steal another's slave if they like the look of them. You may get into trouble if you contact the wrong people and Master finds out about it.

Anyway, I'm hoping to be allowed to 'make you happy' again sometime soon.

Best wishes,

Louise

Aeneas was struck by the openness of the message, its friendly manner but also the caution she'd included. He thought it made sense that his new Owner would be protective of him. He was new to this lifestyle and didn't know what boundaries there were, apart from the ones his Master had given him already. She hadn't yet made it clear who he could talk to and what to avoid. Maybe it would appear obvious, as he looked through all the chat online, but maybe he should write to Fhionna and ask her direct approval before engaging with anyone, just to be on the safe side. He decided that now was as good a time as any to make contact with her and ask for her guidance.

Aeneas clicked on his Master's link and began to type a personal email.

Dear Sir,

I've arrived in Manhattan safely and you may be happy to know that when I had a shower it made me 'howl' like the dog you have seen fit to name me. I love my marks and welts and hope they last for some time to come. In saying that, they will interrupt my daily schedule but I am sure you'll appreciate that.

Thank you, again, for an amazing two days in your service. I have made contact with Martin to say hello and replied to a sweet email from Louise. I would like to ask you, please, how long each week I am allowed to peruse the Violate site, as well as other sites of interest, and with whom I may make contact. My apologies if I have overstepped a boundary but I just wanted to clarify what I have permission to do. I'm hoping it pleases you, rather than offends you, that I'm asking for guidance, as my wish is not to upset you in any way.

Yours,

Dog

Aeneas, as always, checked the message over for spelling, grammar and any other noticeable mistakes. He hoped that the level of submission was right and he wasn't being cheeky. It felt strange to be sitting at home, bruised and stiff, writing a message to a woman thousands of miles away and hoping she would approve of his communication and his behaviour. He was definitely seeking her approval and he guessed he would for as long as their relationship lasted.

That night, he lay on his bed thinking about his new life. He wondered just how much of it he could tell Hank. He'd called him to cancel the spa trip they had planned for tomorrow and Hank had laughed and said they could catch a ball game together instead, the following day.

Aeneas was tired and felt he could sleep for a few hours but wanted to check his email on the Violate site first. He wanted to see if Fhionna had replied. So, getting up off the bed, he padded his way across the floor to fetch his laptop, rather than starting up the main computer at this time of night. The time in Scotland would be around three am and he was sure she would've received his mail and hopefully have answered it.

He visualised her at home, maybe with Tim there overnight although he doubted Tim's bed would be the cage. He smiled and wondered what Master's room was like. He imagined it to be as colourful as her taste in clothing and other rooms, whose decoration were quite vivid and a little on the dramatic side. He also wondered if any of her slaves were allowed in her bedroom to be of service and he laughed as this thought seemed to travel all the way down to his member and make him stiff.

Shifting position, slightly, he lowered his hand to run it the length of his shaft. There was no doubt in his mind that if his Owner had witnessed this she would've given him a punishment for his journal. He felt naughty but continued to stroke himself as he thought about his Master's face and body, the way she moved, her slender hands and feet, that he now realised he loved to kiss.

Just as he was about to move the laptop onto the covers to enjoy himself more fully, he heard a small 'ping' noise and a message symbol popped up on his inbox. It seemed that Fhionna was awake and was replying to his message at that very moment. Aeneas immediately stopped touching himself, as if he'd actually been caught in the act, and clicked on the message. It read:

My Dog,

I'm glad you're home safe and you're happy with your marks. I enjoyed creating them. It's good you asked about limits for website perusal, and with whom you are allowed to make contact, as it shows you're being thoughtful.

I'm glad Louise wrote to you. She likes you but I knew she would. It will be a treat for her, as well as you, if I allow contact between you, from time to time.

To answer your questions: limit yourself to three hours a week on websites, including the Violate site. This should always be your first port of call in case I make contact with you. Any time spent in responding to me, however, may be outside the allocated time limit. You may make contact with the people I have introduced you to and you may make comment on pictures you like and stories on sites that appeal to you but you will make it known that you are an owned slave and are not seeking a relationship with a Mistress.

You will be careful about this, Dog, because if I'm unhappy with your choices I will punish you and as the moderator of the Violate site I can see all that goes on. On other sites, of course, this is not the case and I'm relying on your honesty in this matter.

Warmest regards,

Master

Aeneas read the message through again and replied that he understood. It seemed that Louise was correct in her warning. This made him smile because he hadn't thought of it himself. He was aware of feeling very tired but oddly happy that he was starting his new life in earnest. He wasn't sure what would happen next but he had some decisions about work to make.

He closed the laptop and leaned over the bed to place it on the floor. He had a lot to think about but for now he needed to sleep. He was wondering whether to continue pleasuring himself before settling down for the night but his Master's message had made him feel as though she was watching him so he decided against it. Leaning back on the pillow, after switching the bedside lamp off, he closed his eyes, seeing Fhionna's smiling face looking down on him as he knelt before her. He was sure his dreams would be full of such images that night.

Unbeknown to him, however, a second message was popping into his inbox:

Dog,

I realise that I may be too late for tonight but I will start to control your sexual activity as from tomorrow. I will send you notice of the days you may perform masturbation, to be known as 'p' for permission. You may ask for extra allocation if you are struggling but you will abide by the answer I give you, whether it is yes or no.

Also, I'll be sending you tasks to complete. These will have a time period in which they must be accomplished and if they are not then punishment will be issued. The tasks will take various forms, from writing or selecting poetry, as you have done before, to buying certain equipment for my use on your body. It may also include sexual activity with other slaves, but whatever it is I will expect you to comply.

You will have your 'p' allocation schedule shortly.

Master

* * *

When he woke in the morning, Aeneas groaned at the thought of the long day ahead. During the car journey home from the airport the previous day, he'd emailed his boss to ask to meet him. He wanted to arrange a work schedule that would mean he had more days away from the actual office. He wasn't sure he wanted to quit completely but it would depend on what was said and the reaction he got. If it didn't go well he could hand in his notice and think about early retirement.

Such big decisions to make but from previous conversations with his buddy Hank, he knew he was ready. The adjustment had already taken place in his head but it was the practical day to day activities that had to follow suit. He knew Harry would be more than a little surprised to hear he wanted to cut back his office days and his responsibilities but hoped he would understand. He couldn't tell him the real reason for it, obviously, and would have to tell him it was all getting too much for him, that he wasn't getting any younger, and that finance was becoming a young man's game. It sounded convincing enough but time would tell.

After the meeting, Aeneas was booked in to have lunch with a client whose company was in a bit of trouble and needed advice on how to make it work more effectively. Lunch would take three hours at most but it would be hard to concentrate after finding out what Harry had to say. He would either be excited at having a lot more time to himself, be able to wean himself away from work slowly, or be disappointed his boss had taken it badly.

Rubbing the sleep from his eyes, he finally jumped out of bed and nearly stood on his laptop. He picked it up and plugged it in to charge. Any surfing would have to wait because he was running late. He could smell breakfast being made and hoped Toby wouldn't be too upset when he grabbed some toast and headed out.

Dressed in one of his better suits and thumping his way downstairs, Aeneas sped through the kitchen. He apologised to Toby about having to snatch and run, and toast in one hand, briefcase in the other, headed out to the car and into the city.

The traffic was dire and the drive to the office was taking longer than he'd hoped it would but he guessed being on edge didn't help. He arrived at Harry's office just about on time and let the attendant take it to his spot for him. Usually he just drove it there himself but today he was in more of a hurry.

Smoothing himself down and trying to walk calmly into the building, Aeneas' stomach began to squirm a little. A lot was riding on this meeting and he didn't mind admitting he was nervous. Harry was usually a good boss though.

Standing in the lift, he marvelled at just how excited he was. Maybe the nerves didn't come from wondering what his boss would say, after all, but from the knowledge he would be dedicating his life to the completely crazy idea of being a willing slave. Aeneas laughed out loud and the tiny woman standing beside him stared at him as though he was mad.

"Sorry, Ma'am," he said, "I'm just about to have an important meeting with my boss and I feel a bit nervous."

The woman titled her head to one side as she looked at him and managed a polite smile. "That's ok. You just startled me a little. You look excited more than scared though."

Aeneas smiled back and said she was very perceptive. Then the lift reached his floor and the woman said, "Good luck," before the doors closed behind him.

Up ahead, he could see his boss was on the phone so he lingered until he was waved in. Taking the main seat in front of the large overloaded desk, he waited until Harry paused and eventually hung up.

"Sorry about that. Having a bad morning and it's only nine o'clock."

Aeneas grimaced because he knew he wasn't about to make him any happier.

"That's too bad. I'm sorry I'm not about to make it any easier for you."

He watched his boss fix him with his full gaze.

"Well, I guessed it must be important or else it could have waited. Let's have it then."

Aeneas felt he already knew what was coming but breathed in and started to talk.

"Well, I've been a bit restless for a while now. I feel that I'm getting too old to keep up this pace of life anymore." Aeneas paused, thinking about the words he'd rehearsed, but Harry cut in.

"And you want either to leave me in the lurch or cut back on your work," he said.

Aeneas thought for a moment before continuing. "Well, I don't want to leave you in the lurch but I do want to cut back. I'm getting tired of the hectic workload and I want to be able to enjoy life more before I become too old to do the things I want to do."

Harry stared at him and didn't look particularly pleased but didn't look too surprised either.

Aeneas watched him sit down for the first time since he'd come into the office.

"I've been waiting for this, actually. Not that it doesn't upset me but I've been excepting something to happen."

Aeneas managed to smile at his boss, not really knowing how to follow it up.

"What did you have in mind? Do you want to hand in your notice or do you just want to reduce your days?"

Aeneas said that a reduction in days and workload would be good for now but that he might want to take early retirement in the not too distant future.

Harry sighed before saying it would take a month or two to work out a new schedule but he didn't want to lose him completely.

Aeneas agreed and asked what would happen next.

"Well, I'll have to decide who I think is responsible enough to cover some of your clients and then we'll need to discuss which ones you want to keep on, how often you're willing to travel, etc."

Aeneas thanked him and stood up to shake his hand, thinking it'd gone pretty smoothly, but Harry continued.

"There's just one thing though, I do have a new client I want you to see. I'd need you to consider taking them on."

Aeneas waited for more detail, kicking himself for being too confident too quickly.

"This client could be big business for this company but it would involve quite a lot of 'hands on' work. I don't want to give it to someone else unless I really have to but it will keep you busy. We can schedule a dinner meeting sometime this week and I can fill you in on the details, but it might have to become a priority for you. I'm willing to cut back on more than a few of your other cases, however, if you are willing to do this."

Aeneas said he'd be happy to discuss it, not wanting to upset Harry any more that day.

"Just one thing about it though," his boss said, and Aeneas braced himself for the worst. "You'll have to travel to Scotland quite a lot."

II

Aeneas felt like he'd been floating on a cloud for the past three or four days. He just couldn't believe how it'd all turned out. Not only could he cut back on his workload, giving him much more free time to pursue other interests, but also the one main case he was to work on would take him to where his Owner was. He'd been constantly grinning like a fool and was sure that Toby was a little worried about him. He hadn't had the chance to fill him in on any detail yet but he'd have to soon, before the old man's head exploded. He hadn't even had time to enjoy looking at the Violate website. He felt bad about neglecting communications and sincerely hoped that Fhionna had sent him an email but, also, he hoped it didn't contain a task. He'd be in trouble if he hadn't completed something she'd asked him to do.

Aeneas opened his laptop and spread himself out on his bed, ready to use some of his three-hour allocation for being online. Logging onto the Violate website, he noticed straightaway that there were indeed two communications from his Owner. Aeneas panicked. He'd been caught up in setting up possible meetings with the Scottish company and he'd neglected her. Part of the problem, he knew, was that he was focused on planning when he could stay on for extra time in Scotland to serve her. This had made him feel close to her, devoted to her, but without her actually knowing any of it was happening. He now felt rather stupid. He berated himself and then laughed.

Reading through both mails, he realised the first one told him he would be sent tasks to complete in certain time scales and to expect a schedule of 'p' allocation. The second mail was the allocation itself.

Dog,

You will have three 'p's per week. These will be on a Monday, Wednesday and a Saturday and I'll expect you to send me a 'thank you' text after each one. If you do not manage to complete your allocation on the given day then you'll do without until the next allocation day. Do not carry them over. There will be no exception to this rule. However, I might extend or reduce your allocation period when I see fit, as it may be based around a task to complete.

My number follows below. Do keep it private.

Aeneas felt his stomach flip. He'd been happily pleasing himself without much thought to whether it was actually allowed or not. God, what day was it now? Yesterday alone he'd masturbated twice! He eventually worked out it was Saturday and felt thankful it was an allocated 'p' day but felt guilty for having pleasured himself a lot the day before. The thought crossed his mind that he should tell her. She'd said she would start to control his sexual release the next day. That would have been Tuesday. That meant he'd overindulged significantly on two days, which weren't allocated. Damn it. He'd have to come clean and be honest about the fact he hadn't read her email till now. He just knew he'd be punished if he did tell her, but she was also unpredictable and this made him nervous. He wondered if he should use the number she had given him and try to talk to her about it or whether it would be better by return email. He decided writing it down was better, the cowardly way out, but he just couldn't bring himself to chat lightly with his Owner then divulge the mistake he'd made. He would write to her now and include his number in return. This, at least, would show her he was trying to change his habits and become more aware of her wants, rather than just his own. He marvelled at just how much control she had over him already. Just a missed email could make him panic. He, a fully grown man, a powerful businessman, made to quake in his boots by the thought of displeasing a woman on the other side of a very large ocean, knowing that some physical punishment may be made to his body and knowing he would accept it.

Aeneas stared at the computer screen then started to carefully form the words of his email.

Dear Master,

First of all thank you for your personal number. I will keep it private. May I also thank you for the time taken in allocating my 'p' days and the thought you give to the tasks you wish me to perform. I will, of course, comply with your wishes. I understand, also, that my contact with people on websites shall remain under your control and I promise to be very careful in this respect.

I have much news to tell you, Master, and I will write to you and send it by airmail, for your enjoyment.

I also must tell you that I have a confession to make. I realize that I'll be punished in whatever way you see fit but my honesty is obviously important to us both.

I offer my sincere apologies and tell you that I have only just opened your email regarding my 'p' allocation amount, as well as the specified days. Since Tuesday, which I believe is the day you intended my 'p' control to start, I have masturbated five times: once on Wednesday, twice on Thursday and twice yesterday.

I'm sorry, Master.

Please accept my personal number, in return, and it will be kept on day and night to be at your disposal.

I won't make excuses for my lack of focus on your wishes and I will try my best to do better.

Yours,

Dog

Happy he'd managed to convey his regret, Aeneas pressed send. All that remained now was to try to wait patiently for his Owner's reply and the dreaded punishment. As he closed the laptop he wondered what to do next. He thought it best to keep himself busy rather than pacing about the house and checking the email every half hour. He still felt like he wanted to communicate with her so he thought he'd write his first letter, as promised, in the hope that the news of his diminished workload and the increased trips to Scotland would please her.

Dear Master, (I just love calling you that. It is very appropriate as you are the Master of my world, it seems.)

My main news is to let you know I'm changing my work and my career plans quite successfully, which will allow me to travel to serve you more often. The main changes are based on the number of clients I have to look after and the taking over of one very important client instead. They are based in Scotland and I can't quite believe my luck. My boss was quite determined that I be the one to look after this client's interests, and establish a rapport with them quickly, so this has been my focus for the past few days.

This has made me feel very close to you, Master, although I foolishly forgot that you had no idea all this was happening in my life and you had no reason to feel the same closeness that I did.

I anxiously await your reply to my email as I write this letter, but it in no way weakens my growing need or desire to serve you. In fact, the opposite is true. I feel that the control you have over me strengthens with each passing day, even when we are not communicating with each other.

In times of quiet reflection, I find that my mind wanders to you. You are a positive influence in my life and I can only hope I bring you the joy you seek from knowing I will always strive to serve you well.

I must tell you a funny little story that concerns my housekeeper, who's been with me for years and is due to retire soon. His name is Toby. He's guessed there is a new woman in my life and assumes, of course, that she (you) is my girlfriend. I had to admit that there was someone as I couldn't deny the twinkle in my eye or the spring in my step.

Later on, in my room, I laughed at the thought of ever describing you in such a way and wondered how I could ever describe to Toby the nature of our relationship; if it is permitted for me to call it such a thing.

Even this makes me smile as I'm not sure what it should be called or even if it can be labelled anything other than Master and slave, Lord and worshipper.

I have used the term Lord because it feels that way to me, that I should and will worship you in an attempt to bring you happiness. This also encompasses feelings of what might be described in the Old Testament as avoiding the wrath of God, in avoiding your displeasure and so any punishment.

I crave to be the best slave you have ever trained and owned. I realize this is a tall task I've set for myself and you have never actually uttered these words or expressed this as a need or want.

Even as I write this, I know I will never be perfect but hope that maybe this will give you some further insight into this humble slave's mind and how much I strive to be just that for you… perfect.

I hope you enjoy my first letter, Sir.

Yours,

Dog

Just as he was sealing the envelope his phone rang. He decided to let it ring and completed the address before jogging through to his office to work out the cost of postage to Europe. As he looked up the costs in his directory, and found the right stamps, he heard the phone stop ringing and make a little 'ping' noise as someone left a voicemail. Walking back through to his bedroom, he dropped the letter onto his bedside table and picked up the phone. He saw notifications of four voicemails, one of which was from the person who'd just called. He listened to that one first and felt the colour drain from his face as he recognised the voice on the other end. The clear Scottish lilt of the calm but obviously annoyed voice filled his ear. He couldn't believe it. She'd called him and he'd missed it, no, ignored it. His second big mistake in a matter of hours and only within a few days of being at home. At this rate his body would be black and blue beyond recognition by the time a month was up. He felt sick to his stomach and had to listen to the message again before being able to take in what his Master was saying.

'It seems you're too busy to receive my call. I will not call again today but your email account should be checked within the next half an hour.'

It was short and to the point with no pretence at being other than what she was; disappointed.

Aeneas dropped the phone onto the bed like it was a red hot brick. How could he have been so stupid! He'd just assumed that her reply would be by email and hadn't even contemplated that she might call him, even though he'd given her his number in the hope of hearing from her. And now he had to deal with the fact he had two possible punishments to take and all on account of his own idiotic behaviour. He looked at his watch and decided he needed to try and relax for the next half hour. He didn't think it would be possible, though, so decided he'd go down to the kitchen and busy himself by making coffee. He should probably eat something too but that might be expecting too much.

He glided downstairs is a daze and found Toby already in situ at the table.

"Good morning. Did you sleep well?"

Toby's question was simple enough but it took Aeneas all his efforts to summon an answer.

"I did, thank you."

As he replied he reached for the coffee pot, already full to the brim, and poured himself a large mug full of the hot brown liquid. Normally Toby's coffee was something to look forward to, at the start of a day, but today his mind was elsewhere.

Aeneas distractedly took the cream and sugar that Toby proffered towards him and mumbled his thanks.

"Are you all right, Sir?"

"I'm fine, really. Just a little surprised by a phone message I got this morning. Nothing for you to worry about though, I promise. Oh, I do have some good news too, though."

Aeneas hoped this would distract Toby from further enquiry and also stop him worrying.

"It seems, would you believe, that Harry wants me to take over one major client for the company. One who will take up most of my working hours and allow me to delegate to other people. Also, and most importantly, I guess, is that the client is based in Scotland. In Edinburgh to be exact."

Aeneas finished his sentence and waited for Toby's reaction. He looked at the old man and saw his face was stretched in a wide smile, almost from ear to ear.

"I'm pleased for you, Sir." He took his and his boss' empty cups over to the sink to wash them before turning back to face him. "And what will your new lady think of that, I wonder?"

With this small but meaningful statement, he left the room saying he was going into the village if Aeneas would care to add anything he wanted to the list lying on the kitchen table.

Aeneas watched him leave and wondered what he'd meant. Did he disapprove of his new 'relationship' or was he insightful enough to realise that the message he'd mentioned was from her.

Checking his watch, he realised he hadn't bought a punishment book yet. It had completely slipped his mind. Aeneas moved towards the notepad on the counter and wrote on it to buy a mid-sized, hard-backed journal and also to post a letter, then he ran upstairs, almost crashing his way into his room to retrieve it and back down to place it next to the shopping list, before running back up and throwing his laptop onto the bed. Half an hour had gone by and he wanted to read the reply his Master would probably have sent by now. He wanted to know what was in store for him but was also hesitant about finding out, in case he couldn't deal with it.

Flipping open the lid, he decided there was no way he could wait any longer. She must be expecting him to be looking at it about now and somehow he thought he would disappoint her again if he wasn't. He quickly logged on to the Violate site to receive his email and saw one message. It read:

Dog,

I want your home address to send you a letter. Please reply to this email accordingly.

That was it. That was all it said. Suddenly he had a sinking feeling. This punishment was going to be big.

* * *

The letter arrived five days later, by which time Aeneas was like a cat on a hot tin roof. Every time the mailman came he would run to the door like a young boy waiting for a new toy.

Toby watched him in silence until the day the letter finally arrived. He beat his boss to it and lifted it before he had a chance to get to the bottom of the stairs. He surveyed the frank mark and declared to Aeneas it seemed as though what he was waiting for had arrived.

"Thanks. I'll take it from here."

The old man started to walk back to the kitchen to complete whatever task he needed to finish before heading out but said he hoped Aeneas wasn't getting involved in something he couldn't cope with, then he slipped through the kitchen door.

Aeneas knew he was only concerned for him but thought he should mind his own business on this one and ran back upstairs to open it.

As calmly as possible he sat down on the floor, it seemed the right thing to do somehow, and slipped his thumb into the paper to split it open, sliding out the lilac tinted and perfumed paper within. He recognised the scent as the one Fhionna wore at Violate the first time they met and he breathed it in. He'd asked Tim what the scent was and knew it was one of her favourites; Classique by Jean Paul Gaultier.

By now it was dawning on him just how important she'd become to his own happiness and he read the long sloping calligraphy.

No doubt you will have been waiting for this letter to arrive with bated breath and I hope it's been absolute torture for you. In fact, I know it will have been.

Aeneas closed his eyes for a second and took a deep breath before continuing to read.

I do, in fact, know you'll have punished yourself just as much, if not more, than I have by making you wait for my reply. Your actual penalty, however, is laid out within these pages.

First, I want to say that I received your letter and I have taken this into account. You're fortunate I enjoyed it and it arrived before I sent you this.

Again Aeneas paused and found he was holding his breath. He let it go and thanked his lucky stars he'd written something that had pleased her so much as to influence her decision. He read on.

My leniency has been based on three things. Firstly, on your efforts to change your life significantly in an effort to serve me in person as much as you can. Secondly, that you choose to reflect on what you do and how it affects me, as your new Owner. And lastly, even though you know you're not perfect, you will always strive to improve. This last point is the most important to me as it shows me you will always do your best, even though you may fail in the final outcome.

And now to your punishment proper.

For neglecting to check your email regularly you will write two strokes of the cane in your punishment book. Beside it you should enter the date and the reason why you received punishment. This will be the standard format for all your subsequent entries.

For the outcome of overindulging in masturbation because of not checking your mail for possible tasks, you will write eight strokes of the cane in your book.

Finally, for not answering your phone to me when you had just given me your number, presumably to be used as I see fit, you will write four strokes of the cane in your book.

This last entry is the one that has taken into account your wonderful letter but I was severely disappointed I didn't get a chance to talk to you.

The fourteen strokes will be delivered to you in our next dungeon play, along with any other punishment you have accrued since the receipt of this letter.

I expect better behaviour from now on.

Master

Aeneas didn't quite know what to feel but as he re-read the letter he realised it was definitely fear. He'd accepted the punishment would be high but it was also dawning on him how dissatisfied she must have been if this was a lower allocation than she'd originally intended. He'd received six strokes of the cane before but fourteen strokes seemed to signify a whole new level of pain, by comparison, and lots of thoughts now ran through his mind; how much he hated disappointing her in any way, how could he possibly submit to so many? Could he really let it be his fate to belong to someone who relished his anguish? Deep down he knew he wanted to please her and belong to her more than anything but he didn't like pain and this was a new concept to him.

Once he'd overcome the shock he knew he would call her to try to make up for his mistakes, but for now he felt a little sorry for himself and like he needed to go out to lick his wounds. Perhaps somewhere he could feel a little spoiled.

Slowly Aeneas got up off the floor and wandered to the bathroom to splash water on his face. He looked at himself in the mirror above the sink and studied his own features, the long nose, the dark hazel eyes, his high cheekbones and the greying stubble that curved its way over his dimpled chin and down his throat. He ran his hand over the stubble and realised his fingers were trembling slightly. He really did need some fresh air, so he dried his hands and face and picked up his car keys and his mobile on the way downstairs. He called out to Toby to let him know he was going out, probably into town, and would have lunch there. Without waiting for a reply, he shut the front door behind him as he pulled on his jacket.

It was really sunny outside but there was still a cold breeze and Aeneas felt it lift his spirits as he walked to his car. Pulling some shades from his pocket he rested them on his nose as he adjusted the mirror and switched on the engine. It roared to life. The seatbelt clicked into its socket and he checked over his shoulder as he reversed up to the house then shifted into drive and picked up speed down the long driveway to the main road at the bottom of the hill.

Focusing on the road ahead took his mind off what was to come. It'd been difficult to focus on anything else lately, but he enjoyed whizzing down the lanes in between the newly blooming trees and out onto the motorway that took him into the centre of Manhattan. He decided he would have a wander through his favourite shops. The clerks always smiled when they saw him because they knew he enjoyed quality products and often spent more than a few hundred dollars at any one time. As they mainly worked on commission he could imagine them being happy to look after him for as long as he wanted. He felt he needed some distraction.

After buying a rather beautiful leather belt and the softest leather gloves he'd ever felt, he headed to an intimate little restaurant for some good food and maybe then, and only then, allow himself to think properly about the phone call he would make.

Aeneas sat in a corner booth of a small restaurant waiting for his meal. He brought his phone out onto the table top and looked at it, unsure he'd be able to talk into it in any reasonable manner until he'd at least filled his belly. His waitress, June, was walking towards him with a tray in her hand and he smiled at her.

"Here we are, Sir. Enjoy."

"Thanks, June."

Aeneas slipped the cutlery from its white linen wrapper and began to cut into the steak he'd ordered. He watched a small pool of blood ooze out as he sliced into the meat and was transported back to thoughts of the caning that his Master had promised him. He wondered if the welts would bleed this time. They'd been purple with bruising last time. He understood, also, that punishment might be poles apart from just playful strokes.

Chewing on the first mouthful, he thought about what he'd say when he spoke to her. He wanted to tell her he was sorry for his mistakes, for sure, but he also needed to tell her how he felt scared of the punishment she'd issued. He also wanted to say he'd be able to travel to Glasgow next month, if she would like him to serve her, although now it would be a journey tinged with nervousness.

With these thoughts running round in his head, he took the plunge, wiped his hands on the napkin, and programmed Fhionna's number into his phone. It surprised him that he hadn't actually thought of this till now. Maybe it was because he didn't really want to see her name on the screen and feel panicked, but he really didn't want to miss a call from her again either. He thought about the title to use and 'Ms Fhionna' seemed like the best option. He realised he didn't want it to read as something ordinary but, at the same time, didn't want it saved under 'Master' either. He felt he'd picked a suitable compromise and laid the phone back on the table.

Continuing with his meal, he sliced through some soft asparagus that was covered in hot garlic butter and groaned with pleasure as he let the taste linger on his tongue. The butter burned slightly and he loved its intensity. As he swallowed the last of the hot liquid, his cell started to ring. Aeneas glanced down at the number, assuming it would be either to do with work or it would be Hank asking to meet up, but on the screen, in bold letters, was printed the name for his Master he'd just finished typing in. He wasn't ready to speak to her yet but he had to answer it, especially if there were to be consequences for letting it ring out. He picked it up with slippery fingers and nearly dropped it as he pressed the small green handset symbol that was etched into a tiny button at the bottom, then raised the phone to his ear.

"Good morning, Master."

Aeneas listened to her wonderful voice as she said it was a lovely day and that there was a slight mist around the walls of her home, which she loved because it made her think of Heathcliff and Cathy on the English moors. He felt encouraged by her obvious good mood and thought he'd be able to say all that he'd practiced. When she asked him how he was he said he was well. He was in the city and thinking about her letter, which had arrived that morning.

Getting straight to the point, she'd then asked him what he thought of the punishment she'd given him. Even though Aeneas felt it was his chance to say what he really felt, he couldn't quite bring himself to say how scared he was about the thought of the cane, and so many strokes, so instead he said he was grateful she'd been lenient and happy she'd liked his letter.

There was a pause before she answered him, as if she was expecting him to continue. Normally Aeneas had no trouble finding plenty to say but he was having trouble saying much of anything at that moment.

"I realise that fourteen strokes of the cane must seem a lot and perhaps knowing it's been scaled back, considerably, makes you realise how disappointed I was when I wrote to you. Does that make it seem worse?"

Aeneas managed to say a very quiet, "Yes, Master," into the receiver and heard her laugh. He knew, then, he was supposed to feel guilty and nervous, that she'd wanted him to feel exactly as he did. He also realised he was in deep trouble. She was clever and could play him like a fiddle, and, not for the first time, he felt like he was falling in love.

✂ Chapter 6 ℭ

May 2012, Glasgow

Ties That Bind

I

Fhionna felt that the last couple of weeks in April had flown by. She'd talked to Aeneas a lot, in the preceding days, and come to realise he was a rather special person, very emotional and with a rather large ego, perhaps, but he was also very willing to please her and tried very hard not to let her down. In a long phone conversation, he'd said that his new work client was based in Edinburgh and she looked forward to being able to have some time of service with him every other month. She just loved his accent and thought of him literally as her exotic pet. It would be very good fun to introduce him to more of her friends as she knew they'd be intrigued by his handsome face and muscled body, but when he opened his mouth, when allowed to speak, they'd be delighted to hear his dulcet American tones. They would probably tease him quite a lot at first but she was happy for them to have some fun at his expense. She wondered if he would join in the fun or if he would pout, unattractively. Time would tell, she supposed.

Aeneas was coming over soon and she had so much still to do. She was busy, driving her slaves crazy, she was quite sure, sending them on errands to buy food and wine, to the dry cleaners with several different outfits because she couldn't decide what she wanted to wear for the next couple of days, and instructing them to make plans for Violate the following night. She was enjoying herself immensely though. She was happy he was staying for three nights, although essentially only two full days, and the plan was to make him sleep in the dungeon room, although not inside the cage as it wouldn't do his joints or circulation any good.

Bunty had spent the last few days with her and she knew her slave was quite worn out by all her demands and needs. She'd been unusually aroused and had whipped her and made love to her, often. Fhionna knew Bunty loved her so much that she put up with the craziness but she also knew she just couldn't help herself from being cheeky sometimes. This got her into trouble, of course, but she was the only one who could get away with it, on a fairly regular basis. Fhionna was aware that Tim wouldn't even dare try to be cheeky, even though he could be overly pedantic at times, and Louise was just so happy go lucky and eager to please that it genuinely never even crossed her mind to be anything but sunshine and light. Aeneas didn't know his Master well enough yet to offer his opinion, or even know that he was allowed to, but he'd relax more as time passed and he would come to recognise the signs of when he could joke with her and when he should be silent. She guessed the main indication of this was her raised eyebrow. It was such a natural gesture that sometimes she didn't know she was actually doing it, which meant her slaves were often at a loss as to whether or not they should continue speaking. Sometimes her brow raised when she was thinking or when she was surprised by something a slave said, but it didn't necessarily mean they would be in trouble if they continued on their verbal path. She found this very amusing, of course. It added to the mystery and her power over them was heightened by this simple action, in itself.

Time was passing though and she wanted the dungeon cleaned from top to bottom. It was all hands to the pump, as it were, and she enlisted the help of her maid Poppy; soapy water and sterilising spray at the ready. The dungeon wasn't dirty, as it was cleaned promptly after each use, but she just wanted to make sure. Aeneas would be spending quite a bit of time in there. She wanted to be able to run a white cotton gloved hand over every surface and find no dust. She knew it was a tall order, as the room was large with many nooks and crannies, but she wanted it finished by nightfall.

Along with the house to make ready, she had a lot to prepare for Violate the following night as it was going to be a rather special event. She was excited by Dog's visit but also by the binding ceremony that her friend Sophia was having; taking her sub spike as her slave. Given the name of her slave, Fhionna wanted to have the dungeon room of the club kitted out with two rows of large metal spikes jutting out from the top of the tall walls. She also wanted the huge church candles she'd ordered to be wrapped halfway up their shafts with soft rubber spiked material. She'd found the fabric online and it was being delivered in about an hour's time. The rubber came in small sheets and had small prongs sticking up that would bend to the touch so that no one could be hurt if they bumped into them, but the effect would be absolutely amazing. She was prepared to go all out for this event as Sophia had been her best friend for the last ten years. She'd been through some rough times in the past but had found love with this gentle giant of a man, who adored her. She was so happy for her that she wanted the event to be the 'talk of the steamy.' She laughed and made Louise jump as she walked past her with a huge vase of flowers in her hand, which she nearly dropped. Luckily she managed to catch it before it actually crashed to the floor.

"I'm sorry, Louise. I didn't mean to startle you. Just some private thoughts about tomorrow night that amused me."

The girl blushed and said there was never any need for her Master to apologise and scuttled off to the kitchen, hands now dripping with the water that had splashed out from the top of the vase.

Fhionna called to Tim and he came into the living room to see what his Owner needed.

"Could you make sure you're nearby in about an hour to answer the door, please? The material for the candles is being delivered. You'll need to start cutting it to size and wrapping them straightaway."

Tim nodded and said, "Yes, Sir," before vanishing again to compete whatever task he'd been doing.

A couple of hours had passed and Fhionna knew that Bunty had dropped off and picked up shopping and dry cleaning, Tim had been an angel and had made all the candles spikey, Louise, with some help from Poppy, was halfway through cleaning the dungeon and she, herself, had made sure the catering team, who were delivering the party food, had everything done to spec. She also made sure the DJ was aware of the type of music to play, which catered to Sophia's particular tastes, and what times he would be performing, that the bouquet of flowers for her friend would arrive by special delivery at ten o'clock on the dot and that the champagne would have ice buckets and be at the right temperature.

Tim had cleaned the car to pick Aeneas up from the airport and was about to help his Master organise her clothes for the club. He loved the fact that the outfit she'd chosen reflected the theme of the ceremony. The bodice of the dress was fitted and the top of it was shaped like cups of a bra covered in tiny metal spikes, while the long, silk skirt flowed to the ground and would reach the tops of the soft leather stilettos which were also covered in metal spikes. She'd need to be careful that no one got injured when they hugged her.

"Your outfit is spectacular, Master. I've hung it on your wardrobe door and laid out your shoes beside it."

Fhionna smiled to herself at the thought of publicly impaling Aeneas' cock with the spiked heels of her shoes or making him kneel while chained with his hands behind his back and his genitals hovering over the tops of them, anticipating a blow from the spikes that adorned the leather uppers. She was having so much fun with this theme already. She wondered why she hadn't thought of it before, for a normal event.

She'd organised someone to conduct the ceremony for her as she really wanted to watch it instead and see the look on Sophia's face as she gave her the huge bouquet of flowers just after she'd placed the collar round her partner's neck. Her other long-term friend, Mistress Vixen, famous for her scatty sense of humour, her pink locks, and her love of Sadomasochism, would be doing the honours and Fhionna had written something for her to mull over that gave some history of the couple's relationship as Mistress and submissive. It was a lovely story. It described how they'd met at Violate. Spike, then known as Gareth, had approached her rather tentatively to ask if she would like to play with him. He was so shy that she couldn't quite hear what he was saying and told him to speak up. As he repeated his question, thinking he should possibly rephrase it to show his submission even more, the background music stopped and all that could be heard was his rather loud voice saying:

"Dear Goddess, would you care to be cruel to me please? I have worshipped you since you walked into the dungeon."

Inevitably, there was a pause as the crowd of revellers looked in their direction and waited for Sophia to respond:

"I don't hit just anyone. I'm quite fussy that way."

Of course, the crowd had laughed and Gareth had visibly shrunk before their eyes as he realised that the music had stopped and everyone had heard what they'd both just said. Most males would have fled in embarrassment at that point, but he was rather bold, obviously summoning all his reserves, and continued by kneeling and kissing her feet saying:

"Please, Goddess, if you give me a chance I won't disappoint you."

As it happens, this made Sophia smile.

"Oh for God's sake get up off your knees and go and bend over that bench over there. Make sure you strip first."

This little play scene was to be the beginning of a beautiful partnership and Gareth became spike because of his love of the spiked and studded paddle she enjoyed using on his naked backside.

Reliving this moment, a little, had been fun but now Fhionna's attentions needed to focus on her newest slave's arrival. She was extremely excited. She planned on testing him further, of course, but her aim was also to show him off at the club night as her animal. She couldn't help but smile as she thought about the outfit she'd bought for him to wear. The hood was made of leather and it would fit tightly round his head, but the fun part were the dog ears and long nose, making the wearer look like a real hound. The leather mittens would fit snuggly over his fists, making it impossible to grasp anything, and had fasteners that locked the moulded paws into place. She felt aroused as she remembered his body that would remain largely naked, apart from the smallest of leather pouches, but the ultimate touch was the insertable tail, a long pointy tail that would hang down between his legs and no doubt swish when he walked. She'd have so much fun attaching a lead to a collar round his neck and leading him around as her property.

* * *

The day had flown by. She stood at the top of the stairs that led down to the dungeon and called on Tim.

"It's time to collect Dog and can you make sure he has everything with him he needs, and if he doesn't can you try your best to pick up what he's failed to bring, please."

Tim appeared, said, "Yes, Sir," and smiled at his Master. He knew she was excited because she always fussed about small details when she was on edge, for some reason. He also knew part of this nervousness was the hope that all would go well for her best friend the following night.

* * *

Opening the dungeon door, she was amazed to find that it was nearly finished. Louise was on her knees, scrubbing away at the floor of the cage and looked adorable with a smudge of dirt on her freckled nose. Poppy was there too and was on her knees but behind the St Andrew's cross polishing all the leather straps with a soft rag and some wax.

Fhionna noticed immediately that Poppy's stockings were ripped in several places and three or four long ladders were snaking their way up to her thighs from her heels. She smiled as she thought how cute she was, her blonde and pink wig a little lopsided, the huge stilettos she loved to wear bending her ankles over in the most awkward of positions, the ripped stockings, the frilly knickers that could just be seen beneath the petticoats of her pink PVC maid's uniform and the all too prominent view of the Prince Albert piercing bulging at the end of her cock head as it strained against the frills. Dear little Poppy. Such a good slave who did her best to please her Master and so wanting to be owned and cherished as well as used and abused as a true girl might.

It was several seconds before either of them had noticed her come into the room and each one looked up, surprised that they hadn't heard the door open. Poppy looked up first and said, "Hello, Master," rather shyly.

"Hello, sweet girl. What an amazing job you've done."

Next Louise turned her head and more confidently said, "Hi, Master," with a cheeky grin plastered on her face.

"Hello, Louise. The place looks perfect. Thank you both so much for all your hard work and for being able to cope without me for the past few hours."

Satisfied that all was well, Fhionna left the room telling them they could go to the kitchen after they'd finished and help themselves to some food and a big glass of orange juice each but reminded them to wash any dishes they used and put them back in the cupboards.

* * *

Aeneas was just emerging through the sliding airport doors when Tim arrived. Waving to him, he jumped out from the car and walked towards him holding out his hand to take his bags.

Aeneas beamed from ear to ear as he hugged the smaller man and insisted that he carried his own bags.

"Hi, Tim, I can do it. Wow, it's so good to be back. Feels like it's been forever and it's not really been that long. I guess I know where my heart is."

Tim smiled at him and said he understood completely.

Quite naturally, Tim probably thought he meant he was beginning to feel like his family was here instead of in the States and didn't realise that Aeneas might mean slightly more than that. He was a little nervous about his feelings being revealed too quickly in case somehow it all went wrong.

Aeneas jumped into the front seat and sneaked a sideways look at Tim, hopefully without him seeing it.

"What's up dog?" Tim smiled and Aeneas had to smile back. He'd been caught.

"I was just wondering if you were at liberty to divulge any information about what was to happen over the weekend. I know you're probably not allowed to but any little titbit you can let slip would be appreciated."

Aeneas stopped talking and let out a deep breath; like he'd been holding it in the whole time he was speaking. It sounded like a low whistle and he was sure Tim could tell there was a very nervous type of excitement behind the sound.

Tim smiled and said he shouldn't really give any detail away but that Dog's outfit for the club the next night was amazingly cool and was befitting of his slave name. Tim grinned as Aeneas' eyes grew wide with horror.

"Gee, and here I was actually starting to relax!"

Tim rocked with laughter as his American lilt became a full throttle and almost guttural sound rather than a mere cadence.

Aeneas looked at Tim and then started laughing too. All too quickly, they had tears streaming down their faces and Tim had to wipe his away before he could see to start the car.

"You're so easy, Dog. If I can do that to you just by talking briefly about your outfit then imagine what Master can do to you without actually saying anything at all."

Now Aeneas was back to a fully wound-up state and he sighed a little and said yes, he was beginning to realise what she was capable of.

"All I know is I want to give myself to her completely but it scares me. I don't mean that I don't trust her, I'd happily give up everything I own or am just to be hers, if she asked me to. What I mean is that she is an amazing woman who is wise, clever and sadistic, and I'm fully aware of just how much she'll be able to toy with me and I hope I can cope with it, in the long-term, because there's nothing I want more."

Tim said the best thing he could do would be to try to not overthink everything. "I find it best just to go with the flow, whatever Master wants is what she should get and to fight it only makes it more difficult for yourself. Try to accomplish what she wants to the best of your ability and don't let pride get in the way."

Aeneas was quiet for a moment, then said, "I guess you've been serving Master a long time. You also seem able to tell that I can be quite a headstrong kinda guy."

"I'm not saying try to change your personality, Dog, because she likes who you are. All I'm saying is that to be able to control your own desires is important, so you can put her needs first. It's the best advice I can give you in making your relationship with Master last."

Aeneas blushed and turned his head to look out of the window at the lights as they sped past. He loved the colourful streaks they made on the darkening sky as they buzzed into life.

* * *

Fhionna looked out the window and thought what a beautiful evening it was. She loved the sound of the trees as they rustled in the light May breeze. Summer was fast approaching and with it came the opportunity to play outside. It wasn't quite warm enough for that yet but the sun was beginning to gain strength.

She'd enjoyed some time helping the garden flourish during April, planting spring bulbs and pruning the summer flowering rose bushes. She'd also found a little time, although not as much as she'd really wanted, to sit under the magnificent cherry blossom trees to read her favourite book, *Wuthering Heights*, by Emily Bronte, and also some of the modernist fiction of Virginia Woolf. Two great women writers, separated in more ways than by time alone, but both as wonderful and as advanced in their ideas as each other.

Fhionna sighed, not unhappily, but more in anticipation of what was to come. She felt she was almost ready to write her own novel based on her love to dominate others. She envisaged how it might read to those who dared to break its spine and delve into the secrets of her home life and her dungeon. It wouldn't be pure sensationalism. It would need to have a ring of truth for those who read it; almost like bearing witness to something you knew was real but had only just begun to imagine was possible.

As she let these thoughts skip through her mind, she saw the headlights of Tim's car approaching the house from the bottom of the driveway. Excitedly she found a comfortable pose on the sofa in front of the fire he'd lit for her. Soon she'd hear the footsteps as both her slaves entered the house and sought her out.

* * *

Tim stood outside the front door and waited for Dog to catch up. "Ready?" he asked as Aeneas reached his side.

"Yup, I think so. What is it the English say: 'As ready as I'll ever be?'"

Tim smiled and resisted the urge to punch Aeneas on the arm like a big brother would. Instead he said, "Come on then," and opened the door.

"We can carry your bags down later but I know Master will be waiting on you so let's put her out of her misery." Tim smiled as he used this expression, thinking it was hardly appropriate to be attached to their Owner but doing so anyway, just for the fun of it. He saw a slight puzzled look on Aeneas' face and clarified that it just meant let's not keep her waiting any longer than necessary.

Tim knocked on the living room door and waited for her to answer. However before he could open the door Dog gave him a huge bear-like hug, nearly breaking his ribs, and said thanks for all the advice. He was a little surprised by the big man's gesture but responded warmly to it and left him to his fate.

Aeneas walked nervously into the room and saw his Owner sitting by the fire. On instinct he said, "Permission to approach you please, Master," before crossing the room to kneel at her feet and kiss her hand.

"I hope your trip was a pleasant one. I've been looking forward to seeing you again; to you being in service here."

Fhionna smiled down at him and Dog raised his eyes to hers. It struck him just how lovely she was as he glanced at her strong but slender shoulders. The way she held her body, facing him full on, filled with confidence, and the smile that creased the corner of her eyes, were all so intoxicating.

"Master, I'm just grateful to be allowed to be yours."

Fhionna slipped her hand from Aeneas' grip and he took this as a signal to place his hands behind his back, as she'd taught him to do. She seemed pleased by this but, unfortunately, it was to be rather short lived.

"Please fetch your journal and your punishment book."

Dog heard himself say, "Yes, Master," as he got up from the floor, but a sense of panic engulfed him as he realised he hadn't created the picture of a dog with a collar round its neck for the front of the book.

When he left the room he darted across the floor and started riffling through his bag to find the books she wanted just as Tim was passing the bottom of the staircase that led up to the bedrooms.

"What's the matter?"

"Oh my God, Tim. I can't believe it but I've forgotten to find and print out a picture of a collared dog for the front of my punishment book. She asked for it specifically, along with the title, 'Punishment Book,' and I haven't done it. I've messed up already and I've only been here five minutes! What am I going to do?"

Tim looked apprehensive and Aeneas was touched by his concern.

"I'm afraid, then, we'll both be for the high jump because I was under instruction to make sure you'd achieved everything you were meant to have done before arriving at the house. She was obviously making sure you had the opportunity to fix it before you got here."

"Oh, I'm sorry. It's all my fault".

Aeneas felt crestfallen and now dreaded handing over his book. He thought that the best policy was not to offer any excuses for having forgotten the whole task but just to apologise and hope she wouldn't be too hard on Tim for his part in the failure.

They both looked at each other, headed over to the living room door, and went in together. If their Master was surprised at seeing both of them she didn't show it. She merely waited for them to present themselves in front of her before looking at Tim to explain why he was there too.

Tim opened his mouth to speak but was beaten to it by Aeneas. Fhionna switched her gaze from one to the other and waited. Aeneas took a deep breath.

"I'm sorry, Master, but I haven't printed out a picture of a dog in a collar for the front of my book. I have no excuse other than I completely forgot."

Fhionna looked at Aeneas as he spoke and then turned to Tim. Apparently it was his turn.

"I'm sorry too, Master. I forgot to check all was in order before we got to the house."

Fhionna leaned back in her chair and observed them both with their chins hung low on their chests and started to laugh.

"Do you think I'm about to unleash some great punishment upon you both; that you won't be allowed to attend Violate tomorrow night or you'll be caned until you bleed?"

Neither of them answered, aware of the rhetorical nature of the question, and simply waited for her to continue.

"It's hardly the crime of the century, is it?"

Again they waited but now felt some relief.

"It is, however, a failure, even though a very, very small one. Dog, I will put four strokes of the cane in your book and Tim, because you should know slightly better, you will spend a couple of hours tied and locked into the upright cage."

Tim's punishment sounded fairly severe to Aeneas, and he wondered if he should protest on his behalf but Fhionna continued before he had the chance.

"Take Dog's bags down to the dungeon, please. Once you've done that you should strip and get into the cage and wait for me."

Tim said, "Yes, Master," and left the room.

Fhionna told Aeneas to kneel in front of her. "You haven't actually given me your books yet."

Aeneas realised he was still holding them behind his back.

She smiled and made a big show of writing four strokes of the cane in his book then and there.

"It's so wonderful to be with you again."

Aeneas was amazed at such a tender display of emotion that he forgot his anxiety and looked straight into her eyes as she handed it back.

"I've longed to be here again, and in this position, but I'm really happy I can be here more often, as you want me to be of course."

"I'm glad too. Are you a hungry?"

Aeneas laughed and said he was a ravenous Dog.

Fhionna told him to follow her to the kitchen where he could have some food and she would introduce him to Poppy.

II

The next morning, after Aeneas had slept in the dungeon overnight, Fhionna felt the urge to play. She smiled to herself and almost purred with anticipation. She loved this feeling. She was rather excited at the thought of Dog being downstairs, and wondered if he'd managed to get any sleep. She was also excited about the arrival of Poppy because she just loved triangulation.

She slipped out of bed, wrapped a silk robe round her body, washed her face and hands, and wandered down to the kitchen where she was greeted by the sight of her lovely little slave in a new French maid uniform busying herself at the stove.

"Good morning, Master. I hope you slept well. Is there anything I can do for you?" Poppy blushed and smiled at her Owner as she gathered up the escaping coffee beans that hadn't quite made it into the blender.

"Yes, please. You can go and fetch Dog from the dungeon and bring him up for some breakfast. And make sure he's presentable."

"Yes, Master."

Fhionna, meanwhile, gathered up the rest of the beans, finished making the coffee, then helped herself to the hot bread and the rest of breakfast before settling down at the table and making sure the dog bowl was full with eggs and bacon.

Poppy reached the bottom of the stairs and entered the dungeon. She flicked on the light but used the dimmer so that Dog wouldn't be too startled. Walking gingerly over to the mattress that was laid out beside the cage, she found him wide awake and humming to himself. Poppy started laughing and Dog smiled at her.

"Good morning. You caught me singing to myself. I've been awake for some time and trying not to be too nervous about who'd come to collect me, or by the fact that I'm actually here, which is really difficult."

Poppy said she understood and painting her toenails kept her calm.

"Master wants you in the kitchen to share breakfast. I had mine before I left home so I don't think I'll be needed, unless it's to serve, of course."

Dog wanted to ask her so many questions about her slavery but wasn't sure if he should.

"How long have you been a slave? Is Poppy your slave name or your female name only? How did you meet Master?" Dog stopped, realising he might be making her feel shy and apologised if he was being too nosey.

She smiled and said it was ok to ask. "Well, I've been Master's slave for just over two years now, Poppy is my female name when I'm dressed but my slave name is actually Bitch. I met her at Violate about 5 years ago and we played on club nights before I lost contact with her; when I didn't attend for a year. Then, when I went back, she asked me if I would like to come to her house to be a maid for her and I jumped at the chance. It grew from there, really, and I had a public collaring ceremony, at Violate, to become her slave."

Poppy paused, then said, "I'm happy to fill you in on all the details later but right now Master says will you please make yourself presentable, I guess that means shower and shave, then I'll take you up with me. She didn't say I had to attach a lead to your collar but I know she'd appreciate it, if you don't mind me doing it?"

Poppy grinned at Dog and Dog chuckled.

"No, I don't mind one bit so go right ahead."

She watched him stand up and stretch his long limbs. He was so much taller than her, about six-foot, she reckoned, with tanned skin and rippling muscles. He was quite a lot wider than her too but she was quite short and very petite in stature. She looked up at him.

"Wow, you're a big dog. I hadn't quite realised how tall you were last night when I met you but I guess we were in a hurry to leave you alone with Master."

Aeneas laughed. "Well, it's kinda hard to tell how tall I am when I'm on my hands and knees."

Poppy laughed too and thought how nice he was.

Dog headed into the dungeon's en-suite bathroom to get cleaned up then returned and bent low down so that Poppy could attach the lead to the collar he'd worn all night. Suddenly Aeneas realised how much he wanted a collar of his own, one he could take home with him, to wear as instructed. He let out a little sigh and she asked what the matter was.

"It's nothing, really. Just that I want my own collar and wondering if it will ever happen."

"Aww, I'm sure it will. Master is clearly nuts about you."

Aeneas smiled. "I know she likes me but I don't think she's nuts about me yet."

Poppy said she was sure she was but they'd probably spent enough time down here and had better get a move on or she would have finished breakfast before they got back.

Aeneas knew to get down on all fours to enter the kitchen and couldn't help smiling at how much he'd learned already.

Poppy led the way, pulling Dog behind her, slightly.

"There you are. I was beginning to think you were lost. I'm afraid Dog's breakfast will be stone cold." Fhionna paused. "The lead is a very nice touch, though."

She laughed at the sight of them together, little and large, so different, from completely different worlds, and yet both the same in wanting something more out of life than just the usual, ordinary things that most people settled for. They both wanted to be loved and cherished but in a very unique and special way and she felt honoured to be able to give them what they wanted.

Poppy smiled at her Master and asked if she wanted Dog on the floor at his bowl.

"Yes, please. Fasten his chain to the leg of the table."

Doing as she was told, she slipped the chain round the wooden leg and apologised for taking so long.

"Its fine, Poppy, but you should cook more and make some fresh coffee."

Having given her something to do, she turned her attention to her other slave.

"I hope you managed to get some rest." She ran her hand through his hair affectionately and he found himself nuzzling into it in return, amazed at how good the simple touch felt.

"I did, thank you. I was so excited to be here that it took some time to settle down but I managed it eventually."

"It's wonderful to have you here with me again." She touched his head and shoulders and pulled him in closer.

Aeneas wasn't quite sure what he should do but she said that he could touch her and he gladly hugged her legs.

Poppy was loathe to interrupt the scene but approached the table and curtsied to signal that the food and coffee were ready.

"You may serve, please. Good girl."

Fhionna knew she loved to be called a good girl. She also knew she loved to be called Bitch too but that was kept for their more intimate play time when she made her flinch from her whip or used her strap-on on her pretty little bottom, making her wriggle with pure delight.

Dog grudgingly separated from his Owner's legs and put his fingers into his bowl to eat. He was ravenous and devoured it, without paying much attention to what was actually in it. He was then offered a smaller bowl of coffee and told he could raise it to his lips, rather than try to lap it up. He thanked her and just as eagerly drank the hot liquid from the bowl as he grasped it between both hands.

* * *

When the meal was over, Fhionna told Aeneas to wash the dishes and go down to the dungeon and wait in the position she'd taught him, on his knees. She then left the room taking Poppy with her by the hand. Dog noticed this and felt a small stab of jealousy for the intimate contact but knew it wasn't his place to feel bad about it. He wished, though, that it was him being led away.

Reaching the bathroom, she asked Poppy to strip down to her Ownership collar and to run a bath with plenty of bubbles.

Poppy did as instructed and folded her uniform, leaving it neatly in the corner of the room, with her stockings, wig, and high heels on top. She knew what her Master wanted her to do and couldn't help but feel excited at the prospect of being allowed to bathe her. Much to her embarrassment, her member was standing to full attention when she came back in.

"It's wonderful you're excited. Please don't try to hide it."

Fhionna let out a low purring noise at the sheer pleasure of being pampered, slowly shifting her body through the water towards her slave. She reached out one slim hand, grasped her nipple, and twisted it.

"You will be 'Boy' when I take you downstairs soon. You'll remain naked and in your male form. I'll also refer to you as 'he' so expect it."

Poppy nodded that she understood. Even though she preferred to be treated as female she knew Master loved her to be her Boy just as much. On the rare occasion she called her Boy, in the club or the restaurant, people wondered if it was the same person and often asked. It was, of course, very amusing to her Master. She loved to cause a little awkwardness, sometimes changing gender terms halfway through a sentence if she felt so inclined. She would tell her friends, when they looked confused, that Poppy was her boy/girl slave but they should just call her Poppy no matter what form her body took. Her friends would laugh and say how bizarre she was, which she always took as a great compliment.

Fhionna hadn't quite decided what Bitch would be at Violate that night, but she knew her slave loved to wear frills when out in public and usually the more the merrier. What she'd be allowed to wear depended on how well she performed with Dog that afternoon, she concluded. If she did well then she could wear as many frills as she wanted. She didn't expect her to do badly, of course, but she knew Poppy was strictly heterosexual and might struggle a little with what she had in store for her.

* * *

Downstairs, Dog waited patiently for his Master to come. He found himself humming again to distract himself from being nervous but it wasn't really working. He was even feeling a little scared. He hadn't had any contact with his Master last night, apart from when she placed a collar round his neck and told him he was allowed to sleep on a proper mattress outside the cage, and had only seen her for a short time during breakfast this morning. He knew something was about to happen but he just couldn't guess what it was.

Tim's advice drifted into his head as he knelt on the floor of the dungeon. He would try not to overthink it and just go with his Master's flow.

Just as he was shifting position on the floor, the door opened and someone entered the room. Actually, he thought two people had entered the room but he knew better than to look up without permission to do so. It was his Master who spoke to him, telling him to raise his head from the carpet but to clasp his hands behind his head.

Dog did as instructed, and drank in the sight of his wonderful Owner standing in front of him, but saw that he'd been right, because she was quickly followed by a youngish looking submissive male. He believed he recognised the face but the body he didn't know at all and he wondered what on earth was about to happen. Was Master expecting him to 'perform' for her with this young man? Surely not! He was covered in freckles and it made him look in his late twenties, somewhere, but upon closer inspection of his face he thought, maybe, in his mid-thirties. He felt it wasn't too strange she should ask him to act out her fantasies with Tim or even Louise, now that they'd known each other in a sexual way, but this was a mere boy who stood, shaking slightly, as if a stiff breeze might push him over.

Aeneas was a little confused and it must have shown on his face because she smiled at him and did the introduction.

"Dog, this is Boy, or, as you have come to know him, Poppy."

To say that Dog was amazed was an understatement but nevertheless he broke into a huge smile and said hello to Poppy. Realising his Master had introduced him as 'Boy' he quickly changed this to, "Hello, Boy," instead.

Boy was standing behind Fhionna visibly in shock at being

presented to Dog in his male form. His face and neck were bright red and the pink leather Ownership collar clashed terribly with his skin.

"Kneel down beside Dog. Both of you, put your heads and hands on the floor. We'll start by issuing the punishment from your books. I'll give you a warm up as it's been some time since either of you have been caned."

Dog wondered if Poppy had ever been punished when in his raw male state. If not, it would be a big deal for her and his heart went out to the slender, petite, person shaking beside him. Maybe her femininity helped her deal with any type of castigation and he hoped she could cope without it.

As Fhionna crossed the room to select some of her favourite toys to play with, Dog took the opportunity to raise a hand to place it on top of Boy's hand. He gently stroked his fingers and felt him respond by linking them, briefly, with his own.

It was at that moment their Master chose to turn round and look at them. She smiled as she saw the connection and turned away again, deciding to give them a few private moments together. She realised, then, how protective Aeneas could be, even though he himself was probably as nervous about a new situation. His empathy was lovely and she admired the selflessness of the act.

She decided she'd say something before she turned round so they could separate but feel they'd achieved a little intimacy. It was an important part of their bonding and it would be wonderful if they could care for each other. It would certainly help for them to feel a certain closeness because she planned to test them both to their limits.

Walking slowly back towards them, she found them in their original position. She instructed Boy to get onto the punishment bench by saying, "Boy… bench," and watched as he almost ran towards it to kneel on the padded legs and drape his arms down the sides.

Fhionna arrived beside him and stroked his head tenderly.

Boy rubbed his head against her hand affectionately and it helped him to relax a little.

"You have thirty-two in your book and it will be emptied now."

Boy let out a whimper before confirming he understood and raised his head to allow a gag to be placed between his lips and locked into place at the back of his head.

Fhionna then fastened his hands, ankles, thighs and lower back onto the bench and watched him adjust his body slightly. She then told Dog he should kneel up as before and face him on the bench.

Aeneas did as he was told and was surprised by the arousal he felt when he saw the naked male strapped down and gagged so tightly. He knew he was about to receive many strokes, more than he thought humanly possible to endure, but couldn't do anything to hide his erection.

His Master noticed and laughed but it was a more ruthless sound than he'd ever heard escape from between her lips. He looked into her eyes to try and gauge her thoughts and saw passion. He saw lust but without its usual softness.

"You can't see it, but you should know that Dog is erect at the sight of your beautiful male body. Who knew he liked you so much!"

With these words, Fhionna swiftly turned away from Dog and started to beat the young slave's upturned soft, fleshy mounds. She worked rhythmically, starting with a small leather paddle, which had fur on one side and studs on the other, alternating the side she used so that he was breathless within minutes. She enjoyed herself as she watched him struggle against the tight leather straps. Soon he would feel the cane sting his cheeks but she was happy to use paddles and belts to make his bottom red before she disciplined him properly.

Her favourite belt was one with a long wooden handle. Used so many times before, it was beginning to split along one edge, but it was still effective. She made a quick mental note to ask Tim to have it mended for her, before it snapped altogether, and then started to measure up the strokes by taking a step back.

Raising her arm, she brought the belt down with a middle force onto his waiting bottom. Before long, another stroke was being delivered, then another, and another, until a slight sobbing noise could be heard through the supple rubber ball gag so she ended the onslaught and touched his burning flesh with her cool hand.

"You're warm enough, now, so I'll start your caning."

Boy cried loudly into the gag and started to shake his head. He was terrified.

Dog watched as Fhionna went to the top of the bench and bent down beside him. He couldn't hear the conversation but when she stood up again Boy was nodding his head instead. He wondered what she'd said to calm him down and felt slightly queasy at the thought of having to watch what was to come. By this time his erection had disappeared but whether it was because he was feeling bad for him or because he was feeling bad for himself, he wasn't sure. He knew it would be his turn next so maybe it was both.

He watched as she picked up the thinnest of canes from the rack where over ten different lengths and thicknesses were stored. Dog found himself wondering which one would hurt the most, the thin or the thick. He assumed that the length wouldn't make that much difference.

Aeneas closed his eyes as their Master raised her hand to deliver the first of many blows.

"I can see your eyes are closed. Open them. Right now."

A little surprised that she was watching him in the mirror, Aeneas opened them without answering back and listened as Boy yelled out, as much as he could at least, as the first stroke was hit home, closely followed by the second and the third and the fourth, and so on, without pause, until they were finished. He guessed he'd have lost count by now as he slumped against the bench, completely drenched in sweat and crying hot, salty tears.

Fhionna walked round the bench unfastening all the straps and buckles and gave him a minute to rest before telling him he could get up. She watched him as he very slowly stumbled towards her, like his legs were made of jelly, and collapse on the floor at her feet.

"You've done well. I'm proud of you. You may go upstairs and dress in your pretty red corset, tutu skirt, your black high heels and some black stockings, then come back down. You may also wear your black and red wig."

Dog watched as Boy looked up at his Master and smiled a thank you before crawling from the room. It made him think that maybe it was due to exhaustion, as much as submission, and he totally understood why.

When Poppy entered the room once more, the scene before her eyes was very familiar. There was a weeping man at her Owner's feet. She knew the strokes wouldn't have amounted to what was in her book, though, because there were special circumstances for her own punishment. She'd been told to stop smoking after the illness she'd had, which caused her pain when she breathed. She'd been quite ill. So much so that the decision was made, on her recovery, that she would be punished for every cigarette she smoked. She knew she was being cared for and Master had given her a number to achieve each month, decreasing each time, but she was to receive two strokes of the cane for every one she smoked over the given allowance.

Fhionna smiled at Poppy and allowed her to move closer to Aeneas, to sit beside him on the floor and stroke his head. She moved away slightly and watched as he lifted his head from her feet to turn and smile at Poppy, before giving out more instructions.

"I now need your direct consent because I want to watch you being intimate with each other. I know you'll do anything to make me happy but it's important to know you are both willing to participate in sexual activity."

She watched as both men looked at each other, smiled, and then looked at her before nodding and saying they were happy to be sexually intimate with each other in any way she saw fit to direct them.

"Perfect. Thank you. Poppy, you may start by sucking on Dog's nipples."

Poppy looked up at her Owner and said, "Yes, Master," and complied with her wishes. She approached Dog rather shyly and started to flick her tongue over the large mounds of flesh that protruded from Dog's chest hair.

Aeneas moaned slightly, turning his body round so that she could reach him properly.

Poppy looked at her Master for reassurance and was greeted by a warm smile, so she continued. Taking each nipple in turn, she licked and sucked and nibbled them, causing him to moan with ecstasy.

As Fhionna watched her slaves, she felt her own excitement grow.

"That's enough, Poppy. Go and wait over by the cage. Kneel up, Aeneas, and clasp your hands in front of you, please."

Fhionna walked across the room, selected a hood, and then headed back towards him. She slipped it over his head and, satisfied he couldn't see, buckled a large dildo-gag into place. The internal dildo was medium sized but large enough the fill his mouth without making him choke once movements from Poppy riding his face had started. The cock on the outside of the gag was quite large but she knew that

Poppy could handle it because her strap-on was of equal size.

Very excited at her plans to make her pets interact for her, she bound Dog's hands tightly in front of his body and told him to lie down on the floor on his back. She guided his body to where she wanted it to be and pulled his arms up over his head, slipping the rope that bound his wrists together through the bars of the cage.

Poppy watched her Master very closely and realised what was about to happen.

Fhionna asked Dog if he could breathe properly and waited for him to nod in response. She smiled at Poppy, whose eyes were as wide as saucers, and told her to rub lubricant along the shaft before squatting over it and letting it enter her.

Following her instructions, she took the jelly that her Master handed to her and smoothed some out onto her palm and rubbed it the length of the dildo. She then took the tissues her Owner proffered, cleaned her hands and, without speaking, slowly began to squat over Dog's gag filled mouth while holding on to the bars of the cage for support. Poppy moaned and started to build up speed as she clenched her cheeks to hold the cock in place.

Fhionna saw that Poppy had stopped mid-air, obviously worried he was suffocating, so she checked he was still able to breathe and then told her to continue. She could feel her own excitement spiral as she watched her slaves enact her fantasy. She could see the fresh cane marks on Poppy's buttocks as she rose and fell in rhythm and decided she wanted to see the marks on Aeneas' cheeks too, so collected two long lengths of rope and lifted his legs and held them apart; attaching a length to each ankle before twisting it and tying it round each thigh then running it up to the cage bars. Dog's legs were now wide open and his own striped flesh exposed.

Donning latex gloves, she decided she wanted to fill him there too. Excited at the prospect of his abuse at both ends, she prepared his anus with lube, while testing it to see what size of dildo he would be able to take, assuming it would be a fairly small one. She then collected the right size of butt-plug and pushed, taking her time.

Dog groaned loudly and the room was filled with a squelchy, plopping sound as it got sucked into place.

Fhionna laughed. "Poor Dog. Being used by me and by another slave."

After a while, Fhionna could bear it no longer and decided she wanted some intimate fun for herself. She told Poppy to stop, clean herself with the douche in the bathroom beside the dungeon, and then go upstairs to wait at the foot of her bed. She smiled at her, as she left the room, then untied Aeneas and removed the butt-plug, the gag, and then the hood. She watched him as he screwed up his eyes against the dim light and handed him some tissues to wipe away the drool on his chin before telling him he could use the shower and enter the cage to get some rest. She told him they would chat about his experience later, that she'd expect a journal entry, but for now she had other business to attend to.

Aeneas didn't say anything except a brief, "Thank you," and lay on his back with his eyes closed.

* * *

Dog saw the smile on his Master's face as she left the room and it made him happy. He felt used, turned on, and also very tired. He couldn't quite process the many thoughts that were starting to whirl through his brain so decided a nap was the best idea. Who knew when he'd be allowed to have another!

III

The first day of Dog's visit had flown by so far. Soon it would be time for Violate. Fhionna was nervous, slightly, because she wanted it to go well. It was now late afternoon and she was a little tired after such a long and exciting play with her slaves, but she was extremely happy. She smiled to herself as she relived the canings, the inserted dildos, and the use of Poppy in her bedroom afterwards. She'd felt so horny, she'd known she must orgasm.

She blushed, although there was no one else in the room and thought how impressed she'd been by her skill. It was Poppy's first time, being intimate with her, and she'd been overjoyed at such an honour.

* * *

Downstairs, Poppy quietly unlocked the cage to crawl in beside Dog, who was scrunched up on his side and snoring rather loudly. She was actually exhausted from the play time too but still very excited. There'd been a few 'firsts;' first time with a male, first time to play with someone else in front of Master and, most amazingly, the first time being allowed in Master's bedroom to be intimate and not just to change the bedclothes and dust for her.

It wasn't the first time she'd been asked to be 'Boy' but it was the only time she'd been introduced to someone else as 'he.' She'd been incredibly embarrassed about it but Dog had been so kind in stroking her hand and trying to calm her down. She really liked Dog and only just realised she didn't even know his real name. She thought she would ask him, when the time seemed right, but she wasn't sure she'd tell him hers because she didn't like it much.

Poppy smiled to herself as she tried to slip in beside Dog without waking him up but he was so big and took up most of the room that she ended up having to tap his arm to ask him to move over because Master had asked her to share his cage. Dog had smiled at her and moved further back to let her in before dropping a very heavy arm and paw over her tiny body.

"Dog, can I ask you something?"

He said yes, of course she could, so she tentatively asked what his name was, telling him she didn't actually know it.

"Aeneas. It's Scottish in origin as half my family are from here. It means 'outstanding.' Make of that what you want."

"Yeah. A name to live up to. That would be too much pressure for me, I think."

And then it came, what she'd been dreading.

"And what's your real name, if you don't mind me asking?"

Poppy went a little quiet and Dog took this as a sign.

"Hey, it's ok if you don't want to tell me but can I ask you a few other questions? I'm just dying to know more about you and your service to Master. I'm guessing you're allowed to be intimate with her, given that she told you to go to her bedroom. Look, none of your life is really my business but I like you and think we can be friends."

This last bit made her laugh. "We are friends, Aeneas. I hope I'm saying that right!"

Dog grinned at her and said that she'd pronounced it perfectly before waiting for her to continue.

"My real name is Peter but no one calls me that, except at work. Everyone just calls me Poppy, usually, or whatever Master wants them to call me. Master calls me Poppy, mostly, but sometimes Boy and sometimes Bitch. I love being called Bitch the best. It makes me feel slutty and really submissive." She paused. "I don't really like my male name. It's not that I want to be a girl, as such, it's just that I feel more like me when I dress or I'm called by my other names. It just feels right, somehow. Don't know if that makes sense to you or not."

Aeneas said it made perfect sense. He was getting used to being called Dog and how natural it felt to be an owned animal, much to his amazement.

"As for being intimate with Master, that didn't happen until today."

"Really? Wow. It's been a pretty amazing day for you then!"

Poppy laughed and said it had surpassed her wildest dreams.

* * *

Fhionna relaxed in yet another bath. She loved to be in the tub but she spent far too much time there. She always enjoyed the heat of the water and the view out the window, especially if the candles were lit. The silhouettes of the tree branches were always more beautiful if it was getting dark outside but it was nowhere near black enough for that yet and it was one aspect of the winter months she missed.

As she sank lower into the water she thought about her slaves. She knew exactly what she was doing when she told Poppy she could relax beside Dog and hoped they had enough sense to take it as permission to be intimate if they wanted to be. She smiled and wondered if they would be brave enough to try.

* * *

It was nearly time to get ready for the club but Fhionna decided to let them sleep and to prepare the food for the evening meal herself. Tim and Bunty were due to arrive soon and she knew all would be on hand at the venue because Louise and Martin were there making sure that everything was ready for the night ahead.

As she was checking the contents of the large casserole dish, she heard the front door open and close and called to Tim and Bunty to come through to the kitchen. Tim was surprised to find his Master on her own, making food for everyone, and Bunty chuckled when she saw the sight for herself as she came through the door behind him.

Fhionna glanced in their direction. "I'm quite sure you're capable of keeping my present activates to yourselves."

Tim almost ran forward to offer his assistance and she laughed, saying that one of them could lay the table for five people and the other could go downstairs and make sure Aeneas and Poppy were awake and washed for dinner.

"Make sure they have their nether regions covered please. Other than that, they should have bare chests and be collared."

Tim had said, "Yes, Master," and headed downstairs before Bunty even moved in the direction of the door, and Fhionna smiled because she knew she'd have absolutely no intention of doing anything other than lay the table and would always prefer to do a mundane task than interact with other slaves in that way; if she could possibly avoid it.

Minutes later, Tim resurfaced with both slaves in tow, dressed, as required, in shorts and collars and nothing else. They both crawled into the kitchen and were greeted to the amazing sight of their Master wearing a long silk robe with a long, midnight blue apron over the top and fastened neatly round her waist, dishing out portions of a casserole into bowls and handing different dishes to Bunty to place on the table.

Dog noticed immediately that the table was set with five places.

Now that all the slaves were present, Fhionna told them to sit, except for Tim, who could take over filling the glasses with wine as she took her place at the head of the table.

No one spoke as they took their places but Dog was secretly thrilled to be able to sit somewhere other than on the floor, although he did like being at his Master's feet.

She smiled as she observed her slaves and noted how different they all were. "A toast: to my wonderful little family and its new addition. Welcome, Dog, and I hope you will be very happy in your service."

With that, she raised her glass in salute as all four said, "Welcome, Dog."

After dinner Tim and Aeneas were asked to tidy up before they went down to the dungeon together to dress for the club. Bunty was asked to call the taxi company and order two cars, one to take them and one for afterwards, before she made her own preparations.

Fhionna smiled and asked her partner if she was staying the night but said the car would drop her off first if she wasn't. She then turned her attention to Poppy.

"You can come with me to pick your outfit and I will help you dress."

Poppy said, "Thank you, Master," and got down onto the floor, ready to crawl if instructed to do so, but instead felt her hand being enveloped in her Owner's.

* * *

Once upstairs, they turned left into a spare room that housed a few different wardrobes and had a dressing table with a large mirror, with lots of tubes of lotion and boxes of makeup lined up in front of it. Poppy looked round the room and was excited at the prospect of being able to be dressed and made-up for the evening.

"Thank you so much for letting me be in here with you, Master."

Fhionna smiled and said she was going to treat her to a new outfit, which she could keep. She also said she was going to do her makeup for the evening.

Poppy's face glowed and it showed up all the tiny little freckles across her nose. "I don't deserve such a treat."

"Yes, you do. You did so well with Dog in the dungeon room and I want to show you I appreciate your efforts to make me happy."

She smiled at her sweet little slave and said that if she opened the first wardrobe she would find lots of lovely dresses and that she could pick her favourite. Then she could open the second wardrobe and pick a fur jacket and shoes to match. She also said she should bear in mind which wig she'd brought with her and the colour of her stockings.

* * *

Downstairs, Tim and Aeneas were cleaning and tidying the kitchen, as directed. Tim carefully washed the bowls and handed them over to be dried. Dog was quiet but Tim got the feeling he wanted to ask something.

"What is it?"

Tim smiled at his friend and waited for him to say what was on his mind.

"How did you know?" Dog laughed and guessed it was probably quite obvious he wanted to ask something because he talked quite a lot, usually. "Well, I do want to ask you some questions, if you don't mind?"

Tim said ok but to make it quick.

"I wanted to know if you'd ever 'interacted' with Poppy before but that's only one of the questions I want to ask."

Tim smiled and said no, he hadn't interacted with Poppy in the way he meant and told him to hurry up and ask the rest of it.

"Oh, ok. I was also wondering if you were going to dress me for the club tonight and if I'm to follow your instructions in general, which I'm more than happy to do by the way."

Aeneas paused before rushing on to ask if he played at the club and if he, himself, would also be expected to play tonight.

Tim said he was going to help him dress and any play that night would depend on how Master was feeling, but if the fact she'd made them all dinner and let them sit at the table was anything to go by, then yes, he was sure she was in a good mood, which usually meant she was also in the mood for public play. He went on to say he didn't mean because she'd been generous she expected more from them, as she always expected them to give of themselves, no matter what, but more that it was some indication of how excited and happy she was, which bode well for 'putting on a show,' as she called it.

Dog was listening intently but found that his answers only raised more questions.

"I must admit, I'm feeling completely out of my depth."

Tim smiled at him. "It's all still very new to you, Aeneas, so try not to worry too much. I will probably be expected to play but you may well not be. Master is always open to listening so if you're just too scared then it's best to tell her. I'm sure she wouldn't make you do it on your first proper night there as her slave."

Dog smiled back, rather nervously, and said he understood.

"We'd better get ready. She'll have dressed Poppy by now and be getting her own outfit on."

Placing the last of the cutlery back in the drawer, both men headed downstairs to prepare.

* * *

"You look stunning, Bitch. So pretty. The outfit you picked suits you so well. Now that your makeup's done, let's put your wig on and you can see the end result."

Poppy let her Master put her hair into place and gently brush it, fastening two gorgeous little pink clasps at the front to keep the shorter strands out of her eyes. She then let herself be led by the hand to the mirror.

"I don't know what to say, Master. Thank you so much."

"You're welcome. Do you like what you see?"

"Oh yes." Poppy was grinning from ear to ear. She gazed at her reflection, at the short white and pink gingham dress, the masses of white frills of the underskirt that made it stick up and out away from her slim legs, the diamanté bracelet on her wrist that twinkled in the light, and the pink, patent, stiletto heels that adorned her tiny feet. "I feel just like a princess."

Fhionna couldn't help but laugh, and said she was very pretty, but now it was time for her to help her boss.

* * *

Downstairs, both slaves were almost ready and Tim was asking Dog to help him fasten the buckles on his leather kilt.

Aeneas had to fiddle about, a little bit, as Tim had obviously lost some weight since he'd last worn it and it kept falling down when he let it go.

"All that's left for me to do is put the studs through the shirt cuffs, put my collar on, and then I can help dress you."

Dog was nervous about that part because Tim had already hinted his outfit would match his name so, trying not to think about it, he made some more small talk.

"That's a lovely collar. Is it a special one?"

Tim said it was his ownership collar and was usually kept for either special club nights like tonight or private play time. "I was wearing it at Master's birthday bash but you were way too nervous to notice."

Aeneas blushed slightly. "Sorry. I guess I had other things on my mind that first night."

Tim smiled as he fastened the last stud and turned round to face Aeneas. "Your turn."

* * *

Bunty came down the stairs in a wonderful short spikey creation which had been made especially for her. It was a shorter version of her own, by all accounts, and Fhionna said how wonderful she looked.

All dressed and ready to go, the small gathering of Master and slaves were a real feast for the eyes. Fhionna in her long silk and spikey gown, Tim in his leather kilt, dress shirt and collar, Poppy in her pink and white dress, pink fur jacket, and long, blonde wig, and finally Aeneas, already wearing his leather dog hood with his mouth taped shut underneath it, his dog paws in place and his leather pouch covering his crotch underneath his trousers. He was also wearing a temporary collar made of thick black leather, with a D-ring at the front, which Tim had borrowed from the dungeon wall. She admired her slaves and said how wonderful they all looked while Tim went forward to open the door, just as the long town car was pulling up outside.

* * *

It still wasn't warm enough to be without a warm coat or jacket but the moon was high and the stars were sprinkled across the velveteen sky in a pattern of disarray. Not so much sewn into the fabric, as one might expect, but instead lightly scattered by a large hand, perhaps.

All the slaves in the car were quiet. Dog's silence could be understood but Tim and Poppy were too, staring out the window, perhaps admiring the moonlit landscape or thinking about what was to come that night.

Bunty had her eyes closed and Fhionna thought she could just hear a light snoring noise coming from her direction. She started to giggle and Tim looked in her direction.

"Everything ok, Master?"

She looked at Tim, handsome in his Scottish attire, albeit a leather version, and said yes, everything was better than ok. "We shall soon arrive, I think. Best wake Bunty up and ask her to wipe the saliva from her chin, please."

Tim grinned, realising what his Owner was laughing at, and said, "Yes, Sir," before tapping Bunty on the shoulder.

Bunty snorted and rubbed her eyes, apologising if she'd made any noise.

He laughed and said, "Only a little," before lowering the window to let some fresh air in to help her wake up.

* * *

She'd been expecting the club to be busy and she wasn't disappointed. There was a queue outside and she stopped to say hello to a few people before she went to the door, followed by her little family. They were greeted by Louise and Martin, who took their coats.

"Hi, Dog." Martin gave Aeneas a warm hug and was more than a little surprised that he didn't greet him back. Dog had hugged him but that was all.

"Don't be offended, Martin. He would say hello, if he could, but he can't at the moment."

Martin looked closely at Aeneas and then it dawned on him what she meant.

"Ah, I get it. My mistake." Martin shrugged. "Poor Dog. I think it's going to be an eventful night for you."

Fhionna opened her bag and brought out a chain leash with a leather handle and clipped it onto the collar around Aeneas' neck before leading the way deep into the dungeon. She saw Sophia and Spike at the other end and waved to them while asking Tim to take drink orders for their small group, saying Dog would have a small whisky, before heading in Sophia's direction.

"Hi, how are you feeling?"

Fhionna hugged her best friend tightly before letting her go and patting Spikes head. "You look amazing. So does Spike, I have to say."

Sophia grinned and said she was a little nervous but that Spike was 'bricking it.'

"I feel like I've been waiting for this to happen for ages. Today has been the longest day and I was scared Spike was going to turn into a pile of goo at my feet before the end of the afternoon."

"Well, that's what commitment can do to a chap. It makes them unsure whether they're coming or going. I'm sure he'll do his best to make you proud of him up there. Not long now. I thought it might be better for both of you to have it at the start of the night so that you can relax and play afterwards."

"That's perfect, thanks."

Sophia decided to change the subject slightly. "Who is this you have on your lead? I don't think I've seen this one before."

Fhionna pulled Aeneas forward slightly before pulling him down onto the floor at her feet. "This is Dog. He is my newest slave. He lives in Manhattan but travels over to see me as often as he can. His work has started bringing him here more often though, so that's a real treat. He has his mouth taped up under his hood so he can't speak at the moment."

She smiled and Sophia grinned back at her.

"You haven't changed in all the years I've know you. Still as mad and as kinky as ever. I do love you."

As Fhionna hugged her friend, she noticed Tim had enlisted Poppy to help bring the drinks to the table and that they were on their way back.

Drink in hand, Bunty asked if she could go and chat to some of her friends. Receiving a 'yes,' she kissed her Master's hand before waving and disappearing into the crowd.

It was time for the ceremony and she could already see Mistress Vixen making her way to the small stage, microphone in hand. "You're up. Have a great time. Just relax and remember to breathe. You too, Spike."

Fhionna smiled. She was very excited and bent down to remove

Aeneas' hood and the tape from his mouth so that he could enjoy watching it too.

"Thank you, Master."

She smiled down at him and stroked the warm skin at the back of his neck and smoothed out his hair.

"You can stand and enjoy your drink. I think you'll enjoy this."

Aeneas rose to his feet but not before he kissed those of his Owner, which he felt was now the most natural thing in the world.

* * *

"Ladies, gentlemen, slaves and animals. Welcome to Violate and the bonding ceremony of Mistress Sophia and her slave Spike. It gives me great pleasure to be able to be part of their journey together. Sophia and Spike have both written vows but first there is something she would like to present to her slave as a gift."

Mistress Vixen looked off stage to where she was expecting Rupert, her own slave, to be. On cue, he walked out with a large metal structure in his hands and gave it to his Mistress, who proceeded to open the device and hand it to Sophia as she instructed Spike to kneel down in front of her.

While Mistress Vixen made a short speech telling the story of how the couple met, Sophia bent down towards him, put the device round his neck, and instructed him to raise his hands.

Spike did as he was told and she then fixed him in place, inside the rigid metal stocks. He was now locked inside the gift from his Mistress and he could feel tears forming in his eyes. It was all too much for him and he started to cry.

Sophia kissed his forehead and smiled at Mistress Vixen to continue.

"Aw, for those of you who can't quite see, Spike is crying."

Everyone in the room laughed and clapped their hands, cheering them on. Dog clapped too but found that he was close to tears himself, so bowed his head to hide it.

"And now for the vows." Vixen placed the microphone on its stand and took a step back.

"My darling, Spike. We met at Violate only a few months ago but it feels like we have known each other forever. It is my honour and privilege to take you as my slave, to love you, to cherish you, to teach and guide you, to punish you for your mistakes and to reward you for your accomplishments. I adore you. I present you with this ring as a symbol of my Ownership."

Sophia's eyes moistened as she stood in front of Spike and placed a simple gold band with a tiny padlock symbol in the centre of it onto his wedding finger.

Spike did the best he could to bend from his shoulders to bring his hand forward. His face was tear-stained but he was smiling.

Everyone clapped and whistled as the ring was slipped into place.

"Spike, I'm sure you have something you want to say too."

"Dearest Goddess. I remember calling you this the very first time we met and I'm cheeky enough to say that I was completely right. I accept and long for your guidance and whatever you deem as best for me. You are my universe, my friend, my confidant, and my Owner. I love you. I wish to present you with this gift, as a token of my servitude."

With these words, Rupert stepped forward again and handed Sophia a gold box tied with a pink ribbon and Fhionna knew it was time to disappear behind the scenes to collect the bouquet. She knew Tim would make sure Dog was ok for the short time she was gone, and walked off in the direction of the stage.

Sophia opened the gift box and was both delighted and surprised to find a gold chain with an unusual stone dangling from its links. Straightaway she knew it was her birthstone, an Alexandrite, which changed colour from green in daylight to purple-red in incandescent light. She also knew it was a very rare stone and was over the moon to have been given such a precious and thoughtful gift. It was now her turn to cry.

"And now someone special to you both would like to present you with a small token of love."

Fhionna walked out onto the small stage and gave the bouquet of roses, star-gazer lilies, and forest foliage to Sophia, hugging her tightly as she did so. "Congratulations and I know you'll be very happy together, as if you're not already. Please raise your glasses in a toast to the happy couple. Air do dheagh shlàinte. On your good health."

She grinned broadly as the crowd replied and cheered.

"Oh for goodness sake kiss him, before he faints."

Everyone laughed as Sophia kissed Spike full on the mouth and led him away in his shackles to the quiet room upstairs where Tim had left a key in the door and hung curtains over the windows.

* * *

Back at the table, Fhionna took her seat and pulled Dog onto the floor at her feet to replace the hood but not the tape.

Aeneas' vision might be limited through the eyes of the hood but he was very glad he'd be allowed to speak.

"That was a beautiful toast, Master. What language was it?"

Fhionna smiled down at her pet dog and told him it was Gaelic and that her father was from the highlands so she'd learned it as a child.

"I love that you can speak another language."

She laughed and said she couldn't anymore, just a few phrases here and there. She enjoyed telling tales about her family but decided she wanted to play so told Tim to fetch the equipment bag from the car, strip naked, and kneel beside the spanking bench.

"I'm going to play a lot tonight, Dog, and it might make you nervous, so I'll allow you to decline on this occasion, but I'll expect to play with you here at some point."

"Yes, Master. If it's ok with you I would rather just watch you this evening. I'm a little overwhelmed at the moment. Sorry."

"That's fine. You can kneel beside me while I play and hold my whips for me. I will probably play with Poppy and maybe Bunty too. I might even play with Louise and Martin if I'm not too tired." She laughed at her own exuberance and reattached the lead to his collar before leading him away.

* * *

Pulling leather cuffs that locked round the wrists from her play bag, Fhionna instructed Dog to kneel at the foot of the bench and shackled his arms together in front of his body.

"Hold out your arms so I can drape my toys over them. Don't let them fall because you'll be punished later if you do."

Dog watched as she began to pull whips and belts from the bag and spread them out. Some of the handles were made of metal and they were cold on his skin. He jumped a little and one of the floggers began to slide. He caught it just in time before it hit the floor and he looked up at his Master to see if she'd noticed.

"Well caught. You'll need to be careful as I remove one whip and replace it with another as they all tend to jostle for space."

She laughed as he let out an audible sigh through the mouth of his leather dog hood and said, "Yes, Master. I will do my best." She was already enjoying herself.

The sight of her new slave kneeling on the floor, being very careful with his movements, and Tim, his toned, naked body laying over the bench waiting for her whips to mark his skin, made her flush with excitement. She knew the warm up was very important, where the skin is prepped for the harder, faster lashes from the floggers and the rubber single tail, but she was eager to get to that part. She'd taught herself how to handle them all and only when she was completely sure of her skill had she transferred it from inanimate items to living flesh. She was well aware that to miss could be risky and thankfully she very rarely did. She knew the whips she loved so much were much harder to wield than the paddle or the cane because of their flexibility.

As she picked her first implement she realised she was being watched, not just by Dog, but by Poppy, Louise, and the many pairs of eyes that belonged to the crowd of people who knew what was about to happen. She smiled to herself as she inhaled deeply and began her display, raising two floggers high into the air at the same time, bringing them down onto Tim's back, flicking them so that the ends of the tails grazed his skin in quick succession. Building up speed a little, she struck below his shoulders with one of the whips, while she aimed and struck his buttocks with the other. She felt herself drift and move in time to the dungeon music, keeping up with the rhythm. After a few minutes she slowed the pace before she chose to upscale to a single tail made of kangaroo hide. It was a rather beautiful hand-plaited whip which had taken a specialist six months to complete. She admired it as she replaced the floggers onto Aeneas' arms and fondled its handle.

Tim was used to the pattern of her beatings but it still took greater control to breathe through the sting of the single tails, even after many years of play together. He adored her and he would submit to anything for her pleasure, but it wasn't easy to take such pain.

Fhionna smiled down on him and reached round his body to take each of his nipples in between her fingers. She knew he loved it when she touched him there.

Dog was surprised by Tim's moaning and watched as he rubbed his head against her arm. He supposed Tim knew he was allowed to and wondered why he was so shocked by such familiarity. He'd guessed by now that Tim was her longest serving slave but he was surprised by such an intimate display in a public place.

As these thoughts crossed his mind, Aeneas watched his Master select another whip and pull back her arm to flick sideways at Tim's body with her wrist. He heard the swish it made through the air and jumped as Tim growled when it made contact. He watched as she waited a few seconds for him to regain his composure before taking aim in the same way, for a second time. Dog couldn't bear to see any more and closed his eyes as he felt his heart begin to race.

"Are you alright, Aeneas? Would you like to have your hood removed?"

Dog nodded his head and Fhionna walked round his body to gain access to the laces at the back. Quickly untying them, she slipped it from his head then returned to watch his face carefully. She called to Poppy to fetch some water with ice in it and when she had it in her hand, dipped her fingers into the glass and rubbed a frozen cube across Aeneas' forehead and down his neck. She then asked her to take his place on the floor holding her whips and told Aeneas to move over to the edge of the stage nearby.

"I bet you're pleased not to be playing tonight."

"Yes, Master. It made me feel faint to watch the movement of your whips and listen to the noises he made as they hit home. I'm truly grateful you don't need me to play on this occasion. Just watching it has been enough to handle, if I'm completely honest."

Fhionna laughed and stroked his head. She beckoned to Louise to keep him company, then returned to Tim's side and restarted the scene. She knew how much pain he could take and hadn't quite finished yet.

The next day, Poppy had been the one to prepare the food for the rest of the family. She wanted to repay her Owner for the wonderful outfit and for the wonderful play at the club the night before. Sometimes she just couldn't help being shy but she became such a slut in the hands of her Master, as well as an unexpected exhibitionist. She smiled to herself as she ground the coffee, made French toast, and juiced some oranges that lay in the bowl beside the fridge. She was happily humming to herself, dressed in her Master's favourite latex maid's outfit, when she heard Tim coming upstairs from the dungeon.

"Hi. You did really well last night. Master was in good form!"

"Morning, Poppy. Yes, I know. That's the hardest beating I've had in quite a while. I'm aching in places I never knew existed."

"Yeah, so glad I didn't get what you did!"

Tim smiled as he retrieved a mug from the stand and prepared his old bones to sit on the floor.

"Actually, Master said you could sit at the table today."

"Did she? Oh Good. I think I might have managed to get down there but getting back up again would have been a problem."

Tim pulled out a chair from underneath the table and Poppy brought over the coffee pot and the toast. She also placed the frosted glass jug of OJ in the centre of the table and chuckled to herself for thinking in American abbreviations. Dog would be proud!

"Is Master up yet, do you know? I haven't been summoned so I'm assuming she's having a long lie. I'm sure she must be tired after all the fun. She sent Dog and I down to the dungeon to sleep after she'd dropped Bunty at home. I'd been told to set up the bed for myself beside the cage and lock Dog inside it for the night."

"Aw, poor Dog. He did get quite a shock watching you and Master play. He was very pale when his hood came off. She even ran some ice over his face and neck to try and revive him a little."

The image of his Master bent over Dog with a concerned look on her face made Tim smile. He loved how caring she was but she was really scary at times too. That's why he loved her though.

While she ran the shower, Fhionna let her mind wander; not to the events of the previous night but to her own bonding service with Bunty. It was a long time ago, of course. In fact almost eighteen years had passed by. It had been a civil ceremony, with two of their friends as witnesses, before heading to Violate in an 'alternative' pony and cart. It had been so much fun and pictures of it had been printed in various newspapers at the time. Bunty just laughed and flashed a great big smile at the cameras that peppered the streets before turning to kiss her Master on the lips.

Dear Bunty, with her cheeky attitude, love of solitude, and heart and brain each the size of a planet. How she loved her so. She was one of a kind and when she'd found her by leafing through the advert pages at the back of a *Forum Magazine*, she couldn't quite believe her luck. She knew instantly she'd be a complete handful. She enjoyed her company though, and even if they weren't being kinky together they would enjoy long walks on foreign beaches or a shopping trip as part of a spa weekend. They could tell each other anything but she knew Bunty didn't really want to know the ins and outs of the time she shared with her other slaves, so respected her wishes.

Sticking her toe under the falling water, she braced herself for the onslaught of the measured but pressurised attack on her aching limbs. Any Dom who said they didn't feel the burn after they played, especially as much as she'd accomplished the night before, wasn't being honest. She smiled to herself as she grimaced slightly before settling in to wash away her aches and pains.

As she let the water rinse the suds from her back, she thought about how Bunty had accepted her fate to have her nipples pierced as part of their ceremony at the club, in front of her mother and all their shared friends. She'd been very brave. She also remembered how they'd been to a few fittings of the latex outfits they'd chosen to have made for the occasion. Her own had been a rather spectacular purple and black affair and she'd worn her hair tied in a high ponytail on top of her head. Her hair was very short now but in those days it had been nearly at her waist. She'd felt quite brave walking along the streets of Glasgow in that outfit. She remembered Bunty's ensemble too and felt a rush of love for her slave. She'd certainly caught several people's eye, including two of the local police, by wearing a white latex wedding dress that had Perspex nipple inserts in the shape of stars. She'd had to make sure her nipples weren't quite on show, of course, but it certainly looked as if they were until you stood really close to her. The dress also had zips that ran all the way from the high neckline down to the hem at each side, so that she could be stripped easily. The two witnesses from the day ceremony had been at either side of Bunty, ready to do the honours when the time came for the double piercing. It had been a beautiful display of love.

Fhionna sighed and, deciding she was clean enough, stepped out of the shower and quickly wrapped herself in her robe, while making the impulsive decision that Tim should unlock Dog's cage and bring him to her, along with some breakfast for them both.

* * *

She rang the little gold bell beside her bed and waited for him to appear. Before long, there was a knock at the door.

"Good morning, Master. I hope you slept well. Would you like some breakfast brought up?"

"Yes, thank you. Could you unlock Dog, have him shower, and then bring him and food for us both, please?"

Tim acknowledged his tasks and walked down to the kitchen to ask Poppy for two breakfasts on trays before heading down to the dungeon room. When he got there, Dog was already awake and trying to stretch out inside the cage.

"Morning. I would ask if you managed to sleep but I know you did because of your snoring." Tim laughed as the big man blushed.

"Sorry. I was exhausted after the club last night. Who knew I'd be so tired, even without playing! God knows I would've been a complete wreck, otherwise!"

"Yes. Just as well Master took pity on your dog ass, then, isn't it!"

Both men laughed before Tim continued.

"She wants you to have a shower before I take you upstairs. You're to have breakfast with her in her room. She didn't give any dress instructions but I'm sure she would love you to be wearing the temporary collar from last night and I think you should have your 'nether regions' covered up too."

Dog stopped stretching his limbs and froze.

"She wants me upstairs in her room with her? Oh! Do you think I was badly behaved last night? What should I do?"

Tim smiled and told him not to panic. "Just do as you're told. Nothing more, nothing less. I'm quite sure I have no idea what's to happen, but it can't be bad if you're to be upstairs rather than in this room, that's for sure. Now, go get showered."

He unlocked the cage door and watched as Aeneas crawled out on his hands and knees, stiff from being in the cramped space all night.

"Thanks for the advice. I appreciate it."

He hugged the smaller man before padding off into the bathroom to freshen up.

* * *

Upstairs, Fhionna was waiting for both men and her food. She was famished and wished they'd hurry up. She didn't know who'd been cooking but guessed it might be Poppy. She wasn't really expecting Bunty to be there because she did a lot of skydiving at the weekends.

It was Aeneas' last day of this particular visit, and she wanted to play with him but first she wanted to have a long chat about recent events, not only from last night but from when she'd asked him to perform with Poppy for her pleasure. She knew Poppy had enjoyed it and she wondered what Dog's thoughts were on the subject.

As she walked across the room to the small table by the window, she heard a tap at the door that signalled her slaves' arrival.

"Come in."

Tim walked into the room carrying a large serving tray, quickly followed by Dog on his hands and knees.

"What a lovely sight. You and the food."

She noticed there were a few dishes on the tray and a cafeteria, but also a silver dog bowl. She laughed and said he'd prepared for every eventuality. Tim laughed too and said Poppy had done a wonderful job of making all the food and he couldn't take any credit for the bowl either.

Placing the tray on the table and asking if she needed anything else,

Tim made to leave.

"I shouldn't need you for a couple of hours but I'll ring if I do. I don't think there's anything in the house that needs your attention specifically but if you'd like to check the fridge for supplies and do a grocery shop for what's needed, I would appreciate it."

"Of course, Sir." Tim smiled at his Owner before closing the door behind him. He could tell she was feeling happy and hoped Dog did a good job of serving her this morning.

* * *

"Did you manage to sleep after all the excitement last night?"

"I did, Master, thank you. I had a little trouble at first because my brain wouldn't shut down, but Tim commented this morning that my snoring was quite loud so I guess it happened without me knowing."

Fhionna smiled and told him he could sit on the floor properly, rather than kneel, and eat his breakfast from a plate with cutlery.

Aeneas did as instructed and asked if she would like him to serve. When she said that she would, he removed the lids from each of the dishes. As he did, his Master began to talk to him. He felt the hairs on the back of his neck stand on end as he realised they were probably about to have a long chat, which might have important consequences for the rest of his service as her slave. He just hoped he could live up to her expectations but felt nervous in case she was about to dismiss him for being cowardly the night before. He didn't think she was going to ask him to leave, as her look had been of concern rather than condemnation, but if there was one thing he'd learned so far, it was that she could be unpredictable.

She thanked her slave for serving the meal and gave him permission to start his own.

"You now know that I want to talk to you and I can see that you're nervous but there's really no need to be."

Aeneas dropped some of the eggy toast onto the tray and apologised for the mess he'd made.

"I want to talk about how you reacted last night, not just to the play but to the ceremony itself. You seemed very emotional and I'd like to chat about that. I'd also like to talk about how you felt when I asked you to play with Poppy for my pleasure as we never really did have the chance to discuss it."

Aeneas realised she was just interested in his reactions, rather than going to punish or dismiss him for them, and felt a sense of relief.

"I'm happy to discuss my feelings with you, Master. Where should I start?"

Fhionna smiled and said to begin with his reaction to the ceremony.

"Well, I guess I was blown away by their love for each other as Mistress and slave. I've never seen anything like it before. It was amazing to watch Spike being placed in the metal stocks and then how he tried to move his body towards her so she could place the ring on his finger easily. He was trying to make it easy for her, even though he was in a compromised position."

Aeneas paused.

"Sorry, Master. I'm not sure that I'm making much sense."

Fhionna said he was making perfect sense and to continue.

"Well I guess it made me realise that it's ok for there to be such strong feelings between a slave and their Owner. I'm not surprised there would be but it made me believe it was possible to live like that without feeling some kind of guilt."

Aeneas stopped and looked at her because he got the impression she wanted to say something.

"What a beautiful thing to say and completely the point. It's the most natural thing in the world for there to be love and compassion between Owner and slave. A good Mistress or Master aims to engender those strong feelings. I personally would never take on a slave without the possibility of them developing. It's true that I play with a lot of people but only a chosen few get close enough to be given the opportunity of being my slave. Being a slave is a hard path to follow at times. It's in no way a 'soft option.' Giving yourself to one person, to follow their commands, and always try to put their needs and wishes first is no easy task."

It was now her turn to pause and she looked at her pet.

"Yes, Master. That's what made me emotional, I think. The fact that they were so obviously devoted to each other and also the way everyone reacted to them. It was truly beautiful and made me realise that anything was possible, if you wanted it enough."

Removing herself from the table and moving across the room to the large sofa, Fhionna summoned Aeneas to follow her and sit at her feet.

"I would like to have a ceremony of our own. Perhaps not a big affair at the club but certainly one just as meaningful, here, at home, with some close friends and a small celebration afterwards at the restaurant I took you to on your first visit."

Aeneas couldn't quite believe his ears. He was overcome with a rush of love for his Master and admitted to himself that he wanted to belong to her, as her collared property.

"I don't know what to say and I'm never usually lost for words."

Fhionna smiled and said that she'd noticed. "I'm not asking for an answer right now but I would like you to give it some serious thought. As I said, not an easy path to follow so you need to make sure it's what you want."

Aeneas bent to kiss his Owner's feet.

"I feel like I'm already owned by you and I don't need to think about it because I already know I want to be yours officially, but yes, I will take more time, if that's what you wish. I would like to give you something, do something for you, before I leave tomorrow, to show you how much it would mean to me to be yours. Is there something you would like to have from me that would help convince you I'm ready to accept your long-term Ownership and guidance in all aspects of my life?"

Fhionna said she would write a contract for him to sign as a temporary form of commitment until the time was right to present him with his own collar during a ceremony but, until then, she would like to continue their conversation and talk about his intimate play with Poppy. She was very interested to know how he felt about performing for her, in general, but more specifically with another male.

It was obviously something new, in every sense of the word, and she wanted to make sure he'd be happy to indulge her needs in this way. Especially now that they'd talked about Ownership in earnest. It wasn't that he hadn't done his best but more like she was concerned for his overall happiness as part of her stable of slaves; as he considered committing to her on a more permanent and long-term basis.

Aeneas perched up on his knees at her feet and considered what to say.

"I'm not sure where to start, Master. I was completely confused by having another male in the room, especially one I hadn't even been introduced to before, but then when I saw it was Poppy I felt more relaxed about it. As you could probably tell, I hadn't been with another man before but I've actually had so many fantasies about it."

Aeneas paused as his face flushed.

"Sorry if that was more sharing than you had in mind, Master, but I'm trying to be as honest as I can."

Fhionna laughed and said she appreciated his candour.

"I've come close a few times, over the years, to arranging an appointment with a TV Mistress just to see what all the fuss was about. It made for some interesting dreams, I can tell you, but I never quite plucked up the courage to go ahead with it in the end. I think it's actually a relief, in some ways, because the decision was taken away from me by being instructed to do it, even though you made a point of making sure you had both our consent. I'm glad it was with someone I liked and in the hands of someone I trusted. It made a huge difference."

Now that he seemed to have stopped, Fhionna said she understood and she was happy to hear he'd been able to enjoy it.

"The interaction wasn't explicitly sexual, with the involvement of body parts, so I'd like to know your thoughts on being with another man generally. This is something you can do for me when you get home. You can write me a letter, a fantasy that includes another male's participation. Please make sure you don't write anything down you'd never accept in real circumstances in the future. It can be based on something you've already thought about or something completely new but one that you place into the context of slavery. Does that make sense?"

Aeneas replied that it did and he would do it as soon as he got home.

"Good. I'm going to play with you today but first I need to attend to a little business in town. Go downstairs and ask Poppy to show you round the rest of the house, where all the cleaning equipment is kept, the bed linen, bathroom supplies, etc. If she is cooking or baking then you may stay and help her but after that ask her to take you down to the dungeon to place you in manacles until I get back. You may sit on the mattress to either write in your journal or read a book but be patient, Aeneas, because I might be a while."

She had an idea how to test her new slave and was determined to see what her pet was capable of.

* * *

When she got home, she went straight upstairs to change into something more provocative. She was feeling sadistic and amorous, always a good combination; for her, at least. She quickly showered and changed into tight leather trousers and a leather corset. She loved the way the second skin clung to her body and finished off the look by strapping her feet into leather, stiletto-heeled sandals. He would definitely hear her approach.

Tightening the strings at the back of the bodice, and reapplying some light makeup, Fhionna checked her image in the mirror before heading to the dungeon, looking in on Poppy on the way.

She found her in the living room, cleaning the fire grate.

"Hello. How has your day been? Did Dog help you in the kitchen?"

She laughed as Poppy dropped the brush in her hand and turned bright red before saying how wonderful her Master looked.

"Thank you. I'm sorry I startled you. I assumed you heard my heels on the stairs."

She watched as the sweet slave nervously rubbed her dirt-stained hands down her pinafore, forgetting that it was white.

"Sorry, Master. I've just made such a mess of my uniform. I will go and change it."

She got up off the floor and started to move towards the door.

"That's ok. You may as well finish the job in a dirty uniform than make a mess of another one. I realise you want to be clean and tidy for me but you can change later, that's a good girl."

Poppy blushed. "Thank you, Master. I hope you have fun with Dog." She smiled and did a little curtsy before returning to the task in hand. "Would you like me to light this fire for you, once I'm finished preparing it?"

Fhionna said no but she should prepare and light the one in her bedroom instead.

Heading downstairs, she took as many 'exaggerated' steps on the wooden stairs as she could and laughed as the sound echoed around the high walls. She opened the door to the dungeon and saw an upturned book lying beside the mattress and her large male slave on his knees but with his hands only halfway to his back and his head not having quite reached the floor.

"Nicely done, Dog. You didn't quite make it in time but good effort."

She smiled as she walked towards him to remove the metal shackles from his ankles. He remained still, now in position properly, but she noticed he was shaking slightly. She touched his back to see if he was cold but his skin was quite warm. Stroking his head and running her fingers down his spine, she examined her pet. She then ran her hands over his body and underneath to this nipples, taking them between her fingers and squeezing them. She watched him arch his back and enjoyed the low growl that trembled through his throat.

Freeing his nipples, she told him to crawl to the cross on the other side of the room. Once he'd arrived in position, she instructed him to stand at the cross, facing outwards, and to raise his hands to the leather straps at the top. She then told him to spread his legs so that his ankles were positioned at the straps at the bottom of each wooden leg.

Fhionna moved towards a selection of toys that hung on one of the walls and selected a blindfold, a penis gag, severe nipples clamps, two heavy weights, and a length of rope, before she walked back to her slave.

"Permission to speak, Sir." Aeneas waited for the answer then continued, "May I say that you look stunning, Master, and I'm very happy to be in your company again."

Pleased with him, she caressed his cheek with the back of her hand then strapped his wrists and ankles into place, covered his eyes with the blindfold and slipped the thick phallus between his lips. She was amused to see his erection and enjoyed the aesthetics of his bound and helpless form. She attached the clamps to his nipples and watched the tiny teeth burrow into his flesh, almost like hungry little insects. She listened to his groans through the gag and the heavy breathing that followed as he tried to adjust to the pain. Next, she took the slim rope and created a loop at the base of his cock, passing the ends up and over then down again, around the balls, and watched his member dance with an exaggerated engorgement. Letting some rope dangle, she then shaped a loop at the other end and tied a knot, so that the weights could be clipped into place, either individually or together.

Aeneas was growling quite loudly through the gag but it was a strangled noise, and she was loving every note of it. She decided his whole body needed to be secured against the wooden frame, using belts around his torso and his thighs, before she attached the smallest weight to the rope and made it swing back and forth between his legs. She watched his knees bend, slightly, but the wide leather straps held him in place and she was glad she'd used the extra bondage.

Not satisfied he was suffering enough, she walked back over to where the toys were stored and selected a sharp little pin-wheel. She smiled as she ran the three layers of tiny spikes across his throbbing penis then up his torso to his large protruding nipples.

Aeneas started to squirm and grunt as he tried to move away from the new pain. As he did so, the nipple clamps moved and the weights swung between his legs.

Fhionna noticed his member was starting to change colour under the strain of the rope at the base of his shaft. She laughed and knew she could continue the torture a little longer but that the blood would need to be allowed to flow again soon, so decided it was time to test him in another way.

Releasing him from the weights, the clamps, and all the bondage except for the gag, she told Aeneas to move to the bench and bend over, separating his legs and resting his arms down the side. Once he was secured, she walked over to a secret little drawer that was almost invisible.

Aeneas ached everywhere and his mind raced as he watched her in the mirror, wondering what was about to happen. In other circumstances he may well have admired her leather clad form and the height of her stilettos, but all he could think about, at that moment, was his next test. She'd said she wanted to see what he was made of and he was sure she was able to take him to heights he'd never imagined possible, as well as push him deep into pits of despair, if she wanted.

He watched her slowly taking her place behind him and coming up in between his thighs. He moaned. He couldn't help it. The proximity of her body made him shiver in anticipation and the feeling of helpless surrender only heightened his need to please her as much as he possibly could. Her smile and her laugh were the highest rewards he could ever receive and her displeasure the worst punishment he would ever have thought possible.

These thoughts passed quickly through his mind and, in a matter of minutes, his Master's intension became abundantly clear. Aeneas growled as much as he could with the penis-shaped gag filling his mouth as her long, slippery, obviously lubed fingers, made contact with his inner ring. He squirmed his ass, making a kind of circular pattern as he rubbed against the leather. This only encouraged his member to grow again and this time get stuck up against the hard bench.

Fhionna could tell that Dog was trying to lift himself up to encourage her to go deeper and perhaps free his member at the same time. His noises were becoming more and more feral with every finger she added to his penetration, so she decided to give him what he so obviously wanted and plunged her whole fist inside. She laughed at his predicament but her amusement soon faded when she saw the white sticky mess he'd made dribble down the bench, from underneath him. Withdrawing her hand, she watched as Dog fell forward, limply, gasping and breathing heavily.

"That was quite a performance but your orgasm was a mistake."

Aeneas heard her words and panicked. He moaned loudly, looked at her in the mirror in front of him, clenched his fists and shook his head, obviously trying to explain himself even though he couldn't do anything but mumble and drool.

"I completely understand you feel you couldn't help yourself, given your circumstances. You may even feel that punishment is unwarranted because how could you tell me it was about to happen with the gag in your mouth. You're right in that you couldn't speak and I haven't told you how to communicate in any other way. For that I apologise, but, if you'd wished to, I'm quite sure you would have found a way to try and let me know. Instead you writhed and squirmed and moaned yourself into a stupor. There appeared to be no attempt at communication, at all, on your part. As you've just demonstrated, the clenching of fists and the shaking of your head, as well as making eye contact, are all acceptable ways to attract my attention while gagged, without having been expressly told what to do. Therefore, I believe you could have made an attempt to stem the flow, as it were, and that's what you'll be punished for, not the ejaculation in and of itself."

She stopped speaking and watched her slave slump even further onto the bench and nod his head, possibly to indicate that he not only understood but he may even have agreed with her assessment. She knew he must feel completely defeated. She doubted if he even had the energy to wonder what his punishment would be.

As his Master rang the dungeon's little gold bell, it seemed, to Aeneas, that every room had one. He hadn't actually noticed them before but it made sense to him that they existed. Ease of calling to a slave; simple and effective. He wanted to watch what she was doing but was too scared to open his eyes. He thought it would probably be Poppy who came downstairs because he hadn't seen Tim for ages, but he was wrong.

"Please bring down a large tarpaulin from the supply cupboard, along with a scrubbing brush, some carbolic soap, and a basin of cold water."

Dog couldn't believe his ears and he began to mumble. Drool escaped from between his lips as he tried to form words. He tried to glimpse her face but she wasn't there. She must have gone into the bathroom to prepare for what she was about to do next, assuming she was the one to actually do it. He was still watching, waiting for her return, when the door opened and Tim came in, closely followed by their Master. She had changed and was now wearing jeans and a t-shirt, and had bare feet. He'd never seen her so casual before and thought how pretty she was, even without all the glamour. This thought helped calm him down and made him try to be ready for his punishment. He stopped struggling and gazed at her.

Fhionna moved towards him and asked if he would welcome a gentle caress. Dog nodded and moved his head towards the hand that she offered.

"I'm glad to see you're calm. That's good. This will be extremely unpleasant but I know you'll do your best."

Dog nodded again and nuzzled into her fingers as much as he could while she beckoned to Tim to spread the plastic sheeting around and under the end of the bench as much as he could and to bring the water and brush with him. Once they were in her possession she said that Tim could leave.

Tim thanked her, glad he wasn't going to be asked to do what he thought he might have to, and left the room while she unfastened the straps round her slave's legs and thighs and the belt across his back but left the arm straps and the gag in place. She told him to stand between the legs of the bench, which he managed to do, on tiptoes. She took the scrubbing brush, dipped it in the water, and lathered it with the soap. The thought crossed her mind that her grandmother had suffered this punishment on her tongue, as a child, for telling lies, and it made her shudder, but here she was, about to do it to her slave to teach him a lesson, only on a different part of the body.

Aeneas lay crying on the bench, his member, balls and buttocks red raw from the brush. They stung and throbbed and he felt sorry for himself.

Fhionna left him in the cold soapy mess as she emptied the bowl of water and rang the bell for someone to come and take the plastic sheets and the equipment back upstairs.

The door opened and Poppy came in.

"Take these and dry them out, please. Then could you start preparing some food for dinner? If you could make something with the chicken that's in the fridge. Thank you."

Poppy didn't say anything but curtsied and left when she'd gathered up the kit. She couldn't look at Dog because she'd guessed what his punishment was and could hear his sobs. It was enough to make her cry too so she left as quickly as she could.

Fhionna walked over to the bench and finally freed her slave of his bonds. She told him to kneel at her feet. Removing his gag and looking at the mess on his face from tears and spit, she told him to wipe his chin and kiss her feet.

Dog did as he was told, still sniffling, not so much through the pain now but through feeling totally ashamed of himself.

She could see he'd learned what she'd hoped he would. The punishment had been crude, in its method, and one she didn't use often. It had served its purpose though, and now she would let him rest and have a hot shower before dinner. She had plans for him later that night and wanted him both clean and calm.

* * *

Tim was getting ready to leave, making sure Poppy had everything she needed, because he had a night out planned. It was his son's fortieth birthday bash. He couldn't believe he had a son that age, and neither could most of his friends. Master had made sure he knew not to come the next day and also that he was given permission to think only of his son and himself for a whole twenty-four hours.

Fhionna shooed Tim out the front door before letting Poppy know she wanted the evening meal up in her room. As she was leaving the kitchen, she asked her to collect Aeneas when the stir fry was ready and bring him upstairs, along with the food and a dog bowl.

* * *

A knock at the bedroom door signalled their arrival and she called out to come in.

Poppy placed the tray on the table while her Master told Dog to sit on the floor at her feet.

"Make sure you eat before you go."

"Yes, Master. I have some waiting for me and I'll make sure the kitchen is tidy before I leave."

"Thank you. Have a good night."

As Poppy left the room, she addressed her newest slave.

"I don't want to talk about your punishment. You earned it and it's finished with. We will eat together and talk about more pleasant things, then you'll be allowed to bathe me. I see no need to deny myself pleasure on your final night here."

She told him he could help himself from the large bowl of food on the table, putting as much into his dog bowl as he wanted.

Aeneas thanked her and wondered if he could ask her a question. "Master, I will do as you desire. I'm just not sure I deserve to bathe you as it feels like a reward." He was relieved, though, when she smiled and said it was time they got a little better acquainted.

* * *

Aeneas was in awe of his Master, the way she guided the movements of his hands across her body, knowing just what she wanted. Even while completely naked she was a force of nature. She had guided his fingers to intimate parts of her body and had felt no compulsion to hide her enjoyment. He felt calm and compliant. Ready to serve. Ready to be hers, completely.

* * *

Fhionna instructed Dog to crawl to the foot of her bed. When there, she tethered him to one of the four large carved posts of the frame using a slender chain running from the link on the leather collar round his neck. She then proceeded to padlock him in place and walked round the side of the bed to her table to drop the key into a little trinket box.

Aeneas watched her as she then removed a red-coloured folder from under the bed and opened it, bringing out what looked like a set of papers.

"One of the things I had to do in the city today was very important. I'm expecting you to read over this document and sign it."

Aeneas could feel a lump rise in his throat. He was nervous again.

"You may take some time but know that it pertains to what we discussed earlier."

Fhionna placed the papers in front of him, where he knelt chained to her bed. She smiled at him and thought how appropriate it was he should look so docile; having been newly punished and allowed to serve her intimately, for the first time.

"I'll return shortly. Make sure you read it thoroughly."

Aeneas said, "Yes, Master," and bent his head to complete the task, fully intending to sign it straightaway no matter what it said.

Contract of service in slavery between
Master Fhionna and slave Aeneas (Dog)

This is a formal declaration of your consensual devotion and obedience as a slave to Master Fhionna in the form of a contract. This contract will be in place, from May 2012, until such time as a collaring ceremony has been agreed to and arranged. It will be signed by both parties.

I, Aeneas, as a willing slave, will submit to my Master's whim and pleasure, unconditionally, and agree to try my best, no matter how difficult the task.

I will serve my Master as she requires, at her home and at functions.

I understand that my Master reserves the right to use me for her enjoyment and the enjoyment of her female and male friends. She will also expect me to interact, sexually or otherwise, with her other slaves.

I will always do my best to follow instructions to the letter and be obedient at all times, particularly in the company of other Mistresses and when on show.

I understand that my Master has the right to cancel my contract if she believes I am in breach of any part of it. Master Fhionna will notify me in person of this decision.

I understand that I have the right to ask for permission to withdraw from this contract should my life circumstances deem it necessary, but only under extreme circumstances, such as illness, redundancy/retirement, etc. and that this must be done in person.

I will be the property of Master Fhionna for the duration of this contract. This means I will serve her when she requires and be faithful to her as my Owner. This means I will serve no other, unless she sees fit to loan me to one of her friends.

I will always be honest and reliable.

I will submit to any task, punishment, or pain that my Master sees fit to administer for her own pleasure and/or for my training and guidance.

I have the right to ask questions of my Master, regarding tasks, etc. should the need arise but be clear that her final decision stands.

I will attempt to follow any instruction that my Master believes will enhance her pleasure in me. This includes my sexual (masturbatory) denial and chastity.

When the term of this contract is over, I understand that my Master and I will discuss the continuation of my service considering... Re-shaping my service contract in general before renewal or cancellation and/or the possibility of formal Ownership through ceremony and the presentation of a permanent collar.

As an owned slave I make a promise to my Master that all my deeds shall be in her best interest. I shall at no time place her or her family or lifestyle in jeopardy and make a promise to be discrete.

I have the right to ask my Master for permission to add terms to this contract that I would wish to accomplish, for her pleasure.

I, Aeneas, as slave of Master Fhionna, agree to these terms and sign my full name to this contract to show my devotion to her.

Signature _____

I, Master Fhionna, agree to the terms I have written for my slave above and state that at no time will I expect my slave to accomplish an impossible task. Nor will I put him or his family/career in jeopardy.

Signature _____

* * *

After amusing herself by reading some of Dog's journal, she returned to the bedroom where Aeneas knelt with his head on the carpet, his hands behind his back, and the signed contract in front of him. She was overjoyed and took her place on the ottoman beside her slave, picked up the parchment, leaned on his broad back, and applied her signature below his. She heard Aeneas sigh and realised he was crying but that this time they were tears of joy.

As she unlocked the chain, she lifted his handsome face until his brown velvet eyes were looking deeply into her own grey.

"Get up onto the bed, Dog, and lie with your hands tucked underneath your back. It's time to celebrate."

❦ Chapter 7 ❧

June 2012, Glasgow

A Masochist

I

Fhionna was looking forward to the June Violate, even though there were no special events planned for the duration of the evening and Aeneas was not to be in Glasgow again until the end of the month. She loved seeing all her friends in the same place and had a lovely outfit planned, based on the flowers of the garden. She smiled to herself as she thought about the white roses that were delicately embroidered on the bodice of the gold dress because it made her feel particularly summery.

She treasured the different flowers she could see in full bloom at this time of year. The sweet peas were always amazing as they climbed their way up towards the heavens, determinedly clinging on to the fencing for dear life, and the tall, proud sunflowers aiming to reach as high as they could. She thought they resembled her different slaves, in so many ways. She revelled in their attempts to make her happy and their own determination to succeed at whatever task she gave them. Each one brought with them their own unique gift and style of accomplishment, but none were worth less or more than the other and she made sure they each felt special.

Poppy, despite her name, resembled the sweet peas. She was desperate to please by obtaining the end goal, sometimes scrambling to accomplish it. Not for reward but for the simple happiness of being considered a loyal slave. She was sometimes very shy and girly but also sometimes very masculine, which betrayed her actual physicality. There was nothing more she loved to do, at home, than put her feet up, paint her toenails, and watch the football. She was a delightful creature who loved to be fluffy and pink in private, or at her Master's home, but she also loved to be 'cock of the walk' when she was working or having a drink with the lads. This last mental picture made her laugh. Dear little Poppy. She was an absolute angel.

Fhionna now pictured Dog, the sunflower. He was tall and proud with an ego to feed. He wanted to be perfect, the best, but without being competitive with Poppy, or with Tim, because he knew there was no need; that he was significantly different to them. He didn't feel the pressure to grow straight and tall in competition with others. He needed a little support from the cane, however, because his stem was thick but not completely self-supporting. He needed its rigidity and its firmness.

She thought about the imagery she'd created in her mind. She thought about how the Poppy sweet pea flourished and the more she cut it down the more it grew new flowers on its tangled stems. Never giving up and delivering more and more fragrance. She also thought about the Aeneas sunflower. About how it was a single flower on a single stem, striving ever onwards and upwards under its own volition but drooping as its head became too heavy to hold up on its own. She smiled as she acknowledged how nature could mimic the relationships of her life; their beautiful fragility and strength.

Bringing herself back to the present, Fhionna started to plan her day. Tim wouldn't be around for a few days and may not even make it to Violate this time. She was sad about that but his attendance was almost perfect so she hoped he had something good planned and would enjoy himself on his time away.

Pulling her chair closer to the kitchen table, she put her laptop down and opened it. She needed to do some work on the club website today, creating new membership cards and answering any questions, as well as looking through the personal ads to see if she could help match-make. Usually Louise did this job, as no one knew all the members like she did, but she was away on holiday this week with her husband, on a biking trip in the south of France. This meant Louise wouldn't be at the club either. She would certainly miss her vibrancy but knew that Bunty would take over the door and introduction duties.

She thought about Bunty as she flicked through the personal ads first, smiling at the prospect of being able to help people meet. This only worked, of course, if they shared some detail in the profile they'd built or within the body of the ad itself. She found that a photo always helped, as well as a little about what their orientation was and maybe a little about hobbies, etc. So many people didn't even have a picture and gave no inclination of their physicality. It didn't need to be a face shot but could be a shadowy outline, an artistic view of their body draped in lace, or something tasteful that didn't include just a picture of their erection or their clit. She appreciated such effort because it showed they were genuinely interested in meeting like-minded people and didn't expect lots of detail in return for, frankly, not very much.

After acting on these reflections by typing out a few short emails, she continued on to the main page of the Violate site which was always full of people making contact about the address, advice on what to wear, and saying that they were travelling to the club for the first time and asking where was a good place to stay. She answered some of these posts with the specifics of hotels nearby and let people know the site had an information and dress-code section but as she moved down the list, one post, in particular, caught her eye. It was from a male who said he was travelling up from England on business and would love to attend the club while he was in Glasgow. He said his name was Stephan and he considered himself to be a masochist, rather than a submissive, and if there was anyone who would be interested in giving him some pain he would do his best to 'put on a good show.'

Fhionna smiled and thought how self-assured he sounded. She liked his confidence and the implication he could take just about anything, as long as it was going to hurt. She laughed at the thought of wreaking havoc on his body and decided to reply.

Dear Stephan,

Welcome to the Violate site. I'm glad you want to attend and hope you have a wonderful night. My name is Fhionna and you can find my profile either in the organisers' listings or in the personal section. I would love to have a conversation with you, with the possibility of leading to some play. I identify as a sadist and dominant so perhaps we could have a little fun together.

Best wishes and have a safe journey.

Logging off from the site and closing the lid of her laptop, she thought about the possibility of having a new play partner for the evening. It would make a change for her to play with a masochist rather than a submissive, or one of her own slaves, and she wondered how different it would feel. In her mind, masochists were more self-serving in their needs and wants, rather than being focused on the needs of the person they were playing with. There were exceptions to every rule, of course, but this was a generalisation that hadn't been usurped yet, even though her experience of masochists was rather limited. She wondered what whips to pack and thought she'd certainly need her canes this time. She laughed as the excitement grew and decided she would go and do it now, even though the event wasn't for another two days.

Placing her toys carefully into the large bag she used on club nights, she mused about the prospect of a masochist ever becoming a slave. She realised that a big part of the thrill for them was, quite often, to offer their body to be marked, perhaps showing off at reaching levels of torture that very few people could accomplish. She wondered if there was more to it than that though; if there could be a real connection with someone who was a masochist. She loved the idea of making blood flow, the delight in their eyes as she brought the cane down onto their waiting flesh, but she wondered if their enjoyment could be based on her delight to inflict pain, rather than just feeling the pain itself as the only and ultimate goal. She was sure the answer was yes and she would certainly enjoy the opportunity to play on such levels, should it present itself.

Having packed everything she thought she might need in way of equipment, Fhionna looked at her outfit, checking its suitability for raising her arms high enough to bring a cane down through the air and onto her waiting victim. She decided that it was fine but could always pack something else to wear, just in case. It was actually quite common for people to bring a change of outfit to the club, one for making an entrance and one for changing into should the night take a turn towards full-throttle-activity.

Unzipping the clothes bag, she felt the soft velvet fabric and ran it across her cheek. She loved its gold hue and soft texture. Another lovely garment she would wear once or twice and then sell at a Violate auction night to raise money for the bi-monthly charity drive. She was happy she could help, even in a small way, and the money raised was usually given to medical research, whether it be for cancer or something else close to someone's heart. Whatever the cause, it was always fun on these special nights and as well as selling off outfits there were always slaves to sell too.

Slave auctions saw Mistresses and Masters giving over their slaves for service to the highest bidder, sometimes just for the duration of the club but sometimes for a day at the winner's home, with certain guidelines of acceptable behaviour built in. Mostly it included housework and chores with the option of punishment if the chores were done badly. It never included any sexual activity because it was considered ill-mannered within the community to use another's slave in this way. It was all very enjoyable and usually the slave came back to their Owner a very thankful sub and glad to be where they belonged.

* * *

Fhionna felt hungry and realised her tummy was making the most inelegant noises. It was definitely time for some lunch. She hadn't realised it was getting so late. Tempus fugit; time certainly did fly, when you were having fun, and she smiled as she walked down to the kitchen where she made herself a large tuna salad and a mug of coffee before settling down to switch on her computer. She may as well continue with her work on the club site.

Munching her way through the crispy lettuce and soft avocado slices, she perused the messages of thanks. She must admit, she'd managed to answer a lot of questions and was glad to see they'd been appreciated. There seemed to be quite a few new people wishing to attend. It was shaping up to be an interesting night and even if she didn't receive a reply to her own email, it would certainly be fun to meet so many interesting characters. She must admit, she wasn't really expecting a reply yet. She did think she'd get one, even if only to politely decline, but she'd only just sent it a couple of hours ago and not everyone was as quick off the mark to answer as she herself tended to be. She was definitely enjoying reading her messages though, and thought she'd reply to some of them as she finished her food.

As she scrolled down to see which ones to target, she noticed Stephan's email right at the bottom and clicked on it.

Dear Fhionna,

What a pleasure and a complete surprise to receive any answer to my post but one from the owner of the club herself, well, what an honour and thank you. I would love to chat with you, if you have the time, but realise you will be very busy.

I took the liberty of reading through some of your personal profile and must admit got very excited at the mere prospect of being of use to you. The photographs on the site of your handiwork certainly led me to believe that I could indeed offer my body to you as your canvas, should you wish to play.

I very much look forward to meeting you and the night will be a greater success for having done so.

Warmest regards,

Stephan

Fhionna laughed as she read it and nearly sprayed coffee everywhere. He was certainly a charmer and didn't seem submissive in the least. He was very polite and obviously had impeccable manners. It would be fun to see what he could do.

* * *

The day had quickly turned into evening as a long conversation had started between them and she certainly looked forward to a more 'in-depth' chat, in the future, about whether he thought a masochist could ever become a submissive or a slave. Would he, for example, be able to give himself over just for someone else's pleasure if it didn't involve pain in some way? Did he think he would ever just be able to follow another's guidance, offering obedience without any self-interest? She was sure there must be someone out there who could quite happily straddle both worlds and she hoped to meet someone like that one day, someone who enjoyed pain but did not seek it out under selfish motives and would be a slave, needing and wanting to follow her rules. In a lot of ways she still felt a slave was someone who could take the pain she gave without any self-motivation at all, that there was no greater gift than to suffer purely to make her happy.

She'd been blessed with Bunty, Tim, Poppy and now Dog, who had all shown such devotion. There were some things that they enjoyed more than others, of course, and she knew she could use these as rewards and gifts. But for a masochist the pain was the gift. Would they be happy just to be at someone's feet for an afternoon if that's what was required of them? Time would tell but it would be good fun finding out.

She certainly loved a challenge. She smiled at the possibility of a friendship developing between them and was surprised by her excited reaction.

* * *

The next day, Fhionna thought about how happy she was knowing that Poppy would be arriving later on. She enjoyed her own company but she did miss her slaves when they weren't around. She also contemplated Violate the following night and even though this event needed no specific plan in place, she felt she should let Poppy know that both Tim and Louise would be away.

She smiled as she thought about the day's events, and her dear little slave waiting for her, as she wrote out a note with little chores that needed to be done around the house. There weren't many because everything was pretty much up to date but a few things to do would keep her slave happy until she got home. She wanted to play with her but first she had to attend to some office business and she wanted some time at the spa, perhaps for a massage and manicure.

Dear Poppy,

I may not be home when you arrive as I'll have been to the office and possibly the spa. Please be wearing your small latex shorts and your metal, lockable collar. There is no need for you to be wearing anything other than these two items. As soon as it turns six o'clock you should kneel in front of the fireplace in the living room, having lit the fire at five-thirty. You should also have chosen a couple of play items from the dungeon and have them with you. I can only think of a couple of small things that need done in the house so please check the bathrooms for cleanliness and new loo rolls, etc.

Tim and Louise won't be attending Violate tomorrow night so I will want you to remain in your masculine form for the event.

I look forward to seeing you soon.

Pleased with what she'd written, she shrugged herself into her summer coat, picked up various bundles of keys from the sideboard, and closed the door on her way out. She felt good as she aimed one set of keys at the car and watched the lights flick on and off. She was looking forward to a productive day away but also to returning home to Poppy. She knew she'd read the note and be a little crest fallen at having to be 'Boy' today and for Violate, as well as a little uneasy at having to pick items from the dungeon.

She knew how difficult this was for any of her slaves to do and found she enjoyed their discomfort. The difficulty came in a few different forms; should they pick something they knew Master would like them to choose or should they pick something purely motivated by their own want? If they picked something like a cane then which one? Should it be the thin one that cuts and stings and is ultimately harder to take? Or should they choose a heavier cane that thuds and bruises but needs more warm up beforehand?

She laughed as she slipped into 'drive' and imagined Poppy's dismay at having to make such choices when usually these were made for her. Today was going to be a wonderful day.

* * *

Feeling relaxed after a short yoga class and a hot stone treatment, Fhionna opened the front door to her home. It was six-thirty so she knew where her slave would be but wondered what items lay beside her on the sofa. She felt a raw kind of heat spread through her body and realised she was very excited at the prospect of having Boy to play with for the whole night, if she felt like it.

Poppy was able to stay until late on Sunday and it was only Friday. It was a rare occasion when they were alone for this long and she thought about this as she hung her coat on the hall stand. It wasn't that she was worried about being interrupted, far from it, as Tim would have stayed busy elsewhere until summoned, if he'd been in the house. It was more that she felt she could concentrate completely on Poppy without having her mind wandering to others who may be around and what they were doing. This was something she created as a distraction for herself because she always wanted to make sure her slaves were happy, busy, and being looked after.

Walking into the living room she saw her slave kneeling on the rug, as she'd been trained to do, in front of the dancing flames in the fireplace. The room would have been bright with sunshine but she'd drawn the curtains to give maximum effect to the orange glow of the fire. Fhionna certainly appreciated her thoughtfulness and loved the welcoming atmosphere of the room. Even though it was early June, it was Scotland and the sunshine wouldn't be in its full radiance until at least the first days of July.

As she approached the sofa, she looked at the toys spread out over the cushions and was impressed. There were four items in total. Three of which she would have chosen herself and one of Poppy's favourites, giving a definite but appreciated unequal balance. She loved her little slave, very much, and smiled as she looked at her naked back with the beautiful tattoo of an angel in a pose of submission, with the tips of the wings turning into birds in flight. It was a tattoo that had been done before she'd become her property but she thought how much it suited the young man's body.

"I love your muscled thighs and narrow hips and waist. I love the curve of your neck up to the very sensitive parts of your ears that make you squirm when I run my fingers across them. I adore how your breathing changes and the tiny shivers I can see run down your spine when I gently touch your skin."

She glanced at the toys as she spoke and savoured her slave's choices. The first object was a Pear of Anguish; an anal device made of metal that could be fully opened up, once inserted, to stretch the cavity to its maximum. The metal arms of the device, which were left outside the body, could be locked, making it impossible to remove without the key. The second was her favourite belt and the third item was a long, thin, fiberglass cane, one she knew she hated. The fourth and final item was a strap-on.

"You've chosen well. It's obvious you put a great deal of thought into the selection. The pear will open you up nicely to receive my strap-on and the belt and cane will leave beautiful marks on your buttocks before I penetrate you. Raise your buttocks higher into the air and spread your legs."

Poppy loved the strap-on. It made her feel slutty and able to do anything that was asked of her. Unfortunately, though, there were no frills to hide behind. There was no enjoyment in receiving pain but she loved the marks that were left behind. They were a reminder of her slavery. A reminder of why she'd chosen this life, a life where she would be beaten and used to within an inch of her life. A life she'd craved since being a teenager. She'd no idea of what it meant to be an Owned slave then, of course, but rather a very strong urge to be able to give herself to someone for their pleasure and therefore her own pleasure would come second. She thought also about how hard it was sometimes. She knew her Master appreciated all she accomplished and, in truth, she might not have been able to submit to someone who didn't respect her or know how difficult it was to face activities you feared. She loved her Owner. Very much.

After delivering some warm up blows to her cheeks with her open hand, Fhionna picked up the belt. She aimed the strap at the centre of her flesh and let it fall, gently at first, to make sure the aim was true. Picking up speed a little, the strokes began to fall more heavily, one after the other, as they reigned down upon the upturned buttocks that struggled to stay in position.

Smiling and purring like a kitten, she increased the strength of each blow but slowed the pace so that Poppy could catch a breath between them. Part of her enjoyment was to watch the effort it took her slave to maintain composure but she also knew to alter the frequency and strength of the strikes to ensure she wouldn't be 'broken' too quickly. She loved the dance of it. She craved the moans, the movements, the struggling and the ultimate surrender. It was the best feeling ever. Through patience and care, her slaves would give her the universe, their whole being.

By the end of it, Poppy was a crumpled mess on the rug.

"Tell me how you feel, Bitch."

"I'm tired, Master, but very happy to have given you so much pleasure."

She was normally a very quiet person who gladly went about her tasks hoping she would have her Master's attention at some point during the day, even though it was likely that some pain would accompany it.

"That's beautiful. Thank you."

Fhionna felt the urge to do something she normally didn't do and sat on the floor beside her slave.

"Sit up."

Bitch did as she was asked and put her hands behind her back.

"You can relax. You've done really well."

Fhionna placed her arm round her shoulders, hugged her, encouraging her to snuggle in against her body for comfort.

* * *

After what seemed like hours, Fhionna finally moved the sleeping slave from her arms, gently laying her on the rug. She stoked the fire and placed more logs to boost the flames. It was quite late and she was hungry, so she decided to prepare some supper and set up a cage at the bottom of her bed for Poppy to sleep in overnight.

The portable cage was rather small compared to the one in the dungeon so she'd let her crawl into it without locking the door behind her. She knew she loved to wake up and see the metal lattice structure because it made her feel secure and safe, but the open door gave her enough freedom to move around the house to perform the tasks she needed to do or to simply use the bathroom. She also knew she loved being at the bottom of her Master's bed; able and willing to be at her side in an instant if need be.

* * *

Over breakfast, Fhionna told Poppy she could wear something she liked from one of the wardrobes in the dressing room until it was time to go.

Poppy was so excited at this prospect that she almost spilled the last of the hot coffee she'd been pouring into her Owner's cup.

"Thank you, Master."

Fhionna was pleased to see the excitement in her slave's eyes but also noticed a little sadness there too.

"I'm glad you're happy but I sense there might be something wrong and I'd like to know what it is so I can help. Sit at the table and tell me what's bothering you."

She did as she was told and started, somewhat tentatively, to tell her what was on her mind.

"I love being your slave, Master. You mean the world to me and have saved my life. I was feeling lost and let down by past relationships and you not only gave me purpose again but made my fantasy come true."

Poppy paused and managed a sort of sideways glance at her Owner.

"I feel that I should leave, though, and I just don't want to go. I have issues at work. I may lose my house, as well as my job, and I don't want to burden you with all my problems."

Fhionna waited for a minute or two before she replied. The thought of losing her slave was too awful to contemplate.

"Peter. There is no way on earth I'm accepting your resignation. You will let me help you and I should give you trouble for not coming to me before now. We will try and sort it out together and if the worst happens then you will simply move in here, with me, full-time. We can talk about the details of it at another time, but I'm not going to let your world crumble about your ears. I know you find it difficult to see me as your friend, as well as your Master, but you must, especially in this case. Why on earth would you think I would abandon you and let you leave? You should know me better than that by now! So, we will talk about this tomorrow. Go and choose your outfit."

II

Time had passed quickly and she felt better after the little talk she'd had with her Master that morning. The day had morphed into hours of fun trying on lots of outfits with her Owner egging her on. It was lunchtime before Poppy had settled on something wonderfully girly, all pink froth and white bows. She'd laughed as she'd been encouraged to practice her curtsy in impossibly high heels before being instructed to bend over the end of Master's bed and be taken from behind. Oh how she'd loved every second of it.

It was now early evening and, after having spent the rest of the day twirling around the house dusting or being on her hands and knees scrubbing the kitchen floor, Poppy was a little sad at having to resume her natural male form to be her Master's boy. She'd been asked to have a nice long bath and to wear her slave collar and a fresh pair of shorts for the club that night. She'd also been told that dinner would be late because she wanted to wait until Bunty arrived.

Poppy sighed as she placed her pink outfit in bags for the dry cleaners. The garments were way too delicate to be washed, even by hand. She was well aware she'd been spoiled all day though, and smiled because she felt more able to face what was to come, knowing she had a home, if she needed one. She felt she couldn't intrude on her Owner's world for long, or upset Bunty by being around permanently, but for now she felt secure and happy and enjoyed it.

* * *

Downstairs, in the kitchen with her Master, she waited for Bunty to bring food. She felt ravenous and tried to keep her stomach from rumbling by clenching the muscles. She was content sitting at her Master's feet and her head was being stroked from above. She let herself close her eyes and enjoy the feeling. The table had been set and her Owner was looking at the laptop in front of her, quickly checking for any new messages she might need to answer before the event started. She could tell she was excited about something, although it wasn't her place to ask. If Master wanted to tell her what was on her mind then she would.

Poppy jumped as the large front door banged, signalling Bunty's arrival. She quickly rose from under the table and went out to meet her in the hallway, taking the bags of food from her hands. She wasn't known for being overly friendly and Poppy knew there'd be no hug exchanged like with Tim or Dog, but that was ok. Bunty was a very private person and Master's longest slave. She didn't know the exact length of time but thought it must be nearly twenty years.

* * *

After dinner, Bunty helped Poppy with the dishes while Fhionna showered and got dressed.

"I love the outfit. There's not much of it. Not your usual style."

Bunty laughed as she teased Poppy a little.

Poppy knew Bunty mostly got to wear what she wanted, although, on occasion, she was given some direction.

"What are you wearing tonight?"

"Probably just something simple and black. I don't like latex and leather much but I love to wear a tiny black dress and killer heels. I know Master loves my legs so I can keep her happy by showing them off, as well as please myself by feeling ultra-sexy."

"Oh, that's lovely. You have beautiful legs."

Bunty smiled, said she was going to go get ready because she knew Poppy wouldn't mind finishing up without her, dried her hands, and left the kitchen to go upstairs to her room. She was the only one allowed to have her own bedroom. Poppy knew she didn't live in the house, as such, as she had a busy normal life elsewhere, but she also knew this was her home away from home as much as she wanted it to be.

Putting the last dish back in the cupboard, she wondered what to do next. It wasn't often she was left with no instructions and she was wearing her club outfit already. She decided it was probably best to go upstairs and offer to help Master with hers.

Just as she was leaving the kitchen though, she saw her Owner was coming down the staircase.

"Just in time to put your coat on and bring the car round, please. You can drive tonight and we'll drop Bunty at home on the way back."

Fhionna smiled at her slave as she walked off to get her coat. She often wondered if it was confusing for other people that he was always referred to as she, even while dressed in the latex shorts and not much else. She guessed most of those who attended Violate would just take it in their stride but it crossed her mind that Stephan might not find it easy. She was sure he had lots of experience in the scene, though, so maybe she was doing him an injustice.

* * *

In the back seat of the car, Fhionna and Bunty held hands and chatted about the night ahead. Poppy noticed this in the rear-view mirror and thought that she'd never seen her Master holding hands with anyone before. She wasn't sure why it made her smile but there it was, stretching wide across her face. She guessed she just hadn't given it much thought. To her, Master was purely that and it had never crossed her mind she'd want or initiate such an ordinary, yet softly intimate, action. She didn't know that much about their relationship, and it was none of her business, at the end of the day, but she was somehow glad her Owner felt able to be so close to Bunty in front of her. She knew they'd had a collaring ceremony many years ago but she now pondered the idea of it being a real marriage. She wished there was a way to find out. Tim would know but she thought it inappropriate to ask. Poppy found herself wondering what they were talking about. They were both fairly animated and Bunty rolled her eyes at one stage, something that Poppy would never do.

Pulling up outside the club, she jumped out and opened her Master's door and, as a nice gesture, quickly ran round and opened Bunty's door too. This made them both smile and they kissed each other before separating and heading inside while Poppy parked a little further along. When she eventually entered the building, Fhionna had already removed her coat and Bunty was hanging it up.

"Boy, you will do the first two hours on the door tonight, please, and then Bunty will swap with you so that you both have a chance to mingle."

Poppy took her position behind the table spread with flyers, Violate logo badges, and new membership cards. A cash box lay underneath with notes and coins already inside. She thought tonight was going to be busy and settled down to the task at hand, ready with her happy smile to greet new people as well as long standing members. She'd only done this job once or twice before but was quietly confident and banished her shyness to the recesses of her mind.

* * *

It was already ten o'clock and the last two hours had flown by. Poppy was glad to see Bunty heading in her direction to take over until midnight, when the door closed, but she'd enjoyed herself.

Just as she was starting to organise everything, a very tall male sauntered through the door like it was the most natural thing in the world to be entering a fetish club wearing the tightest leather trousers she'd ever seen. She looked up at him as he grinned down at her and politely asked where the cloakroom was. Poppy gave him directions and also asked if it was the man's first time at Violate.

"Yes, it is. Hi, I'm Stephan."

Poppy stood up and realised she only came up to just below his nipples and sat back down again, flushing pink, as she held out her hand.

He smiled as she introduced herself, saying her name was Poppy but tonight her Master wanted her dressed as plain old 'Boy.'

"A lovely name. It suits you. I think I'd be too large to suit a name like yours though. Your Master is here tonight, I assume?"

She said that she was and registered the surprise on his face.

"Yes, Master Fhionna. Only her slaves and play partners call her that though. Everyone else calls her Fhionna or sometimes Mistress Fhionna. She goes by the title Mistress on the Violate website but I don't think she likes the term very much."

Stephan smiled and said she sounded like a very interesting lady and she was the one who'd been kind enough to welcome him onto the site before he travelled up from England.

"Bunty, Master's other slave, is just about to come and take over on the door so I'll be heading into the dungeon shortly if you want to come with me. I'm sure it'll be ok to introduce you if she's expecting you."

He grinned and said he'd be honoured to follow him but noticed the young man wince.

"I'm sorry, Poppy. Forgive me if I've said something wrong."

"That's ok. It's just that everyone refers to me as 'she,' even though I'm not dressed the part tonight. Master likes it like that. She sometimes calls me 'he' but not often."

Poppy giggled a little and changed places with Bunty, introducing Stephan as she did so, before leading him into the bowels of the club. She was about to say 'don't be nervous' but she doubted this man was nervous about anything.

* * *

Fhionna was talking to Sophia and Spike when they entered the dungeon. She liked the couple a lot and was happy to see them. Sophia was the first to spot her and shouted 'Poppy' at the top of her lungs before wrapping her up in her arms for the biggest hug of her life.

Stephan watched the little group from a polite distance and waited to see what would happen next. He saw Fhionna stroke her slave's head in a loving gesture, then excuse herself from her friends and walk towards him.

"Hello. You found us ok, then? I hope the drive up was pleasant and you're not too tired."

He took her proffered hand and shook it gently.

"The traffic was horrendous but well worth it to be here tonight instead of Sunday night, in time for meetings on Monday morning. May I say that Poppy is very sweet! I made a couple of mistakes straightaway though, and assumed she was referred to as he and that 'his' Master was a male. That'll teach me never to take anything for granted."

He laughed at his own conjectures.

"I think she's forgiven me though."

"You weren't to know. It can be very confusing talking to my slaves. I'm just glad she overcame her usual shyness to put you straight."

He could tell she was already teasing him a little and decided that he liked her.

Fhionna said she was just going to nip over to Poppy to give her some time off to join in the fun. She explained that she loved to dance to the trance music, which usually played upstairs at this time of night, if she was allowed too.

"I've been thoroughly spoiling her today but it will give us a chance to chat in the quiet room upstairs too, if you like."

Stephan said, "Perfect," and waited for her to come back before eventually following her upstairs, watching Boy's pert little latex-clad bum disappearing up the steps in front of them. He wasn't attracted to other men but this little bloke was very sweet and charming in his own way.

Fhionna turned to him on the stairs, just as Boy disappeared from view. "She's so full of life. You'd never guess she's only ten years younger than I am. She looks so much younger and has the energy of a teenager. I'd love to know how she does it."

He smiled and thought to himself it was probably being a slave to someone like her that did it, but kept the rather surprising thought to himself.

* * *

Fhionna and Stephan talked for over an hour about what it meant to be a masochist. They talked about the need for pain, how it could encompass both a very physical need, on the part of the recipient, but also a psychological need to please the sadist. He said he loved being able to give his body as a canvas because he admired the artistry of the marks after play. He could see her point of view though, and understood why she mainly saw the body as a canvas in terms of her slaves' deep submission.

"I find that it's a matter of ego, which is the starting point of the desire. I think that masochism is ultimately selfish in its motivation. It's the quest to fulfil your own desire while the desire of the sadist comes second. It might also come from a need to be 'seen' as the best; being able to take more pain than others can achieve, perhaps. So, making the play partner happy is not actually the end goal but more of a by-product."

She smiled as she watched him digest what she'd said.

"Perhaps. But the sadist has selfish motivations too."

She had to agree that she loved to inflict pain but refused to accept it was always completely based on self-interest. There was part of her that wanted to be the best with a rare kind of whip. Part of her that loved to hear the flesh tear and see the blood flow, and yes, part of her that enjoyed her slaves' tears. But, through all of this, she cared deeply for the well-being and happiness of her subjects and encouraged them to be the best they could be. If that meant teaching them through punishment too, then so be it. She cherished those she chose to have close to her, those who made up her kinky little family. She both wanted and needed them to be happy. It wasn't always easy to see them suffer, through being punished, but sometimes it was necessary. She loved to spoil them just as much.

"They're all so different from each other. They all have very different skills and abilities, likes and dislikes. I consider myself to be a compassionate sadist, which is definitely a contradiction in terms. I feel like I'm quite complicated in some ways, but also easy to please, in others."

Stephan asked her to try and sum up, in one sentence, how she could be made happy, but really wasn't surprised by the answer.

"Oh, that's easy… I always encourage my slaves to be honest and to do their best. The outcome itself is less important."

As they made their way downstairs, she realised she hadn't played with a masochist in public before.

Boy was still upstairs dancing to the loud music that throbbed through the floorboards and she wanted someone to hold her whips for her so she scanned the room for a submissive she knew would be happy to oblige before she considered asking Sophia if she could borrow Spike for half an hour. As she searched, she saw Martin talking to an interesting looking female. She didn't really want to interrupt him so she continued to flit her grey eyes around the room in case there was another prospect, someone who looked more available, but found the crowd was full of new people that night. She was about to give up but gave another glance in Martin's direction only to find him standing on his own and watching her. She smiled and raised a hand to call him over and within a second or two he was weaving his way through the crowd on the boundary of the designated play zone.

"Martin, this is Stephan. He's travelled up from down south to attend Violate for the first time, and we're going to play. Would you hold my whips for me please?"

Martin nodded enthusiastically as he shook his hand.

The little party of three made their way towards a sturdy cross that was bolted onto the wall and had a mirror placed behind it so that the dominant could see their play partner's face. Fhionna thought this was a nice touch as she, herself, always enjoyed the expressions of her subs and slaves and it also helped her gauge the strength of the blows she administered, especially if she hadn't played with the person before. Many people assumed it was for the submissive or masochist, in this case, to be able to view their Dom, but it wasn't.

She motioned for Martin to kneel on the floor at her feet but off to the side so he wouldn't trip her up or generally get in the way. She hadn't yet hit anyone in the face with a whip but there was a first time for everything. She then approached Stephan, who seemed to be watching her closely, and asked him to undress to a level where he was most comfortable.

He smiled and said, "Certainly," before stripping to reveal a posing pouch underneath his leather trousers.

"Clever. You've obviously done this before! Kindly face the cross with your legs spread out towards the posts and your hands through the straps above."

Taking her place behind him, and checking he wasn't too tall for her to see his face in the mirror, she asked him, very briefly, how he would like to start their play.

He grinned and said he was happy for her to strike his back and/or buttocks, as she wished, and if she liked his nipples, he loved taking pain there the most.

"Then we shall be a perfect match for each other."

Fhionna spent no more time in pre-play questioning, selected her whips, and started to slowly build up the thumps of the floggers on his broad back, watching the soft suede make his pale skin turn pink, before picking up the pace and flicking the ends of the whips so that they landed tip first rather than with the full flank, making it sting slightly more. She watched him, carefully, and loved the fact he hadn't flinched yet.

Moving towards Martin, for a heavier set of floggers with which to repeat the process, she decided she wanted his skin to turn red before she used her single-tails or bullwhip on his torso. She noticed he'd begun to move his shoulders around a little, but only fractionally. She approached him and whispered in his ear that she would like to begin the pain in earnest and asked if he was ready. On hearing he was, she moved back towards where Martin knelt and picked up the rubber snake whip as she replaced the floggers onto his upturned arms. She looked at Martin and winked at him. She was enjoying herself and played to the crowd a little as she stood directly behind him flexing her hands and arm muscles. It was at times like these that the crowd sometimes went quiet and the odd 'ooo' and 'ahhh' could be heard as she concentrated on landing the strokes in the correct places.

There was definite skill involved in using a snake whip. More so than floggers, because it could do a lot more damage if she missed. She didn't miss often but she was only human, much to her own disgust. She let out a little chuckle and aimed to take the first strike. She would still build the strokes but this time starting with the tip of the whip and progressing on to its full flank. It was essential to know how your whips and implements functioned, and the possible damage they could do, in using them properly and to most effect.

Fhionna raised her arm high above her head and let the whip fly forward in a fast-paced kind of circular motion. She watched as thin linear marks started to appear on his flesh and smiled as he winced, slightly, for the first time since they'd started playing. Moving her body a little, she changed angles so that the tip of the whip would land on a different part of his back each time. Not too far away from the first few strokes but far enough to feel completely different. As the lashes repeated, and a variety of whips were used, it would be more difficult to achieve this effect. The more she hit him the more the strokes would overlap. There was only so much space on a person's back, after all.

Just over an hour later, she finally ended her onslaught and revelled in the angry welts that seared his flesh. There were now several blackening stripes on his back, as well as all the smaller ones that zigzagged underneath them. She'd enjoyed his growls and grunts. This, in itself, had fuelled her desire for more, so stepping closer, she ran her fingernails through the welts and ridges she'd made. Blood started to trickle from the fresh wounds and create a tiny river that ran down to the waistband of his pouch.

"There are some wonderful marks on your back. Can you feel the trickle of blood?"

"I can feel everything. Thank you for the privilege of being your play partner."

As he smiled at her, she found her hand reaching up to grip his nipples in between her nails. It felt like the most natural action in the world but the intensity of his response amazed her. She was happy to let him gaze into her eyes while she hurt him. She knew, in that instant, they would become good friends and play partners, even if he never became her slave.

III

It was nearly the end of the month and Aeneas was contemplating why his new Master hadn't been in touch very often over the last three weeks. He knew she had her own company to run, and she'd be busy with her slaves, but he felt a little perturbed that the only contact between them had been an infrequent 'hi' and checking up on his behaviour.

He'd finally decided to read the report of the latest Violate night, which Martin had posted, and the jealousy he felt was horrible. It also surprised him. It was obvious Fhionna had enjoyed her play with the 'masochist,' and there certainly seemed to be a chemistry between them, but Aeneas wasn't a lover of pain so wondered why he felt unsettled. Maybe it was because he hadn't long found her and moved heaven and earth to become hers. He didn't know if this 'Stephan' would ever become part of her family but the thought crossed his mind and he didn't like it much.

Dog tried to make plans for work while he was in Scotland rather than think too much about what had happened a few weeks ago. He felt unsure whether Master had missed him or not. He surprised himself with this sudden, selfish need for attention and snorted loudly at the childish feeling. He thought, maybe, it had something to do with the fact he was only visiting Scotland for one day this time round. He had a ton of work to do and wondered if he would even see his Owner for more than an hour or two. The fact that the last time he'd seen her was so meaningful didn't help. Not only had he signed his slave contract but he'd also been allowed his first intimate contact with her. Was it any wonder her lack of communication worried him so much? It was possible he'd done something wrong but, then again, if he'd annoyed her she would have told him. If there was one thing he knew for sure, it was that. Master had no qualms about voicing her discontent, even if she did so in an almost gentle manner, most of the time. No, he was certain she was just busy, so he put his brain to better use in thinking about the fantasy he'd been asked to compose and then send by airmail.

From what he remembered, he was to write something that included being with another male. He knew, by now, the thought of this excited her and it would make him feel special again. He would need to find her instructions again to make sure he followed them correctly but he felt his writing skills were quite good and was confident this was something he could do well. He mentally chastised himself for not having remembered to do this sooner and now it occurred to him that this was what she might be waiting for.

* * *

Dear Master,
My apologies for making you wait for this letter.

Fantasy…

I can hear voices from the other side of the door and wonder who her friend is. Rose is keeping her promise. I haven't known her long but she has a kind heart and a really kinky nature and I can tell her anything, including my own kinky desires. I can see her becoming my BFF. A friend forever.

I remember telling her about this longing I had to enact a scene where I was tied up to become the willing victim of a beautiful woman and her male friend. I remember telling her I wanted to be whipped by a male because I thought it might feel different, more painful because males are stronger than females, usually. I also told her I wanted to feel a strap-on because it was a huge turn-on and I'd really love to feel a male inside me, someday, but I wasn't quite ready for that yet.

And now, after having shared some good wine and laughed together at the prospect of the fun we were about to have, I'm securely fastened to a leather bench and my mouth is stuffed to bursting point with a rubber gag that only just allows me to breathe around its circumference. I tug on the cuffs that have my wrists firmly wedged up against the side of the bench but it's clear I'm not going very far and can only wait for whatever's going to happen next.

I watch as she crosses the room to where there's a stash of toys. She's wearing jeans, stiletto heels, and a leather corset. I have to admit she looks hot. She's strapping herself into a harness and rolling a condom onto the dildo's shaft, running her fingers along it.

Now standing in front of my face, I feel her remove the gag for a moment and see her smiling down at me, knowing only too well she's about to drive me crazy. I hear myself begging for her to let me feel her friend's whips on my back and buttocks before she uses her strap-on on my reddened rump and she laughs at me. I already want to cum so damn much and I don't know if she'll let me or not. I'm a little surprised to find this thought so exciting. Not to be allowed to cum even though she knows I want it is amazing.

I'm also looking forward to having deep welts on my body. I've felt a whip before and enjoyed it but it wasn't enough. It didn't alleviate my need, at the time. I'm definitely not a masochist and I don't usually seek out pain but sometimes it feels good to surrender in that way and I'm hoping that her friend will leave the marks I crave.

Rose is wonderful. I can't help but growl at her as she stuffs the gag back into my mouth and tells me I'm going to get all I desire but she's the boss. She's telling me not to be greedy and I can't help but wriggle on the bench, hoping she'll understand I'm eager and that I find her attractive. She's laughing at me again and calls me a good little slave. God knows where that phrase came from but that's exactly what I want to be.

She walks away from me and I strain to see what she's doing. She's at the door, obviously letting her friend in. I didn't hear the front door of the apartment open but guess he must have had a key.

He's tall and handsome and I can feel my dick stirring as it's trapped beneath me. I know I said I wasn't ready to be with a male yet but just looking at this guy is making me change my mind. I shift my body, trying to let my member free, wondering if either of them has noticed my excitement.

R: "He's waiting for you Derek. It's really funny. He's squirming all over the bench. He's asked me if I'll let you use your whips on him first so be my guest."

D: "Great. He's really pretty trussed up and helpless. Thanks for letting me take part. It's always a pleasure to help someone enact their fantasies."

I can hear every word of their conversation and I love the fact they're talking about me as if I wasn't there.

Derek is standing beside me and he's telling me how handsome I am, what he's going to do to me. I mumble through my gag that I'm ready for him to beat me but I'm almost sure he doesn't understand the actual words. He's smiling at me though, and before long the first heavy blow lands on my back. He's not about to hold back, it seems.

Each blow sends me through the roof and I'm howling. It's what I want and need. I'm tired but will take what he can give before I'm used by Rose. I can see her watching from the corner of the room. She's obviously enjoying the display and I'm glad she's feeling excited.

D: "I think he's had enough but I'd love to be able to use his mouth while you use his ass. Is that ok? Can I ask him?"

R: "Sure. Take his gag out. He'd said he wasn't quite ready for a male to be inside him yet but I guess his mouth is different to his ass so you might get a yes."

I feel faint and hot and unbelievably happy. Derek is standing at my head removing my gag and I'm panting, "Yes," as many times as I can before my breath runs out.

D: "That's great. I'll make sure you enjoy it and I know I will."

R: "Wow. I never thought we'd be doing a spit-roast today."

I could tell she was happy at the prospect and I wanted to engage with her properly but I didn't have the energy. I was allowed some water before they left me on my own to prepare for what was about to come. I found myself grinning and wishing they'd hurry up and come back in.

When they did, Derek was at my mouth in seconds and Rose was behind me. I lifted myself up as much as I could at both ends.

R: "How cute is that. He's so submissive. I really don't think he even knows how much of a subby he is."

D: "He's very cute. He takes a lot of pain too, which is always good."

I could hear them laughing as they each entered their allotted holes and I felt my face burn. I wanted this. I really did. Derek was handsome and Rose was beautiful. What wasn't to love?

Before long it was all over and I was being released from the bench I was on, but not before the gag had been shoved back between my lips to signal that Rose wanted my complete silence and obedience.

R: "We're going to leave you alone for a while but I want you to keep the gag in and I'm going to lock the door behind us. You can either use the time to have your own orgasm or you can just sit quietly and think about what's happened."

I nodded my head and was amazed at the power of her words because all I now wanted to do was sit and think about them both, with the gag in my mouth. She exuded such power and control. She was so dominant, not only towards me but towards Derek too, and something inside me responded to it. I felt that I should nod to let her know that I understood my choices and she smiled at me.

Master,

I hope I continue to be in your thoughts. I'm presuming you're busy and I haven't displeased you in some way. I hope this letter goes towards allowing you to remember my devotion.

Sincerely,

Your Dog x

* * *

Overall, Aeneas was happy with the letter and was confident the fantasy would amuse his Owner. He read it through again before deciding to post it. He was excited about her reaction to it and hoped she understood how much he'd missed her, even though it had actually only been a few weeks since they were together.

Licking the envelope and carefully adding the address to the front, Aeneas thought he'd enjoy a walk into the village to post it so called out to Toby to tell him he was going out for a while. Closing the front door behind him, while placing his shades on his nose, Aeneas started to whistle. He felt better for having taken some positive action and completing another task. One that he hoped would be happily received.

IV

Fhionna was sitting up in bed, reading, when she heard the letterbox rattle downstairs. Tim was in the house so she knew there was no need to interrupt her enjoyment of the book. Male chastity was definitely something she was interested in. Tim and Bitch were both pierced with Prince Albert rings but it wasn't something she'd taken any further than that.

She'd just read a section about an exercise that encouraged the submissive male 'partner' to keep a diary that recorded entries relating to levels of arousal and also levels of frustration, when Tim knocked at her door.

"Come in."

He'd waited for her to answer before pushing the door open and passing her the mail. "You have a letter from America, Master."

"So I have." Fhionna smiled. "I'd love some breakfast now please. Coffee and a bacon sandwich. I'm quite hungry."

Once he'd gone, she slipped a little silver knife along the seal of the envelope and slid the pages out, perched her glasses on the tip of her nose, and started to read. She thought Aeneas' handwriting was extremely neat and how he must have taken extra care to make it legible. She could imagine him sitting at a writing desk, in a large study, reflecting on his chosen words and slowly writing out his thoughts.

The fantasy he'd enclosed was exciting and she wondered about the logistics of making something similar happen, one day, but then she felt a tinge of annoyance as she read the last paragraph. It seemed he was feeling ignored. This, in itself, she didn't mind. It was good for a new slave to know they weren't the centre of the universe. What she didn't care for, however, were the obvious and crude terms of critique. It had been a busy few weeks, he was right, and so he should have had the foresight to write the letter earlier and proclaim he understood that he was but one slave in her family and hoped she would enjoy the fantasy she'd asked for. This would have been a more successful approach than seemingly blaming his new Owner for neglecting him and reminding her that his devotion should be remembered.

She decided, then and there, she would hand write a reply. It would take a few days to arrive but it would get there before he was due to be in Glasgow and would mean he was waiting for her answer. Hopefully he'd receive it the day before he was due to fly. She liked the thought of him panicking about it all the way across the ocean. She smiled as she realised she was being rather harsh but it would nip such behaviour in the bud and be a lesson he wouldn't forget.

* * *

Aeneas,

I loved the short story you wrote for me. You described your desire so vividly and it made me excited as I read about your final moments in the room that allowed you to fully realise your submissive nature. Well done.

It's a shame, however, you left it so long to write and even more unfortunate that you seem to blame your Master for ignoring you and your obvious devotion.

This was a mistake made on your part and hasn't gone unnoticed.

I nonetheless look forward to seeing you soon.

Master

As she sealed and addressed the envelope, Tim knocked on her door.

"You're smiling, Master. Was it a good letter?"

Tim felt quite bold to be asking about the contents of her private mail but, as it was so obviously from her new slave, and he was aware she wanted them to be in a close relationship with each other, he thought she may not mind his enquiry.

"It was a very good letter. I enjoyed it on so many levels. He wrote a wonderful fantasy for me and then made the mistake of blaming me for not being in touch as much as he thinks I should have been."

Tim felt the colour drain from his face. "Oh, I'm sorry." Tim didn't know what else to say under the circumstances. He wasn't sure if he was distressed because Dog had made a mistake and was going to be punished, or if it was the thought of Master being angry. She didn't seem too upset though, so he guessed it wasn't enough to make her rethink his position as her slave. He liked Aeneas and didn't want to see him punished, or his see Master annoyed, but he was especially aware of his disappointment at the possibility of not being intimate with him and it made him blush.

"Thank you for the lovely breakfast. Can you go out and post this letter for me please. I'll enjoy what you've made and then I'll plan my day."

Tim took the letter and left without saying anything further. He could tell her mood had changed, slightly, and thought it best just to do as he was asked without giving her any further cause to feel irritated.

* * *

Aeneas was extremely agitated. He thought his Master must have received the letter by now but he hadn't heard from her and he was due to fly to Scotland the next day. He hadn't slept much the last couple of nights because he'd pictured all sorts of things going wrong. Maybe she hadn't received it. Maybe she was still expecting his task to be completed. Maybe it had arrived and she hated it. He was fighting the urge to jump on a plane, there and then, because the thought of making her unhappy was awful and the wait for the consequences was nearly as bad.

Running his hand through his unkempt hair and beard, he decided he should get up and sort himself out. He felt tired and sad but he had business in Scotland, if nothing else. He didn't know how he would be able to get through all the meetings if he hadn't been able to see her the day before, as scheduled, but he would have to. It meant he would have a day to wander about in Glasgow, unaccompanied and feeling sorry for himself, hoping she would summon him before his first appointment with the board of the company based through in Edinburgh, and it would be torture.

Finally managing to haul himself out of bed and head to the shower, he missed Toby shouting up to him that the mail had arrived as he ran the water. It wasn't until he was drying himself and had forced himself to go down for something to eat that he noticed the letter from Glasgow sitting on the table by the front door.

"God, Toby. Why didn't you tell me the post was here?"

Toby came out the kitchen, drying his hands, and said that he had but maybe he hadn't heard him because of the shower.

"Ah, ok. Sorry. I'm just a bit grumpy. I haven't been sleeping well."

Toby said he'd noticed and suggested opening the letter to help alleviate his tension. Toby was smiling at his boss because he realised he was being forward but guessed that Aeneas was waiting for something from Scotland and it probably wasn't to do with his work.

* * *

Aeneas slumped onto his bed, feeling utterly exhausted. The letter was short and to the point and he wasn't sure how he felt about it. He was glad she'd loved what he'd written but devastated that he was stupid enough to infer she was to blame for the lack of communication. He chastised himself for not taking the initiative to make contact with the fantasy letter first and just letting her do all the running after him. He was relieved she still wanted to see him but also scared of what the punishment might be. He was an emotional wreck and wondered, momentarily, if it was all worth it.

Rather than going down for something to eat in the kitchen, after all, he decided to get undressed, crawl back into bed, shut his eyes, and get some rest. Feeding himself could wait. At that moment all he wanted to do was try to sleep.

* * *

The next day was hectic. Toby was helping him take his case out to the car, making sure he'd packed his passport and everything else he might need, before driving him to the airport. The old man hated driving in rush hour traffic but he had some errands to run and could easily do them on the way back and make sure his boss wasn't having to think about negotiating his way between the aggressive drivers on their way home from work. It was an evening flight out which meant, with the time difference, that Aeneas would arrive in Glasgow around eight am. He wasn't being picked up until eleven and so it would give him a little time to find a gift for his Master on arrival. He would normally have put more time and thought into this but he'd been unsure as to whether or not he would actually be seeing her. He'd felt, ultimately, he would see her, even if he wasn't actually invited to, even if it was just to ask why he'd been 'let go.' He'd enough male pride to ask for an explanation but luckily he hadn't needed to.

* * *

With bags in hand, Aeneas wandered about the expensive shops looking for something a little unusual. He didn't have high hopes of finding something rare in among the high-street, logo-laden outlets of the airport but maybe there would be something pretty that would strike a chord. There wasn't a club event scheduled so the option of maybe buying something that would have matched her outfit was off the cards. He wasn't sure, if there had been an event, he would've been allowed to attend it anyway. He was certain, however, that this type of punishment would be close to the top of Master's list; leaving him locked in the cage to mope as the rest of her kinky family went off to have fun. Aeneas almost laughed at the thought of it. In some ways it would've been a blessing to be just locked away rather than bear the pain he might have had to go through instead.

Trying to focus on the task at hand, to concentrate his whole will on being in the 'now' and not thinking about or analysing what might happen in the near future, he walked into a little jewellery shop that chose to be a little quirky, nestled in among the larger, glitzy boutiques, and almost immediately found something he thought she might like. It was a small dragonfly brooch. Its body was made up of turquoise jewels and on its head were tiny little white crystals that sparkled in the light. He was pleased he'd found something so delicate and bought it quickly. It was nearly eleven am so he walked to the pick-up zone, at the front of the airport, as calmly as he could.

Just as he arrived, he spotted Tim waiting for him and waved. He was happy to see him smile and wave back before coming forward to take his luggage.

"Hi, Tim. Am I glad to see you!"

Tim laughed and said, "I bet you are," before warning him that Fhionna was in the car waiting on them.

"Oh!" Aeneas frowned and stopped walking.

Tim put out a hand, placing it on his back, as if to catch the large male in a faint.

"Yes, I thought that might throw you. Master doesn't usually come to the airport unless she's travelling herself because she loves the anticipation of your arrival at the house. She's also made it quite clear that she wants us to get to know each other a little better and a car journey is a good way for that to happen naturally."

Aeneas was speechless so just nodded.

"Unfortunately, that's the case today. I think the best way to approach this is to simply get in and say nothing till you're spoken to. If she offers you her hand then kiss it like you normally would and give her the gift you're holding. I do think it's best to let Master make the first move, no matter what it might be."

* * *

Walking to the car seemed to take forever, perhaps because he felt like he was literally dragging his feet. Tim opened the car door for him and motioned to get in while taking his bag to the boot. He was nervous for Aeneas. He knew the man would feel as though he'd been summoned to the gallows but also that it couldn't be too bad if she was still willing to see him. If she'd been really angry she would have cancelled his visit and made him wait till next month.

Dog hardly dared to raise his head in acknowledgement that his Master was sitting beside him. If he had, he would have realised she was smiling, knowing full well she'd tortured him severely already and she wasn't going to let him suffer much longer. It was hardly the biggest mistake in the world, after all. The relationship was still fairly new and she wanted to make sure he understood he should be careful when writing to her; so that it always made him think about what he was saying. She did have a sense of humour though, and actually liked the opportunity to tease him to this level. There was never going to be any chance of dismissal for something so minor. The fun part though, was he didn't know her well enough to be aware of that yet. But he would, through time.

Fhionna held out her hand and Aeneas took the opportunity, as Tim had advised, to kiss it before handing her the little dragonfly in its blue and silver box.

"How sweet. Very pretty. Thank you, Dog."

She took her hand away from his grasp to pull the tiny ribbon and let it drop to the floor of the car. Aeneas stayed quiet but watched her as she unwrapped it.

"Oh, it's beautiful. Thank you. You may pin it on my jacket. I love it."

Aeneas did as he was asked, even though his hands were shaking slightly.

When Tim looked back at them both, he saw them sitting quite close to each other so knew that everything was fine.

As he drove past the busy terminals, negotiated the various roundabouts, and headed onto the M8 towards the city centre, he realised that Aeneas hadn't noticed they were heading in the opposite direction of home. He would probably start paying attention to his surroundings before long though, and then there would either be a rather awkward silence or lots of questions. Either way, he knew she would have some fun at his expense.

* * *

Later that night, Dog was shackled to the wall in the dungeon where he'd eaten food from his bowl before settling down to write in his journal about the day's events. He was tired and was glad for the rest and time to reflect. He wasn't sure if he would see his Master again that night but he was learning to live in the present and not worry too much about what was going to happen next. It seemed that Master's training was already starting to have the desired effect.

Taking the pen in his hand, Aeneas started to write down his feelings. He'd been used and abused and was sore. He was also extremely happy. He'd been totally fooled, having thought that Master, at best, would have punished him herself at some point during the day. It had been a complete surprise when Tim dropped them off at another private house rather than at Master's home, and even more of a shock when a huge male answered the door wearing little more than a harness and tiny latex shorts. The look on Dog's face must have been priceless as the male had laughed at him before he'd invited him into the house and led him to the basement.

His back had been flogged and his ass cheeks had been beaten to within an inch of their life before Fhionna had taken him with her strap-on and he realized, as he wrote it all down, that his fantasy had come true and it had been the worst and the best idea she could have come up with and he hated and appreciated it, all at the same time.

When it was over, Aeneas had been left, locked in the basement, until Tim came to let him out. They'd been allowed to chat for a little while before their Owner had told them it was time to go. He remembered how she'd let him lie down, stretched out on the back seat, and how he'd kissed her hand then fallen asleep due to the motion of the car.

Aeneas put the journal and pen on the floor beside the mattress. He touched the raised bruising on his buttocks with his hand and, just for a second, ran a finger up and along the crevice between his cheeks, letting it slip gently inside the aching flesh of his anus. He sighed and felt something almost like yearning. He longed to be touched there again, to feel the full force of his Master's silicone shaft inside him. He wanted to feel the pain and ecstasy of it on top of the fierce burning on his skin. He removed his finger and lay down, arranging his chains around him. He knew he'd pleased her and this was his last happy thought before he drifted off into a deep and well-earned slumber.

Chapter 8

July 2012, London

Three Days Together

I

Day One

It was now the middle of July, only two short weeks after he'd been in Scotland, and Aeneas was due to be in London. He had a little business to attend to but the main reason for the trip was to spend three whole days with his Owner and he couldn't wait. He was running late for his flight and hoped it wasn't an omen for the rest of the trip. He hated keeping her waiting. She detested being late and had booked time in a dungeon for when he arrived. He couldn't quite believe she expected him to survive two hours in a dungeon after a seven hour flight, but that's what she'd said in her last communication so he was going to make sure he slept on the plane.

* * *

Taking his seat, he checked that the addresses he needed were safely stored in his phone. His flight was due to arrive at noon and the dungeon was booked for an hour later. It didn't give him much time to catch his breath.

Aeneas ordered a small Scotch and closed his eyes. He'd managed to take a sedative just before going through security and was already feeling sleepy. He tried to calm his mind but started imagining how the dungeon would look, thought about the comfort of the apartment he'd rented for the duration of their stay, and fantasised about what would happen to him, in general. He felt pleased with himself for having found the apartments for hire only one small block away from the play space.

Accepting his drink with a thank you, he read over the initial plan for meeting up with Master. She'd instructed him to come to the flat first so they could travel to the dungeon together, after having dropped his bags off. He'd forwarded the details of the apartment two days ago and left instructions with the receptionist to give her the keys and any documentation he might need to sign. He'd guessed she'd want to gain entry as soon as she arrived, which was to be around ten-thirty, so she could freshen up. He wondered if she'd enjoy the short flight and the private car he'd arranged for her. He'd wanted to do something special and figured that making her travel as comfortable as he could would be appreciated. The rest of the arrangements were being billed to the company but he was paying for her travel himself.

* * *

Fhionna enjoyed the car ride. She loathed trying to get out of the airport and across London at the best of times, and it was very kind of Dog to have arranged this little surprise. She was both amused and happy when she saw someone holding up a sign that said 'Ms Fhionna' on it and headed in her direction.

"Good morning, Madam. Can you please confirm the name of the person who has arranged the booking for you? I just need to make sure I have the right person."

Fhionna smiled and wondered what she would say. She wanted so much to give his slave name but thought it might be a little risky if he'd made the booking through his company.

The driver smiled at her as she paused and said that either of his first names would be fine.

She laughed and promptly said 'Dog.'

"Thank you, Ma'am. If you would care to follow me."

As they moved into the morning air, she thought that although the weather was very pleasant at home it was always so much better in London. The south of any country was always hotter, it seemed, and she paused for a moment to remove the lightweight, flowery scarf from around her shoulders.

As the car crawled along the busy streets, Fhionna lowered the window to look at the tall office buildings as they passed by and watched the faces of the people on the pavements as they went about their daily lives. She smiled when she noticed a little girl staring into the window of a huge department store while she held onto the sleeve of the jacket of a man who could be her granddad. In the other hand she gripped the string of a giant red balloon. It was a lovely sight. The little girl looked content, perhaps having had a good morning at a fun-fair, before going to the swing-park, then stopping off to buy a toy.

At the flat, she was able to shower and have a mid-morning snack before it was time for Aeneas to get there. The dungeon was booked for one o'clock and she enjoyed the fact that he would be hot and bothered, and perhaps very excited, after his long flight.

Flexing her toes to paint her nails, she looked at the small radio clock beside the bed and saw it was time to get dressed. Having blown hard a few times on the varnish, she tiptoed over to her case and chose her outfit. It was too hot to wear leather or latex so she decided to wear a short silk dress and some strappy sandals. The heels were high enough to lend them an air of kinkiness to play in but the style wasn't appropriate for the large fetish event they were attending so she'd packed a couple of outfits with matching shoes. She knew she'd enjoy making the choice, depending on her mood.

* * *

Aeneas had arrived and was sprinting towards where he knew the driver would be waiting for him. The flight had landed late and it made him feel more than a little anxious. The Scotch and the sleeping pill had done their job but now he felt jumpy as he almost took the exit gate like a hurdler and threw his bags at the man waiting with the sign that said 'Mr. Manning' on it.

"My apologies, but I'm in a hurry."

The man said he understood and just to follow him before jogging off in the direction of the car park.

When he reached the apartment he was out of breath. Trying to calm down, but failing miserably, Aeneas knocked on the door and waited. It seemed like an age before it was opened but he knew it was just his mind playing tricks on him.

"Come in. You're very late."

There she was, his Master, calm but obviously not amused.

"I'm sorry, Master. I have no excuse apart from the travel time took longer than planned."

Fhionna didn't smile but motioned for him to quickly freshen up and change into a clean t-shirt and jeans.

Doing as he was told, without taking the time to kiss her feet, even though he really wanted to, he took clothing from the largest bag before speeding off into the bathroom. He could hear her heels as they tapped out a rhythm on the wooden floor of what he assumed would be the kitchen area and nearly burnt his face off as he splashed the water onto his sweaty skin rather too hastily.

"I have called ahead to the dungeon and the owner has agreed to push our hire time up by half an hour. He said we should be there in five minutes because of being so close by."

Aeneas was pleased to hear that their plans weren't completely spoiled but feared he'd pay for making his Master change them. He heard her continue to speak and concentrated on what she was saying while he threw himself into his clothes.

"I wanted two hours in the dungeon and this was the only time he had available today so you're lucky we could keep our booking."

Aeneas knew, only too well, his Master didn't have to explain and felt even more embarrassed. On leaving the bathroom, he went straight to her feet and kissed them.

"Thank you. Now get up and let's go."

Aeneas simply said, "Yes, Master," and opened the main door into the hall, patting himself down as she passed him to make sure he had his phone and wallet.

* * *

The dungeon was incredible, a real Aladdin's Cave. On the outside it was a rather dingy flat on the top floor of a block, which was three-high, but on the inside it was like something out of a BDSM film. The reception room was small and quaint, with two velvet chairs arranged beside an old-fashioned wooden table that was set with orange juice, bottles of water, and other refreshments. The owner had welcomed them warmly and assuring them there was no rush because the next hire had cancelled.

Ian offered to show them around the rest of the rooms and Fhionna smiled, told Dog to 'stay,' and then followed him as he walked from the reception room.

Aeneas flushed bright pink at being told to stay like that in front of the dungeon keeper but knew just to wait where he was. He decided it would maybe go in his favour to be on his knees when they came back and so he got down onto the floor and stayed beside the little table with his head bowed and his hands placed behind his back, as he'd been trained to do.

"It's an amazing play space. Thank you so much for showing me all the hidden treasures. I'll need to book in for a full day next time, just to be able to enjoy them."

Dog heard Ian laugh and say it was his pleasure and he was glad 'Mistress' had enjoyed the tour.

"I'll be through in my room should you need anything else. I must say that your slave is very well trained. He's such a handsome specimen too."

Aeneas heard the words quite clearly and then heard his Owner laugh and say maybe he would like to join them next time.

"I think you probably just made him nervous, Mistress, but I'd love to accept your invitation. Thank you. I hope you have fun and please ring the bell when you're ready to leave."

* * *

Before she left the little reception room, Fhionna told Aeneas to undress and be wearing his collar by the time she came back.

Aeneas waited on his knees, naked apart from the wide strip of leather now encircling his neck, and it wasn't long before he heard a small bell being rung. He assumed he was being summoned, that she'd changed her mind about coming back to fetch him, so stood up, walked to the hall, then thought better of it and got back onto his knees to make some effort at crawling between the little rooms to find her. On his third try, he found her sitting on an ornate velvet throne with various metal shackles at her feet.

"Fasten the shackles around your ankles, lock them, and then give me the key."

After doing so, he waited for his next order.

"Stand up and move to the middle of the room. Position yourself under the head cage that's dangling from the ceiling."

Once in position, Aeneas clasped his hands behind his back and waited. His Master was circling him with a concentrated look on her face. He admired her features, the narrow nose and almost black eyebrows that arched so seductively when she was thinking or planning a slave's demise. He'd grown to love the little moments when he could secretly watch her absorption in a task or cautiously take note of how she spoke to and treated her other slaves when she forgot, for a moment, he was in the same room. He was also beginning to realise just how much she loved to plan things. Not to the extent of being inflexible but she certainly liked to picture a scenario in her mind and implement it, allowing for small changes along the way but only if really necessary. Aeneas thought this was why Violate nights were always so spectacular. The detail of the decoration and the outfits she chose for herself and her subjects were always indicative of a loving, creative process.

Aware his thoughts were running away with him, he brought himself back to the situation at hand and realised his Owner was struggling to lock the head cage she'd chosen to use round his neck. He wondered if he should help but closed his eyes instead and thought about what he looked like in the device. He knew how much she liked metal structures of this kind and thought it would look rather sexy if she did ever manage to get it on.

Forgetting for a moment where he was, and having to try and concentrate on being patient, he started to hum to himself. No particular tune, just something random and made up. It was only after a second or two of silence, a distinct lack of rattling chain or cage movement, that he opened his eyes and saw his Master glaring at him.

"When you're quite finished, I will continue."

Aeneas went red but found he couldn't hang his head to hide it because of the metal bars in which he was now, solidly, encased. He managed to mumble a quick apology and knew better than to let his mind wander for a second time. He thought she was really sexy when she was a little irritated but she was also scary and he knew, instinctively, not to get anything wrong on purpose. He clamped his mouth closed and let her continue.

* * *

Dog felt as though he'd been put through his paces. Once the head cage was in place, his hands had been bound to it to keep them high and out of the way. She'd then whipped him thoroughly and severely tortured his nipples. After she was satisfied, she'd released him from the device and ordered him to crawl into the bathroom where she'd showered him with her own golden nectar before chaining him to a wall to let him marinate for a while. She'd then hosed him down with icy water.

As he shivered and shook from the cold, he had to admit that this punishment was just as bad as any caning might be. He hated being cold but especially as he'd been left to dangle, to drip dry. The incredibly intimate gesture of receiving his Master's urine, however, had been wonderful. She certainly knew how to give with one hand and take with the other. All his actions had consequences, it seemed, and this was something he must remember going forward in service to this wonderful woman.

* * *

The afternoon had been full of surprises, most of which had focused on some form of bondage. Not only had he been chained and abused in the wet-room but he'd also been hogtied and electrocuted with a Violet-Wand device that sent tiny currents racing through his entire body. He'd been secured in place by lengths of ribbon, neatly tied in bows around his neck, his ankles, his wrists, and his torso, making him look like a gift that needed to be opened. She'd taken pictures of him, and told him they would be uploaded onto her website, before loosening the ankle ribbons and refastening his legs to wooden posts at the top of the mattress he was lying on. He'd been thoroughly abused with different sized butt-plugs and dildos, until he'd begged and cried, and he'd known she would only stop when she was completely satisfied.

Aeneas felt sore all over and struggled on the walk back to the flat.

He'd been instructed to keep quiet until spoken to, so hadn't said much to his Master. He'd dutifully answered her when she'd asked him a question but other than that they'd walked in silence.

It was quite late when they got back because Fhionna had decided to take an extra hour at the dungeon since it was available. She'd told him to take a hot shower then run her a bath. She'd also said she was hungry and had asked him to order them some food from one of the menus in the kitchen drawer, before unpacking his dog bowl from the kit bag.

Aeneas, having completed all his tasks, waited for her next command. He wasn't sure if she would want to eat at the table or on the sofa with a tray but he thought it best to follow what he'd been taught up until now, and that meant the bowl should be placed just under the table but beside the legs of her chair so he was within reach. It amazed him just how much he'd not only come to terms with eating like an animal at her feet but how much he actually loved to do it.

* * *

Fhionna had certainly enjoyed her day but she also felt more than a little tired and couldn't wait to get some sleep. She was happy to eat her food from a tray while she sat on the sofa because she felt a little lazy and had rented a film to watch before she collapsed into the huge, feathery bed. She briefly thought about making Aeneas watch the film with her but had allowed him to eat his meal from his bowl then curl up on the sofa at her feet. She smiled to herself as she listened to his muffled snores. He'd done well and was obviously exhausted. She would let him sleep on the sofa tonight instead of on the floor.

Lifting his head from her ankles, she covered her slave in a blanket and left some instructions on the table for him to follow in the morning. She turned the television off and walked slowly towards her bedroom, switching off the lights on the way.

Day Two

After breakfast, they headed out into the heat of the city to do some shopping. She wanted some new whips to use at the club they were attending and also wanted to wander around some vintage shops to look for bargains in clothing and bric-a-brac. Her taste was rather eclectic, loving to fill her beautiful home with wood and silver and mosaic. She knew Dog would have a few bags to carry back to the flat and thought they might end up using a taxi. She loved wandering through the packed streets with her pet following on behind, trying to keep up and navigating his way through the bodies that seemed, so often, to get in his way. She laughed as she heard his sexy American voice saying, 'Pardon me, Ma'am,' as he dodged between buggies and women who couldn't steer them but clearly thought it was a good idea to bring their offspring out into the 'maddening crowds' anyway.

* * *

Dinner that night had been exquisite. Fhionna had asked Dog to book them a table at one of his favourite restaurants. He'd lived in London before, it turned out, and knew his way around the best eateries. She loved good food but also the ambiance of her surroundings. She often craved places that had opulent décor, with mismatched furniture and vibrant Indian cushions scattered on wooden benches, but she also valued the sparse, modernist feel of white brick walls, billowing white muslin and silk drapes over high windows, and twinkling fairy lights twisted up inside huge glass vases that were discreetly positioned on window ledges. She often thought these places kept the surroundings simple so as not to detract from the food itself. Choosing the place to dine was an art form; the outcome could be truly fantastic or majorly disappointing.

* * *

Aeneas had been extremely nervous selecting the restaurant but was happy his choice turned out so well. They'd talked for hours and it felt like they'd been friends for years. They'd talked about her family history and his life in Manhattan. They'd shared secrets not many people knew, and chatted about how she'd come to know she was dominant, even as a child. He was fascinated by her life and felt honoured be a part of it. He didn't think he'd ever seen his Master so relaxed, outside a fetish setting, and was pleased to have been allowed to orchestrate it.

* * *

"Goodnight. Sleep well. I enjoyed your company today. A little different for us to have a 'normal' day together."

Fhionna smiled at him as she disappeared into her room, happy he'd pleased her so much and could cope well with being in her presence in any circumstance. Behind the closed door, she enjoyed the process of slowly peeling the summer dress from her body and letting it fall to the floor. She kicked the flat sandals from her feet and examined her painted toenails. She decided they needed to be redone but she would do that tomorrow. For now, all she wanted was to rest between the sheets, close her eyes, and drift off to sleep.

* * *

It was four in the morning when she woke. She'd been having the most wonderful dream but opened her eyes to see light streaming in through the curtains she'd forgotten to close. The images were still vivid though and made her excited.

Snaking her hand down her body, she began to touch herself. She moved her fingers delicately at first, but the urge to orgasm was building and she knew she wanted some attention from her slave who was probably still fast asleep in the next room.

Laughing to herself at how naughty she felt, she removed the strap-on from its velvet bag and fastened it onto her body, bending round to fasten each small buckle at the side and adjusting the strap that ran between her buttocks. She then reached into the bag again and removed a condom and rolled it onto the solid rubber shaft before lubing it to make it shine. She felt powerful and sexy and decided she'd take some rope, a gag, a pillowcase, and the leather belt she'd brought in case she wore her jeans, with her.

* * *

Aeneas shifted slightly in his sleep, only half aware of the footsteps crossing the room. He was having some very erotic dreams about the time Master had made his fantasy happen. He remembered the excitement of not being able to move much, as well as the thrill of being taken from behind while having the guy's member in his mouth. His Master had quite clearly said be careful what you write about because it might come true, but he hadn't really expected it to be so exact. He'd been explicit and rather naïve to think she wouldn't know someone who could 'help her out.'

Just as he was moving onto his back to relieve the cramp in his arm, which was trapped underneath him, Aeneas felt his head being wrenched backwards and something like a hood being pulled over it. He realised, pretty quickly, it was a pillowcase with a large hole cut out in the front. Next he felt a thick, phallic-shaped gag being thrust into his mouth and buckled behind his head. Aeneas grunted as something was placed round his neck and pulled tight. He was then pushed back down onto his stomach and his hands were being tied behind his back. His ass was raised into the air as a hand grabbed his testicles and pulled, and his head fell forward forcing it into the cushions of the sofa.

Dog moaned loudly as he felt something cold and wet between his cheeks and then something hard being thrust into his hole. Completely surprised and totally excited, he gave himself over to the lust of his Master, thinking how lucky he was.

Day Three

Fhionna had slept until ten, which was unheard of, but now wanted to start her day. She was aware that Dog had a couple of meetings to attend so, pulling on her robe, she walked through to the living room where she'd kept him tied for the rest of the night but with the gag and belt removed so there were no restrictions to his airways. She smiled as she saw his body lying on its side and proceeded to remove the rope from his wrists, making him groan as he brought his arms forward and shook them out to get rid of the ache.

"Good morning. I enjoyed using you last night. I hope you managed a little sleep, but I may let you nap later on this evening before we go to the club."

She told him to shower and make them both a large breakfast. She knew his first meeting was at noon and she said he should text to say it had finished and when his next one began. She also told him he should be back at the flat no later than six o'clock and he would receive two strokes of the cane for every minute he was late.

* * *

Aeneas moaned as his body creaked its way into a standing position. He no longer had the flexible body of a thirty or even a forty-year-old, even though he worked out every day. He decided to do some stretches while he waited for the shower to run hot. He usually wasn't given time to exercise when he was in her presence but, then again, he hadn't exactly discussed the possibility. She obviously liked his body and his muscles but maybe it hadn't crossed her mind that he had to work at it as often as he did. He smiled to himself as he thought she might even like to watch him flex and bend and lift weights, taking pride in her fit pet.

* * *

During breakfast he chatted to his Owner, quite openly, and said he would do his best to be back at the time she'd requested but his last meeting was on the other side of town and it wasn't due to finish until five-thirty.

Fhionna reiterated that he could be late but he knew what the consequences would be. She was a little annoyed he was already making excuses but was also having some fun at his expense and guessed she might be in for a treat later, as she expected there to be at least thirty strokes in his book by the time they left for the club event. She could always cane him whenever she wanted to, of course, but this way she got to imagine him running across the city trying to avoid something that, ultimately, was inexorable. She enjoyed testing him, putting him through his paces, and he'd done well so far.

* * *

It was five o'clock and Aeneas was stuck in a conversation with a woman who insisted on arguing the worth of some stock or other that he didn't particularly have much interest in. He tried to be polite but knew she was probably more than a little irritated because he kept looking at his watch. She seemed to be raising her voice every time he did it. In the end, he felt he had to excuse himself by saying that she was probably right but as he had an engagement all the way across London he would need to excuse himself. The woman, whose name he'd already forgotten, raised an eyebrow in a similar manner to his Master when she was ticked off, and this made him smile. He'd managed to say how lovely it had been to meet her before dashing out of the room at break-neck speed, throwing his name badge and door pass onto a table nearby.

Out in the street, he hailed a cab and asked the driver to get him to the nearest train station or subway that would have him back in the area of Euston as quickly as possible.

"In a bit of a hurry, Sir? I hope you've a little time to spare because this traffic ain't going anywhere."

Aeneas sighed. He didn't have any time to spare but could see the driver was probably right.

"Oh, God. I'm not going to make it." He wasn't talking to the cabby, of course, but voicing his general frustration. He'd managed to get out of the last meeting early only to be defeated by traffic. He could almost feel the raised angry welts on his ass right now. He'd probably be due a hundred strokes and be a blubbering wreck by the time she'd finished. He did seem to spend a lot of time crying these days, but he'd always been an emotional person anyway. His mother used to tell him, as a child, that he wore his heart on his sleeve and his thoughts would always be written right there on his face. She hadn't been wrong, as it turned out, but it was sometimes a good thing because it meant his employees could tell very quickly when he wasn't happy with their work performance.

Entering the building where the apartments were, at five-fifty-eight, Aeneas half killed himself sprinting up the stairs rather than waiting for the elevator. He burst through the fire door onto the third floor and ran up the hall, arriving outside the flat door at six-o-one.

Fhionna opened the door and laughed when she found a heavily panting dog. He observed her check her watch, declare him one minute late, and inform him he would be the recipient of two strokes of the cane, which would be entered into his punishment book.

Dog almost crawled into the room through exhaustion and pulled himself up to sit on the arm of the large sofa. He hung his head and mumbled that it wasn't completely fair he would receive any strokes of the cane because he thought being a minute late, after having done his best to get there on time, was a good effort.

"It was a very good effort and I'm very impressed. However, a promise is a promise and you'd respect me less if I didn't deliver. What kind of message does it send to my slave if he is allowed to think he can manipulate his punishments or rewards, for that matter, by being a petulant child? So, you shall have the two cane strokes now. Get up, drop your trousers, and bend over. Snap yourself out of your huff, right now."

Dog mumbled, "Yes, Master," and rather grudgingly did as he was told.

* * *

That night, after food in the room, Fhionna relaxed with a glass of wine and a good book while Dog was gagged and knelt on all fours in front of her as a foot stool. She felt he'd needed something more than the two strokes of the cane to make him remember his place. Maybe they'd spent too much time as equals over the past couple of days. They were equals as human beings, of course, but their relationship was top heavy and he must be reminded of that.

Not having been able to concentrate on her book for long, she decided to pick her outfit for their night out. She'd already packed a very basic costume for Aeneas to wear, which consisted of a leather thong, Doc Martin boots, and his collar. It was a symbol of his newly Owned status and she would happily make him follow close behind on the end of her lead.

* * *

Aeneas drooled miserably onto the floor. His arms were shaky and his knees were sore. He guessed this was an extended punishment for his earlier moodiness. He wished it would be over soon though. He'd worked so hard at being back at the flat on time but guessed she was right. One minute late was still late. He'd felt grumpy, at the time, but could see the wisdom in her comment now. He didn't think he would ever have attempted to manipulate her in any way, and didn't think it was possible, but she was obviously making sure he knew who was the boss and was correct to do so.

Trying to relax, Aeneas thought about what he would be expected to do at the club. He'd never been to Club Rub before. He'd been to other events while he'd lived in London but only once or twice. They were never something he'd enjoyed that much on his own. He'd stuck to visiting professional Dominatrix to try and scratch an itch, not really expecting to meet someone who would be more than a temporary solution. He thought how arrogant he sounded and almost laughed through the gag that was stuffed into his mouth. He was certainly in no position to be prideful.

* * *

Standing outside a grey building on a busy crossroads, Fhionna gave Dog his instructions for the evening.

"Be on your best behaviour. Take our coats and bags to the cloakroom then go to the bar. You may have a whisky and I'll have a G&T. Do not speak until you are spoken to. You will carry my kit bag and hold my whips if I decide to play with someone. I will be playing with you tonight so expect that too. You know how to behave at a club night by now so remember what I've taught you because your behaviour is a reflection of my training."

Dog simply said, "Yes, Master," and patiently stood beside her holding the bags with the outfits and whips inside. He noticed there were only a few people left in front of them now and was desperate to get inside. He'd been waiting for this and felt excited at being in another city with his Owner; wanting to show off his skill as a slave to anyone who wished to watch or take interest.

* * *

Aeneas looked back over his shoulder as he walked off in the direction of the changing room. It crossed his mind how lovely she looked. It was a simple leather dress but the way she wore it was so commanding. The stiletto heels showed her muscled calves off to perfection and he thought how envious any sub would be that saw them together. Unlike most Mistresses he'd played with, Master was a true

Goddess. It was a title he wanted to use but she was far more subtle than that. He loved the way she knew she was skilled at what she did but didn't have a massive ego. He thought this might have something to do with her dislike of role-play. She was just naturally dominant and felt no need or want to lapse into a fantasy role. She could humiliate if she so desired but her power didn't lie in the debasement of others or in a need to shout and threaten. Her raised eyebrow was more than enough and had the power to subdue an errant slave, all on its own.

On his way back, drinks in hand, he noticed that there were already quite a few dominant females seated in various booths with their subs and slaves either sitting on the floor at their feet or kneeling in front of them as a foot stool. He was sure she'd noticed them too and wondered if he would become her furniture again, at some point. For now, it seemed, she was quite content to sway to the beat of the music and sip from her glass as he sat on the floor doing the same. He was quite comfortable in his collar, boots, and thong, and his lead dangled freely down his chest. The chain was cold on his skin and it made him think about how she liked his bare torso, which he'd started shaving as part of his normal routine at home in New York.

Dog watched as people started to dance. He didn't have a lot of rhythm but he certainly enjoyed good music. It was loud, of course, but it wasn't just the mindless-thumping that some clubs played. He was beginning to relax and looked forward to holding Master's whips or being played with himself. He had an exhibitionist side and he knew that she did too. She loved to swirl her whips, laughing as she caught sight of subs closing their eyes and hiding their faces in case it gave their Owners or partners ideas. He smiled to himself as he remembered her saying she'd often been the 'threat' with which other Doms kept their subs in line, saying, "I'll give you to Mistress Fhionna for punishment if you don't behave."

Letting these thoughts tumble through his head, he was only half aware that his Owner was starting to move.

"Get up, please. I want to go and see the main dungeon room."

Aeneas stood up and held out his hand to steady her as she stepped down from the tiny plinth the table was nestled on. He loved her smile and was happy to follow on behind, like the obedient dog she expected him to be.

* * *

Fhionna had enjoyed the music but she wanted to watch the play, so taking her place behind a polished brass barrier, like might be seen in old fashioned theatres, she watched as Masters and Mistresses led their pets and slaves over to various pieces of equipment. She was particularly interested in a gorgeous gay couple and wanted to see what the sub could do. She thought the Dom was in his late forties, somewhere, and that the slave was quite a bit younger. They were both in great physical shape. The older man's torso was naked, and he sported heavy leather jeans and boots. His handlebar moustache was a bit of a cliché but he suited it somehow.

* * *

Aeneas could sense his Master's interest as she watched a gay couple play together. They were right in front of her and he could almost feel her bristle with excitement as blow after blow landed on the back of the slim, young slave. He also felt his own desire and shifted from one foot to the other as he stood behind her. It always amazed him just how much she seemed to know what he was thinking because she'd turned round with a huge grin on her face and told him to remove his gag from the play bag and to kneel in front of her but facing outward towards the players. He was now on his knees with his hands clasped behind his back as he'd been trained to do. He'd come to love the feeling of the phallus filling his mouth and hoped she'd noticed and enjoyed the growing bulge in his tight thong.

* * *

Fhionna stroked her slave's head as he knelt in front of her and bent down to whisper in his ear that he was a good boy and she'd noticed his excitement. She stood up just in time to see that the gay couple had finished playing and the slave was now kissing his Master's boots. She started to clap, even though no one else did, and the male Dom looked in her direction and smiled. She smiled back as he took a little bow and was thrilled to see he was leading his pet towards her.

"Hey, thank you for your applause. It's nice to be appreciated. You're not from London are you? Most Londoners don't clap like that.

They're much too controlled to show any emotion." He smiled as he held out his hand and introduced himself as Mike. "This is Brute, my slave."

Fhionna took his hand and offered her own name. "Hi, I'm Fhionna, and this is my slave 'Dog.' I love your slave's name. I'd love to hear the story behind it. He's very obedient and you're very skilled with the whip, I must say. It's not often I see someone as talented as you."

"Well, that's a great compliment. Thanks. Do you use whips yourself?"

"Yes, all kinds of whips and I love to use the cane too." She laughed as she felt Aeneas shift his position slightly. "Dog's a new slave, so is still in training, but he knows what they feel like."

"Aww, that's really cute." Mike grinned at her. "He's lovely. You're obviously a good Mistress. He's very well behaved. I hope I'll get the chance to see you play later."

"Thanks. He's doing very well. A couple of hiccups along the way but generally very good."

"Would you and your pet like a drink? We're heading into the bar for a little while. Brute gets thirsty when he's been whipped."

Mike smiled as Fhionna said to lead the way at the same time that she pointed to the floor to indicate Aeneas should crawl behind her.

* * *

Finding a table that would fit them all, Mike sat down and asked Brute to go to the bar and Fhionna said Dog would accompany him to help carry the drinks, saving his slave two trips.

Mike watched as she removed her slave's gag before they headed off together. He smiled and said he hoped that Dog and Brute would like each other as they made a very cute couple.

She laughed and then smiled at him to show she was more than happy to discuss Dog's sexuality, as well as her own desires.

Mike apologised for being so forward but admitted he found Dog very attractive and hoped he was Bi and that she might be interested in watching the subs interact with each other.

"I've found a lot of women love to watch males together, and why shouldn't they? It's certainly not a heterosexual male's prerogative to watch two girls 'get it on.'"

Fhionna admitted to being Bi herself and that her slave/partner, Bunty, was a woman. She said she'd been told by her closest friends, fairly often, she was greedy, wanting to have all the wonderful slaves for herself, no matter what their gender. She also told Mike she was truly lucky to have her own home with its wonderful dungeon and to have met so many wonderful people to play with, some of whom she'd chosen as her slaves after they'd shown signs of wanting to serve her and make her happy.

"You seem like a remarkable woman. I wish I were Bi sometimes." Mike let out a snort and chuckled in a most endearing manner.

Fhionna thought he was the loveliest bear she'd met and that he was very engaging. He was obviously very horny, and openly expressive of his desires, but she liked the fact he also had a sweet side and could giggle like a school boy.

* * *

Dog stood beside Brute at the bar and chatted happily to the young man. It turned out he'd been Mike's slave for two years and lived with him full-time, which was a dream come true. He said that Mike was originally from Norway but had lived in London for over ten years. The young man turned red as he alluded to an interest in foreign accents and said how much he loved that Dog was from Manhattan. He also talked about belonging to the sweetest man on the planet but how he also had a very scary side.

"That's great. Your relationship sounds perfect. I've only become Master's slave recently. I have a lot to learn but she knows what she wants, how to direct me, and I'm getting the hang of it, I think. I love to make her happy, to see the smile light up her beautiful grey eyes, but I know she has a wicked side and can punish me without even raising a whip. It does help that I'm not her only slave. I've learned a lot from Tim, who's this kind-of butler, housekeeper, slave, and general servant, all rolled into one awesome package. And he can also take the whip amazingly well. He's been her slave for a very long time."

Dog stopped talking because he realised he was monopolising the conversation and the drinks had arrived.

"He sounds awesome but I'm sure you'll make her just as happy for many years to come. We'd better head back though because if Mike's beer is warm when we get there he won't be pleased."

Dog smiled and agreed that they should go. He'd ordered himself a coke because Fhionna hadn't given her permission for anything stronger this time.

Back at the table, drinks in hand and smiles on their faces, both slaves saw how well their Owners were getting on. Brute poked Dog in the ribs with his elbow, looked up at the big man, and whispered that they might both be hatching some sort of plan. He smiled and told him he was used to being made to play with other males for his Master's pleasure and he hoped Dog would enjoy it because he liked him a lot.

On noticing their arrival, Fhionna and Mike both turned their heads to smile at the slaves.

"There you are. We were wondering where you'd got to. Come and sit on the floor, both of you."

Fhionna patted the side of the cushioned bench she was perched on as she spoke and Mike grinned at them.

Doing as instructed, the men sat on the floor beside each of their Owners and found themselves being stroked and petted as leads were clipped onto their collars, simultaneously. Dog caught Brute's eye and winked at him. This was a sure sign that something fun was going to happen.

* * *

In the dungeon room, having finished their drinks and deciding it was time to play, Fhionna strapped Dog down onto a beautifully padded and studded leather bench. Once secured, he was going nowhere. He looked sexy and she felt excited. Not only were they about to play in public but Mike and Brute were watching them and she was determined to impress them.

* * *

It was one in the morning and the small group left the building and headed back to Mike's place. The event didn't finish until three but they wanted to have some private fun and they'd achieved all they wanted at the club.

His house turned out to be a large, spacious flat with beautiful art on the walls, tastefully placed lighting, and sumptuous furnishing. It was a gem hidden in the depths of the cramped, noisy city.

"Your home is fantastic. I love it."

Mike smiled and said it had taken him a long time to get it how he wanted it but the best part was the room next to his bedroom. He led the way and Fhionna followed him, instructing Dog to stay, smiling at him.

They entered a reasonably large dungeon chamber, wonderfully kitted out with a suspension hoist, a long padded bed with a cage built underneath it, and a gorgeous purple spanking bench. She felt an immediate reaction between her thighs and let out a low whistle.

"Wow! It's beautiful. I can understand why it's your favourite room. Can the hoist lift someone completely off the floor?"

"Oh, yes. I have various padded cuffs that fit both ankles and wrists, as well as a love swing. Brute loves the swing as it makes him feel like he's floating."

Mike grinned at her and said she could use the room during her stay in London, even if it didn't get used that night.

"That's very kind of you. Thank you."

They walked back through to the lounge where their slaves waited for them.

"You're in for a real treat, Dog."

"Open a bottle of wine, please, Brute. Once you've done that, you and Dog can go and kneel in the dungeon and wait for us."

"Is Brute your only slave or do you have others? I know some people prefer to have one person to share their life with but I love to have a main partner and other people I choose to be close to as slaves. They're all so different and that's what allows it to work so well. I don't want them to be jealous of each other but having more than one slave means I get to have all of my needs and fetishes fulfilled. I'm very lucky."

Mike smiled. "Brute is my favourite. We're like partners, I guess, although I prefer to live on my own, to be honest. He's been mine for a few years now and we want to have a binding ceremony. I have two other slaves that I play with but they don't go to clubs. They're both married and like to keep a low profile. Brute is actually Bi too and had a girlfriend for a long time but she dumped him because she said he wasn't dominant enough." Mike laughed. "I know he's a lot happier with me. I care for him deeply and he's a wonderful person. It's like he was born to be a slave. He's so eager to please and hates it if I'm ever angry or disappointed. I think the worst punishment I could ever give him would be to ignore him for more than a day. Not that I ever have."

Fhionna returned his smile and said he was very like her in many ways, and that Dog was also similar to Brute in his need and want for real submission. Silence from her would torture Dog just as much as his silence with Brute.

Mike raised his glass towards her to make a toast.

"It's not often I find someone I think will be a genuine friend, and even less often that they turn out to be a woman, so I'm very happy to have met you, Fhionna."

* * *

"Stand up." Fhionna gave the order and both slaves complied, keeping their hands behind their backs. She thought how beautiful they were together. They looked completely different. There was a twenty-year age gap, at a guess, which made it even more exciting. It was also fun to learn that Brute, whose real name was Mark, was Bi and she hoped his Master might let her touch him as she would let him touch Dog.

Mike walked over to where several lengths of rope hung from hooks on a wall. "I would love to see them tied together while we torture them. Does that suit you, Ms Fhionna?"

He grinned at her as she said she'd like that very much, and walked back to the little group with the rope in his hands. She noticed he'd also picked up various sets of nipple clamps.

"Stand back to back, boys, and put your hands at your sides. You may hold hands, if you wish."

Mike watched as the slaves did as they were told and was happy to see that Dog had no problem holding onto the young man. He knew Brute would like the connection but also that it would give him comfort.

Mike had every intention of letting Fhionna play with Brute as he also wanted to play with Dog. He would never dream of dominating the scene and he had a feeling that she was also more than capable of voicing her preferences. It's what he liked about her. She seemed confident and open to new experiences.

Mike handed her some rope and opened his hands to let her choose the clamps she liked. He'd noticed the size of Dog's nipples and knew she obviously enjoyed them.

"I'd love to watch you tie the boys up, Mr. Mike." She laughed at the title she'd given him but he'd called her similar.

"It would be my absolute pleasure. I would love to play with Dog's nipples while you played with Brute's, if I may?"

They both grinned as they watched their slaves bow their heads at exactly the same time and knew a fun night lay ahead.

* * *

Dog and Brute lay on the floor of the dungeon, exhausted. Both Masters had left them to rest and retired to the living room, no doubt to talk about them. For now, all Brute wanted to do was be hugged by the strong man who lay beside him and curl up into the hollow of his curved body and feel the weight of the arm that draped over him. It had been an intense few hours and the first time, in years, that he'd felt the touch of a woman.

He liked Fhionna, he thought she was sexy for an older woman, but it had been strange, even so. He was used his Master's touch, and the touch of men he was ordered to play with for his pleasure, but Mike had never shown any interest in seeing him being touched by a female before.

Dog shifted slightly and broke the boy's thoughts. "Are you ok Mark? Is my arm too heavy for you?"

Mark snuggled in closer. "No. It's perfect where it is. Thank you, Aeneas."

The men had decided to call each other by their real names when their Owners weren't around. It seemed appropriate, somehow, now that they knew each other better.

Aeneas sighed but it wasn't a sound of dissatisfaction.

"You have a very high pain threshold. It made me wince when Master made me watch as she caned your ass. You took it really well and it made me really randy to watch the way you squirmed. That's when my fate was sealed, I think, as Mike noticed my excitement and made it clear he would like to use my mouth."

Dog stopped speaking when he realised Mark's breathing was heavy and let his hand wander down towards the boy's member. He gently teased his erection to full thickness before slipping his other arm out from underneath him and sliding on top of him to play with his sensitive nipples.

Mark moaned and thrust his chest up towards Aeneas.

"Please. Let me give you the same pleasure that you gave to my Master. I would love to do that for you. You're very handsome." He blushed as he spoke but slowly moved down to take the head of Aeneas' cock in between his lips, flicking at the end of it with his tongue in quick, darting movements, then longer, slower caresses.

Aeneas grunted as the boy's mouth fully enveloped him, as he slid his body down between his legs. He watched as Mark sucked his balls and licked his shaft then snake his hands up to Aeneas' nipples to gently tug at them. He couldn't hold off any longer. He felt the cum rising and, with a brief thought of whether he would be allowed to orgasm or not, shot his load into the boy's eager mouth.

ℬℴ Chapter 9 ℭℬ

August 2012, Between Cities

Home Is Where the Heart Is

I

Fhionna felt she'd spent some real quality time with Aeneas. She felt that they'd reached a whole new level as Master and slave and it made her smile. She also felt happy to be home because she'd missed Bunty very much but the play they'd had together, on her return, was truly magnificent.

Only too aware that she had a lot of work to catch up on, she decided she wasn't going to see Dog this month. It was still only the start of August but she had window displays to design and implement and some new customers to meet. Pre-fall, as the fashion industry called it, could be a very busy time for her and her small team of staff, with all the new ranges hitting the shops. Both fashion and homeware tried hard to tempt people into believing they needed a whole new wardrobe update or they would benefit from changing their kitchens into something that looked like it might be home to cute little church mice, with lots of tasteful wicker baskets filled with bread. It was all very exciting and fresh but also hard work.

She thought about the display plans she needed to draw up as she headed into the office. She also thought she would miss Dog, as he would be in Scotland soon on business, but it couldn't be helped. She needed to tell him that even though he was coming over, she'd be too busy to see him and wondered how he'd react to the news.

* * *

Aeneas lay in bed with his laptop open beside him. He was excited to be travelling to Scotland and only a very small part of that was based on the fact his business deals were going so well and his boss was very happy with the way he dealt with the client's needs and demands. It was good to have his job, inasmuch as it continued his income and he could write off the flight expenses, but it wasn't like he really needed it. He'd made his fortune already and could quite easily see himself emigrating from his present home in the US and buying a new home in Loch Lomond, for example.

* * *

Downstairs, and regular as clockwork, the mail arrived and Toby's footsteps could be heard going to retrieve it from the matt at the door. Aeneas had been expecting an email from his Master but none had arrived. He was a little surprised he hadn't heard from her and felt a little pout begin to tweak the corner of his mouth. It was amazing just how much he felt like a petulant child when she hadn't been in contact. They'd only met six months ago but had shared so much already. She'd certainly changed him for the better.

Lost in his own thoughts, he jumped as Toby knocked on his bedroom door.

"Sorry to disturb you, Sir, but there's a letter for you from Glasgow. I thought you might like to know straightaway rather than see it for the first time when you come down to breakfast."

As Toby made his way back down to the kitchen, Aeneas tore open the envelope. It was from Fhionna and he was so glad to be holding it. It was good to have something tangible he could actually grip in his hands. Email was fine, hell any communication was better that good, but an actual letter was by far the best.

Tugging on the paper inside, and unfolding it rather hastily, Aeneas felt his heart sink as he started to read:

Dear Dog,

I love how close we have become. Our time together in London was wonderful and I saw many varied facets of your personality.

Since returning home, however, I've noticed just how much my own work needs my attention and so I have decided I won't have time to see you this month.

You remain in your Master's thoughts and I will be in touch again soon.

Aeneas read the very short letter again before ripping it up and throwing it at the bin beside his bed, missing it completely. To say he was disappointed was an understatement. What he felt was utter deflation tinged with anger.

Biting his lip till it bled a little, he slammed the lid of his laptop down and marched into the bathroom. He wasn't acting rationally, and he knew it, and it only made him feel worse. Running the shower and breathing deeply, he tried to quell his emotions but was finding it difficult. Stepping into the cubicle, he let the water run over his short, thick hair and down his neck and over his broad shoulders. He decided he would stand under the torrent until he calmed down. He guessed he would be there for a little while.

Drying himself off, Aeneas started to think about his flight details and his general travel plans. He felt he should change some of it and perhaps book a hotel in Edinburgh rather than his usual place in Glasgow's West End. The anger had subsided and he now felt sad. He understood, of course, that his Master's wishes were quite literally his commands and she also had a career to focus on. He felt stupid for reacting in the way he had but it was just frustration. He knew better than to complain about it, after the punishment he got in June, but he needed her firm control and guidance. He loved her and Scotland was becoming his home.

* * *

As the plane touched down, Aeneas sighed. This trip wouldn't feel the same without being able to see her. He'd emailed, and they had exchanged texts, but that had been the extent of their communication. And now, he was here, about to do his job and that was all. Greg had managed to change his flights to arrive and depart from Edinburgh Airport and also change his hotel. He felt rather tired, and a little bored, as he walked through the checkout to baggage claim and then out into the sunshine. At least it was a warm day but it made him think of his

Master enjoying her garden. But maybe she didn't even have time for that.

* * *

Arriving safely at his hotel, Aeneas dropped his bag onto the bed. It was a beautiful and unusual room with a large window overlooking a narrow cobbled lane that led up to the castle. Greg had searched online for suitable accommodation and had presented him with five choices. Aeneas had picked this one because he liked its quirkiness and felt like he would need a bit of luxury to take his mind off of where he really wanted to be sleeping. He'd pondered the idea, recently, of having a cage built in his bedroom and having a lock fitted on his bedroom door. He would have to ask Toby to leave his clean laundry in the spare room or he'd have to make the cage able to be dismantled so he could let Toby into his room on certain days, once or twice a week.

Checking his watch, he realised it was too late to make contact with the first client he was due to see but still too early to start thinking about settling down for the night. He was wide awake and restless. So, deciding to surf the net for a while, he unzipped the laptop case and set it up on the table beside the window, moving the complimentary sherry and sweet Scottish tablet to one side.

Making himself comfortable in one of the leather bucket seats, and moving the little arrow around the screen, he thought he'd look up theatre listings and possible entertainment for the few nights he was staying. The Witchery, it seemed, was central to lots of pubs, clubs, and restaurants. He was spoiled for choice and it was making his head spin.

Not wanting to finish with his search but feeling he needed a quick break, Aeneas decided to order some food to be delivered to the room and promised himself he'd go down to the hotel restaurant the next night. He'd noticed the bold use of solid wood carvings and the dark velvet drapery on the walls, as he'd walked past the diners deep in whispered conversation, and liked the look of the place. It seemed a very romantic venue, however, and he was in no mood to enjoy it right now.

Replacing the receiver in its cradle and returning to the computer, Aeneas trawled all sorts of sites looking for something but, at the same time, not quite sure what. He clicked on one that advertised itself as an alternative night out to the normal humdrum of Edinburgh. He doubted whether anyone visiting the city would consider it in such terms but he smiled and followed the links to go deeper into the information and galleries of photos it provided and discovered it was a professional dungeon. Much to his horror, he'd stumbled across a site that promised to provide 'what he needed' in the comforts of a deluxe house not far from where he was staying. He'd assumed, when he'd clicked on it, it was some sort of theatre that played host to risqué performances. He'd seen a lot of dungeon websites before and there were none of the usual warnings of, 'you must be 21 to enter' or 'content of this site is for adults only.' He was completely thrown off guard and all of a sudden felt uncertain about what to do.

* * *

Aeneas found himself walking down Castle Street towards a tall building with high windows and metal structures bolted into the walls at either side, like railings only more decorative, and thought how appropriate it looked. The metal added a sense of doom to the façade, as if it was saying, 'abandon all hope ye who enter here.' He would normally have smiled at the mere thought of it but all he felt was a little bit sick. How could he even be contemplating what he was about to do. He berated himself as he pressed the buzzer and was let into the building but he was still going ahead with it, even though it was arguably the most stupid thing he'd done in his entire life. In his head, he could hear the disappointment and anger in his Master's voice as he climbed the narrow stairs in front of him.

* * *

Mistress Donella was tall and curvy and in her late fifties, he guessed. She was perched on a throne when he entered the formal chamber, and she looked like so many of the Pro-Doms he'd seen before. When he'd been in the 'fetish circuit' he'd almost always visited someone his own age or older. He hadn't liked many of the younger Doms he'd seen because he'd felt like he was being subjected to a mere child's whim rather than seriously taken in hand. For the most part he'd enjoyed the sessions he'd booked but they'd always left him wanting more and in a wholly unsatisfied state. He knew that's why he'd wanted to seek out someone special, someone he could submit to, that he felt could take proper control of him and not just be going through the motions of what they thought it meant to be dominant. He also knew, because of the fact he'd already found this person, that this Dom would ultimately fail to make him happy.

The first words out of her mouth confirmed this fact.

"I am to be referred to as Goddess and you will be punished each time you fail to address me properly. Is that understood maggot?"

Aeneas felt he had two choices. He could either turn round and walk right back out the door or enter the role play, as she wanted, to see if it improved. Making what he knew to be a mistake, he said, "Yes, Goddess," and waited to see what would happen next.

* * *

Back in his hotel room, Aeneas sat gingerly on the edge of the bed and removed his shoes. The caning she'd delivered was ok but had certainly not 'hit the mark' in terms of being what he needed to feel. It was such a pity he'd had to call her 'Miss' or 'Ma'am' to get her to finally use one on him. Usually older Doms were more intuitive than that but he guessed some were better at reading body language and signals than others. The whole session, in fact, had felt like he was leading her by the hand rather than her leading him by the ear, which was what he ultimately needed. Rather than having his guilt for being there assuaged in an effective manner, he felt he'd directed the whole thing himself and been left with marks on his backside that meant nothing. No, actually less than nothing. He knew he was trying to feel pain as a way of feeling something from his Master, something as an extension of her, but Mistress Donella hadn't been capable of anything more than shallow engagement. In the end, he'd actually had to ask her directly to give him twelve strokes of the cane because, "he'd been a very naughty boy."

* * *

Aeneas hadn't been needed until his first meeting at ten o'clock so he'd had time to visit the gym next door to the hotel and have a hearty breakfast in his room after a hot shower. He'd forgotten about the marks on his cheeks and had yelped as the water hit them.

Checking his schedule again he noticed he had some spare time until his next meeting at three o'clock, so he decided to log on to the Violate website to check out what was written about the August event. He knew he was punishing himself by doing so because he was missing his Master but he couldn't help it. He expected to find stories written about the dungeon play and various testimonials about how wonderful the dungeon owner and her staff were because that's what usually appeared. He wasn't disappointed and found all of those things but was also shocked to see that a visiting 'Goddess' from Edinburgh had enjoyed her night immensely and thanked Mistress Fhionna for her friendly and personal attention. It mentioned how she hadn't expected to be shown around by the owner of the club herself and how it had made her feel very special indeed.

Aeneas heard a buzzing sound in his ears and felt sick as his stomach churned. Not only had he been stupid enough to visit a Dom but he'd also thought that being from different cities, even though only about forty miles apart, it was very unlikely his Master would know a professional Dom from Edinburgh. Even though he knew there must surely be many other Mistresses who called themselves Goddess, he had a sinking feeling that Fhionna might have met Donella, and wondered if they'd swapped contact details, promising to stay in touch. He knew he was letting his imagination run riot, and it was his guilt causing him to make absurd connections that probably didn't exist, but it was the mere possibility of a friendship that scared him. It wasn't as if Master and Donella were similar in any way, so it wasn't really likely they'd become bosom buddies who swapped stories.

Feeling slightly green around the gills, he went to the bathroom to splash some cold water on his face. As he stared into the mirror and watched it drip from the end of his nose, he heard the phone on his bed start to vibrate. Assuming it would be the alarm he'd set to remind himself that he was due to get ready for his next meeting, he walked across the room to switch it off. He picked it up with the sole intention of dropping it again but was stopped in his tracks by the name that flashed up on the screen in bold capital letters.

* * *

Fhionna had been so busy with work that she'd hardly had any time to draw breath. It was two o'clock and, even though she was sure she would be interrupting his business day, she decided she would speak to Dog. She dialled his number but only half expected to hear him answer it in person.

"I'm so pleased to have caught you. I wasn't sure you'd be available in the middle of a working day but I wanted to let you know I was thinking about you."

Aeneas was dumb-struck and only just managed to croak an answer.

"Good afternoon, Master. It's good to hear your voice. My next meeting is in an hour." He tried hard to find more words to say but found that he couldn't.

"I won't keep you but I wanted to invite you to dinner with me this evening. Say, around eight o'clock. I'd be happy to come pick you up from your hotel. Where are you staying?"

Feeling himself blush, he admitted he'd changed his hotel to one based in Edinburgh instead of Glasgow and felt relieved when she said she understood it was easier for his business meetings and that she would arrange to see him before he left for home, instead.

Aeneas could only find the power to mumble, "Yes, Master," before falling silent again. He thought he'd had a narrow escape when his Owner had said to have a successful day before she hung up on him but as he'd dropped the phone back onto the bed it had vibrated to let him know there was a text.

It may be that you were busy, so caught off guard by my call, but I suspect there's more to your palpable silence. You are usually very vociferous. You will have the chance to explain, after your business is completed, because I will drive through to Edinburgh and meet you at your hotel. You should reply to this text with the name and address, including the full post code and your room number.

* * *

Fhionna stood outside the hotel on Castle Street and looked up at the solid stone structure in awe. The love of old buildings and the faint whiff of history they secreted into the air had always made her heart glow and she knew that this was a lot to do with how her father had raised her to love them as much as he had. She'd always loved Edinburgh because it was a city of hidden depths. It was very commercial on the main streets, which were lined with tourist shops and big brand-name stores that most large cites had, but it also had secret, cobble-stoned passages and lots of little winding staircases, that stood up to the trampling hordes of visitors from other countries trying to soak in the ambience as much as they possibly could before returning home to their skyscrapers and neon lights and story-high adverts. She could picture the giant billboards in Times Square in Manhattan advertising the latest blockbuster film or Broadway show and marvelled at how two cities could be so unalike but equally as wonderful.

Unwillingly dragging her mind back to what she was about to do, she allowed herself to pass through the polished glass door which had been opened for her. She smiled at the man as she passed him, and walked towards the brass directory on the wall by the lifts to search for the room number Aeneas had given her. She'd instructed him to be naked and collared, kneeling on the floor just inside the door. She usually liked to be greeted on her immediate arrival but, in this case, she'd decided she would make him wait for her in his room.

* * *

Aeneas was naked, collared, and wondering how the hell he was going to explain this one to his Master. He'd belonged to her less than a year and he'd already messed up so badly that it might be beyond repair. Every time he started to run through it in his mind he was disgusted by how pathetic it sounded. He wasn't perfect. He knew that. He admitted he still had a lot to learn but he was also a good judge of when a mistake could be reasoned away and when it was just down right selfish and stupid. This one definitely belonged in the second category and no matter how he tried to rationalise it by thoughts of telling her how much he'd missed her or how he felt he'd needed to feel pain, or at least some sort of physical contact, on her behalf, he knew it all sounded clichéd and unimpressive.

These thoughts were still rushing round his brain as the door to his room opened. He wanted so much to look up and watch his Owner walk up to him as he knelt on the floor. This would normally have given him a rush of love and devotion but this time there was only a kind of dread and he knew it was completely his own fault.

Sucking air into his lungs, he did his best not to shake. He heard the click of the catch as the door closed and dared not move. It seemed like forever before Fhionna told him to crawl to her, kneel upright, and explain why he'd been so tentative on the phone earlier.

Positioned in front of his Master, he knelt up, as instructed, and kept his hands behind his back. He couldn't look her in the eye and guessed she'd take it as an indication of guilt. Which it was, of course. He'd been impressed by how she'd picked up on his 'uneasy feeling' during their very brief conversation on the phone. This fact, however, was also very scary and meant that the smallest infraction would be noticed, never mind a whopper like the one he was about to own up to.

He closed his eyes, briefly, and exhaled.

"Master. I feel so guilty. I've made a terrible mistake and one that I can only hope you will be able to forgive. When you told me I wouldn't be seeing you while I was in Scotland my heart sank, but before I go any further I want to assure you I'm not making any excuses for my behaviour but only letting you know how I feel and how much you mean to me."

Aeneas paused, waiting for Fhionna to say something but as she only looked at him, with her eyebrow raised in question, he continued.

"I was feeling miserable and more than a little abandoned and even though I had absolutely no reason to doubt your affection for me, or your command over me, I decided I needed to have an interaction with a Dominant woman. All my instincts were telling me what a bad idea it was but I continued all the same. This is what I'm most ashamed of because I knew I'd be letting you down very badly by making a stupid decision and yet I let my ego and my pride get the better of me. I'm so sorry, Master."

Aeneas felt the words pour out of him but sensed it was time to stop. He lowered his head down onto his chest and kept his position, even though he could feel his heart pounding. He waited until she was ready to respond but her disappointment was tangible and he thought that if he was made to look at her the tears would come. Instead, he heard her walk away from him. He felt partly relieved that she hadn't shouted at him or lifted his head up to stare at his face, but he was also partly afraid in case she was so upset she could only find the words to dismiss him from his service, and therefore her life.

* * *

Fhionna sighed as she looked out over the rooftops of the city. She gazed at the mix of new, brightly glazed tiles and old slates, preferring the dark oblongs on the traditional buildings. They matched her mood. She was saddened by what Aeneas had said but she was also upset. She'd known from the way he'd talked to her, earlier, there was something he wanted to tell her but she'd never imagined it would be about such a big mistake. She'd made it quite clear, written it into his contract of slavery, that to serve another without her permission would not be acceptable. She wondered if he understood how important this was. Surely he must. He'd agreed to sign it, gratefully accepting it as something he wanted as much as she did, and now she had to decide if this was the end of their relationship.

* * *

Aeneas was finding it hard to hold back the tears and wondered when she would give him her decision. He knew a punishment would be involved, if she decided to keep him as her slave, but he was more concerned with the fact that he needed to be part of this woman's life. It would allow him to be the person he'd always wanted to be. A slave, the contented property of another, cared for but guided and instructed, accepting the consequences for mistakes, should they be made. He wondered if he dare look to see where she was, try and read her expression, but couldn't bring himself to do it. He had an overwhelming feeling of wanting to beg for her forgiveness, to tell her how much her disappointment was worse than any punishment she could give him. All he wanted was to be hers.

II

It seemed like Aeneas had talked and cried for hours but in actuality it had probably only been for a short time. His face felt tired and his eyes were sore as he rubbed them and ran his hands over the short stubble on his chin. Master had accepted his apology and was giving him another chance but the punishment was still to come. He hadn't told her who it was he'd seen, and she hadn't asked, but he thought this might come back to bite him on the ass.

He'd been told to clean himself up before she'd left the room with her phone in her hand. He was conscious of wanting to blow off the meetings scheduled for the next day, to serve her in any way she saw fit, but knew he would do whatever she wanted him to do. He suspected he would be in for a difficult night and it would probably please her to make him carry on with his business the next day, as planned. He was beginning to understand her fairly well and guessed that she'd think this would add to his punishment because being allowed to serve her the following day would be more than he deserved.

* * *

She was pleased she'd managed to make contact with Donella and acquire a room to rent to punish him that night. What she hadn't bargained for, however, was the information that Dog had already sessioned there. She guessed it made sense, geographically, but when the other Dom had told her how Aeneas had been less than polite, and it was she who he'd played with, Fhionna was furious.

The other woman had apologised profusely, saying she had no idea Aeneas was an owned slave, but the fact that he'd hidden his status from her only made Fhionna more annoyed. It meant he knew he might be turned away if he'd mentioned it, so he'd given it plenty of thought. She'd assured her there was nothing to be sorry for but, if she didn't mind, she wanted to include her in his punishment. Donella had said she was happy to take part and offered the dungeon room for as long as was needed, free of charge.

After saying thank you and agreeing that it would be good to have dinner together before the session took place, Fhionna hung up the phone. She couldn't help but smile as she thought about what was in store for Dog. She would certainly make him regret his decision to break his contract.

* * *

It was only when Aeneas had been told his Master had secured a dungeon room for a few hours and the Mistress who owned it had agreed to take part in the session, that he realised what might be about to happen. She was smiling at him but it wasn't the normal kind and happy smile she usually shared. He wasn't used to this expression and felt it deep in the pit of his belly. He was in trouble. He could, of course, give up this relationship and the slavery he craved if he so desired. He also knew, if it ever did end, it would need to be her that finished it because he never would.

Following instructions to get dressed and leave his collar in place, Aeneas walked hesitantly behind his Master as they went out for the evening. He noticed she hadn't seen the need to tell him where they were headed and hoped he was wrong. As they left the hotel and turned right, however, he felt foolish for being so naïve. Aeneas stopped dead in his tracks behind her and looked up at the gate with dread.

"Is there something you would like to tell me now before we go into this building?"

Aeneas blushed and lowered his gaze to the ground saying he wouldn't insult his Owner's intelligence by even trying to give an answer.

Fhionna told him to press the intercom and announce their arrival.

Once inside, they were greeted by Donella herself. She gave Fhionna a massive hug, as if she'd known her for years, and merely nodded in Aeneas' direction. This made him wonder if his Master had already discussed his previous session and, if so, what had been said. He doubted whether the conversation about him had been favourable. Maybe Donella had told her how he'd topped from the bottom or that she was dissatisfied with his performance in some way, adding to the fact he shouldn't have been there in the first place.

Aeneas was told to strip then to get onto all fours. The other woman watched him carefully. Once on the floor, he waited for his next order but realised both women were walking away from him and worried that he was expected to follow but hadn't actually been told to do so. Just as the thought had popped into his head, however, Fhionna turned her head in his direction and said, "Heel, Dog," without even breaking her stride. He felt embarrassed by the command but knew, of course, he was being made to feel like that on purpose. If this was how the whole evening would go then he was sure, by the end of it, he would be a complete wreck. He felt like he'd already learned his lesson just by living with the guilty feelings but obviously Master didn't think so. She was right to punish him but he wished for the cane more than ever because humiliation like this was much more difficult to bear.

Turning left at the end of the hallway, Dog crawled onto cold tiles. He thought it might be a kitchen or bathroom floor but didn't dare raise his head to look around. He followed on behind his Master and her companion until she told him to sit underneath the kitchen table, joking with Donella that he would be truly embarrassed by now.

Crouching low under the table, in what appeared to be a rather spacious kitchen and dining area, Aeneas attempted to make himself comfortable. Fhionna obviously noticed him shifting his weight around and reached down to attach a chain through the ring on the front of his collar before running it up between the wooden legs and clipping it to the high back of her seat. This meant that Dog's neck was now stretched upwards so much that he couldn't lie down and had no choice other than to be in an upright position with his head tilted back, looking at the wooden slats above him. The thought crossed his mind that his Master was being particularly cruel, uncharacteristically so, and this annoyed him, even though he wouldn't complain about it. Instead, he felt himself shutting down, trying not to allow himself to be rattled by it. Fhionna and her new friend had been chatting, eating, and laughing together for what seemed like forever and his neck was very sore. If she'd treated him like this from the beginning then there was no way he would ever have wanted to belong to her. He was feeling sullen but he couldn't help it.

Aeneas let all these negative thoughts run through his mind but, realising his Master was talking to him, brought his attention back to her and said, "Sorry, Master, could you repeat that please?"

With a slightly irritated tone, she told him he would be taken through to the dungeon chamber shortly.

* * *

Dog lay on the carpet curled up in a ball at Fhionna's feet. He'd been beaten with a hard wooden paddle by both his Master and Goddess Donella and then caned. He'd lost count pretty quickly but his Owner had taken great delight in discussing how many strokes he'd been given as they walked back to the hotel.

"Come here. You've paid the price for your ego-trip and I hope you realise just how badly you hurt my feelings. The agreement we both signed stated, quite clearly, what was allowed and what was not and it upset me to learn you'd broken it so early on in our relationship simply because you were feeling left out. I was surprised because I thought you were completely devoted."

Fhionna stopped talking and looked at her slave with a furrowed brow. All anger had dissipated and instead sadness was etched on her concerned face.

Dog sat up and looked straight into her eyes for the first time since she'd arrived at his hotel room earlier that night. He admitted to feeling lonely, then angry and sullen, and finally that he'd learned a valuable lesson and was relieved to be back in his rightful place at his Master's feet. He told her that punishment from her was like nothing else on earth and he wanted to show her what a good slave he could be. He may never be absolutely perfect but he would try his best to make her happy.

๏ Chapter 10 ๛

September 2012, Manhattan

Crossing the Ocean

I

She decided it was time to do a little travelling. She liked to go to large cities the most and having a slave who was based in Manhattan meant she had even more of a reason to visit there. She was excited about the idea and thought she would plan it while she had her breakfast. She was also excited, however, that Poppy was staying for a couple of days as she hadn't seen the sweet little creature for a few weeks. She'd been on holiday, visiting friends and family in Ireland, and had returned home yesterday. She'd emailed her Master as soon as she'd landed, it seemed, to request permission to serve, saying how much she'd missed her. Fhionna, of course, had been delighted and said she was looking forward to seeing her.

Poppy's short reply had made her laugh:

Dear Master,

I'm so excited at being back home. There are only so many days I can stand to be called 'he' instead of my rightful 'she' and it's definitely crossed over the limit.

Love, your little slave,

Poppy

PS... May I come tomorrow please, Master?

Settling down to the food her dear little slave had made, and watching her almost skip from the room to tackle her chores, she smiled and switched on her laptop to jot down some provisional ideas. She thought she would have a week there, whether she spent all that time in Aeneas' company or not. She wanted to go fairly soon so thought it best to email her slave to ask him to book her hotel and plan some time off to spend together. She also wanted to know about any fetish events so she could plan her holiday around attending at least one of them.

* * *

Tim ate his breakfast, checked his watch, and stuffed the last piece of toast into his mouth as he hurried towards the front door. He was serving Master today and was running late. He hadn't been well the night before and was suffering a little bit. He was determined he was going though. Fhionna had texted him to say that Poppy was back and that she, Master, had some news. He couldn't imagine what it might be.

* * *

She stood up, pressed the 'send' button, and watched her message leave. It would be the middle of the night there so he wouldn't see it for at least another few hours, but she felt happy. Not only was she planning something exciting but Poppy and Tim were both in the house today.

Leaving her dishes on the draining board for one of her slaves to do later, she wandered into the living room. She glanced at the clock as she thought about Tim and realised he was late, which wasn't like him in the slightest.

Just then, the front door opened.

"Good morning. You're late. Are you ok?"

"Good morning, Master. I had a sleepless night but I'll be fine. Thank you." Tim got down on the floor to kiss his Owner's feet before excusing himself to remove his coat.

"There's some coffee left in the pot and you can make yourself some food if you're hungry. Come into the living room when you're finished, please."

Tim said he'd had some toast but coffee would be good and thanked her, again, before heading towards the kitchen.

Fhionna watched him go and set up her laptop again. She should really check on her business and let her staff know she'd be out of the country soon.

As she sent her last email, Tim knocked on the door and came in.

"You wanted to see me, Master?"

"Yes. Come sit beside me. I have some exciting news." She patted the seat next to hers and continued, "I've decided I'm going to Manhattan soon. Well, very soon, actually. Perhaps next week or the week after. I'm planning on spending time with Aeneas while I'm there but really just want to get away for a week's holiday."

"That's wonderful news, Master. You haven't had a holiday for a while." Tim paused before continuing, "May I make a request, please?"

She looked at her slave and felt her eyebrow go up, which made them both laugh.

"Of course but I don't remember you ever making a request before."

"Please may I treat you to the trip, Master? I'd love to accompany you too, if it was allowed."

Fhionna stared at him. "My goodness. I'm not sure I can let you pay for the trip but I'd certainly love you to come with me."

She watched his face as it broke out into a huge grin.

"Thank you. That means the world to me! I would really like to treat you to the airfare though, please."

"Well, if it makes you happy, then yes. Let's do it."

She told him she'd sent an email to Dog and asked him to find a hotel. She thought that maybe an apartment would be better, since there would be two of them staying for a full week and maybe three of them for part of the week.

Fhionna clapped her hands together excitedly and told Tim he should go home and plan his packing. She would text him with the confirmed dates later that day, and he should book the flights accordingly.

* * *

It was nine in the morning and the flight was on time. She hated waiting around for hours in airports so was thankful for every time things went according to plan. She remembered, one time, Bunty had made a huge mistake with her passport by making a hole in the top corner with a hole-punch; her excuse being it was easier to file with a treasury tag through it. Fhionna had gone ballistic at the airport when they'd denied her travel. She'd had to rush to the passport office to buy a new one and catch a flight an hour and a half later, which had been the only other flight she could get that day. Bunty had been grateful not to be travelling with her.

She smiled as she recalled the incident. She could laugh about it now but at the time she would almost certainly have told Bunty to take her case and leave, permanently. She was a highly intelligent person, usually, and her stupidity had only fanned the flames.

* * *

After a while in the air, Tim looked at his Owner hoping she would sense he wanted to talk.

"What is it?"

Tim smiled. "I need to tell you something, Master. Not a bad thing though."

"Yes?"

"It's about Aeneas."

"What about him?"

Tim blushed. "I like him a lot, maybe more than I've cared to admit. Up until now, that is." He looked down at his book for a second, as if choosing his words carefully. "I know how much you love to see your slaves play together and I feel a little guilty for wanting to be with him so much for my own pleasure, rather than purely for yours. I'm not used to this feeling, Master, and I'm not comfortable. I thought it best to tell you and get it off my chest, as it were."

Fhionna put her book down and raised her glasses onto her head.

"I was hoping you'd develop strong feelings for him, eventually. You make a great team and I know you've been a wonderful friend these past months and have helped him develop as a slave."

Tim was more than a little relieved to secure such a warm and encouraging answer. He wanted to give the 'green-light' to his Master for any intimate play between them, not that she needed it, of course. He would have done anything required of him anyway but he hoped that by letting her know how he felt it might allow her to enjoy it even more.

* * *

Aeneas was excited. An email from his Master said she was 'coming to America' and a slightly later one, the same day, said Tim was coming with her. He'd chosen and booked the hotel, arranged time off work, and was now waiting for their plane to touch down. He felt the urge to get down on his knees and kiss her feet right there in the airport but guessed it would be a bad idea. His friends and employees travelled a lot and there was every chance he'd get caught doing it.

He watched the arrivals board tentatively, his heart pounding in his ears, and wondered if the feeling would ever dissipate. When he saw her flight had touched down, he went to the barrier to scan the faces of the crowd. Hundreds of people flowed through to meet expectant family and friends. He watched a young couple reunite, and a little girl hug the life out of an old woman, before he shifted his gaze back to where it should be.

Tim was waving at him and his Master had a huge smile on her face. He knew she would be tired because it was still morning there, even though they would have been in the air for about seven hours or so. It always took its toll on Aeneas when he did the journey.

Stepping forward to greet them, he briefly kissed Fhionna's hand and gave Tim a hug as he took the bags from his hands.

"It's so good to see you both. I was so excited to get your emails. I hope the hotel I've booked is suitable as I haven't stayed there myself. I sometimes stay in the city when I'm on a night out but the places I've used were all booked out."

Aeneas knew he was rambling.

"Sorry, Master, I'm babbling. I'm parked near the entrance. It'll be a half an hour ride to the hotel, roughly. Did you have a good flight?"

"That's ok, Dog. I'm rather excited myself. Yes, the flight was lovely, thank you. We were well looked after and had good books to read. Let's go and find your car."

Aeneas scampered ahead like a young puppy and she rested her arm through Tim's as they followed on behind.

Outside, it was a sunny morning and the temperature was already above what she was used to at home. It had been a good start to the month though, with temperatures high in their teens on average.

* * *

It had taken just over an hour to get to the hotel because of unexpected traffic and Fhionna felt hungry.

"Let's check-in, dump the bags, and then come down for some food."

Tim and Dog followed on behind as she mounted the escalator, which took them to the first level. Reaching the room, and using the electronic card, she motioned for Aeneas to go first to unburden himself. She let Tim follow him and then entered behind them. When she went in, both men were standing just inside the door. The room was tiny and not at all what she was expecting.

"Did I not ask you to book an apartment, Aeneas?"

Dog looked sheepish. "Yes, Master, I'm so sorry. I thought that's what I'd done. I will go to reception and change it."

"Please see what they have available and ask them what went wrong. We'll be in the restaurant downstairs so come and let me know what's happening."

"Yes, Master." Aeneas noticed that she'd used his formal name and not the pet/slave name she'd affectionately given him. He watched as she 'reversed' out the door and was ashamed to acknowledge there wasn't even enough room for her to turn round properly. There was no way she would be comfortable in the tiny room, never mind with Tim there too.

* * *

She'd enjoyed her meal and now felt a little more relaxed as she asked Tim to remove her shoes and start the shower. The junior suite was so much better than the first room and had a wonderful king-sized bed, a small fridge, a sofa and chair combo, a dressing table, and a fairly large bathroom. Dog had done well, even if it had taken him an hour to sort out. He'd been annoyed and hot when he'd finally found them in the restaurant. He'd apologised all over again and she decided she would reduce the punishment she was going to give him because of the original mistake.

"I love the view. Central Park is so beautiful."

Tim agreed with her and smiled. He turned his head to look at Dog, who'd been told to strip and stand with his hands on his head in the corner of the room until he was needed. He was impressed that Aeneas had offered to pay for the room for the whole week, as a gift, and as a way of making up for the fact he hadn't taken the time to go and check out the room in person. He guessed this was the only punishment he'd receive for the mistake because he'd tried so hard to correct it.

Fhionna laughed as she noticed Tim look at Dog for a brief few seconds before returning his attention to the window. "Do you feel sorry for him?"

"A little bit, Sir, but I know you are being kind because he tried his best to make you happy in moving rooms, and that's what matters to you most."

"Yes, it does, you're right. The only reason he is being punished at all is because he should have done it properly in the first place. He had plenty of opportunity to visit the hotel himself, to see if it was suitable, and he didn't."

She looked at her slave who was standing quietly as he'd been told to do, and laughed because she knew he could hear them talking about him. He was, no doubt, more than a little embarrassed but she also thought he might be a little relieved his ass would remain unmarked. At least for now.

* * *

Before leaving the room, Dog had presented his Master with a short list of fetish events and shops she may wish to visit. There were two or three outlets he thought looked promising. He'd managed to get a couple of days off work, at short notice, because he only really had one boss above him. As long as he put in the effort at a later date, he was generally very flexible.

As he shut the door behind him, he thought about what might

happen in the next few days and felt a heady mix of excitement and nerves. In all honesty, this was something he was getting used to. An unusual mix of emotions but they were far from unpleasant. He felt sure Fhionna would want to visit Paddles; a fetish club that was on the following night. He'd been once before but it was a while ago and it might have changed a lot since then. Clubs like that tended to change managers or owners frequently in the US.

* * *

Aeneas got into his car and took a few deep breaths to calm down. He felt a little rattled after having been punished by being ignored and left in the corner of the room while his Owner and Tim had talked openly about him as if he wasn't there. In some ways, it felt worse than being beaten. He was a little surprised to see his hands were shaking slightly and decided to go back into the hotel for a glass of iced water and to read a paper to compose himself.

Settling down in one of the large leather armchairs he observed the hotel guests and staff coming and going until his order was brought to his table. He'd decided he was hungry, as he'd been too excited to eat much that morning, and had missed out on lunch because of having to sort out the room mess. He enjoyed 'people watching' and was very happy to see Tim come down the escalator and into the bar area.

"Hey, Tim, over here." Aeneas jumped out of his seat to wave at him. He was genuinely glad to see the man. "I had to calm myself down before I drove home. My hands were actually shaking. I'm not quite sure why. I'm glad I did though because I haven't had a chance to say hi to you properly yet." The large man enveloped the smaller one in a bear hug and invited him to sit down.

"Hi, Dog. I won't stay, thanks. I've been sent on an errand to find bubble bath. Don't suppose you can point me in the right direction?"

"Take a right out of the hotel and walk half a block. There's a gift shop with all things soapy and smelly to make every woman's dream come true."

Tim said thanks and hugged Aeneas one more time before heading out the door to find the perfect tincture for his Master's 'first of many' bathing experiences in Manhattan.

Fhionna looked over the list of shops and events. She was surprised by how few fetish clubs there were but Dog had warned her that the scene there was way more focused on professional Dominatrix services than public events. He'd said there'd been a time when Manhattan had been filled with exciting kinky nightclubs but those days were gone. Luckily, there was a club on the following night and she'd brought an appropriate outfit with her. It wasn't as extravagant as some she owned but she loved it nonetheless. Sometimes simple really was perfect.

Scanning the rest of the list as she thought about her dress, she noticed a fetish shop called Purple Passion. She definitely wanted to go there and she hoped it would be open tomorrow. It would be great to see what they had and maybe take a new whip or two along with her to Paddles. She'd packed a few fetish essentials, not really wanting to bring whips through American customs, but she guessed it would be ok to leave with some in her case. Who would care about that as long as she was going somewhere else?

She was happy she had a full and exciting first day planned. The rest of the time she would create her own amusement in the hotel. She had a great imagination, two slaves to play with, and the knowledge that Tim had the hots for Dog.

* * *

The next day started with a text to Aeneas telling him to meet them at Purple Passion at midday. Apparently it didn't open until then but stayed open fairly late in the hopes of catching the passing trade from kinky people finishing work and making their way home or to various Mistresses.

Fhionna was more than happy to negotiate her way round the subway system and thought of it as part of the adventure. It wouldn't matter if they got a little lost or were a little late. That was the beauty of having slaves. They waited patiently for you to arrive without complaint.

When they got there, she couldn't help but feel excited. It was an Aladdin's cave of whips, corsets, leather and latex clothes, and sex toys. On the outside it didn't really look like much but on the inside it was totally transformed into an amazing space filled with everything a Master could want.

She grinned at Dog and clapped her hands together excitedly, which made both men smile.

Just as she was about to step further into the shop, a rather shy female appeared at her side. She said her name was Ann and that Dog had organised a guided tour for her, as well as the use of a private space at the back where she could try out some whips, if she wanted to. He'd also negotiated a ten percent discount on all her purchases.

* * *

After two hours of fun, choosing whips and floggers to try out on her slaves' bare backs, and dancing in and out of the fitting room in various outfits, she decided she would have a new leather quirt, two new suede floggers, some electrical toys, and a new gag. She also bought a short leather skirt and a new leather corset that had red flames hand painted up the sides. She was a little disappointed they didn't stock shoes but overall it was a fantastic experience and she loved every second of it.

Leaving the shop, Tim and Dog followed on behind their Master with various bags in their hands.

"I'm rather hungry so let's find a place to eat. Perhaps somewhere Italian. I'm in the mood for pasta and we'll all need some energy for tonight."

She was ready to sit down and relax.

* * *

Back at the hotel after a wonderful day of shopping, she thought it would be fun to watch her slaves take a shower together. It was an intimate act without being overtly sexual but it would still be very exciting.

"Tim, move the chair from the dressing table into the bathroom please and sit it across from the shower. Dog, pour me a glass of wine and put it beside the chair. You should both strip."

She smiled as she watched her pets undress and hesitantly enter the bathroom.

"I want you to shower together. I also require you to remain partly visible through the glass so wipe the condensation away from time to time."

It took a minute or two for the men to get comfortable in this new situation but before long they were soaping each other's bodies without hesitation. She watched as Tim was the first to caress the large man's muscled back, massaging the skin and watching the suds trickle down his spine and run between his pert buttocks. His excitement was obvious and her own exhilaration matched it. Soon he turned the other slave round and started work on his chest, moving slowly down his torso.

"You are gorgeous together. Swap places."

Fhionna hated to break the mood but she wanted to see Dog reciprocate. She knew he was a little shy still, but she wanted to see how he handled touching Tim. Hopefully it would be as easily as he was able to be touched by him.

She smiled at her slaves as they glanced in her direction before Tim turned to face the wall to encourage Aeneas to copy his actions. He did so eagerly then knelt on the base of the shower to wash Tim's lower body. She watched excitedly as Tim thrust his buttocks backwards and opened his legs to let Aeneas run his hands over the fleshy mounds before reaching forward to wash his engorged member. His moans were audible against the running water and it was obvious that both of them were enjoying themselves.

After a while, she placed her wineglass on the tiles and told the men to rinse themselves off and dry each other before tidying up the bathroom. She asked them to return the chair to the living room, put their collars on, cover their genitals, and kneel beside each other in front of the window. She was excited and wanted her pets on full submissive display. Not only was she pleased room service would be dropping off another bottle of wine but she was happy that the window ran the full height of the wall; from the soft carpet to the rail which held the curtains. There were no buildings directly across from the room but she was thrilled by the prospect that people in the park would be able to view the outlines of her slaves' kneeling figures, should they choose to look in their direction. They were on the second floor, so discreetly above ground level, and she felt very much at ease as she rested her long legs on the backs of her pets, watching the world go by outside.

It wasn't long before someone knocked on the door and announced themselves. Fhionna laughed as she wrapped herself in a fluffy robe and walked to the door to sign for the bottle, leaving it wide open so the kneeling figures were on full display. She was in a wickedly mischievous mood.

"That was very good fun. I wish you both could have seen the young man's face when he noticed you. I wasn't quite sure if he was appalled or wanted to join in. It was hard to tell but I enjoyed his blushing cheeks."

She didn't expect a reply, and she didn't get one, but she saw Tim glance in Acneas' direction. The night was young and there was lots more fun to be had.

* * *

Fhionna was wearing her new clothes. She loved the way the flames climbed their way to her cleavage from the base of the black leather corset. She felt sexy and thought they matched her mood perfectly. She now felt the dress she'd brought from home was too low-key. She admired her slaves, who were dressed in matching leather trousers and chest harnesses. Tim's harness was a classic black and Dog's was a deep red colour, so between them they matched her outfit beautifully.

"Is the taxi booked, Aeneas?"

"Yes, Master, it will be here in fifteen minutes, as you requested."

She'd told her slaves to kneel on the floor with their hands behind their backs, as they had been taught, until she was ready. She'd given them some time alone to chat and dress and had enjoyed the fact that another little bonding ritual was underway.

"One of you can carry my bag and the other should fetch my coat."

She watched as they did as they were asked and smiled as Aeneas held her coat for her to slip her arms into the sleeves.

"Are you excited?"

Tim was the first to answer.

"Very. It promises to be a fun night."

Next it was Dog's turn to reply.

"Yes, Master. I'm pretty overwhelmed already but I know I'll be looked after and Tim will help keep me calm. I just want to make you happy."

Dog blurted his response and Tim elbowed the large man in the ribs, which made them all laugh, just as reception called to say their taxi was outside.

* * *

Dog opened the door of Paddles to let his Owner and his fellow slave descend into the cellar below. In the taxi, she'd asked him about the layout of the club, what rooms it had. If there was a theme. Was there a dance floor? And presumably there was a bar area, although this last question was more of a statement, as if she was clarifying the thoughts in her head.

Aeneas had enjoyed her attention and being able to be the one 'in the know' for once. He'd been silent most of the evening, as they'd both been told to be, but now he had a chance to be the 'host slave.' It was amusing to think he'd had specific ideas about how the night would go and none of it had happened. It was as if he'd forgotten he was trained to 'expect the unexpected' as far as his Master was concerned. He knew she'd have her own plans but he'd fantasied about showing her around and being allowed out of a strict slave role, at least some of the time.

He considered himself to be a good host and knew how to spoil a guest a little. He'd been pleased about the opportunity to show that side of himself at Purple Passion earlier in the day, and had loved her reaction to the small treats he'd been able to set up. They'd been half an hour later than she'd specified so it had given him the chance to get in there before her and be waiting outside, satisfied he'd done well. He'd also wanted to make up for the mistake of failing to check the suitability of the hotel room, of course. He wouldn't do that again and hoped he'd be able to offer her his home for a holiday, at some time, but felt it wasn't appropriate to make the offer yet.

Realising he was lagging behind, Aeneas ran down the stairs to catch up. He was just in time to watch Fhionna walk past a few slaves and subs that lined the walls waiting to off-load coats. He noticed some of the men eyed her almost hungrily and worried, slightly, she'd be uncomfortable. He was glad Tim was right behind her but even more pleased to see she was actually enjoying the attention. He should have realised she was more than capable of handling herself in any situation but particularly in a fetish club, even if it was 'across the pond.'

"This is a wonderful venue. I love the raw brick and the medieval sconces on the walls. From what you said in the taxi, I'm sure I won't be disappointed by the actual play rooms either."

She smiled at Dog as she handed Tim her coat and told them both to take their jackets off. Then she rummaged around in the bag of toys and handed Tim sets off leather cuffs, so her pets could fasten them onto each other.

Tim also noticed the way the other men looked at their Owner but wasn't worried about it. Both her slaves were there to protect her, should she need it. He smiled because he knew they were attracting attention to themselves. She looked formidable and was a new face in the club, and they were dressing each other. He winked at Dog because he knew he was nervous but also because he was sure there would be a few surprises in store and he wanted to encourage him to just go with the flow. It was still early and play wouldn't have started yet, so there was time to relax a little, tour the premises, and people watch for a little while. He also hoped they'd both be allowed a whisky or two.

* * *

Fhionna balanced herself on a narrow ledge that was covered in soft padding. It wasn't quite a proper seat but a full-sized set of furniture would take up too much space. She also noticed there was an un-cushioned shelf, just below it, which was really just a hard step. It was obviously created as a perch for subs and slaves so they didn't adorn the actual floor and take up room. She started to relax as she watched people head to the bar, as Tim now did, and wondered why there were very few female subs at the club.

Dog was perched on the lower step and she had his lead in her hand. She'd turned his collar round so that the D-ring was now at the back and the buckle was at the front. She loved how muscled his back was and was about to start up a conversation with her slave when a male came and sat on the padded section beside her. It seemed that not all subs sat on the step, after all, and she smiled at him as he addressed her by asking to kiss her hand.

"A bit lame, I know, but I haven't seen you here before, Mistress."

Fhionna laughed and said it was probably because she hadn't been there before.

"Wow! A Scot! Your accent is amazing. Say something else."

Fhionna smiled patiently and said, "Like what?" She'd a feeling the conversation would go downhill very quickly, if it ever got started properly.

"Wow! Just wow! You over on holiday or have you moved here? Sorry, my name's Denis."

Fhionna shook his hand politely and replied that she was there on holiday and to visit her slave, indicating Aeneas and the lead in her hand.

"Oh right. You have a slave. I shouldn't be surprised by that. You're rather gorgeous."

"Actually, I have more than one. My second slave is getting drinks at the bar."

"Second slave! That's cool. Is there a third one?"

She was right, this conversation was going nowhere, but she tried to stay focused.

"Numbers three to five are back home in Scotland looking after my house."

She looked at the bar to see where Tim was. She could see him trying to fit three glasses into his hands and wondered why he didn't ask for a tray. She also noticed Dog's shoulders were moving up and down. He was obviously giggling at the stilted conversation taking place above him.

She smiled at no one in particular and raised her hand at Tim to indicate where she was. When she saw an opportunity, she stood up and motioned to Dog that he should do the same. She said a very quick goodbye to Denis and made a move towards the first dungeon room but not before she nearly fell head first over a sub who'd prostrated himself on the floor in front of her feet and asked if he could kiss them. She looked down in amazement and wondered if this is how the whole night would be. She'd certainly been approached by hopeful subs looking for a Mistress before but not quite so abruptly. This one, it seemed, had a huge bag of toys with him and she was very keen not to give him the chance to open it so she calmly said, "No," stepped over him, and led her two slaves away. She certainly didn't mean to be impolite but she wasn't willing to be drawn into an unwanted encounter.

* * *

The first chamber was fairly small but had a beautiful wooden cross fixed to the wall. She liked the feel of the room and decided this was where she'd play. When she finally stopped and turned to her slaves she saw they were both grinning at her.

"I hope it doesn't continue like that all night, Master. You'll be tired out by the time an hour or two has passed."

"I know! I'd no idea the sight of a new 'Mistress' would cause such a spectacle."

Fhionna indicated she was ready to play and asked Tim to kneel on the floor beside the cross so he could hold her whips. She watched him as he took position and stretched out his arms so that she could lay her floggers across them. She then turned her attention to Aeneas.

"Remove your harness and face the cross, placing your hands and feet at the top and bottom of the X."

Dog suddenly felt shy. He felt rather exposed, even though the room was small enough not to encourage many onlookers. He knew, however, his Master was in 'top form' and this usually attracted lots of attention. He thought he might have felt a little less conspicuous having been allowed to keep his leather trousers on but actually their presence just highlighted his naked back even more.

"Open your legs wider, please, Dog."

Fhionna moved his ankles apart with her foot and attached his cuffs to the various metal loops on the cross' legs. She was about to have fun on his back. She'd warm him up, of course, but her intention was to leave some thick stripes on his skin.

Reaching up, she strapped a gag into his mouth. She smiled as she did so because she knew he'd realise a serious whipping was about to take place. He would know the gag was for noise reduction, as well as aesthetics, and it excited her greatly to have her large, handsome slave in such a vulnerable position. She would enjoy his moans and groans very much.

Selecting two suede floggers, she started to slowly twirl them both through the air and worked her way up to a considerable speed, pausing sometimes to examine his back and run her cool hands over his hot flesh. She was happy with the result but wanted to move onto the quirt so raised welts would form on top of the reddened skin. The stripes would turn black and purple, almost instantly, fulfilling her desire to create a piece of art.

Tim watched in silence as their Owner worked her magic, feeling his own excitement growing between his legs. He realised, of course, the flogging was just the start of the play but couldn't help watching and enjoying the other slave's beating. He knew, also, that once it was over it would be his turn on the cross.

Just as the thought entered his head, she turned towards him and asked him to stand. She also asked him to bring a chair over to the cross and lay the whips across it.

On his return, he noticed she'd taken Dog's arms out of the restraints at the top of the cross but had left his legs in place. He was then instructed to remove his harness and stand behind Dog. He did as he was told and happily pressed his body up against his friend and fellow slave, knowing his subsiding erection would spring back to life against the man's leather clad buttocks.

Fhionna removed Dog's gag, cleaned it, and placed it in between Tim's lips instead. She then shackled both slave's ankles together, one behind the other, and clipped the men's wrist cuffs together too. Surveying the result, she decided to attach Dog's collar to the top of the cross by slipping the end of his lead through one of the rings that were bolted into the wall behind it. Now she was ready to play again, repeating the pattern of warm up with the floggers before selecting the quirt.

Tim could take a lot more than Aeneas because he'd been her slave for a lot longer, so she was able to use her full strength as she brought each stroke down onto his back. Much to her delight, Tim groaned loudly and moved his body against Aeneas but the most exciting part was when she noticed Dog take Tim's hands in his to encourage him. It was a beautiful thing to witness and she knew they were becoming close.

* * *

After both slaves had been released and had thanked their Master by kissing her feet, Fhionna attached Tim's lead and put in it Dog's hand. She then took Dog's lead in her own hand and walked off in the direction of the social area. She was sure they made an interesting sight and this was confirmed when they reached the bar.

"Hi, I'm Scott. I must say that you looked amazing bringing your slaves in with you just now. They're very well trained. What can I get you?"

She introduced herself, said thank you for the compliment, and they'd all have a whisky.

"Which part of Scotland are you from? It sounds like Glasgow but I might be totally off track so please forgive me if I am."

"I'm impressed! You've obviously been."

"Yes, a few times, actually. I have friends in Scotland but they're based in Inverness. I do travel, though, when I go over. I love Glasgow. The people are so friendly. Their accents can be a bit hard to understand, at times, but yours is very clear."

Fhionna smiled and asked him about how he came to be working there and if he enjoyed it.

"I love it. I actually own the place and have a great relationship with the Doms that work in Pandora's Box next door. They give me free sessions, from time to time, because I let them in for nothing. I also do some repair work to their equipment when they need it. It's really good fun just being in their company. You should organise some play time there, while you're in Manhattan. It's an amazing space and the hire of a room doesn't cost that much for travelling Mistresses."

"That's a great idea. Thank you. I'll do that. This is Aeneas, who lives here in New York, and this is Tim, who's from Hull."

"Pleased to meet you both. An American and an Englishman. What a multi-cultural little group you are."

Scott laughed and said he hoped she enjoyed the rest of her stay before disappearing to serve some customers.

II

Delighted at having had such a wonderful start to the week, Fhionna felt like she wanted to spend some time in the hotel room. It was a vast improvement on the first one and she felt comfortable there.

"Dog will be joining us here this afternoon. We shall have some fun together."

Tim blushed at his Owner's enthusiasm for having her pets perform for her again so soon but was very excited by the idea. He was glad he'd told her his secret because it meant it might happen more often than it would have done otherwise.

"Go and shower, head out to the deli for breakfast, and then we'll have a chat about what I want to happen."

Tim said, "Yes, Sir," before heading to the bathroom. He felt happy.

* * *

Dog arrived, as commanded, at three o'clock. He had his collar with him and a gift for his Master. He was very excited at the prospect of being in her company again and wanted to show his appreciation. He loved being with her but also wanted to get close to Tim again too. He liked him a lot and now knew Tim was attracted to him. They understood each other pretty well and had the same goal… to make their Owner happy. If that meant he was allowed to enjoy himself while doing so then it was a bonus.

In his free time that morning he'd called into Pandora's Box. He'd phoned in advance to make sure he'd be let in but once there he was shown round all the rooms to help him choose one to rent. Scott was right, the equipment was pretty impressive, as was the cost of the chamber hire itself. He'd been able to pick a room without much of a problem and hire it for three hours on any day that suited her for the coming week. He hoped she liked the gift. She'd seemed very interested in the suggestion when Scott mentioned the place. He'd imagined that a room and a 'Mistress' session would cost a whole lot more but thankfully it hadn't been necessary to include anyone else.

Standing outside the hotel room door, he reread the instructions she'd sent him. He was to knock on the door, go in and undress, put his collar on, and kneel at the foot of the bed. He was to remain silent until told otherwise.

Aeneas felt excited. His heart was beating really fast and his palms were sweaty. He wondered why he was so nervous. It wasn't as if he was meeting her for the first time. He guessed it was because he didn't want to mess up. He also had a feeling something new was about to happen to him.

When he entered the room, he saw that Tim was already collared, naked, gagged, and tied down, spread-eagle, on the bed. He also noticed his Master sitting by the window with the chair facing where he'd been told to kneel.

Aeneas removed his clothes and followed the rest of the commands.

"I want you to be completely comfortable with what I want you to do so please give your consent for sexual contact with Tim."

Dog suddenly felt very shy but told his Master he was happy to take part in anything she desired. He felt it was necessary to speak rather than just nod his acceptance.

"Wonderful. Thank you. Reach up and caress and squeeze Tim's nipples between your fingers. Then play with his member between your hands before you take it into your mouth. You will find condoms on the bedside table. Take your time and enjoy it."

Without making another sound, he slowly reached up, stretched his full length out over Tim's restrained body, and started to play with the man's nipples. He teased and rubbed them until his moans filled the room and his member grew hard against Dog's belly.

Aeneas looked back at his Master, but being unable to ask a question, decided he would just have to take a chance and do something he thought she would enjoy and would also drive Tim wild. So, climbing up further onto the bed, he took an erect nipple in between his lips and started to flick it with his tongue. Tim groaned loudly and writhed underneath him, and Dog could feel his own erection spring to life. He knew Fhionna had a great view of both her slaves' excited cocks and it fuelled his desire to put on a good show. He intended to fully seduce and tease Tim for her gratification.

Releasing the nipple from between his teeth, Dog slowly slid his body back down over Tim's and took his member in his hands; following the next stage of his instruction. He wanted to make Tim cum but knew this shouldn't happen until he was given express permission to do so.

"What a beautiful sight you both are. You may now use your oral skills to make him cum."

Happy to hear these words, Dog let go of Tim's cock and crawled round the side of the bed to fetch the protection. He would have happily sucked him off without it but did as he was asked. Aeneas rolled the thin rubber down over Tim's shaft and watched as he thrust his hips up towards his mouth in anticipation.

Tim looked into Aeneas' eyes and tried to smile underneath the gag.

Dog smiled back before he finally surrounded the other man's erection with his lips.

* * *

Tim was completely spent and lay panting on the duvet. He was in heaven and felt as though he could drift away into a deep sleep but for the gag that still kept his mind semi-alert. He wasn't sure what would happen next, but he thought he might have to reciprocate and for that he would need to find some energy from somewhere.

"Dog, remove the condom and pour its contents into the ice-cube tray then put it back in the freezer. Untie Tim and remove his gag. You will then change places and perform for me again, in exactly the same way."

Aeneas wondered why on earth he had to save the milky fluid in such a manner. He didn't particularly like the idea but did as he was told. He then climbed onto the bed and let Tim tie him down, rather excited about what was to come next.

Tim smiled at Aeneas and dared to quickly kiss him full on the mouth before slipping the soft gag into place. It was his turn.

III

Fhionna had been delighted when Aeneas presented her with the gift of the three-hour play time in the dungeon, and now that the day was here she was really excited to be using Pandora's for her fun. She'd seen a documentary about it many years ago where a journalist had endeavoured to gain access to film a session but the only way they would let him in was if he booked in to see the Mistress called 'Raven,' who owned the premises, for a session of his own. It had been tremendously entertaining and now it was time for her to pay a visit to the famous dungeon chamber herself.

Stepping out of the taxi, she saw the entrance for Paddles and smiled. Tim looked in the same direction and laughed.

"Fond memories, Master. It was the beginning of our trip almost a week ago. So much has happened since then and now play in Pandora's Box with my Owner and her other slave. It's wonderful. Thank you for allowing me to come with you."

"It's certainly been an adventure I won't forget and most of it couldn't have happened without you."

She smiled at her slave and took his hand. "Let's go in. Dog will be here shortly and I'm dying to see the room he's booked before he arrives."

* * *

Fhionna was impressed by the friendly girl at the reception desk and even more so by the room she showed her. There was a rack along one wall, with a sturdy crank at both ends that could stretch any victim to their maximum length. There was also a spanking bench and a throne, which she particularly liked because she could instantly see herself ruling over her slaves from its comfortable seat. She laughed as the images of her two handsome slaves, in predicament bondage, danced through her mind.

The girl, whose name was Jules, smiled and said she was pleased she was happy with the room and could imagine having fun there.

"Yes. Very happy. Thank you. Would you be able to provide a basin of warm water and a hand towel? Tim can come help you organise it and carry it back, if that were possible."

"Yes, of course. We can do that for you now, if you wish."

"Yes, please."

She watched as they both left the room. She knew he might have guessed some of her plans because she'd sent him out that morning to buy razors and shaving foam. She had to admit, it was great the hotel was only a block or less away from all the shops she needed when it came to ordinary household items and delicious food.

Tim came back into the room, on his own, carrying the bowl and towel.

"Jules is very sweet, Master. Should I give her a tip?"

"What a good idea. I'm guessing she won't make that much money just doing reception work so it would be a nice gesture. Go and do it now."

Tim smiled and disappeared again.

The next time the door opened it was Aeneas who entered.

"Hi, Master."

Dog was full of energy and went to the floor to kiss his Owner's feet.

"So good to see you. Do you like the room, Sir?"

"I love it. Thank you so much for arranging it. Tim will be back shortly. He's just with Jules at the moment."

"Yes, Master. I passed him in the corridor. I'm glad you're happy. They have other rooms but I thought you might enjoy the throne in this one."

Fhionna smiled, took her seat, indicated it was time for Dog to strip, give her his collar, and then kneel on the floor in front of her.

Just as he did so, Tim came into the room, smiled at his Owner, and waited to be told what to do. He was happy he'd managed a brief hug with Aeneas before he'd run down the hall to the dungeon room.

"You may strip too. Give me your collar before you bring the bowl of water, the towel, and the shaving items over."

She looked at Aeneas to gauge his reaction to what she'd said and was happy to see he was frowning slightly. She'd planned on testing him by shaving his head but thought better of it. Instead, she would let him watch as she shaved Tim's. They would both be in shackles and Aeneas would wash Tim clean of soap and hair when she'd finished. She thought it would be another little intimate act between them but one that was very different. This was a symbolic act of slavery and often caused an emotional response. She felt it was a good way to start the session and would make Aeneas think about what would happen to him in the next few hours from a deepened understanding of his new role in life. The whole week had been extremely good fun but it was their last day together, as a threesome, and she wanted it to be remembered in a more serious manner.

* * *

Back at the hotel, both slaves undressed and knelt on the floor, beside each other, in front of the sofa. They watched as their Master poured whisky into tumblers and wondered why she hadn't asked one of them to do it for her.

Fhionna smiled to herself as she moved slowly, and quite deliberately, towards the men to hand them each a glass, before she continued across to the fridge and opened its tiny freezer compartment. She reached in to retrieve the tray of ice cubes and watched her slaves' faces as it dawned on them what she was about to do.

"Let's raise a glass in celebration of a wonderful week together."

She laughed as she lifted her hand and drank from her own 'rocks-free' glass.

Tim raised his glass and said, "Thank you for a wonderful time, Master," while Aeneas merely wrinkled his nose and sipped the liquid unwillingly.

She grinned broadly at Dog's obvious disgust and told him she wanted him to make a small toast.

As he looked up into his Master's eyes, he saw the merest hint of challenge and decided it would be in his best interest to comply. He wasn't sure what to say but quickly realised it might be a delay tactic to allow the cum from the melted ice cube a chance to spread through the liquid before he was made to drink it properly. He wondered if he was brave enough to try and gulp it, to avoid the nasty substance, but thought she would probably just order him to drink down the melted jizz on its own, after the Scotch was gone.

"To you, Master. To a wonderful week full of fun and laughter and amazing new experiences as your slave. To Tim, for his friendship and love and our deeper bond. To a safe journey home tomorrow and a pining Dog being left behind."

They all laughed at the imprinted image of a 'pining dog' and she allowed her slaves to hug her and each other before they finished their drinks and parted for the night.

* * *

On his way home, Aeneas thought about all the work he had to do over the next few weeks, and how much he hated being apart from his Master. He knew he was lucky to have her in his life but it didn't help lessen the feeling of loss when they were apart.

❧ Chapter 11 ❧

October 2012, Glasgow

A Fetish Halloween

I

Fhionna felt a little sad that Dog wasn't visiting this month but knew she would enjoy herself anyway. She didn't always play at the Halloween Violate event but she always loved the atmosphere. It was almost tangible. It crackled with anticipation and abandon.

Excitedly going from room to room to check that the decorations were up, she laughed as she brushed a few errant cobwebs from her very short hair and thought that if she'd worn a long wig she might have tried to weave some little spiders, on their webs, into it. As it was, she'd painted her hair white and teased it into very short little spikes instead. She loved Halloween and every year Violate became a spooky place to play, with realistic eyeballs hanging from cage doors and fake blood dripping down the mirror behind the cross. Instead of the usual low-key music there were intermittent moans, groans, and screams, while in the dance room upstairs there was a decidedly 'heavy metal' feel with lots of chains wrapped round the sound equipment and standard lighting for emphasis. It was a big hit with the younger members of the club and was always one of the busiest events of the year.

She'd asked Tim to pack their outfits so they could change at the club. She wasn't sure there would be enough time to do the decorating then get home again and her outfit was particularly difficult to get in to. It was based on her love of the Borg Queen in Star Trek and was made up of a latex cat suit and heavily boned latex corset that cradled her ribs. The corset was outlined in silver piping and was adorned with several sizes of tubing, which zigzagged and flowed round her body. Her cheekbones were already exaggerated with simple latex prosthetics and she had tiny, but rather sophisticated, pieces of metal glued to her temples. It would be tough to wear all night but she felt the effect would be worth it.

* * *

Tim was upstairs unzipping bags and removing steel plating for his Borg-minion armour. He liked the costume very much but he had other things on his mind. He didn't want to let his Master down, or upset her, but he had to tell her he was retiring from service. It had to be soon because he would be in hospital in a couple of days-time and had to organise his life in case he didn't get back out.

He hadn't told her he was ill, and should have done before now, but hadn't wanted her to change her lifestyle or treat him any differently than she would have normally. He knew his timing was bad and it could wait till the end of the evening or perhaps the next morning.

* * *

Ready in their costumes, Fhionna and her Borg servant headed downstairs to greet people as they arrived and hand out a free-drink token. Each guest could choose from, a Bloody Mary, a Black Devil Martini, or a glass of Pumpkin Spice Punch. She always had some sort of small gift to give out, emulating the giving of sweets but with a very adult twist. She also always offered half-price-entry and encouraged people to go 'all-out' on their costumes to make it a truly fun night to remember. These were some of the reasons why it was always one of the busiest nights on the Violate calendar and the only other night that was as nearly as busy as the Christmas party.

Feeling excited and ready for anything, she welcomed a young man who had the most incredible long hair she'd ever seen. It was quite literally down to his bum. She liked the fact that he seemed a little shy but discovered he'd taken the chance to travel all the way up from Devon to be there. He was planning to see Glasgow and possibly Edinburgh while he was in Scotland, as he'd never been before. She thought it was rather brave of him to come up on his own but also recognised that men were often brought up to be more independent than women. Society had changed a lot since she was young, of course. She'd had a great upbringing, with parents who'd never stood in her way of anything she'd wanted to do, but back then it wasn't as easy to travel and make connections with people because there were no mobile phones and the internet was pretty much in the realm of science fiction; apart from the few who could afford computers.

Welcoming his compliments on her outfit with a smile, she told Tim she was going to show Craig around. She led him away to the changing room and offered to help him into his outfit. She felt rather forward doing it but nothing-ventured-nothing-gained. She liked this youngster straightaway and wanted to see what his body was like.

As he got dressed, Fhionna talked to him about his experiences and he told her he'd only really tried things out with his long-term partner but they'd recently split. He said that, like thousands of others, he was looking for someone he trusted, could serve and devote himself to, and the only way he was going to do it was to put himself out there. He said he felt a bit like a piece of meat being thrown to the lions but he was really just a puppy in need of guidance and care. All he wanted was someone who understood what made him tick and could be happy training him to their standards.

After chatting for a while, she decided it was time to join everyone else downstairs. She told Craig the dungeon would be busy all night and asked how he'd feel about being part of her little group of friends for the evening. She could see he was delighted at being asked and was happy he showed absolutely no hesitation accepting.

"I don't usually play much at Halloween but I feel like I want to tonight."

Craig smiled at her and said he was too shy to play on his first night at a fetish event but he'd love to watch and do whatever else she told him to do.

"I hadn't realised it was your first time. I just thought you hadn't been to Violate before. Please don't worry about playing. Would you like to hold my whips for me instead?"

Craig said it would be an honour and wagged the tail of his furry dog suit.

She laughed. "I think I'll call you Pup. Just kneel on the floor out of harm's way and pass me a whip I want when I need it. The person I'm about to play with is called Martin. I've known him for a while now so don't be scared at the level of play we have together. I don't play with everyone in the same way."

Walking towards Martin, who was waiting patiently by the whipping bench in the corner of the room, she took the end of the lead that Pup had attached to the collar round his neck and took him with her.

Craig happily followed on behind, wagging his tail, which made the onlookers giggle. He enjoyed it when she turned round to see what they were laughing at and stopped in his tracks, raising his hands up to make paw shapes in front of his body and pretend to lap at her face.

Fhionna rolled her eyes at him and continued to pull him behind her. She could tell he was going to be fun to get to know a little better.

* * *

He couldn't believe his luck. He'd felt really nervous about coming all the way to Scotland from the other end of the country but was so glad he had. He'd been hoping to meet people and make some new friends but this was beyond his wildest dreams. Not only had he been taken under the wing of the woman who ran the event but she'd obviously been open to having an eager young pup follow her around.

So far he'd talked non-stop about himself. He knew he was over compensating for his naturally shy disposition but she really seemed interested in what he had to say. He hoped he hadn't bored her rigid but he got the feeling she was more than capable of telling him to be quiet, if need be. He was just so happy to skip along behind her, swaying his ass from side to side to make his tail swing, and add in the occasional hop and jump and chew on the lead like a real puppy might. He felt full of beans and didn't care who knew it.

* * *

After Fhionna had finished playing with Martin she turned her attention to Spike. Sophia wasn't well and said he could attend on his own. She'd also said he would be asking her politely if she would play with him because, 'he needed to be punished for not being attentive enough to his Mistress recently.'

She smiled as he made air-quotation-marks when he delivered the message. She told him she'd be delighted to deliver his punishment and he should remember to thank his Mistress properly when he got home. She knew Sophia would appreciate a 'blow-by-blow' description and enjoy being presented with his bruised bottom.

* * *

Pup had done well holding her whips as she played with various people. He'd pretended to hide behind his paws when it got a bit much for him and she liked his sense of humour. There was a certain vitality she was drawn to. She found him amusing but also quite earnest in his need to serve someone special in his life. She knew she would enjoy his company outside the club too and thought she might offer to show him around some of Glasgow the next day. It would depend on his plans, of course, but he obviously didn't know anyone in Scotland and thought he might find some company fun. At least on part of his trip.

II

At home, the next morning, she told Tim all about the young puppy she'd met, that they'd chatted for most of the evening, and how she'd found out about his masochistic nature. She told him how cheeky and funny the boy was and how she'd offered to show him around Glasgow but that he'd said he was too shy. She went on to describe the fun she'd had with Martin and Spike, and a few others, and how sorry she was that he himself wasn't feeling up to any play.

She was aware she was rambling but she wasn't so self-absorbed that she didn't notice Tim wince.

"You certainly don't need to feel guilty. I accept that sometimes play isn't possible, so don't worry you've upset me because you haven't."

Fhionna watched him as he tried to find the right words to express how he was feeling. It was obvious he needed to get something off his chest and she felt she should encourage him a little.

"We've known each other a very long time and I hope you know I'm your friend as well as your boss. You can tell me anything and I'll always respect your privacy."

Tim smiled at the use of the word 'boss' and knew he'd have to tell her what was on his mind.

"I have some news but I don't know how to say it."

He looked at the floor for courage but she told him to lift his head and continue.

"I've had some bad news. I'm ill and I'm due to go into hospital in a couple of days and to be honest I'm not sure that I'll be coming back out."

Tim looked at his Master's face, took her hand, and moved in closer to her legs as he sat in his normal position on the floor at her feet.

"It's not cancer but, to be honest, they're not sure what it is. I'll be having lots of tests and they want me to stay in to go through them, to keep an eye on me." Tim paused and took a deep breath. "This means I'm going to have to retire as your slave. I'm so sorry, Master. I hope you can forgive me."

Fhionna sat silently on the couch and listened, trying to take it all in. She listened while he described the tests and possible treatments he was about to go through, how he hated to let her down in any way, and how he was glad to see she was happy and had Bunty, Poppy and now Dog to take care of her. She listened while he told her how happy he'd been as her slave and how she'd given his life purpose. He told her how much he loved her and worshipped her and thanked her for including him in her life.

Eventually, wiping away the tears which were rolling down her cheeks, she spoke to him for the first time in what seemed like an absolute age.

"I have so many questions, not just about the illness and how you found out, but why you haven't let me help you. Why you haven't told me before now. I must admit I'm feeling rather lost."

Tim, for the first time since the death of her father, when he'd happened to be there on the morning he passed away, took to his feet and sat beside her on the sofa, hugging her to him. He felt her melt into his arms as he stroked her head, gently trying to console her.

"Isn't it selfish of me to need comforting when it's you who are ill?"

Fhionna pulled herself together and asked if he would let her look after him for the rest of the day.

Tim smiled and said, "Yes, Master," maybe for the last time.

* * *

The day had passed really quickly. They'd spent hours together, just chatting. They reminisced about some of the fun they'd had, like the time she'd organised to kidnap someone from the airport, at his request, and had taken him into the woods to flog him.

Tim had been the chauffeur, with his impeccable suit and cap, and she had worn stiletto heels, seamed-stockings, and a tight pencil skirt; like one might wear to the office for a business meeting. He'd opened the car door for her, as he usually did, then followed at a discrete distance. She'd admitted being a little on edge because she really didn't want to be caught out as she frogmarched the sub back to her car, bundled him onto the floor of the back seat, tied him up and put a pillowcase over his head. As it turned out, the airport hadn't been a problem but they'd nearly been caught by a dog walker in the forest. She'd decided, then and there, she would take her captive back to the dungeon instead and, even though this hadn't been part of the original plan, it seemed the submissive was happy to go along with whatever his simulated captor had in mind. The drive back had taken a full two hours but he hadn't complained.

"You know, I think he actually enjoyed being driven around, feeling helpless, not knowing where he would end up."

"I'm sure you're right, Master. It added to the thrill of it all. He went from knowing what was going to happen to feeling truly vulnerable, which was sort of the point really."

As they'd moved onto other stories, and talked about New York, she realised their trip to Manhattan had been meant as a parting gift.

"You know, I feel like I want to punish you for keeping this quiet but I'm not going to."

Tim smiled. "And that's exactly why I couldn't tell you. We'd have missed out on so much. Not that I'm a lover of pain, as you know, Master, but your enjoyment of it, of me being able to take it for you, has meant the world to me."

Tim paused.

"I'm ok with you letting Bunty and the others know what's going on. I wish it wasn't happening but there's not much I can do about it. I've had many wonderful years putting my fate in your hands."

It was now Tim's turn to cry and she hugged him.

Asking for the details of his hospital admission, Fhionna insisted she would see him as soon as they let him have visitors. "I guess you'll need to start getting used to calling me by my actual name. Won't that be awful!"

She smiled as she said it, and he agreed it would be completely abhorrent.

* * *

The few days that followed were filled with laughter, more tears, and then laughter again. They'd enjoyed good food together and some of the other, usual, activities they'd shared as Master and slave, but she refused to play with him because she didn't think he should be going into hospital with bruises and welts.

She'd been surprised, once the time had finally come for him to leave, when he'd said he would like to offer her some advice.

"Please pursue the young pup, Master. Don't give up on new relationships, or potential play partners, because of me. I would hate the thought of you not living life to the full because of being sad. I'll look forward to the day you can come visit your old slave and hopefully you'll bring some lovely chocolate, if I'm allowed it."

Fhionna promised he'd see her again soon but trying to smile, as she waved goodbye, had been the hardest thing she'd done in a very long time.

III

Craig lived way down in Devon so it made it more difficult to train him properly but so far he'd done really well and completed all the tasks she'd sent by email or text. One of the first things she'd requested was to shave his body. She'd made it quite clear she preferred smooth skin on her potential subs, and thought it would be a very good first test. She'd laughed when he'd initiated a 'discussion' about it, saying how much he loved all of his hair because it made him feel more like an animal, but she'd eventually asked if he would do it for her. She'd said that he could keep the mane on his head but she'd like the rest to go.

She found it pleasurable to know she could possibly affect change in the young man's psyche and also asked him to keep a record of his thoughts and feelings as he developed in his submission.

* * *

She sat at the kitchen table and watched the steam rise from her coffee cup for a while before she opened her laptop to read Pup's fist diary entry. Finally, perching her glasses on the end of her nose, she clicked on the little envelope symbol and started to read.

Hair removal

Wow. I really didn't want to do that and you know what? I think she knew. It was a challenge. I loved my hair. It made me feel like a lion. But I am a pup and an obedient one and I will do what I'm told. The things I don't want to do (asked to give up) but do out of devotion are what mark me as a growing submissive – not the things I exclusively take enjoyment from. So my body is now bare. I'm staring at the pimples caused by the mid October air. It's a new feeling I'll have to get used to but I am prepared. I will make my new Mistress proud. My body is hers to shape (and shave). I know that I can consciously and lovingly submit to this woman. I want to be ready for all the things I won't want to do so that I can do them well. I know I will be kindly guided and benevolently moulded to better and improve myself. I will give everything I am able to give because I want to and am happy to. I love how the arrangement came about, being asked if I was prepared to do it, coaxed not forced. I was given a choice, being asked can you do this. I can't express enough how much that meant the world to me. It's more inspiring and intoxicating than any order. Being asked, 'Can you do this?' or 'Can I rely on you?' inspires a submissive to give everything they have in the tank, and more.

Fhionna reread the email a few times before making some notes of her own. She didn't often feel the need or want to chart a sub's progress by writing herself, but in this case she thought she might find it helpful.

Tim had given her a beautiful notepad for Christmas one year. It was leather-backed and large enough to record one's thoughts in.

Perhaps he'd been subtly trying to tell her something. She'd loved the gift and thought that it could now be put to good use recording Pup's words and her own reactions to them. She also hoped Tim would like the fact she'd found something worthwhile to chart within its handcrafted pages.

Taking her laptop and the notepad upstairs to the tiny little attic room she didn't use very often, she printed out the email and made her own entry on the opposite page:

- *I'm impressed by such early signs of devotion. I hadn't expected Pup to be so well developed as many his age are not. He is already showing signs of deep submission and I must keep track of his feelings and thoughts. This is only the beginning, and I won't see him in person often, but it's a promising start.*

- *The next task will be very different. It will be to become an animal, proper. I feel he expresses an interest in dehumanisation and so the next step will be to help him achieve this on a deeper level than just dressing as a dog.*

- *I also feel his dehumanisation links deeply with his want and need for chastity. To him it may mean more than submission, although it will undoubtedly feature greatly in the relationship he chooses to have with a special Dominant. He seeks to keep himself in check, not through any special morality or religion, as such, but through a purifying ritual of abstinence he hopes will impress the person he eventually gives himself too. It seems important to his core sense of self.*

Finishing the last paragraph and rereading her words, Fhionna was satisfied that she was going to be able to help Pup achieve his goals. She felt an overwhelming desire to do so. She liked the boy and felt sure she could gently coax him to accomplish his dreams. It was, she decided, a new and exciting adventure, even though she'd been rather nervous at first. She wasn't used to such a large age difference and she didn't know how it would impact their play together, should that day ever come.

* * *

A few days had passed and his next diary was due to drop into her virtual-mail-bag. This time she expected a report on how he'd felt eating most of his meals from a dog bowl on the floor in his room. He still lived with his parents and she knew this would have presented an interesting dimension to the task. She'd also asked him, as if that wasn't enough, to endure different forms of pain or difficulty while he ate and she was looking forward to reading the result.

Boiled cabbage and gravy dinner from a bowl on the floor

Holy crap! Another intense dinner. I swear my mind is beginning to associate eating with BDSM. Taking in nutrients and giving back pain, struggle, and extreme concentration in return. I was challenged to make my evening meal more of an ordeal but to do this in a way I chose myself, for her amusement. I know I'd rambled on about having my anus filled in a previous email or two, or three, and thought that to have a dildo securely in situ while I ate from my dog bowl on the floor would make her happy. I knew she would applaud the fact that if I so obviously couldn't concentrate on eating my food (and be grateful for it) then I should eat it with something long and stiff rammed into my butt and locked there until every morsel was finished. I was sweating from the exertion of inserting the dildo, and the struggle to lock it in place within the leather harness that ran between my buttocks up to my waist, then around my waist with a belt, but what I hadn't bargained for was that the continued dipping of my head into the bowl to lap at the slop would cause what felt like never ending stimulation to my prostate. The deep discomfort of the dildo as it was sucked in meant that every bob and lunge encouraged a stream of pre-cum to drip onto the carpet. I had to dig really deep to find a quiet place in my mind where, for just a moment, I could block out all of the signals my body was sending to my brain and focus on the task of eating. I exhaled with frustration, at one point, as I didn't know if I would manage it. I knew that I must and the more I thought about it the more I felt like I was being watched by her. Because of that, I knew I would continue until every last drop of the soggy cabbage and cold gravy was lapped up and swallowed. Even now, at the beginning of her guidance and teaching, I realise all I want to do is what I'm supposed to do. However complex or simple the challenge, the task is the task, whatever that task is. If it's what is required then it's what I will do. I am rewarded, every time, with a great freedom that comes from obedience and the comfort I take from releasing control to such a powerful force. I'm realising that every opportunity to please and obey her is a gift.

Fhionna was hardly able to contain her excitement as she read his latest offering. The fact that Pup viewed his growing submission as freedom was a revelation. She knew it was, or could be, but also thought very few people actually got to experience it on such a meaningful level.

The words she recorded beside his came easily:

• *Pup's mental maturity is astounding. He is very developed in his thought process, certainly in terms of his own needs and desires. His self-expression is advanced and this shows signs of someone who has taken the time to get to know himself, and even enjoys such self-exploration.*

• *This is someone who loves to be challenged both physically and mentally and enjoys someone of equal or more advanced intelligence. That someone needs, however, to be caring and non-judgemental in their approach. Respect is an important foundation of a relationship, for him, and it should be delivered both ways; earned by each person.*

• *I feel he will respond well to time periods, set out for him, where he can devote himself to quiet reflection but in a BDSM context, perhaps kneeling for half an hour with his favourite gag in his mouth. This will not only help him 'centre' his own thoughts but may well help him to feel close to me when he needs to.*

She decided she needn't wait to send her new sub his next task. It was one that could be completed that day. She often had his work schedule to hand, when she read his emails, because it helped to be able to judge how much time he could dedicate to his instructions. She felt that their interactions so far, paired with his level of philosophical maturity, showed he was able, and willing, to give some deeper thought to what it meant to be a masochist and a submissive. How he thought the two connected. This was a subject close to her own heart and she wondered if his theories would align with hers.

Masochism

When I met her for the first time at Violate we didn't talk much about masochism and submission, and the differences between them, but I think this is something that interests her and I've been given the task of writing about what makes me tick. I believe masochism, for me, ties in with a desire for chastity and denial, as well as a physical need for acts of sadism. I've come to realise that emotional masochism is just as important to me. This sounds very selfish and I guess that's what she wants me to think about and explore and it's why, recently, I've been reconsidering the terminology and what it means to really call myself such a thing. I find controlled levels of pain relaxing but I'm realising that it's actually the response from her, the pleasure she derives from the acts she asks me to perform, that fuels my desire to take more and do more. To not focus on my own selfish feelings of enduring small levels of pain but to completely trust her and give her the control to give as little or as much pain as she sees fit, knowing I will take it just for her amusement. I do enjoy the rush of the roller coaster ride and the physical discomfort (like many a serious masochist might) but not, now, with the goal of self-fulfilment because, without hers, it has become irrelevant.

* * *

She enjoyed reading all of Pup's diaries. She was impressed by how someone fairly inexperienced could write with such passion and clarity. She was enjoying giving him tasks to perform and helping him develop, not just in his sexuality or as a submissive, but as a person in general. She often found one was hard to separate from the other, though, because if he knew himself well, on a generic level, then it would be easier to understand himself as a submissive person. It would become more obvious, therefore, how he might develop an understanding of what his Dom might want from him and how to give it.

Feeling a strong urge to reply to him with a handwritten letter, she sat down in her favourite seat in the living room and thought about the words. As she gazed out over the garden, she noticed the leaves were falling from the branches of the trees that surrounded the lawn. She loved to see the red and gold flashes of colour as they spun in the breeze to their resting place below. Not much of the lawn could be seen now, and the smoothness of the external carpet, which was so beautiful in the height of summer, had become jagged and rough.

Fhionna felt inspired by the change in her garden and knew she would support Pup through his own transition from submissive to slave.

Dear Pup,

Thank you for your diary entries. They show me you have a keen mind and also a strong will to succeed.

It can take years for someone to reach the level of self-awareness you've expressed.

You obviously have the ability to analyse your actions and motives but not overthink them, giving you a unique ability to be able to learn and develop but also to be led. A wonderful gift to anyone you wish to submit to.

You have the ability to be able to think for yourself and not have to be taken every step of the way like a bull with a ring through its nose, on the end of a chain. You are able to think about what would please me, what might be allowed, and put this into action when required.

You're allowed to have pride in your actions and achievements. To know you have done well is a wonderful feeling and I encourage that. Submission takes work and dedication but, at times, you may fail at something you've tried to do. There's no shame in that. Your best effort is what matters most.

I am here for you if you are struggling and need some help. If you were having difficulty and didn't reach out to me, and I found out about it at a later time, I would not be happy.

Self-doubt can be destructive. Staying in the present and not worrying about future events will help. There is no need to worry about what may or may not happen. I am your guide and you can trust me. Guiding you and training you, to please me, makes me happy.

I will always look after you, gently push you, and listen to you... in return for you listening to me.

ఞ Chapter 12 ౪

November 2012, Glasgow

Masochist slave

I

Stephan was due to arrive in an hour for dinner, so she didn't have a lot of time to spend getting ready. She felt a little drained from all Tim's news and more than a little sad. She wasn't entirely sure she felt up to any play that night, but knew he was driving a long way to see her and that they, too, had a lot to talk about.

Deciding to pour herself a glass of wine from the bottle Tim had decanted before he left, Fhionna thought she'd order food to be delivered to the house. She loved the little Italian place in the village and she knew he would love their food as much as she did. She was really happy he was staying in Glasgow for a couple of days. He'd said he would book a hotel but she'd insisted he be spared the expense by staying at her home. He'd accepted the offer but said if she grew tired of his company all she had to do was let him know. She'd laughed and promised she would kick him out if she felt the need.

She got dressed in her favourite skinny jeans and a large woolly jumper before heading down to the kitchen to pick up the number for the restaurant from the little pile of notes that were kept in a large wooden bowl on the countertop.

Just as she started to enter the numbers into her phone, she heard the doorbell jingle. She looked at her watch and muttered, "Right on time," before heading to answer it.

As she swung the door open she realised he was brandishing a picnic basket and a huge bouquet of flowers. Fhionna laughed when his grin appeared from behind the flowers, accompanied by the words, "For you, Madam. A rather tired but extremely excited male at your service."

"Come in. I was just about to order some food but I see you've thought of a much better idea. I have the wine and you, it seems, have everything else."

Wrapped in duvets, they happily settled down in front of the summer house on the checked blanket he'd brought to protect them from the crispy grass he thought they might encounter, and chatted about his drive up, the adventures they'd both had since she'd seen him last, and then finally to tell him the news about Tim, whom he'd come to know quite well over the last few months.

"That's so sad. I'm sorry. If there's anything I can do, even if it's to drive home again, then please, just ask."

She smiled and said she was glad of his company but admitted to being a little tired.

"Then I shall retire to bed when you require it. Just instruct me. I'm here to make you happy."

There was a short silence as they both let the words he'd said sink in.

"Wow. I don't think I've said that to you before but, to be honest, it's the thought, closely followed by an actual physical feeling, that I've been experiencing more and more. It makes sense to me in a way that it's never made sense before. I've never been interested in submission or even finding someone to regularly see for my pain needs but there's something about you that inspires me."

Once he'd finished talking, she smiled at him and took his hand, a very intimate gesture that she hadn't shared with him before, and which made his ears turn crimson. She told him he'd pleased her very much and she was glad he'd voiced his thoughts, especially because he was obviously feeling awkward. She laughed to signal she was teasing him a little and he laughed too.

The food had been exquisite, as she'd known it would be because he was an exceptional cook, and they'd continued to chat inside by the fire which she'd lit while he was retrieving the quilts. She was pleased to see he was happy to sit on the floor without having had any prompt to do so. Their relationship hadn't been based on these familiar rituals she loved to do with her slaves, but it seemed this was about to change and she felt her excitement grow. She felt that a whole new level of their relationship was about to unfold.

"I've come to realise, rather shockingly, that my place is at your feet, should you want it to be. The way you take great pleasure from causing me the pain I crave has been the basis of our friendship and will probably remain very important to me, but I want it to progress beyond that single but very beautiful facet."

Fhionna listened quietly. She felt it was what she'd wanted for a while but was waiting for him to be ready to make the next move, towards one of submission, rather than push him in that direction. She was, after all, very happy to cause him pain and for there to be no other aspect to their play together, but she was ecstatic to hear he was interested in pleasing her in other ways.

Jumping to his feet, rather too quickly, Stephan apologised and rushed from the room. She laughed as she watched his large, six-foot-four-inch frame, run away like an excited boy and return carrying a flat package in his hands; one, she noted with pleasure, that was wrapped in deep red tissue paper and tied with black velvet ribbons.

He knelt in front of her and presented her with the gift.

"I completely forgot about this. It's something I hope you will love and treasure. I remembered who your favourite artist was and wanted to get you something by him. I must admit I have an ulterior motive though, and hope you will accept my proposal to be your slave in training."

She grinned and said she was very excited by both gifts; the gift of his submission and the canvas. In that order.

Holding the painting before her in outstretched arms, she admired the reprint of Hieronymus Bosch's 'The Haywain Triptych' and its depiction of man's decent into hell. She was impressed he'd remembered her love of this particular scene, especially since they'd discussed so much over the last few months.

"It's truly magnificent. Thank you so much."

Wandering about the room, she imagined where she would hang it for optimum visual effect. She hadn't noticed at that point but he was smiling as he watched her flit from one wall to another, cocking her head on one side like it was the most important decision in the world.

Fhionna eventually sat on the couch because she guessed they had more to discuss than the painting and she wanted to see what else he had to say.

Stephan asked for permission to touch her feet and rub them gently between his warm hands, so she relaxed back into the folds of the quilt and raised a delicate foot for his attention. She encouraged him to explain his idea of serving her; without the pain they both clearly enjoyed.

He looked up at her from his position on the floor and then turned his attention back to what he was doing. She thought how beautiful it would be to one day hear him say the words, 'Yes, Master,' and hoped what he said next would give some indication if it was possible.

"Actually I thought about nothing else while I was driving up this afternoon. I was nervous as hell that it wouldn't be something you'd want from me; having slaves already. I almost talked myself out of it but thought nothing ventured nothing gained. I've seen, first hand, how others respond to you, your gentle manner. The way you so obviously care about each one of your submissives, their happiness and their well-being. I wondered if this was something I could really give you and decided that I needed to try, if you'd have me."

He stopped speaking and waited for her reply. Once it had been well and truly established she was over the moon, they continued to talk for hours about what she would expect from him, what he was willing to try and what, if any, his hard limits were.

Fhionna was a little disappointed when he said that the only thing he could never do was to be with another man, but she had Poppy and Aeneas to interact with each other, if she so desired, so accepted his limit.

He went on to say he'd do anything else to the best of his ability but that it might take him a little time to adjust to this new role in their relationship.

* * *

By the end of the night it had been decided that the first step was to give him his slave name. Fhionna said it would be her choice but he had the right to question it, as long as he had a good reason. She smiled as he wrinkled his nose at her and said that as long as it wasn't 'Fluffy' he was sure he could live with her decision.

* * *

The next morning, Stephan woke to the sound of the alarm on his phone going off, telling him it was time to get up and to do the first of what he suspected would be many tasks for his new Mistress. The night before, she'd enquired if he'd be comfortable calling her Master and he'd asked if he could work up to it.

He thought about this exchange as he made his way down to the kitchen, dressed only in a black leather collar that had been waiting for him on the table in his room. It felt a little odd to be wandering around her house completely naked and collared but it was also exciting and he felt certain physical stirrings as he padded downstairs to start their breakfast. He'd been told there were plenty of provisions in the fridge and it was all food she liked so he couldn't go far wrong.

He found himself whistling as he went about the business of setting the table and wondering how he would let her know breakfast was ready. He would normally have brazenly rapped on the bedroom door of any guests in his own house or shouted up the stairs that grub was up. He couldn't well do the latter but he could do the former, if done with slightly more consideration.

* * *

Upstairs, Fhionna stretched like a cat and smiled as she heard Stephan's rather tuneless noise drift up through the floorboards. She was amused at the happy, carefree sound but also because she knew he would be wary about making any mistakes so early on in their new relationship as Mistress and slave. She felt satisfied that she would be able to train him to her ways and had already picked his new slave name based on her experience of their play together. She would tell him what it was soon, but not yet. At that moment, she was quite content to lie back and giggle at the thought of how he'd let her know her breakfast was ready. A rather small conundrum, in the circumstances, but an opportunity for some fun.

He was putting the finishing touches to a concoction of eggs, onions, tomatoes and fried potatoes that he'd learned to make as a young boy in the kitchen with his mum. He'd made some tweaks to the recipe to make it more 'adult' but the basic ingredients were the same. He then placed some napkins into silver rings he'd found in a drawer and used the black ribbon from the wrapping on the painting to cut then tie round them in tiny little bows. He thought it looked stylish and hoped she would like the little touch of elegance. Everything was ready, and all that was left to do was to choose his approach of service. He decided to tiptoe upstairs and knock softly on her bedroom door and wait to be told to enter. This seemed good manners, more than anything else, at this point.

* * *

Fhionna was sitting up against her feathery pillows when he landed his first soft knock. She stifled a little laugh and ignored it. It was more than a few seconds before the second, slightly louder rap came. She ignored that too. It was even longer before he attempted a third one, a full blown knock with his knuckles, and she held her hand over her mouth to silence herself. Next she saw the door being slowly opened and quick as a flash she shouted, "I didn't say you could come in," and watched as the door quickly shut again. She'd done this before, when getting to know her darling Bunty, but it never grew tiresome. She was having fun but thought she'd better put him out of his misery, so she bounced out of bed and swung the door open to find poor Stephan kneeling on the floor with a slightly perplexed look on his face. She laughed and told him to stand up before telling him she was playing with him.

He grinned at her and said, "Yes, Mistress, I guessed that eventually but not before you shouted at me."

* * *

After breakfast, which Fhionna had to admit was somewhat of a surprise and very enjoyable, she thought it was time to play. She knew Stephan was staying for a couple of days so she'd sourced and bought a large roll of barbed-wire. She was very excited because she'd found something new to try, which was difficult when you'd been a Dom for so long. She was also thrilled because her new masochist slave loved to receive pain as much as she loved to give it.

She let the thought sink in and corrected herself. He did love to receive pain but it was pain from her, specifically, it seemed. She believed this was one reason he was developing feelings of submission towards her. She also knew, even though he hadn't expressed it exactly in this way, he admired how caring she was. He seemed to need this; to feel respected and protected. All of these things were good. She'd no doubt in her mind he could succeed at anything he put his mind to and they were already firm friends, which was a great base to build on.

Wandering over to the sink where he was washing the dishes, she came up behind him and told him he could finish it later but now she wanted him on his hands and knees in the dungeon.

Stephan said, "Yes, Mistress," and walked calmly towards the kitchen door but before he got there, however, she'd said, "And you can crawl there."

* * *

Half an hour had passed before she eventually entered the dungeon and she was happy to see he was still on his hands and knees but with the added bonus of having his head lowered with his forehead touching the floor. His hands were out in front of him with their palms open and yielding, facing upwards. A very submissive posture.

As she moved toward him she had a sudden urge to run her nails over his back and underneath to his large, erect nipples. She knew about his love of nipple torture and it was obvious the professional Doms he'd seen, over the last few years, had all taken pleasure in focusing on the area.

Hearing the low growls of satisfaction as she dug her nails deep into the fleshy mounds, she decided she would tell him the name she'd chosen for him. He hadn't moved from his passive position while she'd touched him, and she was pleased he was waiting to be told to do so.

"I appreciate your effort and it's the beautiful noises and movements you make when I hurt you that have made the choice of your slave name so easy. From now on you shall be known as Beast.

The blank tag on the collar you're wearing will be engraved with your new name while you're here."

She smiled as he stayed silent but carefully moved a hand to gently stroke the foot positioned at his head before moving it back to its original place. The gesture was full of innocence and he'd shown his devotion with this one simple act. Beast had accepted his name with grace and she felt she'd chosen well. She felt it suited him but she also wanted him to be content with it. She didn't feel this was a weakness but only showed she cared about her slave's happiness as well as her own. She knew a name was important and firmly believed a slave could embody its nuances.

Feeling rather excited, Fhionna left him in position on the floor and set about unravelling the wire she'd bought. She had gloves and cutters, and it had been disinfected, so all was ready. She cut the wire into lengths and decided he would become her work of art. The fact that there would be some wonderful pain along the way just heightened her sense of joy and creativity. She would bind him in it and take photos of the end result before playing with his nipples again and watching him squirm beneath its thorns. She knew to take it slowly, being her first time with the wire medium, but also knew it was only the beginning of the fun she would have with it.

Instructing Beast to sit up, she placed a hood on his head. This would not only protect his identity, should she decide to upload some tasteful photos onto her website, but it would also protect his face from the tiny sharp sections of wire if she decided his head would become part of her art. She'd seen pictures on other sites which catered to barbed-wire enthusiasts, and had witnessed some amazing positions of slaves hung by, or wrapped in, wire; leaving no part of their body untouched. She'd happily clicked her way through hundreds of images and wanted to try some of it for herself. For now though, her focus would be to learn how the wire could be manipulated and how best to make it take the shapes she wanted.

* * *

Beast was mesmerized by his Mistress' focus and concentration. It made him feel very close to her. The fact that she'd brought something scary into their play together was inspirational but also the way she took care in learning how to use it was very endearing. He watched as she cut lengths of wire and made it bend to her will, much like she did her slaves. He felt a little nervous as she approached him with gloved hands and a glint in her eye but was also surprised by an overwhelming feeling of need.

* * *

Fhionna began to wrap the wire round his shoulders, then moved onto his torso, carefully and slowly applying it to his skin. She loved the raw look of it and knew she'd soon want to press the barbs into his flesh. Before she did that, however, she wound some wire round his head, making sure it lay over his eyes but that the little spikes were all facing outward. The end result would be beautiful but safety was also a concern.

She sighed happily as she worked, stopping sometimes to decide where the next piece would go or to move some of the barbs that were already in place. She looked into his eyes from time to time to gauge his reaction, but he was mostly looking straight ahead as if he had become her clay to mould. She appreciated this but decided it was time to make the beast growl, so she removed her gloves, sat on the floor in front of him, and began to move her fingers over the wire and press down with increasing force. The wire she'd decided to place between his lips was not meant to act as a gag but it would certainly lend an interesting aspect to their play. She made a 'mental note' to fashion a wire gag, later, because she wanted to see him suffer a little.

* * *

Beast was aware of his own heavy breathing as his Mistress worked on his body. He was beginning to feel the sharp spikes but they were little more than slight pressure points, which he knew might change as his Mistress' thirst for pain grew. He was concentrating on staying still and kept his eyes facing forward; so she wasn't distracted by his gaze. He could tell she was creating something, that this was the beginning of some special play together, and felt a little frightened to be the focus of such obvious intent. It wasn't that he didn't trust her because he'd never have considered trying to be someone's slave he couldn't completely rely on to keep him safe. It was more that he felt her power, he supposed, and it was impressive.

He ran the tip of his tongue along the wire between his lips but didn't feel any of the spikes. He guessed she'd used the straight part so she wouldn't cause damage. He was in no doubt about her sadistic yearning but this 'sympathy' was a lovely paradox. This made him determined to encourage her total freedom. He wanted her to push his boundaries and, perhaps her own too, so thought he'd offer to make a proper ball gag from the wire. Spikes be damned.

* * *

The play that afternoon had resulted in lots of blood and Fhionna was delighted. She was tired but very happy. He'd done incredibly well to overcome his nerves and had not only fashioned a gag from the wire but had also asked to be given a little time to make a wire implement that could be used to beat him. She'd been so impressed by the request that she'd left him alone in the dungeon for an hour to see what he could come up with. The result had been amazing and the paddle he'd constructed meant the blood had splattered his thighs, the floor, and her.

She smiled as she thought about it and how she'd set up a little camera in the corner of the room to try and capture the scene. She was sure she'd retrieve some beautiful stills from the footage and looked forward to editing it. The short film would also make interesting viewing for some of her more 'advanced' player friends.

* * *

That evening, Beast had woken to find himself chained to the wall and wondered how long he'd been asleep. He wondered if she'd been in to look at him or if she'd been busy elsewhere in the house.

After these fleeting thoughts, his hand went to his buttocks to examine the marks the paddle had left behind and was a little disappointed because there were none. It had been a fantastic experience though. He'd been impressed by how she'd decided to 'warm him up' with a cane first. This made him laugh. The thought of her other slaves starting off with the cane was rather doubtful. Still, he was glad he could bring something new to the table. Being a masochist had its advantages. It was being submissive he would find a challenge, long-term, but he thought he was doing ok so far. She seemed to like him making suggestions for their play together. Again, he wasn't sure if she allowed anyone else to do this and so he felt quite privileged to be able to be part of the process. He didn't doubt for a second that if she wanted less of his input she would tell him.

* * *

Fhionna opened her eyes and yawned. She'd fallen asleep uploading the photos and had only just realised it was getting dark outside. It was dark earlier, these days. The sun would be almost completely down but the horizon beyond the trees and the summerhouse would still be a scarlet slash. She loved the twilight hours between the sunny but ever-chillier days and the darker, starry autumnal nights. It was a time of day that suggested a shift between moods, perhaps moving from energetic enthusiasm to a more subdued élan.

Her thoughts mimicked the changing light and she smiled as she remembered Beast was still chained in the dungeon. She wondered if he was awake and thinking about what had happened to him that afternoon.

Slipping from her bed, she climbed rather sleepily into her robe and freshened up in the bathroom before going to the kitchen to put the kettle on. She then went downstairs and opened the door to look in on her slave. She smiled at him when she found him propped up against the back wall watching the door.

"I'm assuming it's 'good evening, Mistress,' although I'm not at all sure what time it is so please excuse me if I'm wrong. There's also one other thing I should correct. Good evening, Master."

Beast smiled and went on to say that after the afternoon's playtime together he had no doubt that she deserved to be addressed by her proper title and he was willing to dismiss all of the male-centric connotations of the word for one that meant 'his Owner.' He hoped this would meet with her approval and apologised that he'd had to give it a little thought.

Without making a fuss about the change in circumstance, Fhionna said, "Wonderful. I'm ravenous so you can make dinner," and moved to unlock him. "This time you'll be eating from a bowl on the floor at my feet."

∞ Chapter 13 ∞

December 2012, Glasgow

What A Wonderful Year

I

Aeneas anxiously checked his watch. It was already ten after eleven and his flight had been circling in the air for a while, making him at least an hour late. He hated being late, so damn much, but especially because his Master was picking him up herself. It was bad enough that it was the only flight he could get, but the delay would mean she'd be driving them along the dark country streets. He guessed she was more than capable but also knew she loved being chauffeured.

She'd told him in a recent email that Tim had retired from service because he was seriously ill and wondered when she'd raise the subject. He was out of the loop because he hadn't seen his Owner for two months and he wanted nothing more than some quality time with her without concentrating on anyone else. He knew this was completely selfish but he couldn't help it; even though it conflicted with his feelings for Tim. As always, he would just have to go with his Master's flow and when she wanted to talk about it he would listen. He also wondered if he would get to see Tim again, which made him sad on a whole different level.

* * *

When the plane finally touched down, Aeneas almost ran to the baggage collection, through the double sliding doors, and sprinted across the concourse and out of the main entrance to the pickup point. It was only then that he realised, because he was so late, Master would probably have had to park the car properly and go into the airport to find him.

"You seem to have misplaced someone, Sir. Can I help you?"

Aeneas turned round to say that he didn't think they could and saw Fhionna grinning at him like she'd been watching him this whole time, buzzing around the building like a tormented wasp.

"It's so good to see you, sorry I'm so late, stupid plane kept circling, my bag was delayed and the last one to come through. I've had so much coffee I think I might be flying on my own, I'm just so happy to be here, it's been ages, how are you, can I kiss your hand?..."

Fhionna laughed at him and told him to take a deep breath.

He did as he was told, smiled at her, and finally settled on, "Hi, Master."

"It's great to see you too, Aeneas. We have a lot to talk about but it's getting late so it can all wait until tomorrow."

Aeneas plodded along behind his Owner with a very tired but very happy smile on his face. He was too tired, perhaps, to worry about anything that had been on his mind recently and, as always, he was struck by her quiet confidence and lack of drama.

* * *

After a light supper, Fhionna instructed Dog to get some sleep.

"Go down to the dungeon and sleep in the cage tonight. You may just get up when you're ready to make breakfast. It really is good to have my lovely American slave here again and I'm eager to see if you've remembered all your training."

She smiled down at her slave as he sat on the floor at her feet, his handsome features enhanced by the collar round his neck and the slightly greyer hair at his temples. He looked completely shattered and she thought he would benefit from some really good rest before the adventures of the next two days unfolded. She wanted to talk about Tim and allow Dog some time to go see his friend on his own but it could wait.

* * *

Aeneas had a quick wash before crawling into his cage. He hoped he would be able to sleep through until a reasonable hour. It was weird being in the house with just Master there; with no Tim to give him helpful hints on how to behave properly. He guessed he knew enough by now though.

He stretched out as much as he could and enjoyed the sound the door made as it clunked into place. He felt ready to sleep but found his mind wandering to his feelings about his Master instead. Well, not her as such, but more like Tim's relationship with her and his own relationship within that dynamic. He thought about how much he'd been his mentor, as she'd openly encouraged him to be, and how there'd been no jealousy on Tim's part at the arrival of someone new to serve.

As time had gone on he could see their deep connection and was amazed by how much Tim could put her needs and wants before his own. Aeneas knew he would struggle with this because he wasn't quite as selfless. He'd hoped, back then, that he'd be invited into her inner circle to be given the chance to prove himself but if it hadn't been for Tim, it might never have happened.

There was no doubt he'd miss the man but he wondered how Fhionna was coping with the loss. He guessed she had lots of friends to rally round in times of need but he also knew she was a private person and imagined she might not have told lots of people how she was feeling. This made it even more important that he was able to put all self-centred thoughts aside and be there for her, if she needed him to be.

* * *

Fhionna looked at the clock beside her bed and realised it was ten am. She very rarely stayed in bed that late but she hadn't slept very well. She'd been too excited at the prospect of having her lovely American slave in the house and found her mind flitting between what she'd planned for his stay and how he'd conduct himself, now that Tim wasn't around to help him. She doubted that Dog would ever be perfect but somehow it didn't matter and it amused her that he tried so hard and sometimes failed so spectacularly. There would always be room for improvement but this was part of his charm, in some ways. She definitely enjoyed the challenge he presented and was sure he would serve her well, for the most part. She was also sure she'd need to punish him fairly often but hopefully he would learn from any mistakes he made and it would strengthen his resolve to be a better slave.

She hummed a familiar little tune as she took a quick shower, then wandered downstairs to see what her slave was making for breakfast. She'd heard him clattering about in the kitchen and wondered what on earth he was doing.

As she stood in the doorway, she heard him singing to himself so she stopped to listen to the Hebrew for a little while before going in properly.

"Good morning, Aeneas. What a lovely song. I can only imagine what it means but I hope you'll share its significance while we eat."

Dog spun round on his toes as he heard her voice.

"Good morning, Master. I hope you slept well. I hope I didn't wake you up."

"No, I was already awake and I'm rather hungry."

"Yes, Master. I hope you like it. I'm not a great cook because I don't do it very often but my mum taught me some dishes when I was young. They were mostly kosher dishes so I've adapted one a little. I hope it tastes ok."

Fhionna smiled at her slave and took a seat at the table as he brought over the food and mugs of coffee. She also smiled at the thought of how different his approach to making breakfast was, as compared to Beast. He was obviously enough of a cook to be able to adapt a dish but the finesse of the table and the almost clumsy padding around the room in a fluster was really funny. It was very enjoyable, she had to admit, and it never ceased to surprise her just how each of her slaves had different personalities, which made their approach to pleasing her so unique. She remembered the distinction she'd made between the sweet pea and the sunflower and couldn't help but wonder what Beast could be. She wasn't entirely sure there was an appropriate 'flower equivalent' but she would enjoy thinking about it.

As she let her mind wander, she became aware that Aeneas needed an answer to a 'serving' related question.

"Yes, you may sit at the table beside me. No need for a bowl this morning. Now, tell me, what were the words you were singing when I arrived?"

Aeneas was overjoyed at having made a successful meal for his Master and to be sitting at her feet in the living room wearing only his collar. He sensed it was now time to talk about Tim and he wanted to be attentive and give thoughtful responses, should he be called on to do so. He watched her face carefully and listened to her thoughts on how her loyal life-slave was doing.

"Tim is at home and recovering nicely. He was in hospital for quite some time but with special meals, good care, and medication, he is getting better. We've chatted about his return home and we both agreed that Poppy would go and look after him from time to time and I will make sure I go to see him too. He won't be coming back as my slave but we've had a good laugh about all the good times we've shared. He also wants to be kept up to date with the ins-and-outs on my little family and says I should write a book about it one day."

Fhionna paused and shifted her gaze briefly towards the fireplace.

"So, the thing to ask now, Aeneas, is if you would like to go and see him?"

"Yes, Master. I'd love to see him. I was thinking about him a lot last night and I was hoping it would be possible."

"Perfect. You can go this afternoon. I'll let him know you're coming. He will be pleased."

"Are you not coming too, Master?" Aeneas had to admit he was a little surprised by the idea he would be on his own with Tim but he thought it must be his Owner's way of giving them some time together. Considering how close they'd become, this was very considerate.

"No, I won't be coming with you. I'll give you the address later because I have something I want to ask you just now. I'd like you to stay longer and attend the Violate Christmas party on Saturday, and I hope you'll be able to change your plans slightly to accommodate the event."

"Yes, Master. I would love to stay with you for the club night. I will work on changing my flight today, if I may?"

"Yes, of course. That's settled. After your visit to Tim you will head into Glasgow and pick up a new outfit for yourself. It should be latex and a mix of black and red in colour. I don't mind which style you choose. You should also buy some latex spray, to make it nice and shiny, because my supply is running out."

Fhionna smiled and gave her slave permission to leave the room and to go and get organised for his day ahead. She had plans of her own to make and it would be better if he were otherwise engaged for the afternoon.

* * *

As she clicked 'send,' she realised just how excited she was at having invited Beast to attend the party too. She hoped he'd be able to come but wasn't entirely sure of his work commitments at this time of year. She would know soon enough though, as he was always prompt in replying. She was intrigued at the thought of him meeting Dog for the first time and wasn't completely convinced they'd be friends. It would, at least, be interesting to see how they interacted with one another while in her presence.

Christmas still held a special place in her heart, even though she knew she was extremely lucky to be able to live the life she wanted to live and was thankful for that all year round. It quite often surprised her just how unencumbered by any sense of guilt she was as she freely and openly expressed her desires and needs. There had been times, in the past, when she'd come to realise that others were jealous of the fact she felt this way but she'd refused, point blank, to let anyone dampen her spirit.

Having banished these thoughts from her mind, she'd given Aeneas Tim's address and sent him on his way with a basket of treats. She then decided to play some of her favourite opera music while she made plans for the fake snow delivery, the decoration of the candelabras with the holly, complete with sumptuous berries she'd bought from the shop in the village, and finally the wrapping of the gifts she'd bought for her slaves. She was extremely happy about this last little job because she'd put a lot of thought into what each of them might like.

She thought her way steadily through the gifts… Some collector's items from Star Trek for Bunty because she was mad about all things 'Trekky,' and a leather dog hood for Aeneas, for him to take home to America and wear when she instructed. For Beast she'd bought a metal torture device that clamped the tongue down and fitted round the head, causing the wearer pain and discomfort. It was modelled on a sixteenth century Scold's Bridle, or Scottish 'Brank,' and even though she couldn't condone its original use as a tool to control women, she would certainly enjoy its consensual use on her masochistic slave. For Poppy she'd purchased a pink frilly outfit. She was easy to buy for because anything pink and frilly would send her slave straight to a room with a full length mirror to try it on and practice her curtsy. Tim was the hardest to give presents to because he always said it wasn't necessary and that all he wanted was to serve his Master. She'd always found a little something for him though, but this year she would simply make sure he spent some time with Dog so that they may do together what they wanted, purely for their own pleasure.

Fhionna's mind ticked off the little list then wandered happily back to thoughts of her darling Bunty and how she'd always said the thing she wanted most in life was to be by her Master, friend, and partner's side till the day she died. She loved Bunty so much, not just because she was so devoted but because she was a wonderful person who was a pleasure to be around, who made her laugh, and who lived with the fact that she needed to have other slaves and subs in her life. Bunty was her angel and she was thankful to have found her all those years ago.

Even though she was enjoying all these lovely Christmassy thoughts, she knew she should really turn her brain back to its task of sorting out the club festivities and uploading the flyer for the event on the website. This should really have been done by now but with everything that had happened recently, it'd completely slipped her mind.

The picture was really good. On it were two slaves, one female and one male, donning prickly holly collars with chain leads attached, red hats with white fur trim, black boots, also with fur trim, and tiny little shorts made of red lace that left very little to the imagination. The third figure was that of a stern Mistress who held their leads in one hand and wagged her finger at them saying, 'You've been very naughty?'

The three models she'd approached to pose together were delighted, even though they didn't actually know each other. Fhionna had found them on the Violate gallery and it had all gone really well. It turned out that the female slave was looking for a Mistress so she'd made sure they'd been given some time to themselves to get to know each other and they'd left at the end of the day, hand-in-hand. She loved happy endings, even though she did feel slightly sorry for the male sub who was also looking for a Mistress. He'd been such a good sport because he'd been bossed around all day by the photographer, the Mistress model, and by her. The poor boy hadn't known whether he was coming or going! He'd certainly earned the meagre wage she was paying him but she knew he was secretly enjoying the attention. He was very young and it was doubtful he'd had three women giving him orders before.

She laughed at the memory as she opened her laptop lid, plugged in the power supply, and crossed the room to make some coffee. Just as she was about to switch the kettle on she heard an almost silent little 'ping' that indicated she had mail, so she sat down and moved the mouse across its pad to read the message.

Dear Master,

How strange those words still seem but how much I love them nonetheless. It would be an absolute honour and privilege to come and be with you for the Christmas party and thank you so much for the invite. The truth is, I have found myself thinking about you a lot. It's only a short time ago that we shared some incredible moments together, you as my new Master and me as your new slave, and I'm thrilled at the prospect of being trained by you.

I admit to being in awe of you and the power you wield over me. It's not something I have ever experienced before in my life, and I'm thankful for every opportunity afforded me to serve you.

In other words, a resounding yes to your request for my presence in a couple of days' time, and I cannot wait to be at your whim again.

Yours,

Beast

* * *

Dear Beast,

A quick reply, thank you. It makes me smile to think of you dropping what you're doing to write to me, as a good slave should. I'm completely thrilled that you can come up for the event and you will stay with me, of course.

Today I have been planning the festivities and, as you probably know by now, it's one of my favourite things to do. It crossed my mind that I would love you to be here, even though as you say, we saw each other fairly recently.

Please have arrived by three o'clock and bring suitable Christmas fetish attire. I don't mind what you wear as long as it includes something red. The collar with your new name tag awaits and I wish to discuss a more permanent slave adornment while you're here. I'd like you to give this some thought. It need not be a collar. It can be a piece of jewellery that you can wear at home or while you work. I would like you to wear a reminder of me while we are apart.

If you feel, however, it's not too early in our relationship as Master and slave to be considering aiming towards a commitment collar then I'd be very happy to discuss that too.

Now I'm laughing because I know, only too well, your brain will be doing somersaults as it processes all this new information.

How quickly and successfully you have morphed from masochist to slave in my mind.

Safe drive up,

Master

Pleased with the reply, she pressed send before quickly perusing the subject titles of other emails. None promised to be as exciting as opening the one from her Beast but one or two certainly needed to be answered before she closed the lid and continued with her plans.

Fhionna let her mind roam as she walked upstairs. She wondered how Aeneas and Tim were getting on. Dog was a very affectionate person and they liked each other very much. One might even say that they loved each other. She hoped they were having fun catching up but was sure that Tim was still too weak for any real physical 'contact.' She imagined, however, that he'd enjoy some gentle play with his nipples and perhaps a soft touch elsewhere on his body as long as Aeneas was very careful. One thing was certain, she wouldn't be asking for the details of what had passed between them but she would listen if Aeneas wanted to share how the afternoon had played out.

* * *

Aeneas was thrilled to be sitting beside his friend and holding his hand. "I think you gave Master a fright, Tim. She misses you a lot but she's relieved you're ok. I know I will miss you giving me advice and teaching me how not to be so stupid."

Tim smiled and squeezed his giant paw. "Well, that's something you'll just have to figure out for yourself, isn't it!"

He was really happy to see Dog and grateful that she'd let him visit.

"I'm so glad to be here and thankful that Master suggested I come. I wanted to see you but I wasn't sure what her plans for me were. Luckily she's requested I change my flight home and move some work around so I can go to the Christmas party on Saturday, which means I get to serve her longer."

Tim smiled at his friend and loved the enthusiasm in his voice. It was clear he was enjoying his slavery. He felt a heavy ache in his heart, however, that he couldn't resume his place as her slave, at her feet, in her home, but he knew the time had come to plan a different lifestyle because he wouldn't be capable of achieving the goals she might set for him, which had been the whole point of his existence. He hated the thought of her restricted joy based on his frailty and he didn't want to become a burden.

"I can tell you're excited at being with her again. I know that feeling well but it must be tenfold for you, being so far away."

"Yes, it's not easy sometimes. I'd love to be living here so I could attend to her as she needed me but I'm working in Scotland more and more so who knows. It might become a possibility in the future, but I'd need to know it was what she wanted before I would ever make such plans. She might enjoy having me travel so far to serve her. She does like having an 'exotic pet' who makes so much effort to be here. I'm also not sure I would cope quite as well with being in the same city or country, at least, and knowing that she was being served by other slaves and pets when I was just an hour away, for example. At least having thousands of miles between us means I have no choice but to wait until I can manage work commitments and book flights. It also means that I get excited about planning the details of my trip and enjoy the anticipation of what's to come, knowing she has carved out some specific time just for me."

Tim stroked Aeneas' fingers while he talked. He hadn't seen a jealous side to Dog but he'd been his Master's slave for a long time so he guessed that Aeneas had no reason to feel that way about him.

"You're right that she enjoys having you travel so far just for her. She also enjoys the planning it takes and having a slave in the US means she has the option of travelling there to be pampered by you. She loves to travel and it's a huge thrill to be able to say to her friends that she has an American slave who can accommodate as well as come here. As for the slight possessiveness, well, I've never witnessed that in you and I can't say that I've ever felt that way either, to be honest. If something can comfort you, think about all the people she meets and how few she chooses to have as her slaves. They're very different to each other and have their own talents and appeal. You are no exception to that."

Aeneas thought about what Tim was saying and agreed that it was easier to think in those terms.

"Anyway, enough about me. Is there anything I can do for you to make you happy?"

Tim was touched by the phrase, 'make you happy,' and told him he was feeling starved of affection and was missing being his Master's slave.

Dog smiled at him and suggested he closed his eyes and let him give him some attention as he slowly snaked his hands up Tim's body towards his erect nipples. He watched as tiny goose bumps patterned his skin and listened as his breathing changed.

Tim was aware of his growing erection and wanted so much to feel Aeneas' mouth there. He wondered if he dare ask him, or gently move his head down, but in the end neither was necessary. He sighed as the other man's tongue moved slowly over his head then up and down his thick shaft. It felt so good and all he had to do was lie back and enjoy it. It briefly crossed his mind that Fhionna might have intended this to happen and he smiled as he imagined her arousal at the scene. He would be sure to tell her about it and to say thank you.

* * *

Aeneas was having a hard time picking an outfit. His Owner had told him what colour and material but he wondered what style it should be. He disliked having this type of freedom and he didn't want to get it wrong, not just because he might be punished but because he didn't want to let her down. He wasn't sure how much skin he should aim to cover in latex but he guessed that some flesh on display would be good because she admired his toned physique. But, then again, he'd been told it was a club night with more of a party feel to it so he wondered if he should choose something with more coverage. He knew about her fondness for testing her slaves, and how happy it made her to think she might have given them some discomfort, even in something as small as deciding on what clothing to buy. But that was just it, this particular activity wasn't a small thing to him. And he believed she knew that.

* * *

Back at his Master's house, Aeneas stood on the doorstep with a couple of carrier bags in his hands. He'd eventually selected a latex wrestling suit with thin straps that crossed over his back and ran all the way down to his navel at the front. This meant his nipples would be exposed but his genitals would be covered. The shorts of the suit ended on his muscled thighs and showed them off to perfection. The best part, however, was the two-way zip that would give access to his member and his ass, should Master want it. He was very happy with his choice and he'd also managed to pick up a couple of small treats for his Owner. He'd bought her lots of latex shiner but also a huge bouquet of flowers and some exquisite bubble bath. He was a happy slave as he stood on the step. He decided it best to knock then push the door open. He hadn't been told he could come straight in but he didn't want to interrupt her so thought this was the best option.

In the hallway, he noticed there was an envelope with his name on it on the table where the notepad and address book were kept, so he put the bags and flowers onto the floor and opened it.

Dear slave,

I may be out when you get back so please shower and change into the outfit you bought. You will wait downstairs in the dungeon for my return. Be in the cage and lock it with the padlock that is hanging from the bolt. If you are hungry you may take some toast or a sandwich and something to drink with you and enjoy them in your cage but don't make a mess.

I hope you had a good day and I will see you soon.
Master

Aeneas was excited at the prospect of preparing himself in this way. He thought the tone of the note was light and less formal than other letters he'd been given, but he still got butterflies when he had to wait like that because he never knew what was going to happen. To be honest she always surprised him anyway, and Tim had frequently told him to expect the unexpected, but the fact that she was out and he'd been given such direct instructions made him slightly more nervous. He hoped she would be pleased with the choices he'd made and he would use the shiner to give the latex its finished glow.

* * *

Fhionna was thrilled at the prospect of having her American slave waiting for her in the cage. Essentially he was a good slave. Still a little naïve, maybe, but he would learn. His intentions were genuine and he tried hard. He was certainly very passionate and loving and she believed that these were his main motivations. She had a feeling though, that each mistake he made would be a big one. He paid a lot of attention to smaller details, like choosing the best outfit or agonising over a gift, but when it came to making decisions on whether to see a Dom when it was in his contract not to, for example, he let his dick rule his brain then paid for it later.

As she packed the gifts into the boot of her car, she sang one of her favourite songs. She'd heard many performances of Hallelujah before but one of her favourites was by the young opera singer she'd heard at the Royal Concert Hall. Jonathan Antoine had the voice of an angel and she'd had tears in her eyes as she'd listened to him effortlessly reach the highest of the notes. She knew her reaction was partly because of the amazing way the young man had filled the song with his own emotion but also because his stage presence was shy but charming. She'd enjoyed the way he was so unsure of his own talent and hoped he remained ego-free for as long as possible.

* * *

Dog was feeling rather sleepy. It had been an eventful day so far. He'd enjoyed his interaction with Tim. He'd enjoyed giving the man some pleasure before turning to his task. He wanted to close his eyes and sleep but found that he was too busy trying to listen for his Master's car to be able to. He wasn't entirely sure he'd be able to hear it from down in the dungeon but that didn't stop him from giving it a go.

At last, he heard the main door being opened and footsteps crossing the polished floor above his head. Aeneas sat up and checked himself over to make sure he was presentable. He laughed at himself because he was locked in the cage and there wasn't actually anything he could do about it if he wasn't. Once the padlock had been closed there was no way out because he couldn't see a key anywhere. He figured that she wouldn't leave him alone in the house on his own very long because of practical issues. For one, the front door was unlocked and anyone could come in, even though the house was out in the countryside and it was very unlikely. He found this rather titillating, to be honest. He was assuming it was his Owner's footsteps he could hear moving about upstairs but what if it was someone else? What if she'd invited someone to take advantage of him while she was out? He knew she was capable of it and would enjoy it but until he knew for sure it would pay to keep his imagination in check.

Aeneas wiped the sleep from his eyes and the drool from his chin. It had been a long time before the dungeon door had opened and trying to make sure he was in a fit state to receive his Master had been done completely in vain. He was now a rumpled mess.

"My lovely, sleepy slave. How cute you look." She walked towards him and unlocked the door. "Come out and let me look at you."

Aeneas crawled out as best he could but found his legs had gone to sleep. He groaned as his stiff limbs tried to function and realised she was laughing at him.

"Stand up and put your hands behind your head. I want to inspect you."

Doing as instructed, Dog creaked his way into position and watched as she circled him, surveying her property.

"Wonderful outfit. I particularly like the zip at the crotch. You obviously gave it a lot of thought. Well done. Go and bend over the bench."

Fhionna was aroused at the sight of him. She loved the way his erect nipples were on display, the way the straps crossed over his back in just the right place to accentuate the ripples of his muscles, and the wonderful zip that she had every intention of using.

She watched her slave take his position on the bench and move his arms and legs into place to be strapped in, as she had taught him to do. She decided she would hood him before she strapped him down, as well as remove some of her clothing and buckle herself into her strap-on.

Aeneas gasped and tried to relax his buttocks as first the zip was lowered and then his Master's fingers were inserted. The lube was cold and he flinched a little. This made her laugh and thrust her digits in further. He knew he could take the intrusion because he'd done so many times before. He certainly wasn't a virgin anymore.

"I love how vulnerable you look, Aeneas, and I think I would like to play with you a little more before I use you."

Aeneas could only lie where he was, in the darkness of the hood, strapped down, and be the plaything his Master wanted him to be. This was the life he'd chosen and he loved it.

* * *

Back upstairs and settled nicely at his Master's feet as she dangled them over the end of her bed, Dog listened to the plans she'd made for the party. He loved the sound of the decorations and was impatient to open his gift but knew it would have to wait until Saturday, which wasn't that far away.

"I've invited Beast to attend and I'm very excited at the prospect of having you both there. You have more experience as my slave than he has so you will be kind to him like Tim was to you. Don't attempt any intimate contact with him and a firm handshake will suffice."

She laughed as she said it because she knew Beast very well and how uncomfortable he'd be if another man should try and hug him. He'd reciprocate, of course, but he preferred not to have to.

"Permission to speak, Master?"

"What is it?"

"Thank you. Who is Beast?"

Fhionna was surprised by the question but then realised that Aeneas wouldn't recognise him by that name. She knew Martin had written a long piece about his first visit to Violate, and she also knew Aeneas was an avid reader of the columns when he was at home in the US.

"Beast was known as Stephan a couple of months ago. He is now my new slave in training and that is his slave name. You should call him Beast as I will be instructing him to call you Dog."

She watched him for a reaction and knew he was feeling a little huffy when he lowered his head so she couldn't see his face properly.

"He is very different to you, Aeneas, but I really shouldn't have to explain myself."

Aeneas was flushed and irritated. He'd suspected that there was a connection forming between them and he couldn't help but feel Beast was encroaching on his own fairly new relationship with her. He couldn't bring himself to look up when she addressed him as he really didn't want her to see his red face.

"Look at me Dog and tell me what you're feeling."

Aeneas heard the annoyance in her voice and dreaded repercussions because of his obvious mood. He slowly raised his head to almost eye level but not quite. Instead he stared at his Master's chin, rather awkwardly.

"I'm sorry, Master. I guess I'm feeling angry that he is now your slave and there's a possibility he will be a better one than I am. I've been missing you so much and now I'm told you have a new person to train and I can't help feeling upset by that. I don't want him to come between us and I'm worried that you won't want me anymore."

All of a sudden, Aeneas felt tears prick his eyes. He wanted to wipe them away but felt foolish and didn't want to make his distress any more obvious than it already was.

"I see. I understand but that doesn't mean that I'm happy. I realise we haven't seen each other for two months but you're behaving badly. I am loathed to punish any slave for their feelings, and I did ask you to explain, which you have done, but I'm fighting the urge to thrash you. I will never punish in anger, however, so you're free to go for the moment. Go down to your cage and stay there until I come and get you."

Aeneas managed a very quiet, "Yes, Master," before sloping off to the dungeon.

* * *

Looking out from behind the bars, he let himself cry properly. He felt like an idiot but he was also a very honest person. He was a terrible liar, which was good is some ways and not in others, and he just couldn't hide his true feelings when asked to express them. He felt ashamed though. He wasn't jealous of any other person his Master was close to. He loved Tim and thought the world of Poppy. He only knew Bunty a little bit but liked her a lot. He liked Louise and Martin, so it seemed it was only Beast he had a problem with.

He wondered why that was and thought maybe it was because he believed no one else would catch his Owner's interest now that she had him in her service. Maybe it was because all the others were there before him. He only knew for sure that he was now in trouble and he hated it. He would have to wait, God knows how long, for her to deal with him and he would just have to settle down as best he could. The only way forward was for him to either suck it up and take whatever was coming or ask to be released from his contract, which was the very last resort. His slavery was consensual and he'd chosen this lifestyle freely because he'd wanted to be owned by this woman more than anything else in the universe. He was so confused and emotional and prayed he would be able to make amends, when the time came, because giving up just wasn't an option.

* * *

Fhionna couldn't believe how angry she felt. She'd had to send Aeneas away, out of her sight for a while, till she calmed down. It was very rare for her to feel this mad at anyone but it seemed that Aeneas was capable of making it happen. She was unimpressed by his needy attitude and she was extremely annoyed by his huffiness. She now had to think about whether or not she wanted a slave that was prone to such behaviour and how to deal with the feelings he'd expressed.

She'd never noticed any form of jealously from Aeneas before but acknowledged that this was a new situation for him. He was no longer the newest slave so may feel he would have to fight for her affection, which wasn't the case. She would have to show him he was just as wanted as any of the others and that Beast was not a threat to his relationship with her. But first she would decide if a physical punishment was warranted.

* * *

It was quite some time before she was ready to be in her slave's company again but she knew she must eventually put him out of his misery, so she walked down to the dungeon and opened the door. She found Aeneas lying on his side, asleep, and felt a certain passion towards him. He looked vulnerable. On closer inspection, she could tell he'd been crying because his face was crumpled and puffy. This was not how she'd imagined the day would end but she had to talk to him about his concerns.

"Aeneas, turn round please."

Doing as he was told, he managed to smile up into his Master's face.

"I'm sorry, Master. I really am. Please don't ask me to leave. I couldn't bear it."

Fhionna looked at her slave's sad face and spoke gently to him.

"I've given it a lot of thought and while you made me consider ending your contract, and therefore our relationship, I knew I didn't want to lose you. I've also decided that I will not punish you in any physical way. I asked you for your feelings and you told me. I may not have liked them, which is somewhat of an understatement, but I won't punish you for them. You will, however, spend the night on your own, in your cage. Remove your new outfit and pass it to me through the bars. Tomorrow is another day and we shall start afresh."

Aeneas slowly removed the latex from his body and passed it to her, as instructed. He felt cold. It felt a little like he was being stripped of his right to wear clothes but he knew that he didn't actually have one anyway. He'd given up that privilege, and others, when he'd agreed to sign his contract of slavery.

"I will allow you a blanket. Get some rest and I want a better attitude in the morning, Aeneas, because I have other news to tell you."

Dog thanked his Owner and said he understood.

II

It was the day before the party and the house was buzzing with activity. Aeneas could hear laughter upstairs and longed to be a part of it. He was hungry, still tired, and had been in his cage all morning without having any visitors. He'd been told there would be no physical punishment but the lack of attention had been pure torture. He never wanted to be left alone and ignored like that ever again so he'd make sure he did his best to avoid it.

Aeneas jumped when Poppy came in with a tray with some lunch on it.

"I've brought some food and you've to eat it, shower, put your collar on, and come upstairs to the kitchen. I forgot to bring the thong you're supposed to wear so I'll go and fetch it and bring it down. Nice to see you, Dog, and I hope you're ok."

Dog said that he was ok and thanked her for the food. He would usually have conversed more with her but it didn't feel right to be chatty so he ate his food in silence and watched as Poppy left to get the thong.

* * *

Upstairs, Fhionna was having fun because Bunty had arrived and seemed in good spirits, and Poppy was excited about the festivities; running about the house, doing her chores, and loving the fact she was allowed to be really girly.

"Master, what do you want me to wear tomorrow? If it's ok, I'd love to wear my pink latex shorts and collar and my red love-heart pasties."

She watched her partner blush as she said it, which didn't happen often. She was obviously feeling slutty and Fhionna loved it when she was in that kind of mood because it meant she was very receptive to all sorts of wild play. She always did her best to accommodate her wishes, of course, but it was always much more fun when she was feeling ultra-receptive, so she made a 'mental note' to carve out some private time with her later in the day.

"That would be perfect. I'll add a little red bow to your collar too and maybe a little holly".

Fhionna smiled and watched her beautiful slave leave the room to go and try it all on. She felt happy and thought it was probably time to have some food and allow Dog to join them. He'd been punished enough and hoped he was feeling contrite.

* * *

Aeneas had just finished in the shower when Poppy bounced into the room.

"Hi, Dog. You look good and I must say, smell fresher too."

Poppy giggled and handed him the thong but she also carried a pair of thick socks and some boots.

"Master says to go outside and collect wood before making and lighting a fire in the living room and one in her bedroom. Then you've to go to the kitchen."

Aeneas smiled at her and nodded. Luckily he'd made a fire at home before so knew what to do. He didn't want to mess up his first task after being in the dog-house so badly yesterday. He had to admit that he felt slightly better knowing he was to join the rest of the household today. He would get to be around his Master and hopefully be allowed to join in any of the fun that seemed to be happening.

"There's a really happy atmosphere upstairs because Master is letting everyone choose their own outfits for tomorrow, and as long as there is something red involved she doesn't seem to mind that much what we pick. I've chosen a very short dress and some red sparkly high heels."

Dog laughed as he rubbed his short hair with a towel and took the thong with the other hand as Poppy put the boots on the floor.

"That sounds perfect! My outfit for tomorrow, assuming I'm still going, is a black latex wrestling suit that has a red stripe down the side."

Poppy grinned up at him and said he'd better hurry up because Master may want to play in one of the rooms soon, and she'd want it to be warm.

Aeneas smiled back and said he was nearly ready. He wasn't

looking forward to being outside in the cold with nothing on apart from the thong and collar, of course, but he would do as he was told.

* * *

Outside was freezing and Aeneas shivered his way through his tasks. He hoped he'd be allowed some time in front of one of the fires he'd just built but wasn't holding his breath.

When he'd finally finished, he came into the house and took his boots and socks off and left them neatly by the front door before going to the kitchen. He got onto his hands and knees and knocked on the door. Once he'd been told to come in, he crawled forward towards the table and straight over to his Owner's feet to kiss them. He stayed in that position, with his head resting on the floor just in front of her feet, until he was told he could move.

"Good afternoon, Dog. I don't expect you slept very well but I hope you feel more like your happy, pleasant self."

Fhionna reached down to the floor to lift his head so he could see her small smile.

"Good afternoon. Yes, Master. Both fires are built and lit, as you required."

"Good. Fetch yourself some coffee and join us at the table."

As he got up he noticed, for the first time, that both Poppy and Bunty were sitting at the table and were wearing similar outfits to his. Bunty looked wonderful in just a small pair of latex shorts and Poppy was wearing a similar thong, that rather exposed her genitals. He wondered if this meant he was in 'Boy' mode, for now.

"Well, everyone, I have an announcement to make, or rather three announcements, one of which regards tomorrow and the other is about a small gathering you will all attend here, in January."

Fhionna paused and grinned at her assembled family.

"First of all, Beast is arriving tomorrow morning and I want you all to make him feel welcome. I know you won't be here during the day tomorrow, Bunty, but you'll get your chance to meet him properly in January, if you don't speak to him tomorrow night."

She made a point of looking straight at Aeneas before shifting her gaze to Poppy, who she noticed was smiling.

"The other announcements are that Craig, my new puppy, will be coming up in January to meet you all properly for the first time."

Again, she looked at Aeneas to gauge his reaction to the news that she also had a new puppy. She was pleased to see he didn't lower his head but simply nodded to acknowledge the news.

"Craig is a young man who lives in Devon so he won't be here more than once or twice a year but I'm enjoying our communications and his training online. And now for the best bit. I've decided to have a small party in January. The guest list will consist of my immediate family of slaves and a few friends, perhaps, but it's the purpose of the party that matters most."

Fhionna paused, again, and turned her attention to her dog.

"Aeneas, I invite you to receive your formal ownership collar, during a small ceremony, and I hope you will accept all the responsibly that goes with it. I want you to be happy as my slave and as part of my family, in general."

She grinned at him and enjoyed the astonished look on his face. He had no idea she'd planned such an event and he'd probably thought she would keep him at arm's length for some time to come. This last part might still be true, for this visit, but that didn't mean she wouldn't show him he was wanted. She liked Dog very much and thought it was time to throw him a bone, as it were.

* * *

The day had been full of surprises. Poppy had skipped about the house humming 'I'm So Pretty' to herself, even though she was dressed as Boy for most of the day, Dog had blushed at the news she'd given him at the dinner table and said how thankful he was, and now Bunty lay in her arms after she'd beaten the girl and made love to her.

Boy and Dog were downstairs in the cage together and she hoped they'd form a stronger attachment to each other. She knew they were already close but it would be good for Aeneas to have another person to be intimate with, as well as have the occasional visit to Tim. He was the type of person who needed a lot of affection but it would also help him adjust to the fact that Beast was in her life to stay. Helping him feel like

a proper ally among her slaves was just good psychological
because not only had he been used to it but he seemed to crave

III

The time had nearly come for Beast to arrive and Fhionna was very excited. She'd enjoyed some play time with Dog and Poppy that morning and had loved watching them together. She'd then taken Aeneas upstairs to her bedroom for some intimate time alone, with her slave. It had been much needed and she could tell he was overjoyed at having had the chance to devote himself to her, in this way.

"Thank you, Master, for your forgiveness and attention. I live to serve you and I really am sorry to have made you angry. If I may say, I hated being punished by your avoidance and I don't want to ever be in that position again. I accept that it's not my place to question who enters your family. I am your slave and have no right to dictate or be jealous about any aspect of your life or any other slave or submissive you choose to be close to or play with."

Fhionna stroked Dog's head and told him he'd behaved well over the last twenty-four hours. She told him she was very happy with his performance with Poppy and she could see them becoming close.

"Yes, Master. I enjoy her company very much. She is very cute as Poppy and really sexy as Boy."

She smiled at her pet as he spoke, and leaned over the side of her bed to check the clock.

"Well, Aeneas, the time has come for me to shower and get dressed to greet Beast. He's always on time and I want to be ready. Go downstairs and wash then have a rest in your cage. You may leave the door unlocked, if you wish. You can use the time to write in your journal or just sleep. I'll send someone to fetch you when I want you."

Aeneas said, "Yes, Master," and did as he was told. He smiled to himself as he thought about how much more content he would be to get into it this time.

Dog decided to lock it as he liked the feeling of being secure and thought his Owner might appreciate it, if she came to see him at any point. He felt tired enough to get some sleep and certainly felt a lot happier. He couldn't quite believe he'd been given the chance to have a collaring ceremony. He hadn't expected it but it was something that made him very happy. The fact that the other slaves, including Tim, he hoped, were to be there to watch made him feel great. He was glad the new guy, 'Beast,' would witness it, in particular. He felt like he wanted him to know just how much Master cared for him and this was the best way for her to show it. He would do his best to like the guy, for Master's sake, as much as his own. He was usually such a confident and passionate person and it surprised him just how much he needed the other man to realise how devoted he was.

* * *

Fhionna was in the living room reading one of her favourite novels for probably the hundredth time. She'd read it not so long ago but she found herself mesmerised by it. *Wuthering Heights* was so dramatic and romantic and it had a certain darkness about it. It was raw round the edges and grounded its reader so completely. It could feel like one was swallowed up within its pages, as well as the earth of the graves. The story lent itself to enjoying a glass of red wine and a room full of flickering candles, while the winter raged outside; whipping the limbs of the trees into a dancing frenzy.

Placing the book on the sofa and moving to the window, she surveyed the thunderous sky with interest. There was no sun to cast the long shadows she enjoyed so much during the summer months but she was content.

* * *

Stephan was battling the weather and felt like he was getting nowhere fast. At this rate he was going to be at least half an hour late. He hated not being on time but even more so because he was expected by his new Master, which made it so much worse. He would attempt to put his foot down, when he could, to try and gain some time but he

'idn't want to end up wrapping his car round a tree. He'd
..y reach the house and he'd just make sure she knew how sorry
..vas for not being at her feet when expected.

* * *

It was five o'clock when finally she heard the car wheels on the gravel. She was beginning to worry that something had happened to him. She was less concerned about the actual lateness and more about his well-being. He'd had a long drive and she knew life sometimes threw a spanner in the works to test even the most steadfast resolve.

A few seconds later she heard running and swearing, which made her laugh. His sophistication, as well as his southern English accent, meant that any bad language was rather amusing. She supposed she wouldn't hear it often and she may not have heard it now if he'd thought she was just a few feet away. She'd enjoy teasing him about it and she smiled as she waited for Poppy to answer the door.

The inevitable knock came to the living room door and Beast was ushered in. Poppy, still dressed in male attire, simply opened the door wide enough for him to enter the room and closed it promptly behind herself. She obviously had no wish to be there any longer than was absolutely necessary and knew that Fhionna would either send Beast to fetch her if she needed anything, ask Beast to fetch it himself, or ring a bell to attract her attention.

"Good evening, Master. Sorry I'm so late. The weather was bad and held me back. I'm very happy to be here now though."

As he said it, he bent to kiss her hand and asked if she would like him to sit on the floor and keep her company or would she like him to go and unpack and change first.

"You can sit with me a little while. It's good to see you. I'm very happy you're here. It promises to be a good but long night so I hope you're not too tired."

Stephan recognised this as more of a statement than a question and smiled up at his Master and asked if he may kiss her feet. He wanted to show how much he'd missed her and how happy he was to be invited to share in the fun she'd planned.

Fhionna said of course he may kiss her feet and was about to tell him some of the evening's activities when she was interrupted by another knock at the door. This time it was Bunty asking if she and Boy should start dinner and whether or not Dog was to eat upstairs or down in his cage tonight.

"Hello, Bunty. Yes, please. There's a very large salmon to prepare. Thank you. Dog can join us tonight. Ask Boy to fetch him when the food is almost ready."

She watched her partner disappear again and turned her face towards her slave, who was smiling at her. Answering his thoughts, she said, "Yes, an almost full house tonight and I still haven't decided which one of you, if any of you, will be allowed to be in my room tonight."

She laughed loudly at her own joke because she knew herself well enough to know that someone would be staying there. It was made harder by the fact that Bunty wasn't staying till the end of the party because she had an early start the next day and needed to be home by midnight. If she'd been staying then there would have been no choice to make. Bunty always came first. Always.

"Such a dilemma. I don't envy you one bit, Master! So many to choose from… the petite and shy Poppy, the tall and handsome Beast, or the Dog from the basement."

He knew he was being a little cheeky and hoped she'd take it in the humorous spirit it was meant. He had no reason to believe she wouldn't though. He'd seen that she had a good sense of humour and she didn't seem to mind being teased, just a little.

"You are so mischievous. You deserve to be thoroughly punished but you'd enjoy it far too much." She was grinning at him and wagging her finger and enjoying herself immensely.

"Be gone, Beast. You may take your things up to the room beside mine. Have a shower and wear your collar and the thong that are on the bed waiting for you. You won't need anything else. Come back down to the kitchen when you're finished. Please crawl when anywhere on this floor or downstairs."

Beast said, "Thank you," before kissing his Master's feet once more and crawling out of the room to collect his bag. He assumed he could walk up the stairs with it, as she'd said, 'crawl when you're on this floor or downstairs,' so he did.

* * *

Dog was awake and found himself listening to his Master's laughter. He was enjoying it and was even excited by it. He hoped it wouldn't be too much longer before he would be allowed upstairs. He had no idea what time it was but he was sure it must be getting near time to get dressed and leave.

Just as the thought crossed his mind, the door opened and he was greeted by the sight of his Owner herself. Aeneas shuffled around behind the bars of the cage to get into a position where he could bow his head as much as possible. This left his rump up in the air but sideways rather than face on.

"Did you get some sleep?"

Fhionna noticed he'd decided to lock himself into the cage and smiled as she fetched the key to the padlock.

"Yes, Master. Thank you. I feel less tired and really happy, if you don't mind me saying."

"I'm pleased to hear it. You may come and eat with the rest of us."

Attaching a lead to his collar, she told him to crawl behind her all the way up the stairs. Reaching the kitchen door, she pushed it open and signalled for Dog to keep to heel as she crossed the floor to the table. Dog did as he was told and sat down beside the large bowl on the floor, which he guessed was for him. He was getting used to eating this way as it was only a rare treat that he got to sit at the table these days.

When he was settled, he allowed himself to look up and see who else was in the room. He smiled at Boy, who was sitting at the end of the table and so was next to Dog on his left, and then he nodded at Bunty who was placed at Master's right hand side. His eyes then went to the male who sat directly across from Master and he nodded at whom he thought must be Beast. He wanted to have a good look at him but daren't stare.

Bunty got up from the table to fetch the fish from the oven and asked if they were all allowed some wine with the meal. Poppy got up and added the finishing touches to the mound of salad and brought the warm bread to the table too.

"Can I help?"

It annoyed Aeneas slightly that Beast hadn't addressed the question through their Master first. It also irritated him that she didn't seem to mind. Aeneas inwardly chastised himself, 'way to go, big guy,' and willed his internal voice to shut the hell up.

"Bunty and Boy can manage. You may sit and relax. It will soon be time to change into our party outfits so have a glass of wine and enjoy the salmon."

Fhionna fell silent, as if in thought, then added a short toast once all the glasses were filled:

"'There is only one happiness in life: to love and be loved.' The French romantic writer, George Sand, penned these words and they are utterly true but I want to add to them. I am grateful for the form that this love takes, from each of you, my little family. Thank you."

* * *

The taxi arrived dead on eight o'clock and the happy little group made their way to the club. The slaves chatted happily among themselves while Fhionna talked to the driver in the front seat.

"How are you, Fred? Are you doing ok?"

Fred said he was great. "You have a lot of slaves with you tonight, Ma'am! I love Christmas but even more so when I know there's a chance I'll be collecting you and your pets."

Fhionna laughed so much that all four subs in the back stopped talking in an effort to listen in without being noticed but actually being totally obvious. She laughed even more as she pulled the glass screen across, behind her head, to block out their conversation.

"It seems they're interested in what we're talking about."

"I've no doubt they would be, Ma'am. Who wouldn't be interested in that wonderful laugh of yours, for a start?"

Fred beamed at her as he pulled up outside the doors of Violate and got out to help her. "I know you have slaves in the back that can do this for you but I like to join in and I won't have a lady wait for them to exit their seats."

She smiled and said thank you. "Too kind. Have good night, Fred, and maybe we will see you later?"

"You're very welcome, and no, not tonight. I finish my shift soon but I'll let Derek know to come get you because I wouldn't want you in the hands of just anyone. Have a great time and a Merry Christmas, when it comes."

* * *

The venue was still fairly quiet but it meant that she had time to do a quick check that all was in order before she started to enjoy herself properly. She handed her coat to Boy and instructed the rest to do the same and asked her to go upstairs to put them in the cloakroom. She then brought two leads out of her bag and attached them to both Dog's and Beast's collars before taking Bunty's hand and heading to the dungeon. She stopped briefly to say hello to some early-birds then continued on her way through the heavy double doors.

Fhionna noticed the admiring looks her little entourage were receiving and smiled. She loved the attention. The hallway and bar area would be too full of people later to pass through all in a clump, so she decided that if she wanted to have a wander she would pick one of them at a time to accompany her. She didn't go walking through the venue too often because she always stopped to talk to people and missed out on playing.

She looked around her and thought how amazing the place looked. She then unclipped Beast's lead and sent him to the bar for drinks for them all and then sent Bunty to mingle with the people who had already arrived. She then turned to Dog.

"You will spend a lot of the night on your knees at my feet. You will be allowed to mingle, at times, but otherwise I want you to heel."

Aeneas replied that he understood and took his place on the floor beside her, smiling up at her. Just as he did so, Beast returned with the drinks and asked permission to bend down and give Dog his. Fhionna smiled, and said yes, so Beast handed him his glass of whisky and said cheers.

She watched as Sophia and Spike arrived and made their way over. They both hugged her and gave her a small and delicately wrapped Christmas present.

"Wow, that's lovely. Thank you. Can I open it now?"

Sophia laughed and said no, it must wait until Christmas day.

Both Dog and Beast were smiling at her, so she laughed and said, "You're the boss," before handing it to Poppy, who had just returned from the cloakroom.

As they chatted, Spike took his place on the floor beside Dog and Beast was left standing beside his Master, back on his lead.

Dog was impressed to see he knew enough to keep quiet until he was included in the conversation but guessed even he had known that when he was first 'initiated.'

"Beast has driven for hours in the bad weather to be here. He's eager to please. I'll be playing a lot, I think. Beast takes an incredible amount of pain from me and Dog does really well too, so it's going to be a fun night."

Sophia smiled and said she would love to watch both of them take a good beating and that she fully intended to be playing with Spike during the course of the evening.

"What about Poppy? Will you be playing with her tonight?"

"I do love to lift her pretty dress in public so I might indulge if I'm not too tired. Would you like to join in if I do?"

"Oh, yes please. That would be fun. I'll go and mingle a bit first. See you later."

* * *

Fhionna scanned the room and realised that it was very busy. She waved at someone and blew them a kiss. She was feeling very playful, which always meant the imminent demise of her slaves. She was feeling very festive and a little merry but not so much so that it would impair her judgment during play. She was always very careful about that.

Noticing Bunty across the other side of the room, she waved at her too. Bunty waved back and flashed her Master a huge grin before taking the hand of a rather attractive young woman and leading her towards the stairs, presumably to go dancing. She laughed and commented, to no one in particular, that Bunty was being cheeky tonight and it would do her good to flirt a bit and let her hair down. Beast was the one to answer and said that she was very kind to let her have fun in that way.

"She deserves it. She's my slave but she's also my partner and we've known each other for a very long time. She knows what she's allowed and not allowed to do but it doesn't stop her from being a minx sometimes."

Fhionna smiled and turned her attention to Poppy. "Collect my bag of toys from the cloakroom, please. Then you can go and have fun. I'm sure the DJ will play a request for you if you ask nicely."

She watched as her little slave skipped happily from the room then turned to the others. She told Beast she would like him to hold her whips for her while she played with Dog and then they would swap places.

* * *

Kneeling at the side of the bench where Dog was tethered, he noticed she'd placed a gag in his mouth and put him in a heavy latex hood so he couldn't see him, or what instrument she chose, and he knew that this was a blessing as well as a curse. His Owner was being kind enough to let him escape into his own thoughts during such a public play, but it also meant there was no way to estimate what was about to happen and no way to be able to look at his Master, should he need comfort or encouragement.

* * *

Beast, having watched Dog being thoroughly caned with very little warm up, was now in a similar position but he hadn't been given the hood to wear. She knew he would struggle with it and was kind enough to forego it. He'd been impressed by the amount that Dog could take and watched as she'd hugged the man as he'd shed his tears, but now he thought about pleasing his new Master and he could do that by being a pain-slut.

* * *

Fhionna was a little breathless but very happy. She'd been playing with her two large male slaves for quite some time and was a little tired but very satisfied. She grinned down at both of them as they knelt beside each other and looked up at her smiling face. She walked round them as she told them to 'be in position' so she could admire her handiwork.

The stripes on Dog's buttocks were vivid, deep, and wonderfully symmetrical. The whip marks on Beast's back were also deep welts that were already turning black. The bruises would be magnificent. She was really pleased and told them so.

"You may both have a rest. Go and mingle a little and go to the bar if you wish. Tell Johnny that I said to put your drinks on my tab. Off you go. I'll be fine."

She watched as they headed towards the bar and wondered how they would get on, left to talk to each other. Would they stay together and chat or would they split up and socialise separately? She very much doubted they would separate but time would tell.

Fhionna decided to find Poppy and join her. She smiled as she thought about her twisting her body in time to the rhythm and felt like dancing a little. Poppy would be shy, at first, but would relax again and dance to the beat beside her Master.

* * *

"Cheers, well that was quite something. You can take quite a beating with the cane. I'm impressed and especially since you're not a masochist."

Beast handed Dog his glass and held his own up in salutation. He watched the man take it and clink glasses with him.

"Thanks. It's taken me time to get to that level but Master has been training me for a while now. Knowing it makes her happy is the driving force. You take so much more than me though. I would struggle to take anywhere near that much on my back."

"Well, thank you, but I've been playing for a long time, even if not as a slave with a Master, so I guess that makes it easier to take extended periods of pain. I don't have a favourite place to be hit, I don't think, but you're right, giving her pleasure becomes the goal rather than the pain itself, and that's something I never thought I would say. I've seen so many Mistresses over the years and I have some permanent marks on my body. I was worried that would put her off, at first, but she doesn't seem to mind them. I'm hoping that one day she will put a permanent mark on me as part of my Ownership. I find myself hoping for a tattoo or a brand."

"Wow, that would be amazing but not something I've thought about. I guess I would do it if she asked me to but it doesn't figure high on my list of needs." Dog laughed. "I'm amazed you've thought about that already. I hope you don't mind me saying but I did get kinda worried about my own position when I heard that Master had taken on a new masochist slave. Only because I haven't known her long."

"Thanks for being honest. I have no intention of creating any problems for any of Master's slaves. I'm sure my submission is very different to yours and I'm only just learning what submission is, in any real sense. Rivalry wouldn't make her happy and we would only end up on the receiving end of some punishment if she thought there was any."

It was Beast's turn to laugh and he wondered what the best punishment for a masochist would be as he downed his drink.

* * *

Fhionna was talking to her friends when Beast and Dog returned from the bar area and they both smiled when they saw that Poppy was on the floor at her feet worshipping her shoes, now dressed in red latex shorts, a red flashing-light collar, and nothing else. Both men sat on the floor at their Master's feet too, and were greeted with a pat on their heads and a big smile before she continued her conversation. It was obvious she was having fun and that the party was a success, so they could relax and watch what was happening around them.

* * *

Dog let his mind wander and thought about what Beast had said and agreed that rivalry was not the answer. Master was extremely observant and had made it clear she wouldn't tolerate any bad feelings between them. He felt lucky to belong to her and he would make damn sure he was part of her stable of slaves for as long as possible.

* * *

Beast watched the play through the various legs that stood in front of him and smiled as he admired the various shoes and stiletto heels as they passed by. These were a weakness of his, especially if the legs were long and lean to match the heel. He took a quick look at his Master's legs and the stilettos that adorned her long, slim feet and thought how perfect they were and how lucky he was. He felt honoured to be at the feet of someone so graceful and he also admired her happy nature. She gave him the pain he craved, the care he needed, and he valued her influence. He couldn't be happier.

❧ Chapter 14 ☙

January 2013, Glasgow

Deditio: Ritualised Submission

I

Fhionna loved to write when she had the chance, and felt it was one of those moments when she could immerse herself in her thoughts and put pen to paper. She wasn't always successful in conveying her feelings, as she would have hoped, but she felt inspired by what was to come as well as by what had happened over the last year, so decided to sit quietly and let images drift through her mind.

Watch the bodies glide in dance,
Swaying in seductive rhythm,
Soft skin touching, furtive glance,
Unaware of circumstance.

Murmur gently in his ear,
Whispered tales of hedonism,
Breathe the words that quell his fear,
Twist the terms as puppeteer.

Tracing fingers over lip,
Hinting your own lyricism,
Plump and viscid in your grip,
Caring, not, for censorship.

Fates colliding in embrace,
Fill his heart with optimism,
Both converge in time and space,
His demise, plethoric grace.

Laying the fountain pen on the seat beside her, she read through the words on the page. She wasn't quite sure where they'd come from but she quite liked them. She knew they weren't based on one person but, rather, on different aspects of several. She felt they conveyed her passion for a caring and dominant relationship and the power it brought. She knew that supremacy was the essence of her desire but she also loved the caring aspect of her own nature. The dichotomy of hard and soft, of sadism and compassion. The submissive bending to her will, by his or her own choice, was magnificent. There was no other feeling that could compare.

Shifting position on the soft padding of the sofa, Fhionna smiled as she folded the paper and rose to her feet. Today was a big day and people would be arriving soon. She'd enjoyed the last few days in her own company and had spent some time cleaning her equipment, arranging the flowers she'd ordered from her favourite florist, and generally relaxing, doing nothing specific, even though Dog had arrived from the US recently. He was here because she'd summoned him but she'd felt like making him wait.

They'd talked about a binding ceremony and now the day had arrived. Bunty was bringing her outfit shortly, and Beast was due in about two hours with all the food he'd made for the occasion. Poppy and Tim were coming as guests later on, along with Sophia, Spike and Pup. She was sad that Louise couldn't come but was very excited at the prospect of having the rest her family and friends able to attend for the small ceremony and wondered how Bunty and Beast would get on. She was glad they'd already met but they hadn't really spent any time together. It was important she liked him. Fhionna was sure she would but sometimes she could be a little jealous. This was mainly because meeting someone new always meant a period of adjustment and of sizing-up. She loved her so much and knew she'd be fine as long as she felt there was no real threat to their relationship.

Fhionna walked across the hallway just as Bunty came in from the car carrying two beautiful dresses covered in plastic. She grinned at her soulmate and walked towards her to envelope her in her arms.

Bunty grinned back and said, "Hi, Master," before kissing her and pulling away so that she could show her the dresses properly. She was obviously excited and it was surprising to see her partner this way. She wasn't normally overenthusiastic, especially when another slave was being given a bonding ceremony, but it seemed that the fun of the occasion had taken over, as well as the fun of the shopping trip they'd been on together.

After they'd found the perfect outfits they'd taken them to the local tailor for some modifications, to make them a little more unique, and finished off their day by visiting a spa. It had been glorious and was good to get some quality time together. She thought it had probably helped Bunty overcome any feelings of being neglected and allowed her to enjoy herself.

"Take them upstairs and I'll come up in a minute. Would you like some coffee?"

"Yes, please, but I can make it. I'll just pop up and put these on your bed then come down to the kitchen. I brought some pain au chocolat too."

"Oh, lovely. Thank you. I was just about to shower so I'll come up with you."

At the bedroom door she told her it would be a fun filled day, and Beast was bringing lots of wonderful food that he'd probably been preparing for days. She also said that she hoped Bunty would enjoy his company.

"Master, you know I sometimes struggle when you choose a new slave but I trust your judgement. I know you need more than one in your life, but I also know how much you love me so please don't worry. I admit I need to feel special, apart from the others a little bit, but you always manage to let me know that I am. Now go shower."

* * *

She laughed as she witnessed her lover struggling to do up the zip on the back of her dress.

"Here, let me help you."

Bunty looked round and smiled.

"Sorry, I couldn't wait. I wanted to be wearing it when you came in but I'm having some difficulty. Isn't it lovely? The tiny diamantes you gave the tailor to sprinkle across the bodice are stunning. She's done a good job."

Fhionna said she looked beautiful and as she pushed the stubborn zip up to the top, she noticed Bunty was watching her in the mirror. She smiled at their reflection, hugged the girl's shoulders, and kissed her neck.

"Shall I help you into yours now, Master?"

She nodded and Bunty peeled the cellophane off the delicate folds of the blue/black dress. She held her hand as she stepped into it and let her slave glide the zip from the middle of her waist to the top of the V-shape just below her shoulder blades. The dress was exquisite and similarly sprinkled with tiny stones but across the waistline and down the sides, the full length of the gown. It looked like a clear midnight sky studded with stars. It was perfect.

Turning round, she noticed the look of lust in Bunty's eyes. Their passion for each other was still strong, even after so many years together, and she suddenly felt the urge to ravage her before Beast arrived.

* * *

Downstairs, Bunty sat at her feet, massaging them gently. She watched her as she applied some lotion and slid her hands across the soles, kneading the soft skin with her thumbs. After a while, she instructed her to paint her fingernails with a shimmering, translucent varnish that might match the sparkle of a diamond.

As she held out her fingers for her slave to blow on the newly applied polish, she heard a car crunch its way across the gravel.

"I think Beast has arrived. Could you let him in, please, and help him with his bags? Thank you, Bunty."

She kissed her lover before she rose from her position on the floor and headed outside. She watched her approach the car, shake hands with the tall form that emerged, then take a large box in her arms and head back towards the house.

Fhionna felt a little flicker of excitement at Beast's arrival and watched as he followed on behind Bunty with a similar package. She continued to blow on her nails, helping them to dry more quickly, and waited for the knock on the living room door.

"Good afternoon, Master."

She smiled as he approached her carrying a huge bouquet of flowers. He was grinning like a Cheshire cat and bent down to kiss her feet before kneeling in front of her and placing the flowers on the sofa. She laughed and said he was very perceptive.

"The flowers are beautiful, thank you. How did you know my fingernails weren't dry?"

"Well, I could be very smart and tell you I noticed the polish sitting on the floor at your feet but, in all honesty, Bunty told me she'd just finished painting them for you."

Beast beamed at his Master and continued to say he was excited at having been invited to join in the festivities and honoured to have been given the chance to prepare the food.

"I can't wait to enjoy what you've made but, for now, you can help Bunty unpack, please. She knows to assist you in the kitchen and you can take the time to get to know her a little. She's not shy but she is a rather private person so may not open up to you very quickly. I'd like you to make the effort though, because it's important she feels her status is protected."

"Yes, Master, of course. I will do my best to help her feel comfortable around me and make sure she knows I am no threat to her relationship with you. I would never dream of disrupting your life or your relationship with Bunty. It's beautiful and I'm both happy and eager to take my place in your household, as you wish me to, without intruding on your existing or future partnerships."

Beast felt his face glow as he spoke and bent low to kiss her feet again before removing himself from his Master's company and heading out to the car.

Bunty had done a lot in the few minutes he'd been inside and he mentioned how impressed he was.

"Hi, Bunty, sorry I left you to it. Wow! You've done loads. Thanks for that. I can do the rest, if you like." Beast smiled as Bunty handed over a wicker basket and picked up a large pan with its lid taped shut.

"Thanks. I'll just carry this pot in and then leave you to get the rest.

That way I can start to unpack what's already in the kitchen. I know Fhionna was expecting you to go and say hello before coming back out so don't worry."

He watched her disappear into the house and followed on behind with the basket. He noticed she'd referred to their Master by her 'normal' name and smiled because he guessed she was letting him know her 'partner' status and he didn't mind one little bit.

* * *

Aeneas was pacing the floor in his hotel room, waiting for the taxi to turn up. He'd been going crazy the last couple of days being in Scotland but not being with his Owner. He knew she'd summon him when she was ready but, hell, the wait was agonising. Today was the day though.

He'd bought a new suit to arrive at her home but guessed he wouldn't actually be wearing it for long. He chuckled to himself as he thought about the expense of buying something that he wouldn't really need here. He just felt he wanted to look good for her, before he was told to get naked. He wasn't quite sure how the evening would unfold, but he did know there were a few guests invited and that Beast was one them. He wasn't so happy about that. There was nothing wrong with the man, and he knew he'd have felt that way about anyone who Master got close to so quickly after he himself had become her slave. If he was completely honest, he knew Beast was someone she'd love to have around. She loved his style, his height, his manners, his skills in the kitchen, and the fact that he could take massive amounts of pain.

Damn it. He was feeling anxious enough because the taxi was late, he really didn't want to have Beast on his mind too. He would just need to stay calm. It was his and his Master's day, after all. He actually got the feeling Beast would be happy for them, to be invited to be part of it, and he liked him for that, if nothing else.

He checked his watch again and was just about to call reception to enquire about the cab when the phone rang. The voice announced it had arrived but Aeneas felt more than a little irritated as he replaced the receiver, picked up his coat, and headed downstairs. He patted himself down to double-check he had his gift for her in his pocket. He'd chosen a delicate gold and diamond necklace that he knew she would just adore. The gold would look great against her olive skin and the tiny diamonds resembled a constellation of captivating glints of light.

As he hadn't been asked to write anything for the ceremony, he hoped she would give him direction as needed. He didn't know who else would be there and it was a bit overwhelming. From previous chats, he knew his Owner would have arranged a formal setting so expected beautiful clothing to adorn her guests, good food, and perhaps some tasteful music. He thought it would be classical because she played the cello and made no secret of the fact she loved to go to the symphony and the opera.

Aeneas couldn't help but feel that the extravagance of such an event, even if a small and intimate gathering of close friends and her other slaves, would explicitly draw attention to his naked form. There was no doubt in his mind she'd have planned it to be like that, yet he knew it wasn't meant as a humiliation but as a symbolic gesture of entering his new position in life, in earnest.

* * *

As the car pulled up outside her home, Aeneas felt his stomach flip. The driver looked at him and asked if he had a nice evening planned, probably sensing he was a little on edge. He replied that he had a wonderful night ahead of him but he was slightly nervous about meeting some people for the first time. This wasn't exactly true but how else was he to explain his situation.

Aeneas said goodnight as the driver handed back some small change and headed towards the front door of his Master's home. He rang the bell and waited. He felt his heart thudding in his ribcage, as if trying to escape restraints, and thought how appropriate the analogy was under the circumstances.

It was no time at all before Poppy was standing in front of him, looking wonderful in a floor length pink sequined gown with a big grin plastered on her face.

"Oh my God, Poppy, you look amazing. I'm so glad you opened the door. I might have fainted if it had been Master. I didn't really expect it to be but it's something she might do to throw me off my game."

Aeneas realised he was babbling but he couldn't help it. Luckily she was well aware of what it felt like to be on the other side of

Master's surprises.

"It's so good to see you. You look very handsome and also very scared." Poppy laughed and then hugged Dog. "My dress was waiting for me when I arrived. Master chose it for me. Isn't it gorgeous? It made me nervous when she took me upstairs to help me dress, but when I saw it I squealed like an actual girl might."

Poppy paused and put her hand up to her face to feel the heat of her blush, which clashed with the sequins for a few seconds, then stepped sideways to let him in.

"But it wasn't just the dress. Master had another little surprise for me. She knew it would be skin tight compared to my other frocks, which are all rather frilly, and didn't want me to feel anything other than beautiful, so she'd placed some tape on the bed beside it and some beautiful pink lace panties. You can imagine what we did next and it was so much fun. I'm even allowed to have some champagne tonight. It's awesome. It's such a shame Master won't get to see you in your beautiful suit but I'm afraid you have to strip. You probably guessed that anyway. She says to do it in the hallway and leave your clothes neatly folded on the table then kneel, as she's taught you to do, in front of the living room door and wait."

Aeneas said he understood and was surprised when the young man leaned forward and kissed him on the cheek, very briefly.

"I'm so happy you're part of the family, Dog. Try not to be too nervous."

As Poppy disappeared into the living room, Dog took a few deep breaths and did as he was instructed. He carefully and methodically removed each item of clothing and placed the little gold box on the floor in front of him as he assumed his position. He could feel tears start to form already and hoped he wouldn't embarrass himself too much by crying like an idiot. But he guessed it wouldn't matter if he did because he knew she would understand.

* * *

Everyone was chatting and laughing when Poppy came back. "He's ready, Master. He looked very handsome in his suit."

Poppy flushed as everyone looked at her and smiled.

"Thank you. You're very sweet. Come and stand beside Tim."

Tim put his arm round her, briefly, before handing over the two-inch band of metal Fhionna had chosen as her slave's Ownership collar. It was sterling silver and had a small padlock that locked it in place.

"If you could bring him in now, please, Spike."

Spike smiled, opened the door, lifted the small box from the floor and told Dog to crawl into the room. He was not to look around but to head straight forward to his Master's feet.

Aeneas did as he was asked and cried as he heard the guests clap and say, "Welcome, Dog," as he crawled forward. When he reached his Master he stopped and allowed himself a brief moment to wipe the salt water from his eyes so he could actually see what he was doing. He waited for what was to happen next and heard someone say he had a little box, a gift from Dog, in his hand, and what would she like him to do with it.

Spike passed Fhionna the little box to open then took his place beside his Mistress.

"Oh, it's beautiful. Can you put it on for me, Tim?"

Dog's heart skipped a beat at the mention of Tim's name and he started to shake.

Everyone laughed and clapped and said things like, 'aww bless him' and 'poor Dog,' until Fhionna started to speak.

"My dear slaves and friends, thank you so much for being here to help us celebrate. I'm quite sure Aeneas has put himself through the wringer the last few days and it has now, finally, taken its toll. I have rather wickedly left him to his own devices here in Scotland, knowing his fate is sealed but not knowing exactly when, so the time has come to put him out of his misery, I think."

Addressing him directly, she continued, "Aeneas, you will be bound in ropes as a symbol of your accepted slavery. It is customary for a slave to be naked and bound as he enters his new life. I will say a few words about what you mean to me and then ask you to kneel. I haven't asked you to prepare anything to say because this day is about your actions. These are what matter most."

Fhionna paused and looked at her friends' smiling faces as Tim asked Aeneas to place his hands behind his back so that he could tie his wrists.

"It's an honour to take this male as my slave. I promise to cherish him, protect him, punish him as need be, and play with him till be begs for it to stop. I expect honesty, loyalty, and complete devotion. Aeneas, please kneel up. I have a gift for you."

She let her slave do as he was told and smiled as she watched him struggle.

"This collar is a symbol of your new life, your choice to enter it freely, and be the property of another. It is the circle that will be locked around your throat to symbolise that every breath you take belongs to me. I have chosen something simple and elegant, which will fit below the collar of your shirt, when you need to work. If you accept this gift and all it means then you should say so now."

"Yes, Master, I accept it."

Asking Aeneas to lift his head, Fhionna placed the metal ring round her slave's neck and locked it in place.

"Kiss my hand and then my feet. Tim will untie you then you may stand up."

Aeneas did as he was told and felt Tim remove the rough rope from his wrists. He looked up at his Master with a tear stained face before raising himself up from the floor completely. He saw that she was smiling. The necklace he'd chosen suited her beautiful neck, as well as the gown she wore, perfectly. He stayed quiet as he gazed at her, unsure whether to speak, but his silence was broken by Tim as he came forward to hug him.

"My goodness, Dog, you're trembling. Can I fetch him a drink?"

Fhionna said that he could, so Tim walked to a nearby table to pour him a large whisky.

Poppy was next in line with a hug, closely followed by Bunty and Pup, then Beast shook his hand. Sophia and Spike were next to congratulate him as Tim handed him his drink.

Aeneas looked at his Owner and thanked her for the beautiful collar.

She smiled at her slave and was the last one to hug him. It had been a wonderful few days and she was pleased to say it was now time to enjoy the party; eat, drink and play.

* * *

It was late when all the guests had eventually gone to bed and Fhionna had said the tidying up could wait.

Beast and Poppy were the first ones to surface so washed the dishes and set the large table for brunch. Beast was used to cooking for more than a dozen people so had no problem doing things in an organised manner, especially with Poppy there eager to help. He commented on how the sight of them standing together at the sink reminded him of a comedy sketch. They were completely opposite to each other in stature, and probably in habits and other tastes, and it was easy to imagine them in a kinky rendition of *The Odd Couple*.

"Last night was so much fun. I don't get to wear a dress as elegant as that very often. Master is very generous when it comes to my outfits but I must confess I don't have much style. I tend to go for over the top frilly things that are very frothy and girly, but the dress Master bought me was so beautiful and made me feel a bit like a mermaid."

Poppy laughed as she said the last bit and smiled up at the giant man who, similarly to her, was wearing only shorts and a collar. It turned out their Master had guessed who would be up first and had left outfits for them to wear as they set about their tasks. She'd also left one out for Dog, but since he was locked in the cage in the dungeon overnight he would need to wait to be released and that would be when she was ready for it to happen.

"It was indeed. I loved it. It was great getting to spend some time with Bunty too. I was rather nervous about that but she's really nice. I did meet her last month but I didn't talk to her alone. It was great to see you let your hair down too, Poppy. You made me laugh when you started bossing Dog around and Master joined in and told him he had to do as you said. You didn't need to be told twice and you put him on a lead and started making him crawl behind you barking. He took it in good spirits though, I think. We'd all had quite a lot to drink by then."

Beast looked at the young man standing beside him.

"You know, I still can't get used to you in male attire. Isn't that strange! I never thought I'd ever say that to a man and yet here I am wearing a collar and not much else, belonging to another human being, and standing beside someone else who belongs to the same human being. It's amazing what life can throw at you and how much we can change when we meet the right person who encourages you to become more than what you've been before. I always thought I would be a masochist who struggled with his submissive side but then I met Fhionna and all that changed. It's not just about getting the pain I need anymore, it's become something else first and pain second."

Poppy looked at him when he stopped talking and wondered if she should stay silent or not. She decided to ask the question she'd been wanting to ask him for a while. She knew he'd probably blush when she did it but had wondered about Beast's masochism and submission and what the difference was.

"Why is it that you need pain, if you don't mind me asking? It's just that I was wondering what you felt the difference was."

"Good question and I don't mind at all. I guess it's the feeling I get when I know I've made a sadist happy. I know there's not many people who can take the levels I do and it makes me very proud and feel kind of unique when I achieve it. There have been a few women who tried to tame me, as it were, but it's never quite worked. There's always been something missing, whether that's been a lack of long-term attraction or, probably more importantly, a lack of proper duty of care. I've never found someone who cared so much; was as passionate about making sure her submissive was safe, protected and looked after, as much as extracting the pain she needed them to feel for her. It's really powerful. She makes me feel like no one else has. Ever. What about you, Poppy? What does pain mean to you?"

The smaller man hesitated slightly. "I hate pain. I never seek it out and do my best to avoid it by being well-behaved. But sometimes I get things wrong and I know I'll be punished for it. I wondered, in the beginning, why I would want to belong to someone like Master, who so obviously had a sadistic side, but I came to the same conclusion as you. She is so loving and caring. I do love her. She is very kind to me and yet I know what she is capable of too. It can be very scary, being Master's slave, but the goodness inside her is always present. I know I am safe and that she'll never give me more than she knows I can take, even though she does push my limits."

Beast was glad that Poppy felt she could open up to him. She was a lovely person and made him smile a lot. He'd never met anyone like her before, so shy and so obviously happy and joyful to just be led and told what to do. He could see the respect she had for her Owner but knew that Fhionna also respected her slaves and that made all the difference in the world.

* * *

Just as the last dish was laid on the table and the kettle had boiled for the coffee, the kitchen door opened and Sophia and Spike walked in, closely followed by Pup. They greeted each other with hugs and Sophia asked if anyone else was up yet.

"Master and Bunty have still to arrive, Tim went home last night in a taxi and Dog is still downstairs in his cage, I think."

Beast said he wasn't sure if he should take some coffee up to Master's room or just wait. He could do a relay breakfast, no problem, but he wondered if she would rather be present downstairs for a family breakfast.

Sophia said she thought she'd like to be in the kitchen with them all but urged him to take coffee upstairs for her first. He could always blame her for the idea if it was wrong.

Beast smiled and said, "Thank you, Sophia," and busied himself grinding some beans and selecting a clean filter.

* * *

Upstairs, Beast knocked gently on his Owner's bedroom door and waited until he was told to enter.

"Thank you for the coffee. Just put the cups on the table and we'll be down in five minutes. Could you let Dog out of his cage, please, and take his shorts to him? He can come upstairs and sit at the table. Thank you."

Fhionna ducked back under the covers and giggled with Bunty before downing the coffee more or less in one gulp and letting her brush her hair for her. The pair then put on their dressing gowns and went down to the kitchen.

They were greeted by hugs from Sophia and Spike and smiles from the slaves, as well as a chorus of, "Good morning, Master," and "Hope you slept well."

"Good morning. I slept like a log. I must have been tired. How are you, Sophia? Did you enjoy yourself last night? I seem to remember Dog being the centre of attention for everyone, including Poppy!"

"I loved every second of it. Thank you so much for inviting us. It was a great night. I must admit I had a lot of fun at poor Dog's expense too." Sophia grinned from ear to ear as she affectionately ruffled his hair.

"It was, and thank you to Beast for all the wonderful food. A toast: to Dog and his new beginning, to Beast and the hard work he did, and to us all for being a perfect kinky family."

* * *

Sophia and Spike said their goodbyes and left the little family to enjoy the rest of their day. Fhionna, Bunty, Dog, Beast and Pup chatted in the living room while Poppy did the dishes.

"Are you happy, Dog?"

Fhionna knew the answer but she couldn't help but ask it anyway. It was important to her that he felt he'd made the right decision.

"Yes, Master. Very happy." Dog touched the silver collar that now cradled his neck and smiled. "It really is beautiful. I will cherish it and love wearing it every day."

"It suits you." She reached down and stroked her slave's head. "I think the time has come for you all to help Beast carry his dishes and the remaining food back to his car. You may stay behind, Pup."

She watched as her slaves got up off the floor and as Craig sat back down, only this time closer to her feet.

"Today those of us left will relax and tomorrow I'll want to watch you and Dog perform together so be prepared for that. I will give you specific instructions but I wanted to give you some warning. I'm assuming you'll do this for me?"

"Yes, Master. I'll do my best."

"Good boy. Go and let Poppy know she can get changed because Beast will give her a run home before he heads south."

II

The following morning, Fhionna woke early to find a loving note on her pillow from Bunty, which said that she would leave her and the other two slaves to have some fun together today and that she had plans to meet the sub from the Christmas party. It also said she knew she'd be fine with it but if not then she accepted any punishment coming her way, and it ended with a smiling face emoji and a row of lots of kisses.

She smiled and headed for a shower because she had plans too. She could feel her own desire bubbling to the surface as she imagined what the two slaves would look like together. They looked very different and it would make for some interesting photos.

Drying herself off, she decided to look for her good camera. There were times when your phone just wouldn't do because it was still just a phone and had its limitations. She was excited to capture the juxtaposition of the young man with his long hair and the older, more fit male with the close-shaved head that was going grey. Pup also had an extremely pale complexion compared to Dog's olive skin. They really were the exact opposite of each other.

* * *

Downstairs in the dungeon, Dog was in his cage and Pup was on the floor outside it. They had talked to each other through the bars for a good part of the night and each one had found the other interesting and engaging. Aeneas had learned about the young man's love of chastity and his hopes about serving a Master or Mistress who would one day have his genitals pierced and a permanent metal chastity device locked in place, with no access to a key except in emergencies. Dog wasn't quite sure about the safety of this and admitted that the thought of it scared him.

Pup had learned that Dog had dreamed of being owned by someone, such as their Master too and had only, over the last year, found her. He'd admitted to being totally out of his depth and taking some time to adjust to his new situation but knowing, at the same time, that it was the life he wanted.

"I can guess some of what she may have planned for us today, Pup, but she also keeps me guessing so I don't know for sure."

"I'm sure it will be good fun, whatever it is. I like you Dog. I'm a masochist so I enjoy pain and I'm also bisexual so I'm more than happy to perform with you, if that's what's expected of me." Craig grinned from ear to ear then continued, "I'm going to go and have a shower as I want to be a clean pup for when Master Fhionna arrives. Should you do the same?"

Dog wasn't sure of the answer to that but he guessed maybe it would be ok to take a little initiative, on this occasion, and his door had been left unlocked overnight. He thought that this might have been more to do with the fact that she would enjoy the thought of the two of them sleeping beside each other overnight, should they want to. There had been no specific permission granted but there'd also been no specific instructions not to either.

"I'm going to do the same but I hope I don't get punished for it."

"Let me take the blame." Craig smiled at him. "It will be my fault if it's wrong because it was my suggestion."

"Thank you, but I'm the slave that should know better so I may well get the blame for it anyway. We will just do it, get into position and wait for however long it takes for Master to come downstairs."

* * *

Fhionna entered the dungeon and was happy to see her pet and her slave in their kneeling positions beside each other. Waiting. She had noticed the bathroom light was on and inspected the room before saying anything to them. She wasn't entirely happy that they'd showered already but she understood the motive behind it.

"Good morning, boys. Please kneel up with your hands behind your back. Today will be a day of play. You will both remain silent until told otherwise, asked a direct question, or are left alone in each other's company, in which case you may chat. Do you understand?"

She waited for their replies before continuing.

"I see you've already showered. I understand that you thought I'd like clean slaves to play with and, for that, your punishment will be lessened, but unfortunately for you I had planned to take photographs of you showering together. So you'll be doing it again, although some of the pleasure has now been removed from my voyeuristic experience, knowing that you may have been intimate in the shower already."

Dog and Pup both wanted to say that they'd showered separately, purely to be clean, not to derive any pleasure from each other, but knew to do so would result in more punishment.

"If I issue a general order or direction, without adding either name to the end, you will both complete it. If I have something specific for either of you to do I will direct you accordingly. Today I will be taking photos and may do a little filming. Please affirm your consent."

Both males did as instructed but kept their heads bowed because they hadn't been given permission to look up yet.

"Good. Thank you. The filming I decide to do is for my own pleasure and the pleasure of any friends in the scene who would enjoy seeing it. It will only be shown at one of my parties, for amusement or used for my own pleasure, while either or both of you are absent."

Lifting each head, in turn, so they could look at her, she smiled at them and touched each man's cheek as they smiled back.

"Pup, go and start the shower and wait outside it. Dog, fetch two gags from the wall and bring them with you into the bathroom. Place a gag into your own mouth and then the other into Pup's. You may then enter the shower cubicle. Dog, you will gently wash Pup's hair before you both wash each other. Do it slowly. Pup, you will remove your gag when told and kneel in front of Dog to perform orally. Dog, at that point, you will place your hands behind your back. You may orgasm into Pup's mouth. You will then both exit the shower and dry each other off before kneeling in the dungeon. Do you understand your instructions?"

Both slaves said that they understood and Fhionna was pleased to see two sets of cocks harden. This little film was going to be very popular with her Dom friends and she would have a party, in the coming weeks, just for them.

* * *

Pup was crying but not from pain. He was upset, it seemed, because Dog was to bear the brunt of her disappointment at them having taken the initiative to shower without instruction to do so. He'd broken his silence to protest and say it was his fault, to please punish him instead, which had warranted its own reprimand.

"Be quiet, Craig. That's enough!"

Fhionna wasn't happy and both slaves knew it. Dog stayed silent but looked at the boy with sorrow in his eyes. He felt bad for the boy but knew this might happen. Craig had admitted to being a masochist and Master knew that Dog wasn't. Who better to punish than the one who disliked pain. He now understood, quite well, how his Owner's mind worked and she'd often made a distinction between play for pleasure and atonement.

Dog was ready to receive the strokes of the cane she saw fit to give him. He felt a little nervous, as he always did in these circumstances. There was little doubt in his mind that he would take what was coming without complaint. He did wonder though, if there would ever come a time when he knew exactly what he should do without having to be given direct instructions. Tim did it really easily but Aeneas had to admit he'd been her slave for many years so he'd had the practice. He couldn't remember a time when Tim got it wrong but there must have been one.

"You'll only receive six strokes, purely because it was a mistake made through a genuine want to please. You'll count them out as I strike you. Acknowledge that you understand."

"Yes, Master."

"Good. Pup, fetch your gag from the bathroom and replace it. Then kneel beside Dog's head, keeping your hands behind your back."

Pup did as he was told but wasn't keen to watch Dog's punishment and tried to lower his head. He knew his Master would notice but couldn't help himself. She'd positioned him at the top of the bench on purpose. She obviously wanted him to watch Dog's face as he received the cane. She wasn't being cruel, as such, but she was making her point known. This was a difficult kind of emotional pain, much harder for him to bear than the strokes on his flesh. It was abundantly clear that one of the reasons they both admired her though, was her intellect. And this was part of it.

* * *

After the caning, Fhionna had watched Dog suck the young man but not to full completion. It seemed he was to be left in an excited state for his journey home later that day. The silence command had been lifted shortly after Pup had received the lash to his back for breaking it and their Master had allowed him to cry at her feet while Dog stroked his long, glossy mane. The rest of the day, until late afternoon, had been spent worshipping her body, as allowed, and generally being of service. Both males were exhausted and needed some sleep. They'd been put through their paces but the photos they'd been allowed to see, afterwards, had been spectacular. They both enjoyed the animation of their Master as she described each shot and made excited noises as she flicked between each one.

"You can sleep on the train journey home, Pup. I've arranged for a taxi to take you to the station so you should clean up and Dog will help you pack. The car will be here in an hour."

She watched the slaves walk upstairs with very little energy and laughed.

* * *

When Dog woke up, he was more than a little dazed and it took him a while before he noticed the letter with instructions just outside the cage door. The door itself had also been unlocked. He'd slept well, which was hardly surprising, but now he was to freshen up and go up to the kitchen for breakfast with his Master. He felt a mixed sense of pleasure and trepidation that they were now on their own together. He wasn't sure how long it would last because he knew Poppy would be there at some point, but for now he enjoyed the feeling of being the only slave in the house.

Having showered, shaved, and dressed in his shorts, Aeneas walked upstairs to the kitchen. He knocked on the door after lowering himself to the floor and waited for an answer before crawling in.

"Good morning. I've made some food so help yourself and take what you want to put in your bowl. We'll just be relaxing today, you'll no doubt be relieved to hear."

Fhionna smiled at her newly collared slave and continued to munch on her warm buttered toast, happily spilling crumbs onto the table.

"Good morning. Thank you, Master."

Dog took some bacon and eggs and toast of his own and dropped them into his bowl on the floor before returning the various pans and plates to the countertop. He was well-accustomed to eating like this and actually looked forward to it. It hadn't always been the case, of course.

He remembered the first time he'd done it, in the café, and how angry he'd felt at the humiliation, but now realised it was just a ritual his Master enjoyed. There was no malice in her actions just a kind of happy contentment at being able to have the kind of lifestyle she loved. Pure and simple.

"I want you to book a flight back to the US for two days' time but I want to talk to you about how you feel. You'll also have the chance to write about some of your adventures because I think it would add to the book I intend to write about my life. It's something I've given a great deal of thought to and I'd like it to be my next project. I've decided to take a step back from my display business and I've hired a manager to run the day-to-day of it for me instead. It will give me time to dedicate to writing and I want to include you in the story, Aeneas."

Dog let some egg slip from his mouth and apologised. "I'd be honoured, Master. And may I say I think it's a fantastic idea."

"Good. That's settled. I'll give you some time to write down your thoughts. I'll ask Poppy to stop by the office and pick up a computer for you to use. That way it will make it easier for me to edit what I want to use and upload it to my own laptop, rather than having to sit and type it all out again from scratch."

"Yes, Master. Thank you."

"When you've done the dishes come up to my bathroom. I want you to bathe me while we talk."

Fhionna placed her plate in the sink before leaving him to his own thoughts.

Dog was amazed at this turn of events but also delighted by them. He crammed the last of his food into his mouth and took his bowl, the pans, the plates, and his Master's coffee cup over to the sink.

As the hot, foamy water rose to the top of the washing-up bowl, he thought about how much he loved the idea of being included in her book. He wondered how she would integrate some of his thoughts and feelings and felt proud. He'd no doubt it would include Bunty, Tim and Poppy because they were important to her life story, as well as any plot based on it, but he also wondered who else would be included. Maybe Beast and Pup would be part of it, even if in a smaller capacity. They, too, were certainly beginning to feature in her life. Beast more significantly, perhaps.

He felt a small pang of jealousy and crushed it before it grew into something bigger. He knew, now, he was just being protective but also that he had no reason to worry. He loved his Master but so did the others.

Aeneas dried his hands and walked upstairs. He stood outside her room listening to her sing, for a moment, before finally deciding to knock. She sounded happy and he was extremely glad to be part of that happiness.

"Come in."

Fhionna was already in her tub, watching the hot water cascade over her toes, creating a small waterfall effect. Not moving her gaze from the taps, she told Aeneas to sit beside the bath.

"Tell me what was going through your head while you waited to be summoned to the house for your ceremony. Take your time. You can wash my back while you think about it."

Dog got onto his knees, took the soft sponge she held out for him, and lathered it with the soap that rested on the side of the bath.

"I was a wreck, Master. I didn't know what to do with myself, to be honest. In the end, I decided I needed to keep myself busy, in some way, so I didn't go completely crazy. Although, that's how I felt by the end of it anyway. I went for long runs, had hot showers, and tried to read, although that last one was unsuccessful. I looked at the Violate website quite a lot. I enjoyed that more than anything else I did because I at least felt closer to you, and my family, while doing it."

Dog paused to think about what he'd just said; his family.

"I hoped the time would come to be properly owned by you, and I expected it to be very special, but I had no idea just how much it would mean to me. To be naked and in ropes at your feet was amazing, but to be in front of the others too, well, that blew my mind and I couldn't stop the tears, especially when I heard Tim was there. Everyone was very kind to me though."

Dog paused. He felt his chest tighten and released a long, slow, whistle-type breath from between his teeth. He didn't stop what he was doing but he didn't feel able to continue to commit his feelings to words, just at that moment, either. He was relieved when Fhionna didn't say anything but gave him time to let him gather his thoughts.

"I feel like I've entered another universe. I had so many fantasies about living as a slave but it doesn't even compare to the reality. I guess the fantasy was based on my own desires to serve, if that makes sense.

It made me rather selfish as I would often masturbate to them and so they would need to follow a certain formula, one which was always sexually exciting. In all honesty, it never involved pain. It did involve facets of making someone happy because I've always known, deep down, that I'm submissive but the thought of giving myself so deeply to someone, especially someone who identified as a sadist, had never really been achieved in any meaningful way."

She smiled and encouraged him to continue by asking him to explore how much he thought he'd grown as a person as a result of accepting life as a slave.

"I've definitely grown as a person in general. My main achievement, I think, has been to fit into your family. You have helped me so much. You've trained me to be less self-motivated. Fitting into an already established BDSM family was always going to be hard for me, I think. Even more so than learning to take pain because I knew you would train me to be able to do that through being patient and caring and just giving me enough time to learn. I knew the 'fitting in' part was always going to be purely down to me and that was scary. Without meaning to sound ungrateful or petulant in any way, it meant, in my own head, that I couldn't hold you responsible for my own failure to fit in. Whereas there might always have been a very tiny part of me that could put blame on you for not giving me enough time to adapt to the levels of pain you wanted me to take, if I couldn't do it."

Aeneas felt his face burn and felt he needed to clarify what he was saying. The last thing he wanted to do was upset her, for various reasons.

As if reading his thoughts, Fhionna said, "I understand. You haven't offended me so don't worry. Keep going, if you want to."

"It's hard to explain. When you reach a certain age you think there's not much more to learn. You feel that any potential is as a teacher, in some capacity. So, when you discover that you're learning a whole new set of rules that will guide your life, indefinitely, and discover that you want, more than anything, for your teacher to praise you and love you, it's very confusing. My teacher is younger than me by some years but has way more experience in the subject than I will ever have and it's a subject that has practical rituals but which is mainly made up of subjective preferences. Does that make sense, Master?"

Dog was keen to know her opinion of his analogy and hoped he wasn't being too vague.

"Yes. It does. It's like when I meet a new person and I think I can explore new levels of sadistic pleasure with them. Just when I thought I'd seen and done most things, here comes someone who can offer me a way of building on my own practices and skill. It might not be as life-changing but I understand the feeling you're describing. Yours is more based on giving up complete control to the 'teacher,' which is very scary and exciting, and mine is about feeling completely free to indulge in levels of sadism, that I haven't achieved before, which is also exciting and a little disconcerting."

Aeneas listened as Fhionna briefly described her own feelings. He hadn't given any thought to how it might be a little scary for her to open herself up to new experiences. He'd assumed she'd seen and done everything there was to do, but now that he thought about it, it made sense. He could see why she would want to take on more than one slave and insist that each one of them was different. Not only was she a very social, loving, and caring person, but she was also someone who loved a challenge. He thought, though, that the person she referred to wasn't actually him. He was quite sure she was talking about Beast because he was the masochist, turned slave, as far as he knew.

"Thank you, Master. I guess what I'm saying is that I'm open to being moulded and shaped as you see fit. Yes, it's more than a little scary but I'm very happy. I can see myself wanting to live here, in Scotland, to be able to serve you better but I also understand if this is something you might not want. I do love the anticipation of travelling so far to come and see you and hope that you enjoy that aspect of it too. Having an exotic pet, as it were, that you can click your fingers for and have him travel thousands of miles to happily be at your feet is rather fun. All I know, Master, is that I'm now yours to control."

Dog blushed as he lay the sponge down and bowed his head, placing his hands behind his back, hoping he hadn't said too much.

* * *

In the dungeon, Dog wrote down some of his feelings and thoughts in his journal until it was time for Poppy to arrive at the house with the computer. He hoped his Owner would enjoy reading them when she came to include snippets of his writing in among her own words. He felt he'd said too much before, but she'd taken it all in her stride and they'd talked about some future plans and how they didn't include him moving to Scotland; for the reasons he'd given and more. He must admit he hadn't considered that Bunty might not like the idea. He'd thought she would just have done as she was asked, like everyone else did, but he knew that she was his Master's partner so guessed it made the relationship different.

He'd written several pages in his notebook when the dungeon door opened and Poppy came in.

"Hi, Dog. I've brought the laptop for you to use. Master says you're doing some writing for her. That's exciting. I'd be rubbish at that." Poppy laughed at the thought of writing anything and how nervous she'd be. "Oh God, I hope she doesn't actually ask me to write anything like that!"

Aeneas laughed, helped her set it up, and plugged it in to charge.

"Master says we can have a little fun together and then we both have some chores to do. She says you are under strict instructions not to cum but that I can."

Aeneas grinned at her, proffered a giant paw, and asked if she'd like to come into his cage with him; which she did.

As they lay down together she asked if he was happy before reaching up, rather absentmindedly, to stroke the other man's nipples. She said she could understand how everything might have been a bit much to take in lately, but hoped it would settle down into a more familiar routine soon. It was wonderful to have such exciting moments in his life, as a newly collared slave, but also the secret to a long and happy relationship with his Owner was to have 'normal' structure, rules, and ritual.

"Wise words, Poppy. I totally get that. I might feel a little displaced, from time to time, as I move back and forth between the US and here so the rules will help me remember who I've become."

Dog slowly moved his large frame round so that the younger and considerably smaller male who lay beside him could reach his nipples properly but Poppy had other ideas. Aeneas wasn't used to her directing their play together, as she was usually really shy, but today there was a certain kind of confidence about her and he liked it. He watched as she removed herself from the cage and asked him to do the same, saying it would give them more room. She then lay on the mattress just outside the cage and invited him to lie down again.

Poppy began to kiss and nibble Aeneas' neck and shoulders and stroked his body at the same time. She loved it when Dog groaned and growled. She'd been scared the first time he'd done it but she now expected it as a sign of his enjoyment.

After a little while she switched positions. It was her turn to be kissed and pampered. She spread her legs wide with the intention of letting Dog know he could move freely about her body.

Aeneas took the hint and ran his hands down over the beautifully toned, flat stomach and the slim hips until he reached the erect penis that showed how excited she was. He was amazed at how hard it was. Touching the member with his lips, he gently ran his tongue over the tip of the head before plunging it deeper into his wet mouth. Poppy whimpered and gasped as her shaft was engulfed and Aeneas' hand cradled her balls.

Dog loved bringing his friend and fellow slave to orgasm and intended to elicit every drop of cum from the young man's body. He was still amused by the him/her dichotomy that Master employed for Poppy but it seemed to make the young man happy to be able to switch genders at the drop of a hat. Aeneas had come to know her pretty well over the past year and, although it was still slightly confusing at times, he was more than happy to go with the flow.

Poppy trust her hips forward and latched onto the other slave's head with her hands to push him lower onto her member, impaling him. As she felt Aeneas move more quickly up and down her shaft, she could feel the orgasm grow and it wouldn't be long before it erupted and forced a stream of fluid into his waiting mouth. She knew Dog had grown to love this feeling because he'd often been made to lick his own cum from the floor of whichever room she'd chosen to play in. Master would no doubt enjoy the fact that Aeneas hadn't been given permission to orgasm, while he attended to her needs, and this made her feel more confident.

* * *

Both slaves had showered and Poppy had left by the time Fhionna entered the dungeon.

"Hello, Dog. I hope you've enjoyed your day so far. I have a few tasks for you to do so please get dressed and come upstairs to the hall. Poppy will give you a list of what I want you to achieve later this afternoon."

The instruction had been short and concise so he set about collecting his clothes from the cupboard before walking upstairs to see if he needed his shoes. He assumed he would though.

Poppy was there to meet him and his first task was to chop wood for the fire. His next task was related to the first and he'd to put logs by every fire in the house before setting and lighting the one in the living room. The inventory wasn't too long but included a brisk walk to the local village for groceries and other supplies that Master needed for herself. He enjoyed buying things that made her happy and she'd asked for her stock of bubble bath to be replenished. All in all a pleasant task to complete and he would enjoy the fresh air. It would give him time to think about the next entry in his journal.

* * *

Safely back in his room, Aeneas positioned himself on the floor in a place that allowed him to be comfortable in the shackles that adorned his ankles, opened the lid of the laptop, and began to write:

The brief journey today, even in the heavy snow, has been a piquant alternative to the intense preoccupations of a day at home with my Owner. That is where I love to be, of course, but I found that the sharpness of the air was needed to keep me fresh for her ministrations and her desires to use me.

I read somewhere on some sort of travel blog, I think, that being absent, even for the shortest of times, makes the return to home much more sweet. The mind can clear, the body can rest a little, and the heart is allowed to miss her.

I think that when the time comes to actually leave Scotland my work suit will become as sartorially irrelevant as a Christmas sweater. All I really want is to be naked and collared and at my Master's whim. It is, now, all that matters in life.

I will go back to the US, but not back home, because home is with her.

EPILOGUE

Dog was still and silent, on all fours, on the soft rug at his Owner's feet. His head was newly shaved, as she'd instructed it to be, and he waited as patiently as he could for her next command. He could hear his pulse and it seemed to fill the entire room. There was no other sound. He hadn't even heard her heels as she moved towards him across the floor. He knew the clicking noise they made on the glistening wood quite well by now.

Playing in his Owner's favourite room at the front of the house was still a fairly new experience and he fleetingly wondered why she'd chosen this room over the dungeon downstairs. A long time had passed, it seemed, and he wanted so much to lift his head from the floor and look at her again. He thought she was beautiful. He'd been through so much in the past year, every part of it, he thought, being impossible to believe could happen. But it had happened and here he was, a slave, his life changed forever. It was a new beginning: naked, shaved, collared, and waiting to give pleasure to another person through his pain and servitude.

* * *

Fhionna said nothing but walked towards her newly-collared slave and bent down low to kneel on his shoulders. She loved to put nearly her full weight on him like that. She reached down to pinch his hard, protruding nipples, and he reacted as she'd expected. He moaned loudly and moved his body underneath the pressure of hers. She knew he'd try his best not to move his hands from behind his back even though, with his forehead on the floor, it was a difficult position to maintain.

She raised her slave's head by putting her finger underneath his chin; the signal for him to kneel upright. Once he was in place, still with his hands behind his back, she stuffed a soft rubber gag into his mouth. She lifted his head higher and held it there, towering above him and pulling his nipples away from his chest, digging her long nails into the tender flesh as she did so. She listened to his groans and watched his face contort with the pain. It wasn't too long before the saliva dribbled from his mouth, long strings of it landing on his torso or settling on his knees or on the rug. She laughed at his predicament and increased the pressure of her fingers until it was obvious he could bear the pain no longer.

Fhionna frowned, slightly, as he moved his hands to hold onto hers. She released her grip on his flesh and watched him quickly regain his composure and lock his hands in place, once more, behind his back. She watched as he bowed his head and moved it to the floor with a low sigh.

"You realise your mistake of course?"

Her slave lifted his head slightly off the floor and nodded.

"Go to the dungeon and wait for me there. Choose a cane from the rack and kneel with it in your open hands. Is that understood?"

Again, she watched him nod his acceptance before he crawled from the room on his hands and knees. She'd taught him well and she smiled as she excitedly removed her stilettos and ran upstairs to change. She would need a loose garment to wear, preferably one with wide arms or sleeveless altogether. This was the beginning of another wonderful play scene and another amazing year. She just knew it.